Teach Us That Peace

Books by Baron Wormser

The White Words

Good Trembling

Atoms, Soul Music and Other Poems

When

Teaching the Art of Poetry: The Moves (co-author)

Mulroney and Others

Subject Matter

A Surge of Language: Teaching Poetry Day by Day (co-author)

Carthage

The Road Washes Out in Spring: A Poet's Memoir of Living Off the Grid

Scattered Chapters: New and Selected Poems

The Poetry Life: Ten Stories

Impenitent Notes

Teach Us That Peace

A Novel

Baron Wormser

Published by Piscataqua Press, an imprint of
RiverRun Bookstore, Inc.
142 Fleet St. | Portsmouth, NH | 03801

www.piscataquapress.com

ISBN: 978-1-939739-18-6

Although it references actual events and places, this book is a
work of fiction, a product of the author's imagination.

Printed in the United States of America

Cover design by Gregory Smith

Author photo by Janet Wormser

For Sherry

Yea, the darkness hideth not from thee;
But the night shineth as the day

— Psalm 139

Time is an empty house that being inhabits.

— Guy Davenport

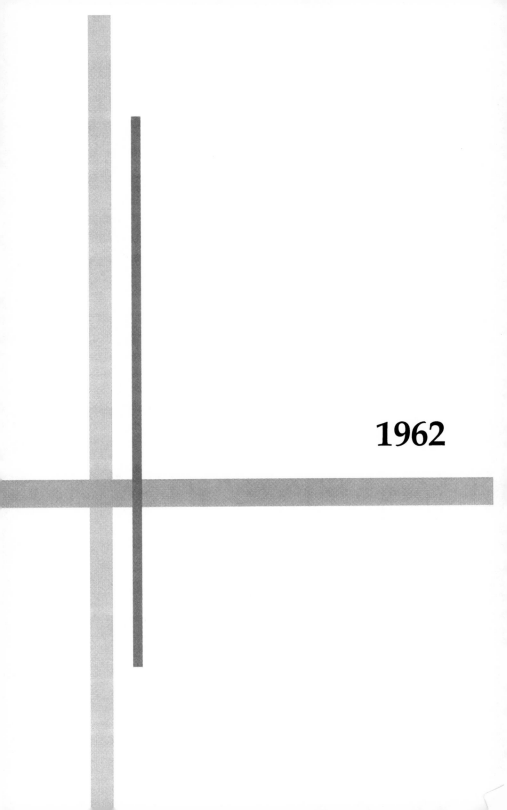

1962

Arthur

"A *shicker*, Arthur. You understand Yiddish?" Mr. Schwartz's face was both hopeful and baleful.

"I do," Arthur answered. "It means someone who drinks too much." He knew numerous Yiddish derogations and he knew the quintessential Jewish look he was being given. Joe Gronchik, Mr. Schwartz's longtime driver and assistant, was "a good man but a wop." Arthur stuck an index finger between his dress shirt collar and his neck. It was warm already on this his first day of work, and it was only eight o'clock on a breezeless morning. Wearing a tie in July in Baltimore was ridiculous.

Joe had been in a serious car accident and was going to be "laid up." In about eight weeks, right around the time Arthur would be going back to high school at City, Joe would be able to drive again. Mr. Schwartz knew how to drive but needed to focus on his job of collecting the rents.

Arthur didn't ask why Mr. Schwartz chose as his driver someone who liked to get loaded. Like Arthur's grandmother Ruby, Mr. Schwartz was from the old country, the home of Yiddish and a vast quantity of opaque water that would only show back your own staggered reflection. The novels Arthur devoured at night in his bedroom had revealed to him already that most statements beyond "Your scrambled eggs are getting cold" were mysteries. Fact rarely was fact. Arthur murmured that he hoped Mr. Gronchik got better soon.

Arthur's father had arranged the job. Mr. Schwartz was one of his clients from "way back," which meant around 1950, when Stanley Mermelstein had started out on his own. One evening in May, before Arthur went upstairs to do his homework, he had asked what Arthur planned on doing that summer between his sophomore and junior year in high school.

Stan said that a client of his "needed a hand." He paused and looked at his son who, as was typical, looked preoccupied. More than once, Stan had told his wife Susan that their son could have used three heads for all the thinking he did.

"I know you've enjoyed working in the office, but this is a special opportunity. Mr. Schwartz is an excellent businessman. You can learn a lot from him." He gave his son an I'm-talking-to-you-kid-wake-up stare. "That good with you, Arthur?" Stan asked, but he wasn't asking.

"That's good," Arthur replied. He wondered what was "special" about driving around and collecting rents, but once again he wasn't asking. He would have money to put gas in the Fairlane when his mom let him use it, and he would have money to buy LPs. Record collecting had replaced baseball card collecting and stamp collecting. No one was going to pay him to spend the summer reading F. Scott Fitzgerald.

The properties Mr. Schwartz owned tended to be shabby but not decrepit. Window casements needed a coat of paint, or doors did not rest properly in their jambs, or roof gutters (where there were gutters) needed to be reset in their brackets. The buildings weren't falling down, however. They were part of that army of red-brick rowhouses that typified Baltimore. Only an earthquake or a Soviet missile strike was going to bring them down. What went on inside—whether the furnace worked or the roof leaked—was beyond Arthur's scope. In fact, he quickly learned he had no scope. When, on that first morning of their driving around, he pointed out a trim board above a door that had come loose, Mr. Schwartz regarded him with surprise. "Are you a carpenter?" The question pulsed with contempt. Arthur made no more house-repair comments.

He didn't stop looking around, however. How could he? He was driving in parts of the city where few white people had spent much time, if any. He was in that near yet foreign country called Where the Negroes Live.

It was recognizably Baltimore: heat shimmering off the asphalt, women in light, pastel-colored dresses, men with their shirts unbuttoned or in summer T-shirts, fire hydrants opened for children to frolic in the gush, automobiles serenely baking. People sauntered, or stopped to chat on the street corners. No one was in a hurry. Tomorrow would be as hot as today. Arthur wondered whether there was a genius to torpor, a principle of energy conservation he had not been taught in science classes. Even the vowels of spoken words became elongated as if weary and suffocated. Hand gestures would do as well, a soft, dismissive *whoosh* through the broiling air.

He wished he could mount a fan on the dashboard of Mr. Schwartz's Lincoln Continental that lacked air conditioning—"because all it does is break and give you a head cold." Instead he sweated and waited because that was his job as Mr. Schwartz's driver—to wait with the bag of mostly ten-dollar bills while he placed his left elbow on the base of the driver's-side window and let the sun freckle him. Sometimes he hummed along to a tune on one of the Negro radio stations, to let the people around him know he was okay. White people had businesses in these neighborhoods, but they didn't live there.

Arthur Mermelstein had grown up in Baltimore. The heat, the drone of fans on window sills, the pesky tumult of houseflies, the rank odor of rotting dog shit on a sidewalk, and the beckoning bells of the Good Humor ice cream truck all formed the essence of summer for him, those and the pelting storms that ripped the clotted air with electricity. After the rain, even the asphalt smelt damp and fresh. The next day the heat began again. The newspaper was full of reports about marches and freedom riders, but Baltimore lay in its own sticky stupor.

He knew the names of streets—Caroline, Dallas, Rutland—but beyond what he observed through the car window, he knew nothing. How could he? He too lived in the city, but far away in the northwest corner in a white, quietly middle-class neighborhood. Some people on his street were moving up, most were getting by, and a few were in trouble—but no one was descended from slaves.

Arthur started reading the newspaper when he was five and began cutting out articles to put in scrapbooks not long after that. Among his favorites were the accounts the *Baltimore Sun* ran about someone born into a slave family who was celebrating a centennial birthday. He studied the photo of the person carefully because he liked to think he could imagine almost anything. He had read countless biographies and novels, but slavery stopped him cold. How could people do such a thing to one another? How did one group of people ever get the arrogance to own other people? How could there be such a thing as *owning* people? How could money so overrule human feeling? Why did the wise founders of the nation allow this? Where did slave owners get the nerve to call themselves Christians? What did that say about Christians? He didn't like it when his grandmother spat out the word *goyim*, but sometimes it seemed Christians deserved the word.

The cloth bag of cash next to Arthur said nothing, but it didn't have to. Like the houses and apartments Mr. Schwartz owned, those slaves had been property. You didn't have to have Stanley Mermelstein, Certified Public Accountant, for a father to realize that money could connect anything to anything, even linking dollars and bodies. It wasn't just the July heat that could upset your stomach. History seemed a vast curtain that never could be pulled up all the way to reveal an understandable stage. You got to see people's legs, but not their faces. You could make guesses; you could make inferences. But you never would know how something as huge as slavery echoed a hundred years later. Maybe it didn't, but Arthur suspected, as he sat there watching various Negroes going about their business, that it did. He suspected that the simplest gesture—a child patting a mongrel dog or a woman drinking a 7 Up—echoed that condition. He felt his tongue loll in his mouth—rife and useless. If one of those Negroes walked up to him and asked what bus took you downtown or where to get a good pastrami sandwich, he doubted he could respond. Such asking would be a big *if.*

Susan

"Now, Susan, you are my best friend and I know how much you enjoy the enhancement of perfume." Lu made a demure wave at the boxes, bottles, and atomizers on her kitchen table. Then she lightly touched her carefully sprayed, peroxide-blond bouffant. She smiled brilliantly — the relentless charm of a professional saleswoman.

Susan gazed at the aroma feast set before her. A divorcée without children, Lu didn't need a big table. Aside from the perfumes, there was a paper-napkin holder made of pine dowels and a ceramic salt and pepper shaker set. Each shaker was in the form of a pig wearing an apron and a chef's hat. "*Bon Appétit!*" was printed on the front of the apron. There were no napkins in the napkin holder.

"Where did you get these, Lu?"

"What do you mean? You know where I work. I'm eligible for the employee discount. So I've bought some and am selling them to a select group of friends. Since you are my most select friend next to Marilyn Monroe, I'm giving you first crack." She continued to smile electrically. "Have you ever tried Evening in Paris? I adore it. It's so. . . ." She paused. ". . . So refined but thrilling."

Susan nodded. Lu read romances by the gross and had the vocabulary to match. Susan nodded again. She had a half-million things to do and here she was, sitting in Lu's kitchen contemplating scents. She put her wrist out for Lu to spray a bit of Evening on it.

Maybe Lu had purchased the boxes legitimately, maybe not. Lu liked to "cut corners," as she put it. "I'm a single woman,

Susan. I have to look out for myself. I don't have a man to rely on." A brave soldier in the army of the female dispossessed, Lu always stood a little straighter when she pointed this out.

"Probably you're not going to Paris anytime soon. Stan doesn't seem like the most romantic guy in the world." Lu pursed her bright pink lips into a sly smile. She held up the perfume bottle as if to address it. "I'd sure like to go. They don't talk about boyfriends and girlfriends over there. They talk about lovers. Maybe we could go together. Two women in Paris." Lu sprayed some of the perfume on her own wrist, lowered her head, and breathed in. "Ooh-la-la!" Swooning, she listed from side to side. "We're not getting any younger, Susan." Lu gave the front of her frilly blouse a fretful tug and touched her hair again.

"Thanks for letting me know. I keep making Jack Benny jokes to myself about being thirty-nine but they aren't funny."

Lu groaned in sympathy. When she wasn't selling cosmetics at the Hutzler's on Howard Street or having a fling with some man who often turned out to be married, she acted and helped with makeup in amateur theater productions. "I'm not looking for a husband, Susan. I'm looking for a good time," was how she answered Susan's questions about "the gentlemen" currently in her life. The plural noun, to Susan's amusement — and, she had to confess, amazement — was often correct.

Susan sniffed. "Oh," she gasped. "*J'adore!*" She flung her wrist toward Lu. "How much do I owe you?"

"We can talk finances later, you French-speaker you. What I want to know is where you are going to wear Evening in Paris. To school? When you go to the grocery or take the girls to their dance lessons? Or when you're hauling your hypochondriac mom around to some doctor?"

"Lu! That isn't nice." Susan brought her wrist down into her lap.

"Honey, I know it isn't nice. That's why I said it."

"Stan and I go out on Saturday night every now and then."

"You're becoming an old person. Look at your hair."

Susan smiled. "Well, it doesn't look like your hair. Weren't you a brunette a while ago?"

"That flip you have is for Catholic schoolgirls. You're a woman."

"I know you give people advice all day about how they should smell but are you a hairdo advisor, too?" Susan pushed her wooden kitchen chair back and rose up. She put both arms out on the same side. "Look, I'm a Hawaiian Clairol girl!"

"Be serious, Susan. I bet your sex life stinks. I bet you take more tranquilizers than you have sex. I bet you haven't been noisy when you make love in a long time."

"Noisy? You bet everyone's sex life stinks that isn't having two affairs at the same time." Susan dropped her hula pose. "I could use a cigarette, Lu. May I?" She motioned at the Tareytons on a side table near the kitchen door.

"You may, English teacher." Lu winked. "And there are some mints on the counter to sweeten your breath afterwards." She winked again but a little longer. "I see a guy twice a week and we do it like crazy. I lose track of time. I lose track of everything. I melt."

"Do you love him?" Susan took a cigarette from the pack but didn't light it.

"What kind of question is that? Love got me two divorces."

"Love matters. Otherwise," Susan paused and looked up at the kitchen's overhead light. It was round and made of opaque glass. Toward its center some dark specks converged — dead flies. "Otherwise, you're just a body."

Lu stood up, went over to the side table and fetched a lighter from her pocketbook. It was slim and said "Greetings from Atlantic City" on its side. "Here, light up. And what's wrong with being a body? Sometimes you sound like such a highbrow. I like being a woman." She rolled her hips Mae West style.

"So do I, Lu." Susan took a contemplative drag, then gagged. "How you can smoke these things?" She held the cigarette away from her. "Where's an ashtray?"

"I forgot that you're mentholated. I'll finish it." She took the cigarette by its filter, then put her free arm around Susan's shoulder. "You know we're friends and friends are honest with each other. Isn't that right, hon?"

Susan knew that line. It was part of their situation comedy. Susan was the straight woman, average female height but shorter than Lu. Unlike Lu, whose piled-up bouffant was as much sculpture as hairdo, her hair wasn't teased or dyed. She used rouge more than she should, but she was pale and the rouge gave her color. She was a little overweight but that was why the Yiddish word *zaftig* existed. Lu was thinner, had blue eyes to Susan's browns. Lu wore high heels all the time; Susan did only for work. Susan liked pearls. Lu thought pearls were for decorating corpses. Together they made a pair.

"Right," Susan said as she sat back down. "So did you steal those perfumes?"

"I got them at a substantial discount. I did not steal them. How I attained that discount is my business. Let's say I have some negotiable assets. That fair?" Lu raised her arm from her friend's shoulder, pointed it up in the air as if taking an oath and spun around in a circle. "I should have been a dancer. I bet they dance up a storm in Paris."

"They probably do the Twist the same as we do." Susan felt limp. The scent had set her off. She had studied French in high school and then for a year in college. What did a *quai* look like? What color was the Seine? What books were in the book stalls? She remembered when Albert Camus died a few years ago and how stricken she felt. She had read some of his books as they were translated into English. He seemed to her what a man should be—virile, unafraid but full of feeling. In the *Sunpaper* obituary picture he wore a trench coat and looked suitably broody, but she could imagine him smiling, too. He must have had many lovers. Lu was right about that word.

Lu put out her cigarette. "I bet those Frenchmen know how to do it right."

"Is the guy who's making you lose track of your identity a Frenchman?" Susan asked.

"I think he's Swedish. Johansson's his name."

"So you're managing to get by over here."

"Don't get wise with me, Susan. You moon over these French painters you're always telling me about and you've never even been to France. What are you waiting for?"

Susan did not reply. She thought about how she liked to

listen to "The Poor People of Paris" on the hi-fi. It was sentimental but she played it over and over: *Every lover's in a trance. . . .* When she heard the song—and she had bought the LP it was on—she seemed to be hovering above the earth, suspended in pure lilting feeling. But she felt herself somehow part of Paris, too, as if she lived there, as if she could walk into an apartment or house and a man would be waiting for her, a man who adored her. Maybe that was her form of romantic dreaming. Maybe that was why she liked Lu. For all her single-woman smarts, Lu was a dreamer.

"I don't think, Lu, there's ever going to be a perfume called Evening in Baltimore."

"Only if it smelt like steamed crabs," Lu said.

"Or a Polish sausage," Susan added.

"Or a Bethlehem Steel smokestack."

"Or Tulkoff's horseradish."

"Honey, we know this town too well. We need Paris." Lu tossed her arms out, then lowered them but kept her hands out and opened—a supplication to the gods.

"Give me another teensy bit of that." Susan stuck her wrist out once more.

"Try it around Stan. Maybe you'll wake him up."

"Who said he needed waking up?"

"Every married couple needs waking up. Once upon a time I was there, too. It wasn't any fairy tale, though." Lu put the tiny bottle back into its box. Carefully she tucked the top of the box into place, then stood back to admire it. When she looked at Susan, her face was serious. "People think I'm stupid, how I spend my life at the cosmetics counter. They think I'm an airhead. But you don't. You're smart but you don't have to think I'm stupid." She picked up the box and held it at eye level. "You know that in every perfume bottle there's something special, something that makes a woman desirable." Her pitchwoman's voice had turned soft. She smiled almost ruefully. "And you know that's a good thing." She handed the box to Susan. "We— you and I—need to feel that."

Arthur

The gummy, stifling air inside the car made Arthur gasp as if he had just come up from underwater. His ears rang with a faint buzzing sound. Beside him sat his impenetrable boss. Fleshy with great, pendulous, Buddha-like earlobes and massive arms, Mr. Schwartz was built like a cube. Even his face was squarish. Though well over sixty, he was strong as a stevedore. Arthur had seen him pick up good-sized pieces of metal lying on sidewalks and in street gutters and carefully deposit them in the Lincoln's vast trunk. "Junk is worth money," he explained. He smelled like old newspapers, old undershirts, rotted leaves — a thin, acrid, sepia odor. Arthur imagined it was the ancient smell of Europe, of cobblestones and plane trees, ghetto walls and potato fields and wooden shoes. No one Arthur knew, not even his grandmother Ruby, smelled like that.

The moment when the fatal words would appear was almost predictable. There would be a lull, some minute falling-out of their collection routine. The firm coordinates of their sitting in a car on a street in Baltimore would give way. *Is Hitler*, Mr. Schwartz would bark or murmur or mutter. *Is Hitler.*

Arthur recognized the construction from Ruby — an immigrant fondness for beginning an utterance with the mild yet emphatic *Is*. That *Is* could lead to a question or an assertion or more likely a blend of the two. No noun ever took responsibility for the verb phrase; the state of being simply lingered, a bridge to nowhere. At home, Arthur joked with anyone who would listen: "Is pizza for dinner. Is a tie game in the seventh inning. Is a new pair of tennies."

Arthur had memorized Lenny Bruce's routine about two guys trying to hire a dictator and lighting in desperation on some loser named Adolf, but he kept that to himself. He could only guess at the feelings that rioted in those three syllables. Though the *Führer*, who had died a year before Arthur was born, came to seem as much a presence as the billboards advertising National Bohemian beer and Philco television sets, it was a guess. Adolf was the grimmest of all gravities. And though Arthur had no one to tell this to ("By the way, Mom and Dad, Mr. Schwartz blurts out the words *Is Hitler* every day at some seemingly random moment, which I assume has to do with some internal conversation he is having and sounds almost funny in a *Mad* magazine way but isn't."), Arthur came to find the eruptions comforting. Instinctively he believed in the poetry of spirits. The blues and spirituals he had started purchasing were teaching him that. And the spirits, as the songs testified, were often malign.

As with gravity, the force of the name never went away. After Mr. Schwartz spoke the words there occurred a silence, a void that Arthur knew not to enter and that Mr. Schwartz maintained as if it were a species of politeness. The two of them sat there—boy (or *boychik*, according to Mr. Schwartz's mood) and old man (as Arthur regarded Mr. Schwartz)—both held by the summoned pall of time. Arthur had no way to dissect this nothingness. Instead he did what he did most of the day, which was sit still, peering alertly through the windshield as if some troop of brown shirts were on the horizon rather than a series of trucks and cars. Mr. Schwartz never explained—never, beyond a few basics, launched into his own history. He too stared ahead through the shared windshield.

Arthur wondered about how Europe could bleed into America. Mr. Schwartz hadn't been in Germany. He'd been here in America. Yet he took it individually. That seemed how history worked, how everyone had to take it individually.

While driving around, Mr. Schwartz liked to quiz Arthur about history. His boss was a fiend for Abraham Lincoln.

"Did you know, Arthur" (and here Mr. Schwartz paused solemnly) "that Lincoln wanted to send the Negroes back to Africa?"

Arthur shook his head no.

"What a difference that would have made. It wasn't a practical idea, though—too many people and boats. And how

11

would I have tenants then?" Mr. Schwartz cackled.

Maybe, Arthur thought, he should bring up the subject of Lenny Bruce after all. Instead, Arthur asked his boss if he ever had been to the Lincoln Memorial.

"Once," he answered.

"Just once?" Arthur asked. He couldn't quite believe it. Washington was so nearby.

"It is not necessary to repeat the experience, Arthur. What do people say? 'I got the picture.' Very impressive. A good thing to have such a monument. Abraham Lincoln was a man of the people."

Arthur couldn't resist. "Are you a man of the people, Mr. Schwartz?"

"What else could I be? I came here as a child. America made me."

The silence that ensued was tolerable. Mr. Schwartz sank into what Arthur assumed was some historical vista. Maybe in those moments he went as far back as his childhood. The notion of Mr. Schwartz being vulnerable, of him having parents, felt like a big leap to Arthur. It was hard not to see his boss as someone who had come into the world fully formed, clutching his little notebook and his money bag. And there was some truth to his being a man of the people. He didn't sit in an office all day and shuffle paper the way Stanley Mermelstein did. Like Arthur's Grandpa Max, he was part of the grubbing and grabbing that was Baltimore.

When Mr. Schwartz spoke again, though inevitably it would be about some business issue, a wistfulness crept into his voice. Perhaps, no matter how much one rent-collecting day resembled another, he still possessed a future. One of Mr. Schwartz's optimistic mottoes—he had a few—was that "every day has a dawn."

That seemed hokey to Arthur. Many days had a fake dawn: someone saying that things would be okay when things were not okay. How many times had he read about the Orioles' manager saying some guy was going to get his batting eye back or his pitching groove? But it didn't happen. The guy wound up in the minors and no one ever heard of him again. And there was the fact of Baltimore, all those faceless, impervious rowhouses marching over miles and miles, all those people—white and colored—trapped in their little rooms. The dawn that came up in Baltimore felt more like a ceiling.

When Arthur offered an opinion about race relations or the sorry state of the Cold War world, Mr. Schwartz grunted and told him he was a "kid who was wet behind the ears" or something in Yiddish that Arthur didn't understand. Arthur didn't feel insulted. He knew that was how adults worked. It was true: Arthur hadn't lived through the Depression or Hitler or WWII or a whole bunch of murderous grief. That didn't make him stupid, though. Guys at school talked forever about cars and getting into girls' pants, and it wasn't that Arthur didn't want to be driving around with a girl next to him. But that wasn't everything.

"Yeah, I'm a kid," he muttered back to Mr. Schwartz, too low for him to hear.

Susan

The girls were squabbling about a barrette.

"It's mine," Iris insisted. "I bought it."

"You bought it?" Ellen hissed. "You don't have any money besides your allowance and you spend that on gum that rots your teeth and on stupid magazines. You didn't buy it. You stole it."

"I get more allowance than you get, peanut. And what do you know about what I do with my money?"

"Don't call me 'peanut'! I'm not a peanut!" Ellen yelled. "I'm shorter because I'm younger, you idiot!"

Susan looked up from the biography of Toulouse-Lautrec she had borrowed from the Pratt Library. For a few seconds she was neither here nor there, neither in France in the late nineteenth century among raffish artists, nor in Baltimore with her bored, querulous daughters. She wanted to linger back there in that world of fabric and flesh, of decorum and hunger. She could have been a courtesan or even a common whore, a woman whose body was her unrepentant fate. Toulouse-Lautrec frequented brothels and painted such women. She was, though, where she was—seated on a green metal lawn chair on the side porch of a brick house off Liberty Heights Avenue. No artist was eying her.

"Girls! Can't you see I'm reading?"

Iris turned to her mother. "You and Daddy argue all the time. I'll be trying to do my homework and you guys will be arguing." She put her hands on her hips to show that she meant business. "How do I feel then, Mom?"

"That's different, Iris, and you know it. We're grown-ups."

"You mean you argue about more important stuff, right?

Well, this barrette is important to me and I'm not giving it to my stupid sister."

"If you don't stop this, girls, I'm going to get up, go upstairs, take two pills, lie down, and you won't see your mother for the rest of the afternoon. Is that what you want?"

Both girls froze.

"Hold it, Mom," said Iris. "Aren't those your feel-better pills? I don't get it. How can they be your go-to-bed pills, too?"

"Me neither," Ellen added.

"Well, they're both. Sometimes lying down and resting makes you feel better. Sort of the way it is for a baby."

"But you're not a baby. You're our mom."

Susan started to laugh. "You're going to grow up and be a lawyer, Iris. To get what she wants though, a lawyer has to do more than shout at someone."

Iris considered the turquoise-colored barrette in her hand. "You can have it, Ellen. I don't want it. And anyway I have a question for you, Mom."

"About?"

"About how come we only have one grandpa? How come you never talk about your daddy? It seems almost like you never had a daddy."

Susan looked down at her book. On the cover was a print of the famous cabaret singer Jane Avril. She had her hands up and mouth open as if singing.

"My father left Ruby and me."

"What do mean, Mom, that he left you?" Ellen asked. "I don't understand."

Both girls were staring hard at Susan. She could have been on a witness stand.

"I mean that he abandoned us. He walked out one day and never came back."

"How could that be?" Ellen asked. Her eyes looked startled. Iris's eyes looked troubled. Susan could only guess what her own eyes looked like.

"This isn't an easy thing to explain because I don't know where to begin. And because I don't understand it myself. He didn't leave a note. He just left." Susan paused. "I'm trying to be honest with you. It's a good question, Iris. Maybe I should have sat you two down already and tried to talk with you about other things, the way I've talked to you about sex." Susan ran a hand over the book cover. "Maybe I felt that Grandpa Max equaled two grandfathers."

"That's not much of a joke, Mom," Iris said.

"You're right." Susan looked past her daughters out to the huge lilacs in the side yard.

The girls continued to study their mother's face.

"How could your father leave you? He was your father." It was Ellen speaking.

"He was my father." The words were shakier than Susan wanted them to be. She took a breath. "I think he loved me but for some reason he couldn't stay with Ruby and me."

"And he never sent you a letter or anything?" Iris asked. "Not even a postcard?"

"Never. I used to dream he would. I used to look in the mail every day. For years. I even used to imagine where the postcards came from — San Francisco, New York City."

The girls looked at each other and nodded.

"That must have been hard, Mom."

Ellen's voice had a quaver in it that echoed within Susan and formed a long, whistling, mournful "Oh!" Her father was like a room she never entered, but the room was still there, desolate and cold. How could she think that her children weren't part of that house, too?

"What he was like, your father?" Iris asked.

"I was a little girl, Iris. He was my father. I remember him. I remember him hugging me sometimes. I must remember him kissing me. Or kissing me on the top of my head. But I was a little girl."

"We remember stuff from when we were little girls," Ellen said.

Susan smiled. "Well, it wasn't that long ago."

"But what could make someone do that? I really wonder, Mom. It's scary." Iris was twisting a strand of her black hair. It seemed to Susan that Iris had been doing that forever — thinking and twisting her hair. Ellen's hair was cut a little shorter than her sister's. She didn't twist her hair the way Iris did.

"Some things we don't know, honey. We just don't

know."

No one said anything. Then, seeking for some compass point, all three of them came to focus on the book in Susan's lap.

"Is he one of those painter guys you like to read about, Mom?" Ellen asked.

Susan smiled more broadly. "He's one of those painter guys, yes."

The girls studied the poster on the front cover.

"Look at that hat she has on with feathers on it. When did ladies stop wearing hats like that? I wouldn't like to wear a hat that big. I like her hair, though. I wish I had blond hair." Iris looked harder at the woman.

"I wish I had blond hair too, Mom." Ellen said. "All the actresses have blond hair."

"Elizabeth Taylor doesn't have blond hair, Ellen." Iris put her face close to her sister's to better make the point.

"Elizabeth Taylor's an old lady. I mean a young person."

Susan rose up from her seat but held onto the book. "Both of you have beautiful hair. Dark curls are lovely."

"It's just Jewish hair, Mom. I'm going to straighten my hair out like Joan Baez's. And it's going to go all the way down my back because I'm going to be a folksinger." Iris opened her mouth like Jane Avril.

A pang of motherly joy seized Susan. Sometimes, she could not believe she had been granted a life on a shore beyond sorrow.

"Look, girls, let's do something. Like listening to Joan Baez. And let's have lemonade. Seeley made some this morning with real lemons." Susan placed the book on the porch table and put her arms out—one daughter for each arm. The girls went to her and pressed against her side. As if to squeeze them to her body Susan tightened her embrace. "Oh, you are getting so big. Where are my babies?"

Iris nuzzled closer. "We don't mean to argue, Mom."

"Really, Mom," Ellen added. "We don't."

"I know you love each other. We all love each other in this family."

"And you're the mother," Ellen declared.

"And I'm the mother." Susan let her arms down so her

daughters and she could pass singly through the porch door into the kitchen.

Arthur

One late afternoon after another perspiring day of driving around both East and West Baltimore, Arthur asked his boss why he didn't tell his tenants to use the mails to send their rent to him. Wouldn't it save time and money? Mr. Schwartz visited some houses every week. That was a lot of knocking on the front door and waiting for people who sometimes emerged and sometimes did not. Arthur addressed his remarks to the windshield more than to his boss, but he turned to him after he spoke and waited expectantly. His father would be proud of him. He was thinking like a businessman.

Mr. Schwartz snorted to the point where Arthur thought that he could see the old man's nose hairs waver in the breeze. "Arthur, please understand. Negroes don't use the postal service." His tone was one of belabored kindness, that of someone talking to a child about another child. "If I trusted them to go to a post office and buy a stamp and put a check in the mail, I would be broke. Most of them don't have checking accounts. Most of them need me to remind them to pay up. Most of them welcome me appearing at the front door." Another snort came forth. "I am the rent man. Negroes need to fix a person to an obligation. If you are out of sight with them, you are out of mind."

"Hey! That's crazy!" was what Arthur wanted to shout but didn't. He looked at his boss's face, which seemed serene with truth, and let some seconds go by. Arthur had seen that face before—the face of a man who had just come down from the *bima* after touching the Torah, someone who had been closer to God. "Mr. Schwartz, you're telling me that Negroes don't write letters, that they never enter a post office. That's absurd. I've seen Negroes who *work* in the post office." Arthur stopped there.

"Pull the car over, Arthur." Mr. Schwartz made a little waving motion with his right hand. "We've got some time."

"I don't mind explaining things to you, Arthur. You think all I care about is money but that's not true. You know what they say in America: 'I've been around the block.' And young people have all kinds of ideas nowadays. Like you, for instance." Mr. Schwartz paused. His large forehead was furrowed even more than usual. "You want life to be smarter than it is. You want people to be better than they are. You read your books and you think life is neat like a book is neat, sentences in a row." His voice, which was powerful to begin with, grew even stronger. The vast pressure in Mr. Schwartz's internal engine was rising. "But it isn't, Arthur. Life is a struggle. Even on a good day." He turned his head away from his pupil and toward the sunshine. "Even on a beautiful summer day, it is a struggle."

Arthur winced. Those last few words had come out almost strangled. Any moment he expected the submarine *Is Hitler* to surface, as dire a vessel as there was in God's Dire Navy.

For some hallowed seconds, Mr. Schwartz seemed mesmerized by the sun-struck Baltimore street that lay before him. When he started to speak again, his voice sounded as if it were coming from elsewhere, more of a treble than his emphatic bass. "Look, *boychik*, I know that colored people use the mails. I know there are colored people who play classical music and are doctors and writers and professors. I respect those people. I respect the people who give me some crumpled bills each week. But there are—what should I call them—lots of holes in the ground under their feet. And the holes are something called 'history.' Even you, an American boy, have heard of history." He closed his eyes. Arthur sensed that his boss was no longer talking to him, the sixteen-year-old in the front seat of a Lincoln, but to someone else. Or he was not talking to a person. He was talking to a spirit.

"Those holes, Arthur, make it hard for many people to do the simplest tasks. But that's not the main part of what I'm trying to tell you, Mr. Wisenheimer. In fact, I'm wrong about the holes. It's not holes. It's that the ground beneath the feet of these people isn't the same ground beneath your feet and my feet." Mr. Schwartz's eyes were half open and had a harsh luminosity to them, as if he had seen a vision. *"Fershtay?* It doesn't matter how much you think about it or read about it. It isn't the same ground. And it's no use pretending it is."

He sighed the epochal Jewish sigh. It had to be the second sound a Jewish child heard: first a parental squeal of delight and then a deep sigh. For a while, it seemed he wasn't going to say anything more. Traffic surged and lurched past the parked car. Sunlight sparkled off the Lincoln's black hood. Mr. Schwartz believed in the dignity of black cars.

"You must not try, Arthur, to make the world a better place. There is no fixing history. Fixing makes things worse, not better." His voice had become contemplative. The pressure inside him had at once wizened and grown firmer.

Arthur straightened up from his behind-the-wheel slouch. However mysterious Mr. Schwartz's words were, he wanted to show that he was being attentive.

"I give them what they can afford. If I give them more, they trust me even less. Why? Because no one has given them anything but grief. Maybe they are like Jews that way."

A Lenny Bruce line passed through Arthur's head: "Negroes are all Jews." It was from a routine where he sorted out the world according to what was Jewish and what was *goyish*: "Chocolate is Jewish and fudge is *goyish.*"

Mr. Schwartz paused again but did not close his eyes. "They sense that I know something about their suffering. Not that I am friendly or pleasant. I am the Jew. I am all business, though you see me chatting sometimes with the ones who pay regularly and are decent people. But they sense that I have been through some storms myself." He stopped. He was looking through the windshield, but not at what was on the street in front of him.

"Mr. Schwartz, I want to be respectful but how would they ever know that? I mean you are from the other side of the world. And you are white more than you are Jewish. You are a white man. That's what goes first here in America — white people." Arthur motioned at the sidewalk next to the car. As if in response, a Negro man emerged from a package goods store and put a brown, pint-sized bag up to his mouth.

When Mr. Schwartz turned to toward Arthur, his face was blank. He angled his head as if to better observe the human specimen on the seat beside him and exhaled — almost a moan. "I have been taking cash money from these people for a long time. I have had the opportunity to know more about them than the mayor of this city knows or most of what you call 'white people.' I know, for instance, the smells of how they cook pig. Not many Jews can say that. The pig is a devil to Jews. You must know that much, Arthur." When he said the name, he split the syllables, pressing down on each one.

Where, Arthur wondered, did all this distress come from? On the radio station, which he had on at the lowest possible volume, Mary Wells sang about "the one who really loves you." The tune lilted along, simple and inviting — air spun into sweet sound. He wished he had kept his mouth shut about the post office. Perhaps Mr. Schwartz and he were destined to sit on this block of Fleet Street, among brick warehouses of women's apparel and plumbing supplies and a few storefronts like the Red Cap Liquor Store, and never move again. The weight of history had pinned them down. Arthur thought of paintings of saints with arrows in their flesh that he had seen in the Walters Art Gallery. The saints looked up toward heaven with anguished eyes. Jews had no saints but they had been martyrs in numbers he could not conceive.

"What I told you about the post office — you don't believe me. Go up to the colored people outside that store. Ask them if they mail letters. Go on." He yanked his head toward the sidewalk, then back to Arthur. "You know what will happen? They will start laughing at you. Get out, ask them. I'll wait for you." To encourage or aggravate Arthur, Mr. Schwartz intertwined his fingers in the air in front of him, bridging one contented thumb against the other.

"I'll take your remarks under advisement, Mr. Schwartz." Arthur had picked up the phrase from his pal Herbie Freilich, who planned to become the Maryland state attorney when he grew up. He wasn't giving in to Mr. Schwartz but he wasn't opening the car door, either. The man on the sidewalk with the bottle in the bag was wiping his mouth with a contented sweep of the back of a hand. The laughter that Mr. Schwartz envisioned could mean anything—or it could mean what Mr. Schwartz believed it meant. The thought nailed Arthur to his seat: how would he—the *boychik*, the sprat, the youth— know? Who was he to ask?

"Okay." Mr. Schwartz separated his hands and put his thumbs up to indicate he was pleased. He savored such gestures.

"Okay," Arthur answered.

That ultimate American word hung in the car between the two of them, an indication of how far Mr. Schwartz had traveled from the town in central Europe he had left before World War I. Arthur had forgotten the town's name because it was so hopelessly foreign—*Ge*-something.

When Arthur pulled the car into the street, he had the uncanny feeling that he had never before been in this city where he was born and was still being raised. For all its solidity and its signs, its shops and its white marble steps, Baltimore was a phantasm. Then someone laid on the horn, Mr. Schwartz grunted with impatience, and he was back in the world that claimed him as its own.

Susan

Summer was passing but the aura of freedom lingered. Susan could make Stan's and Arthur's breakfast in her bathrobe. She could say goodbye to them, then go out onto the little patio behind the house, drink a glass of orange juice she had squeezed, listen to the birds, look over the tea roses she grew, and read the paper. In a little while the bus would come to take her daughters to the day camp she had signed them up for. They said they didn't like it but they said that about most things. When they came home, smelling of chlorine and Bazooka gum, they competed to be the first to tell about a counselor kissing another counselor or what an older girl had told them an older boy wanted to do with her. She had registered them for activities like lifesaving and softball, but it looked like her girls were going to love camp. Whatever they were at eleven and thirteen, they weren't bashful—especially when they were together. They ran upstairs to giggle and talk on the phone.

Susan tried to think what she had been like at that age but couldn't. There was no camp and no giggling. There was what she told her daughters, though she spared them the details of how one morning in early May her father walked out the door of their two-bedroom apartment in Cleveland, Ohio, to go to work, the way he went to work every weekday, and never came back. She remembered lying in bed that night and wondering and getting up in the morning and wondering and being afraid to say anything beyond, "Where's Papa?" Her mother shook her head as if trying to remember something but shook it too violently. It was frightening—someone trying to shake her head off her neck.

The second evening Ruby's wails began. "What has happened? Tell me, mine Susie, what has happened?" Her mother's eyes bored into her: perhaps some clue existed within her daughter's chest. Susan was too bewildered to cry. Ruby collapsed in a thick armchair but Susan stood very still, as if at attention, as if that could make things right. She looked down at her shoes, which had little straps and buckles on them. One strap was frayed and seemed as though it was going to break soon.

After what seemed like hours but couldn't have been — could anyone cry that long? — Ruby told Susan not to tell anyone what had happened. "Tell people your papa is on a business trip. People know he sells insurance. We don't want people talking." Of course people talked anyway — they were people. "How is Isaac doing? We haven't seen him lately. We hope he's all right." Then they talked about the weather or the Dalmatian around the corner that barked at everyone. Then, after a few weeks, a courteous, awful silence entered — a leeriness, as if Ruby and she had caught a contagious disease.

That gulf between the disappearance of her father and life going on was where Susan had to dwell. Everyone around them — neighbors, cousins, teachers, girl friends — skirted that gulf but Susan felt it daily, like the psalm of David they repeated in school: "I laid me down and slept; I awaked; for the Lord sustained me." Rather than moving closer to consolation, she moved away from it. God was a father, after all, and her father was an absence, not a presence. Or worse, her father was a presence that had become an absence — a taunt, a humiliation. As she grew older, her father's vanishing came to seem like the question of God's continued existence: no one really knew.

How many catastrophes occurred in human lives that never made it into the newspaper in front of her? Virtually all, but newspapers were reserved for the larger cataclysms. Occasionally an article focused on an individual life — a common person — and some grief that had torn that life apart — a traffic fatality, a murder. Or as an antidote, an article focused on some celebratory occasion — a graduation or anniversary. Susan looked over at the yellow roses beside the patio and noticed how a few droplets of dew lingered on some leaves. The moisture glimmered in the sun. If only she could sit each morning like this and look at what was around her. An iridescent bug lit on one of the rose blossoms. She watched it intently, not because she wished to identify it, but because it fascinated her. It seemed in no hurry to move. It had nothing to say to her. She appreciated that.

What the *Sun* told her that morning was that Martin Luther King Jr., or "the Reverend," as her maid, Seeley, referred to him, was in jail in some city in Georgia that she had never heard of. Back in December he had been arrested for "parading without a permit, congregating on the sidewalk, and obstructing traffic." The "parade" had been a march on the city hall to protest the city's segregated facilities. After he was released in December, his case finally had come up for trial. The mayor of the city said he would listen to "responsible, law-abiding citizens, not outside agitators."

In the photo of the "agitator" being led off, King's face was grave but gentle. Susan had read that when he was arrested he had said "God bless you" to the policeman. Now he had been found guilty. What else would he have been found? Innocent was the last thing he was. Innocence was for the likes of her, with her roses and orange juice and birdsong. There had been times in her classes when her Negro students informed her, when some issue about race came up, that "you don't know how it is, Mrs. M." She remembered blushing each time. She, after all, was supposed to be the teacher; they were the students. But they weren't sassing her. One of them had put it simply: "White people dishin' it. Black folks takin' it. Ain't that the truth?" That had been LeRoy Smith, a tall, shy boy who sat in the back of the room. She refrained from correcting *ain't,* saying instead, "I see, LeRoy. Thank you for that."

Did he really think she could see what he saw?

Susan put the paper down on the glass top of the wrought-iron outdoor table, then folded it so that Reverend King wasn't looking out at her. What he was doing was the right thing. There was no question—these people in the South had to be pushed—but where would it lead? It wasn't merely a speculative question. Would they sell their house to a Negro family and make the people on their block angry with them? Some of them were angry already. Mr. Steadman, who lived three houses down, complained regularly to anyone who would listen about "uppity niggers."

When Susan looked around her, the roses offered only their loveliness. Though she felt as natural as any growing thing, her arms tingling with the sunshine's warmth, the newspaper insisted she wasn't. Everything human was made up.

"My daughter, where are you?" Ruby was standing at the other side of the table and examining her carefully through her thick glasses. The eye doctor had told them that in a year or two "inoperable deterioration" would render her "legally blind." Ruby's question, though, was metaphorical. Puncturing her daughter's solitude remained for her a consecrated task. Until Susan was in the seventh grade Ruby came to her school each day to accompany her home. She stood on the sidewalk, no matter the weather, and waited — patient, obstinate, anxious, hopeful. When Susan appeared, Ruby waved vigorously. Loss rendered any daily occurrence a miracle of sorts. Approaching her mother, Susan had felt a public weight lifting and a private one descending.

"I'm thinking, Ma. You know me. I like to think."

"About what?" Ruby continued to peer.

Susan picked up the front section of the newspaper. "I'm thinking about why Negroes have to go to jail to be able to do what they should be able to do in the first place. They're citizens. That was made official a long time ago. I'm thinking that these marches and sit-ins and protests are nuts, because people shouldn't have to lie down on sidewalks and get arrested so they can use the local library or eat a bologna sandwich somewhere. I'm thinking this nation is built on lies." She peered back at Ruby as if she, too, were myopic. "And I'm thinking, Ma, about what I am doing here on this patio talking to you about it."

"The *shvartzer* minister is in jail again?"

"Ma, the word is *Negro*. I'm glad to use Yiddish when I need to use Yiddish but the word is *Negro*. *Fershtay?*"

"Not when I was a girl. Black is black." Ruby made a loud clacking sound, a coming together of her lower false teeth with her uppers. "But I'm an old woman. And you know me — *sotsyalist*. For such a man to be in jail is a *shande*. Jail is not for a doctor."

Ruby thought well of anyone who was a doctor. Medicine or philosophy was the same to her. Dr. King was to be

27

respected for being *Dr.* King. Ruby also liked to announce that she was a socialist. It was hard to know what the word meant to her beyond her contempt for both communists and capitalists. "What is left," she used to say, "but *sotsyalist?*" (When Arthur was around the age of twelve, mimicking his grandmother had become one of his favorite pastimes: "What is left for a duckpin bowler but *sotsyalist?* What is left in this refrigerator but *sotsyalist?*") Susan's mother had been in the States since the turn of the century but she still described herself as a *griner*—a greenhorn.

"You're right, Ma. The person in jail is a better person than the jailer is—a much better person." Susan looked at the amiable face of a sheriff. Even in a black and white photograph he seemed florid. "Just doing my job," he had told the reporters from the North.

"So what is for a special at the grocery?" Ruby pulled a chair out and sat down carefully. She had told Susan that the wrought-iron chairs with their round seats were too small. "Only half your *tuches* fits on them."

"The Acme has chicken breasts and legs. Lamb chops too. But I like the A & P better because the butcher flirts with me."

"A married woman with three children and you think about some *goy* with blood on his apron?" Ruby took off her glasses and rubbed her eyes.

"Don't rub your eyes, Ma. And in case you've forgotten, a woman is a woman, not a stone."

"A woman with a husband who takes care of her is first a wife. *Nu?*" Both fair and wise, Ruby turned her palms up, then put her glasses back on. Her daughter knew the gesture: you didn't need to have good vision to have insight.

"I can pay the difference from my pocketbook." Susan rubbed her forehead with her right hand. When your seventy-two-year-old, never-remarried, going-blind mother lived with you, yesterday often smothered today. Though Susan continued to rub her forehead as if to expunge some mark, she felt comfortable with exasperation. By this point, the love between mother and daughter was more a gorge than a bridge—a depth that seemed the creation of eons rather than decades.

Her eyes rested on the ad before her: two-for-one sales on Jell-O and Kool-Aid. The girls begged her to buy Kool-Aid, but she refused. The ingenuities of commercial spelling revolted her. So did the products.

"Susie, read to me about the *shvartzer* minister."

"Ma!"

"I mean the Negro." Ruby clacked her teeth again, pleased with herself. "*Shvartzer* or Negro, what is it with a word? He sits in jail, such a man, as if a criminal?" Ruby shuddered, then frowned.

"He sits in jail." Susan looked up from the paper to see a honeybee touch down on one of her pink roses and begin to sip. As she watched it move its delicate wings slowly, then rapidly, she felt an impulse to sit there and let the morning pass without a trip to the grocery or the dry cleaner or the pharmacy to pick up some of her pills and the milk of magnesia that both her husband and mother seemed to live on.

"There's going to have to be a lot of jails, Ma."

Arthur

What Arthur had to show for his summer labors was a flat ass from so much sitting in a car. He could turn a steering wheel with one hand and parallel park like a pro. He had mislaid three pairs of sunglasses in various luncheonettes and memorized dozens of the songs he heard on the Negro radio stations. He knew streets in East and West Baltimore that few white people could name, much less say they had been there. None of that seemed very fascinating but his father reminded him when he complained about being bored that "a job was a job." His dad was big on tautology—that and reminding Arthur that he was being paid for his efforts.

When he wasn't maneuvering the boat-like Lincoln, he was waiting for his boss to come back to the car. A beige cotton bag stuffed with paper money and an occasional fifty-cent piece sat beside him. When Mr. Schwartz returned with cash in hand, he announced an amount that Arthur wrote down in a hardbound ledger. In the meantime, Arthur listened to the car radio or, if it was going to be a long stop, he turned off the engine and listened on the small transistor radio he carried. ("Not good, Arthur, for the car to run the battery. Batteries, they cost money, too.") Mr. Schwartz didn't like what he called "jungle music," but as long as Arthur kept the volume down he tolerated it. The old man wore a hearing aid, which didn't work well. "Why not get another one?" was not a question Arthur asked.

A sheaf of eviction notices lay in the backseat of the car, but Arthur never saw Mr. Schwartz write one up. A discussion between landlord and tenant was often drawn out over a period of weeks; then the person paid up part of what was owed. Evicting people was, as Mr. Schwartz unceremoniously put it, "a pain in the *tuches*." Sooner or later, the weary bills would make their way into the moneybag; the law was on his side. When someone vacated without giving notice, as occasionally happened, he shrugged it off as the price of doing business with "the colored." The *why* of their leaving was never spoken of, though the inference was that some Negroes — like some birds — were migratory creatures.

The fragility of these lives startled Arthur. His parents argued about money, but that was about what to do with it. Even when his father complained that there was not enough, it had nothing to do with paying the mortgage. It had to do with how much was considered enough. For many of these people nothing-to-very-little was the issue. Often renters stood in the doorway and watched Mr. Schwartz and him drive off. "Good riddance," their eyes said.

The city remained oven-like. As usual, the Lincoln sat by the curb in the middle of a stark block of rowhouses — not a tree in sight. Across the street, two girls were jumping rope. *Slap snap slap snap* sang the rope. While Arthur moved the dial from a commercial for Ex-Lax to anything musical and let the car idle, Mr. Schwartz looked up from his pad and began to recount how the last person with whom he had spoken, a middle-aged man with a genial pot belly, related how the politicians were stealing all the money, including the rent.

Ingenious explanations pleased the landlord. "'Next week,' I told him, 'the mayor is going to have to take his hand out of your pocket.'" Mr. Schwartz closed his pad and put it in his shirt pocket. "I confessed that I half agreed with him. With the politicians money disappears like a shadow in the night."

Deep and mellifluous, another voice entered the car. "Excuse me, gentlemen, for interrupting, but hand over that bag there." Arthur and Mr. Schwartz turned in the direction of the voice and saw a short Negro man with a gun. The man was not leaning into the front seat through the open car window, but the gun, a revolver that looked as though it could blow the head off a steer, was not far from Mr. Schwartz's right shoulder. The gunman must have come up from the rear. Across the street the two girls were gaily chanting in unison: "My name is Mary . . ."

Arthur not only saw the gun but smelled it too — something hard and sharp, something that had been raised up

31

from deep within the earth. His hand remained on the dial. Between-station static leaked out.

"The bag," the voice repeated but urgently this time. The gun started to move even closer to Mr. Schwartz, who had said nothing but now in a voice that was soft but audible declared, "Drive, Arthur." He did not move a muscle as he spoke.

Arthur switched from Park into Drive and in a brief, coordinated motion—foot on the gas, steering wheel turned slightly to the left, eyes checking the mirrors for cars coming up alongside—he pulled away from the curb and into the street. The car did not buck or squeal. It went down the street the way cars were supposed to, quickly but not overly fast. Cars in the other lane came toward the Lincoln, and a truck from a glass-repair company, one of those trucks with racks on the side for the glass panels, drove up from behind. The traffic seemed incredible to Arthur. Life was flowing serenely forward.

When Arthur looked in the rearview, he saw a man standing on the sidewalk holding a gun that was aimed as if the car hadn't moved. The man began to get smaller in the mirror, and then Arthur made a right turn and couldn't see the man anymore.

For a few blocks neither Arthur nor Mr. Schwartz said anything. Arthur drove until Mr. Schwartz instructed, "Turn there. Our next house is off Monroe Street."

"Good," Arthur replied. The word sounded hollow, as if it had traveled from another galaxy to reach him. Though his body felt watery, his mouth was dry. His neck ached from wanting to swivel his head around and look behind. Maybe the gunman was chasing them. Adrenaline pummeled him. He wanted to pull over and start running anywhere, just to run. More thoughts and feelings assailed his head than a head could hold. They bounced up against one another like pebbles or marbles.

Mr. Schwartz said nothing, looking straight ahead as if he were driving. He wasn't whistling but he wasn't frowning either. Arthur couldn't tell if he was placid or stolid. In all likelihood, he was both. The gunman might as well have been inquiring about the prospect of rain that evening.

His boss must be pleased, Arthur thought. He still had

the money, which was what mattered. He had not given in. Though his head still throbbed, Arthur relaxed his grip on the steering wheel. Was the gun real to Mr. Schwartz? Did he care about his own death? Was he, even in that moment, here in America, or was he back in Europe, looking down the barrel of the torment that he spoke to each day? Did he think he was alone in the car, even as he told Arthur to drive away? Did it occur to him to feel responsible for his employee's life? The long fuse of questions sputtered and sparked. Arthur put a hand out to touch the money bag but then recoiled.

"Something wrong, *boychik*?" Mr. Schwartz inquired. He raised his eyebrows in concern. He also smiled slightly. His teeth were yellow-brown.

"We could have been shot, Mr. Schwartz." Arthur tried to control the throb in his voice but couldn't.

"We could have been, Arthur, but we weren't. That is good, don't you think?" Mr. Schwartz sighed with pleasure. "You mustn't back down from people, Arthur. They have all kinds of notions."

"But a gun isn't a notion."

"Yes and no. The person with the gun is full of notions. It is the person that pulls the trigger, not the gun."

"And you were sure he wouldn't pull the trigger." Arthur meant to pose a question but it came out a statement.

"Maybe he did pull it. Maybe the gun misfired. It happens. Unless we go back and ask him, we won't know." He looked over at Arthur and smiled again. "I don't think that would be a good idea, though. I could call the police and report an attempted armed robbery but why bother? They have enough *mishegas* on their hands already. All around" — he gestured with a hand — "is trouble."

Arthur drove down Fayette toward Monroe, looking out for kids darting into the street after a ball or playing tag. The world — the exhaust fumes from an old Plymouth in front of him, the bleating radio, the odor of his own anxious armpits — started to come back to him. He felt disappointed. Something in him wanted the gun to go off. Something in him wanted to wake Mr. Schwartz up. Something in him felt cheated. The feeling depressed him. A gagging sound started from his throat. He didn't want to get hurt but a revelation had come and gone. Something could have come clear.

He pulled the car over to where Mr. Schwartz indicated. The sidewalk stood empty — a rare occasion, since it functioned as an extension of the houses, a place where adults came together and lingered, where children played from morning till night, where young men and women bantered. Mr. Schwartz pulled out his little pad with its spidery notations and opened the passenger side door. He didn't look over at Arthur, nor did he say anything. He didn't slam the car door shut as an exclamation; he didn't gently push it in, either. He was being himself, being regular. Whatever was going on inside of him was so deep it would never reach the surface. Or it had evaporated already — the sweat of another day in hell. Arthur thought of people saying "Go to hell" as if it were some place elsewhere. He heaved forward as if to vomit but nothing came up. Asphalt heat waves shimmered in the thick air. An ambulance clanged in the distance.

He turned the car radio knob a bit to the right. A voice announced that Esther Phillips was up next. "Little Esther no more! She a big girl now!" the Moon Man, a favorite disk jockey of Arthur's, brayed with practiced delight. Arthur liked his tag: "Here from the moon to spin you some tunes." Esther Phillips began to plead, her voice sultry with anguish, "Please, release me . . ." Arthur sat there behind the steering wheel, at once listening and not listening. He had seen the gun. The gun had seen him.

When he looked out at the sidewalk beside the car, he saw broken glass, a RC Cola bottle someone had smashed. The name announced itself on a large shard. He had seen a lot of broken glass that summer. He could picture the gesture — someone, out of anger or boredom or both, smashing the bottle to the ground as if to say, "Take that!" There had to be something freeing in that moment of breaking the glass, but afterwards what remained? Arthur tried to imagine standing there and looking down at the glass he had just thrown to the ground. Emptiness grabbed at him, then something worse — the disgrace of aimlessness. Despite the names on the street signs, every one of the streets themselves seemed lost.

The car door opened. Mr. Schwartz grunted that the tenant had paid in full. He put the money into the bag and read out the next address from his notebook. Arthur wrote down a dollar sign and a number before shifting once more from Park to Drive. He knew that when he got home he was not going to tell anyone what happened. It was not hard to imagine what would occur. His mother would shriek; his father would make a face somewhere between indigestion and disgust. Then his mother would start in on his father about what kind of job he was letting his son do—a job that put his life in jeopardy. Arthur could hear that word in his head— *jeopardy*. His father would get angry and start shouting about life in the big city. His mother would cry and run upstairs to the bedroom. His father would yell something at the empty space where his mother had been, then turn to Arthur and begin to lecture him about being a man.

Mr. Schwartz was humming something but it wasn't the Esther Phillips song. It was more like a chant or prayer, some plaintive scrap from the old country. Then he stopped and glanced over at Arthur. His dark eyes sparkled like sun behind clouds. "That was a close one, *boychik*. I've had a few."

Susan

Sometimes, before she lit a cigarette, Susan thought of *The Great Gatsby*. It wasn't something she would have told anyone. It sounded a little crazy, but the novels she taught every year — *Gatsby*, *A Tale of Two Cities*, *My Ántonia*, *The Return of the Native*, *Oliver Twist* — were part of who she was. They weren't the reason why she got up in the morning — her children would have been the first answer to that ruthless question — but they formed an inner landscape that was her truest home. When she taught the books, she got to be herself, as if the books were conduits for her spirit as much she was a conduit for their spirits. When her students talked about the books, when she felt they were "getting it" (as her son Arthur would have put it), it was as if she were hearing a quickened choir of spirits. That wasn't every day, of course, but when it happened, it was a marvel.

Her attachment was more than pedagogical light and reason. The books haunted her. Their sheer presence — words on a page — made up for loss, yet the books exaggerated loss because they focused so unflinchingly on it. Even when you took the right, happy steps forward that Susan had taken — you married, procreated, and did something useful with yourself — the books said that loss was bound to shadow you. "Time = Loss" was the mortal equation, though that wasn't a phrase she used with her students. She reserved it for herself.

What occurred to her was how in the night preceding Jay Gatsby's death, Nick and Gatsby hunted for cigarettes through the dark rooms of the mansion. Cigarettes reassured body and soul, though they hadn't helped Gatsby. It was the image, however, that unnerved her: the two men poking around, the purpose of it and the senselessness, their being somehow connected and their being disconnected. Yet if she had told someone like Lu about how she felt—Lu having seen Susan light hundreds if not thousands of cigarettes—Lu would have burst out laughing. "You think what? Before you light up?"

Susan blew out a plume of smoke and looked around her kitchen at the cabinets with their mismatched handles, the dinette table that barely held the six of them and the crack that wandered across the linoleum and then branched near the refrigerator. She didn't want Gatsby's palace—those rooms that went on forever were a dream turned nightmare—but she wanted a bigger house with more space for everybody. They needed to not be on top of one another. There was no crime in wanting that.

For a second she felt unsteady, the havoc of her imaginative bones—Nick and Gatsby and Daisy and Tom all echoing inside her—but she turned to the basement door and opened it. "Seeley," she hollered down the stairs, "let's get going. If I'm going to give you a ride, I want to do it now."

Seeley's musical voice drifted up the stairs. "Be up in a second, Mrs. Merm. Ruby's comin', too."

She had given Seeley, who liked plants as much as she did, two philodendrons. It wouldn't have been right to make her carry them on the bus. And Ruby needed to take a ride somewhere. She got crankier than usual if she didn't get out of the house each day. A slow walk around the neighborhood wasn't enough: "About these people in these houses I know enough already." She needed to get in the car, look around as best she could and make her comments about the condition of Baltimore.

Ruby sat beside her in the Ford; Seeley sat in back. "This such a nice car, Mrs. Merm," Seeley said and gave a contented sigh. She didn't drive, nor did Ruby. The two of them liked to discuss the traffic accidents they read about in the *Sun*. "Folks goin' too fast nowadays," Seeley would say, shaking her head. Ruby would concur. "In a hurry. Always in a hurry. And why to hurry?" Ruby could be relied upon to add a rhetorical yet existential question.

Seeley lived in a rowhouse off Poplar Grove, not far from Coppin State College. There were trees by the sidewalks, and many people had flowers on their little patch of front lawn. It

Baron Wormser

wasn't very different from where Stan's father lived, over by the ballpark, except that everyone who lived where Seeley lived was Negro and everyone who lived where Max lived was white. What had Tom Buchanan said in *Gatsby* about the races? "Next they'll throw everything overboard and have intermarriage between black and white." In class last May her students talked about the indefinite *they* and how that created a weak argument for any case. "But you know who *they* means, Mrs. Merm," a Negro girl named Sandra Clark said. "It means how people avoid themselves. It means how one person can hide behind others but those people—each person hiding—add up. It means how you blame others for your own prejudice." She remembered nodding assent, at once delighted, dumbfounded, and agitated by her own confusions. "You teach to learn," her favorite colleague, Joe Costa, often said.

"These plants need a front window or can I leave 'em further back in the parlor?" Seeley asked.

"Back-to-school sale at the five and dime, Susie," Ruby interjected. "The children need school supplies."

"Keep them away from direct sunlight, Seeley. They grow rapidly so after a while you may want to trim them back. They'll trail right down to the floor." Susan looked in the rearview when she spoke.

Seeley nodded. She held the plants on her lap in a cardboard tray.

"The kids," Susan went on, "can buy their own supplies, Ma. They're plenty big, including Ellen. They need to budget their money." Susan didn't lower her voice because of Seeley. There must have been something their maid didn't know about the Mermelsteins, but Susan couldn't say what it was.

"Is your money or your husband's?" Ruby wheezed. "Which?"

Susan went back to looking in the mirror. "The philodendron leaves are pretty, aren't they Seeley? I like that purplish color."

"They are, Mrs. Merm. They are."

"Which?" Ruby repeated.

"Ma, it doesn't matter. The money's there. Okay? Don't worry about it. Stan is generous. You know that. You live in our house and he doesn't say a word about it, does he?"

"He gives me looks. I see them. Every day I see."

Seeley sat a little farther back on her seat and looked out the window.

"Where are you going to live, Ma? And Stan has a lot on his mind. What I think sometimes is that you're paranoid. You *fershtay* that word? You think too much about the bombs and missiles. . . ."

A brown dog rushed out from between two parked cars. Susan hit the brake, turned the wheel to the left with her left hand, and grabbed her mother's wrist with the right. The car lurched into the oncoming lane and then spun, tires squealing desperately as they tried to grab asphalt. The movement was violent but slow. Every instant of the car's turning seemed a stunned eternity.

Susan waited for another sound, a crash, but there was no other sound. No cars were driving toward them; the car behind them had been at a safe distance. The Ford sat there untouched, at a slight sideways angle to the traffic. The dog—it was a boxer—had reached the other side of the street and kept on running.

Everyone had been flung forward and then fallen back. For some seconds there was eerie silence—are we alive?—then Ruby began to whimper: "Mine shoulder. Is hurt. *Vey iz mir.*" She shuddered and rested heavily against the back of the seat.

Susan looked at her mother but spoke to the backseat. "Seeley, are you okay? That dog was on top of me before I knew it."

"I believe I'm fine," Seeley answered. She began to brush off a quantity of dirt that had come loose from the plants. "That dog is gonna get hisself killed. You can't do that, run cross a street like that." Seeley clicked her tongue against the roof of her mouth—a castanet of consternation.

Susan turned the car in the direction of the traffic on that side of the street, drove to a parking space and shut off the engine. She put her head down against the steering wheel.

"And how do I feel?" she asked aloud. The words seemed to explode from her. There was a ringing in her head, a metal band being tightened.

Ruby stopped whimpering. Seeley looked up from the plants.

"My neck hurts. My head has an alarm going off. *Briiing!*" She turned to Ruby. "Do you hear, Ma? I'm hurt, too! I'm hurt!" She was shouting. "Do you hear me? I'm in this car too." Then she started crying, heaving forward and sobbing.

"Mine girl, Susie. Don't cry." Ruby grabbed her own left shoulder, grimaced and tried to move closer.

Seeley strained to get a better view. "That okay, Mrs. Merm. You gonna be all right. You done right to stop. Somebody probably love that dog." She paused to consider. "Somebody need to keep a better eye out, though."

Slowly Susan raised her face. The rouge on her cheeks was creased but she had stopped crying. "What happened? I was driving along. I was telling Ma something. Then . . ." She put her face up close to the rearview. "What a sight I am." She pulled a tissue out of her pocketbook and dabbed at the wetness. She was still in her body. There was no blood anywhere. There were no cracked windshields or smashed-in doors. No sirens were headed toward her. "We're okay, aren't we?" she asked. Her voice was tiny.

The earth had opened up but she had survived. "I'm going to drive you home, Seeley, and then drive Ma and myself to the emergency room. I want you to call the house, Seeley — or better, may I use your phone?"

"Phone not workin', Mrs. Merm."

"I'll stop at a phone booth, then. I've got dimes in my pocketbook." She put a hand up to her hair to fluff it a bit. "It would have been awful if I'd hit that dog. Stan makes fun of me because I hate to step on an ant." She batted her eyes at the rearview. People in the emergency room probably wouldn't scrutinize her makeup too closely.

She looked around. An older Negro man stood nearby on the sidewalk watching them: *What are these people doing?* He was leaning on a cane. He wore a gray felt hat with a silk band.

Her father had worn hats like that. She recalled the softness of the worn silk band, how her little girl fingers had stroked it again and again, how it had soothed her, how there had been hats that remained in the apartment after her father left, how Ruby let them sit there.

She looked down at her hands. They weren't shaking; they were still attached to her arms. Seeley coughed. Ruby moaned softly. Susan started the engine and clutched the wheel.

Arthur

With one hand Arthur opened the kitchen door and loosened his tie with the other.

His mother looked up from the layer cake she was bent over. "And what are you doing here in the middle of the afternoon, Mr. Working Man?" Her voice was that warm, spry, upbeat mother's voice that Arthur sometimes wished he could carry around in a jar and, when he was low, take a whiff of. He wouldn't of course admit that to anyone. Susan was spreading chocolate frosting onto the cake. "Want a lick?" She brandished a rubber spatula.

Arthur took off his sport jacket, placed it on the back of a chair, and walked toward the cake. "To answer your questions in order, Mom, I'm not working because Mr. Schwartz's stomach was acting up. It's probably indigestion but Mr. Schwartz is always saying stuff like 'no one lives forever.' No one does live forever but it's probably indigestion. He left me off downtown and I took the bus home. There's nothing like riding the bus in the summer to wake a person's nose up." He extended the index finger of his right hand and swept off some frosting. "Mmmm, good." For emphasis he smacked his lips. "My sisters must not be home because it's quiet. Ruby must be taking a snooze. Seeley must be working downstairs. Dad is taking care of the Free World of required taxes. My mom's baking a cake. I feel like a reporter: 'All's well in the Mermelstein household. Good night.' Can I lick the bowl?"

"'May I?' is the way to say that, which you know very well." Susan picked up the bowl and held it out as an offering. "You may."

"There's a little time before school starts. Grammar's still on vacation." Arthur began scraping the sides with the spatula.

"Is it just Jewish people who talk about dying every other minute or does everyone do that? Ruby is always talking about the angel of death. I thought only Gentiles believed in angels. There aren't any pictures of angels on the synagogue walls that I've seen." He swallowed a gob of the sweet stuff and grunted with pleasure. "Boy, this is good. I should come home early every day."

"I don't bake a cake every day, Arthur. " Both his parents called him by his given name. When someone called up and asked for him by his nickname, they sometimes paused to think whether the bluntly named "Merm" lived in their household. "Jews don't believe in representations, so that's why there are no pictures in the synagogue, which, like the difference between *can* and *may*, you knew already. And there are angels in the Bible, which you also knew." Susan pulled out the attachments from the electric beater and put them in the sink. "What are you reading these days up in your bedroom?"

"F. Scott Fitzgerald. Ever read him?" Arthur looked around the kitchen. "I know you've read him a ton, Mom, just joking. Can I bum a cigarette from you? Oops! May I bum a cigarette from you?" He handed the clean bowl back.

"You shouldn't smoke. I smoke because I have to."

"That's not an answer, Mom."

"No. I don't like you to smoke in my presence."

"Then I'll go outside and smoke."

"I'm not giving you a cigarette. When I give you a cigarette, it's a weakness on my part. What kind of mother gives her son cigarettes?" Susan turned her back and busied herself at the sink.

Arthur sat down on one of the kitchen chairs but got up immediately and walked over to the sink. "You don't make sense, Mom, but that's okay. Not everyone makes sense all the time, right? I just like to smoke a cigarette once in a while. You know, like an adult. And for the record, Mrs. Rosen gives Howie cigarettes." Mrs. Rosen lived in a duplex across the street. She was divorced. There were three divorced women on their street, which Arthur thought made it a weird street. Ruby said divorce was a *shande*—a shame, a scandal—but she said that about borscht that came in a jar, Elvis Presley, and Wall Street, too.

43

There were a lot of *shandes*.

"Mrs. Rosen has a hard life, Arthur. If she wants to give her son cigarettes, that's her business. As for you, don't smoke those things in your bedroom. You'll burn the house down."

"And we'll all die. See what I mean, Mom? I'm going upstairs to read F. Scott Fitzgerald and not burn the house down. Thanks for the frosting." He grabbed his jacket and nodded in his mother's direction.

"Hold on," Susan said. "When is your job with Mr. Schwartz done?"

"Two days."

"How do you feel about that?"

"Do you want me to keep talking to your back, Mom, or should I go outside and put a ladder up to the kitchen wall and talk to you through the window?"

Susan turned around. "Sorry. I'm just cleaning up."

"I feel I'm glad it's over. I feel that Mr. Schwartz is someone who doesn't want to be here on earth but isn't in a hurry to leave either. I feel that a sword is hanging over his head and the head of anyone near him—like me. I'm glad to get away from that sword."

"And have you gotten to like him?"

"I guess it would take an effort to sit two feet away from someone for two months and not have some positive feeling. He picked up the tab for a lot of corned beef sandwiches, but he's a difficult man. And I think he likes to be difficult. If things were easy, he'd be bored. Or he'd feel cheated." Arthur put down his sport jacket again. "I probably should get this thing cleaned."

"You should. I like it when you pay attention to your clothes." Susan flashed one of her bright motherly smiles. "Did you talk about Negroes with him?"

"Wow, this feels like an interview for a school project. Is this the price I have to pay for licking some frosting?"

"Arthur—"

"I know, Mom, you're just showing an interest. It's what parents are supposed to do, and you're a parent, so *ergo sum* or some phrase like that." Arthur sniffed. "How long is it going to take for that cake to bake?"

"It's for dinner, Arthur. I don't give out pieces of freshly baked cake until dessert. That's a house rule."

"I know, Mom—just checking if you were having a weak moment." Arthur loosened his tie a little further. "Yeah, we talked about Negroes aplenty. Mr. Schwartz should write a book about them. He's an expert."

"You must be one, too, after a few months."

"I haven't talked to one Negro in two months—not one. I'd do better going down to the car wash on Pennsylvania Avenue and talking with the guys there. I'd do better going back to school. I'd do better going downstairs and saying 'hi' to Seeley. All I know is being in that car and hearing Mr. Schwartz and listening to the radio." Arthur paused. "I guess it's a wonder I haven't gone crazy. *Meshuga*—to quote Mr. Schwartz and my grandmother." He started to make a circling motion with his index finger beside his head. "Maybe I have. Maybe I'm suffering from some Baltimore disease and don't know it. Maybe I should go to Johns Hopkins and tell them I have Negro-itis. It's a disease of white people who are close up yet far away."

Arthur looked down at his jacket as if it had something to tell him. He liked to talk to his mother but he didn't like to. She was going to come over and give him a hug, which was okay, but he didn't need a hug. For starters, he needed a girlfriend. He was what his friend John Silverman called "WB." It didn't stand for Warner Brothers; it stood for Walking Boner.

Susan took a few steps toward him.

"Just don't tell me you're proud of me, Mom. No offense but I'm not proud of myself and I don't want you to be. I did the job because Dad told me to do it. I don't know if that's a good thing or a bad thing. Maybe I should have just run away this summer. Kids do things like that. And maybe I should have gotten out of the car and gone up to some people and started talking with them. I talk with Negro guys at City all day long."

Susan halted. She had a dish towel in her hands, which she extended toward Arthur. "Want to help dry?"

"Why not? It beats watching money pile up in a bag. It beats . . ." Arthur paused. "What does Dad call it? 'The School of Life.' Who tells you if you've passed or flunked? Dad never mentions that."

Susan

Susan opened the medicine cabinet door and scanned the contents. The bottle of Miltowns was where it should be. Iris said that a friend at school had read that Jackie Kennedy took them. So did movie stars. Maybe even President Kennedy did. "Someday, we'll be old and we'll take them too," Ellen had advised her.

After taking one pill she smiled for the mirror and then stretched her mouth wide like Lucille Ball. Maybe she should learn to wail the way Lucy could wail. It was a skill. Everyone loved Lucy. Susan drew her mouth back to its normal size. The sleepless vapors she had woken with were going to be banished. Her steps out of the bathroom and into the hall were steady with purpose. Yet she stopped halfway down the flight of stairs to the first floor. Had she closed the bottle properly? Not that her husband would notice. Though men took them, too, those were her "woman's pills," as Stan put it. A woman—her body and psyche—might as well have been outer space to him. He liked to partake of her body (though less and less), but its details were arcane. That's why there were gynecologists, for what he called "female plumbing." He had never used a tampon or gotten pregnant or had menstrual cramps. He tended to be "tip-top." She had been attracted to that. In his ruddy cheeks a sun lay.

She could hear Ruby rumbling around in her little basement apartment. Probably she had started in on one of her favorite regimens—gargling. She did it when she woke up, after every meal, and when she went to bed. Stan was a gargler, too. "Always buy two," he reminded Susan, referring to Listerine, as if she could forget either the noise or the smell.

It was the first week of school and Susan felt she would never get to work. She did, however, have some chemicals calming her down. Dr. Buchbaum prescribed the pills for tension. A patient, kindly man with huge eyebrows and a beak of a nose that made him look like a Jewish eagle, he lectured her about the woes of humanity that pharmacology was combating. Susan imagined the pills as little soldiers with stick legs and helmets on their tops. "We can all be cheerful," Dr. Buchbaum pronounced while pivoting his swivel chair toward her. "It's our right as human beings." He shook his wonderful head in wonder at this prospect and smiled convincingly. Whatever was in them, they worked.

In the kitchen, plates and glasses had been stacked in the sink, crumbs more or less swept away from the table, and the *Morning Sun* put back in order after being disassembled by four different sets of hands. Everyone cooperated reasonably well, including Stan, who was stubborn but neat. Soon Ruby would ascend the cellar stairs, make herself a cup of instant Maxwell House and, in the silence before Seeley arrived, search the paper for the most wrong-headed political comment. Senator Eastland of Mississippi and Nikita Khrushchev were running neck and neck lately.

Seven minutes late. She had lost three minutes soothing Ellen about going to school with a Band-Aid on her knee. "Everyone," Ellen complained, "can see that I fell down." "Wear a longer dress," Iris told Ellen. "Stay home," said Arthur. Her children never lacked for giving one another advice. Stan told all three of them to "pipe down." They piped down. Amazing what the threat behind a male voice could accomplish. No wonder men ran the world. No wonder it was a missile-crazy mess.

She could make up two and a half minutes taking shortcuts down residential streets. Some students would be congregating outside her homeroom door. Some of those students would be Negroes. They hadn't been in the school in any numbers before but now they were. They were new to her. Sometimes it was comical, as when she overheard a Negro boy say that a record he bought was "bad." Afterward she told him she was sorry he didn't like the record. He shook his head at her and laughed. "Mrs. M, you don't understand — 'bad' is 'good.' Somethin' that's *bad* is so excellent that it's *good*. You hear me?"

Little wonder that bad was good; for them America was

upside-down and inside-out. The stories from the South showed that a public space wasn't public until someone insisted it was public. The land of the free was not free. Until a few years ago any sale to a Negro at one of the downtown department stores that lined Howard Street was final because of any number of miserable, unstated inferences: no white person would want to wear something a Negro had worn; Negroes would return goods and never keep anything; Negroes didn't know how to shop; and the worst—Negroes were somehow another category of being, not fit to try on a dress or a pair of shoes. Baltimore was emphatically below the Mason-Dixon Line.

To no one's surprise, however, her Negro students were the same as her white students—young people trying to figure out who they were. She thought of Andrew, a student she had taught the past two years who wanted to be an actor. One day near the end of school he had come to talk to her about his future. "My momma says I'm foolish. She says there's no place for me to be an actor. She says there's no opportunity for a Negro, that it's white people's business, that the last thing white people want to know about are Negroes." He looked straight at her. "What do you think, Mrs. M? Am I foolish?"

He had the most beautiful open face. The charge of feeling in his dark eyes always startled her. A few times in class she had not listened to an answer he gave because she got lost in his face. Now, though, she focused on his words even as a time-honored gulf of ignorance and contempt yawned before both of them. She smiled with hope, though, and belief in her student. "You can do it. I've seen you on stage. I know how truly you think and feel." She looked straight back at him. She knew that he trusted her. And maybe he would do it. As the newspapers attested, Negroes were seizing what was theirs.

A shouted "Bye, Ruby" downstairs, a hurried slam of the kitchen door, high-heeled steps out to the street. It would be nice to have a garage. There were more than enough reasons for them to move, but Stan was cautious. He deferred decisions until they seemed to make themselves. But they didn't. They festered. Everyone knew that the neighborhood, like Susan's school, was changing. A Negro family had moved in two blocks away. Everyone knew that story. Where the synagogue stood down the street would be a Baptist church. It had happened on lower Park Heights and Reisterstown and around the park. Bit by bit it had happened for decades. Stan remembered housing ads from his boyhood proclaiming "No Negroes in the immediate vicinity." In this city of covenants and deals and restrictions it would happen here—another island in the black and white, Jew and Gentile archipelago. It was fear and often loathing but it was the way of the world, at least of Baltimore. If you could leave, you left.

"Not yet" was what Stan said each time, when in the privacy of their bed she brought up the subject of their moving. His voice wasn't mean. He wasn't a mean man, but he didn't listen to her, either. He repeated his reasons. He didn't want to lose what he had. He didn't want to act until he was sure he could buy what he wanted. He wanted to pay down more on their mortgage before taking on a new one. It made sense but it didn't please her. Why be married if your husband didn't please you?

She hated to argue. She hated to wheedle. But one year turned into another. "I'm tired of being here. I need a change. It's my life too," she said. "Of course it's your life too," he answered, but despite what Susan earned as a teacher he had the last say about money. They would move "when the time came." "When is that going to be?" she asked in the stillness of their curtained bedroom. She wasn't asking, though. She was trying to convince herself that it would happen, the way a child believes that a question can make something happen. The pity of it sickened her.

They didn't raise their murmuring voices. They didn't look at one another, either. Their talk was water that ran down a drain. More and more quickly over the past year they reached a moment when everything had already been said. Yet Susan kept asking and Stan kept replying. If she hadn't asked, he never would bring it up. Then she would feel hopeless, which was worse than frustration.

They lay there and breathed softly as if trying to dissolve the tension. They didn't touch one another. They were more ambassadors to one another than they were partners. In not many minutes Stan fell asleep and began snoring. Unless she took a sleeping pill Susan would be up for hours. She could turn on the lamp on her bedside table and read a novel or a biography of an artist. Sometimes that worked; she left her life for another. The light didn't bother Stan, who was a sleep-through-an-earthquake kind of sleeper. When she looked at him, his face had a slack, otherworldly quality as if all mortal ties had been loosened. He never told her a dream.

Sometimes she lay there and her body ached with want — she wasn't a young woman but she wasn't an old one, either. Eventually a pill or a book or both made her forget. But bodies forgot nothing. Another night would tell her that all over again. So, over a Sunday morning cup of coffee, would Lu.

Her Ford Fairlane jolted to life. She felt excited every time she drove to school. She had only been teaching for a few years and had argued with Stan about it. Couldn't she stay at home and remain a housewife? It was true the girls were getting along in school and Seeley ran the house well, but should she be working? His statements and questions seemed logical but ignored how she felt. She had taught before she met Stan. She wanted to start teaching again. She wanted to get a master's degree. And she wanted her own bank account. That demand made Stan throw up his hands. "Don't you think having your own bank account is pushing it?" he asked. "We're husband and wife." He looked at her, puzzled. His pride was rankled. Would her son grow up and be like that? Arthur loved books and music. Still, he was a man. There seemed a basic oblivion in men.

Susan had two short blocks to go. She had promised to look at a theme JJ had written for another teacher. Jacqueline Jones was a Negro girl who last year had told Susan on the second day of school, when Susan handed out the literature anthologies, that she was "sick and tired of reading stuff by dead folks. What about the living folks?" Jacqueline held the book out in the air in front of her. "Give this a try, Jacqueline," Susan said. "To appreciate the present, you have to know the past." She smiled encouragingly. Jacqueline harrumphed and let the book fall from her hands as if disposing of a piece of rubbish. It thudded. Everyone laughed. But Jacqueline turned out to be one of her best students.

"What about the living folks?" Susan thought as she

pulled into the school parking lot. There was a space down by the end of the shop building. According to the habits of which teachers took which spaces at which exact time that meant she had three minutes to spare. She gave a pull at her skirt — it was tight but a good tight, a female tight — then realized that the radio had been playing the whole time. Arthur must have left it tuned to one of the Negro stations, what was called R&B. She had not heard a word or note of it. Now someone was singing — lamenting really — about good love gone bad. Susan hefted the canvas bag she had bought a few summers ago on the Jersey shore that was filled with books, papers, and pens. She clicked off the radio. "What about the living folks?" She started singing Jacqueline's words in her head as she walked toward the main building. A tune was there, though she couldn't say where it came from.

Arthur

"You ever read this stuff, Merm?" Edward Trumbull flicked a finger at the grainy pages of *The Watchtower* lying on a nearby bus seat. "You ever see black folks pick this up? I'm telling you, Merm, you never will. All this foolishness from the Witnesses about the world ending, well, the world's ended for black folks more than once. It never stops ending." Edward paused for emphasis. "But we persevere."

Arthur nodded. That was how Edward talked. His father was a professor at Morgan State and he often used their bus rides home from their high school to educate Arthur about the ways of black folks. Arthur had learned from Edward, for instance, about W. E. B. Du Bois—about whom there was not a word in his U.S. history book. He learned from Edward (who insisted on his full name, not "Ed") that while Edward could use the phrase "black folks," a white person should stick to "Negro." "You have to be careful with the parlance, Merm," was what Edward said. "We haven't been able to call ourselves who we are."

Some of those black folks were in classes at City with Edward. They made fun of him for being stuck up. "Oh, Ed," they would heckle, "Tell us about Negroes." Edward would smile a confident smile at them. "Show some respect for a fellow sojourner," he would say or some such phrase that might have walked out of the oratory of the nineteenth century. They would roll their eyes. "Man, you must be shittin' me," they said. Edward stayed Edward.

"Hard to know how to designate this reading material," Edward noted while reaching over and picking it up. "It isn't a magazine or a newspaper or a pamphlet. I suppose you might call it a 'tract.'" He held it up before his face but at a distance, as if holding it too close might endanger his health.

"You're a Christian, Edward. Don't all Christians believe in the Second Coming? Isn't that what all that heaven stuff is about?" A picture of a resplendent, blond Christ beamed at Arthur and Edward from *The Watchtower's* front page. He was wearing a long pleated robe but it was not like anything Arthur had seen in Hutzler's. "He's going to rise again and separate the sheep from the lambs or some animal stuff like that."

Edward chortled. "Sometimes I forget you're Jewish. You're a stranger in a strange land, aren't you? You've probably never even read the New Testament." Edward shook his head in wonder. "You probably couldn't even name the apostles."

"The who?" Arthur replied. "The what?"

"Read the book, Merm, and find out. White people have used it to their own ends but that's what white people do. Black folks ask, 'How long?' That's not a bad question. And it might be sooner than the Jehovahs are thinking." Edward whistled softly for emphasis. "It might be sooner." Edward placed *The Watchtower* on the mountain of textbooks he was bringing home.

"What about Martin Luther King?"

"Junior, Merm. How many times have I told you he's a junior? Don't forget his father. The man has a heritage."

"Okay. *Junior.* Now answer my question."

"No cracker jail can contain him. Like the Great Emancipator, only death can stop him. And he is but one man at the forefront of a people. Let me tell you, Merm, a world is ending right now in front of our eyes." Edward gestured with the palm of his right hand to show Arthur the world.

Arthur looked at Edward's palm, which had a pleasantly pink tinge to it. Then he looked down at the bus floor with its candy wrappers, bits of cellophane, empty cigarette packs, greasy White Castle bags that had once held hamburgers and fries, and those ubiquitous pieces of foil that chewing gum was packaged in—sometimes fashioned by human hands into a miniscule ball and sometimes left as a thin silvery remnant. When he looked up from the commercial debris, he saw across the aisle two teenage girls in circle skirts and white blouses. Their hair was teased and lacquered. Both were blowing enormous pink bubbles. Suddenly a bubble burst and they giggled as the nearer one pulled the gum off her face and put it back into her mouth. Then, as if on cue, they began to whisper. Arthur could smell their perfume from where he was sitting. It mingled with the sugary gum and the September heat and made him a little queasy. What would it be like to touch one of them? Or both of them?

"Are you listening to me?" Edward put his face close up to Arthur's. "I'm telling you an answer to your question."

"Yeah, I'm listening but I still don't get it. I mean, he's a Christian and these people" — Arthur nodded toward *The Watchtower* on Edward's lap — "are Christians too. But I don't think they are — you know how people say — on the same page. I mean, look at Jesus there. He's the whitest white guy that could be. He's like some Nazi Aryan. Does he have to be that white?"

Edward looked down at the front page. When he spoke his voice was quiet. "No. I don't think he has to be that white. Jesus was a Semite, a Jew. He didn't look like that. This representation is a myth." He looked harder at the picture. "It might be better, Merm, if there weren't any pictures. But then where would people be without any pictures?" He gazed up at the ads on the bus's inside panels for driving schools, cough drops, and appliance stores. He looked down again at the picture. In Christ's right hand was a scepter.

"Maybe," Arthur offered, "that's God, not Christ. Isn't God a king?"

Edward smiled benevolently. "It's the same difference. We get our faith where we can find it. We Negroes are Christians. Reverend King is first of all a reverend. His power comes from God and from Jesus, who was God's son." He halted. "As a Jew can you understand that?"

"Why not? Jews believe in God, too. Not Jesus, of course, and not in the world ending and not in the stuff about sheep and lambs. Jews aren't farmers."

"Sheep and goats, Merm. Sheep and goats."

Arthur grabbed playfully at *The Watchtower* but Edward held onto it. "I have to wonder, Edward, how the goats feel about that. And I have to tell you that I saw a lot of churches but I didn't see any sheep or goats when I was driving around East

Baltimore this summer."

"You were driving around East Baltimore this summer? Which parts? A lot of that is not a white folks kind of place." Edward grimaced slightly. "There's the hospital, of course, and plenty of Polacks, but there's a heap of black folks there, too. What, may I ask, were you doing there?"

One of the girls across the aisle—her hairdo was a little taller than the other's and had a small yellow bow in it—pulled a transistor radio from her pocketbook and held it up between the two of them. They moved their lips as if singing along. With their faces pale with powder, they looked like puppets.

"I was helping an old guy collect rents." Arthur shifted slightly toward the window. It was filthy and stuck. Someone had inscribed *Fuck You* in the grime.

"In East Baltimore? From black folks?"

"Yeah." Arthur raised a finger and began to put quotation marks around the obscenity.

"And in what shape were these properties?"

"Not great but not bad. I never went inside. They could have used a coat of paint but a lot of Baltimore could use a coat of paint."

"Don't be evasive, Merm. I suspect that you were working for what is known as a 'slumlord.'"

"Mr. Schwartz, a slumlord?"

"I don't care what his name is. I suspect that you, my ignorant friend, have done your part to keep black folks in the place where white folks want them—a ghetto."

Arthur looked away from the obscenity and at Edward. He frowned back at Edward's frown. "I thought Jews owned the rights to the word *ghetto*."

"No one owns the rights." Edward smiled bleakly. "You did your part to turn the screw a little tighter. Congratulations." He turned from Arthur and looked straight ahead. His face had the weariness of an old man's.

"Hold on!" Arthur blurted. "I just sat in a car and drove around. I wasn't turning anything to anyone. And people can't live for free. Someone has to pay rent and someone has to be the landlord. Maybe you haven't heard of that."

Edward made a scolding *tsk-tsk* sound. "Don't get hot

under the collar, Merm. Ignorance makes people angry. Look at those Georgia rednecks taunting Reverend King. He should be taunting them. They're the fools, not Reverend King. They're the ones who don't know anything." Edward smiled, more peaceably. "I'm telling you something you should think about. That's all. Why am I talking to you? How can the world improve if no one thinks twice?"

"How can it improve?" Arthur mumbled the words more to himself than Edward. He didn't know what to say. In his head he saw Mr. Schwartz with his notebook, the man with the gun, girls skipping rope, the broken cola bottles on sidewalks. He saw people pushing aside curtains and looking out at the Lincoln parked in front of their house. He saw street signs and traffic lights. None of those images added up to words. But he knew Edward was serious. And he knew Edward had every right to be serious.

"Whoa! Here we are at Garrison." Edward started to rise. "Time flies when you get to talking. This is where the colored people get out while the white people go further down the line so they can be further away from the colored people." Edward hefted the books from his lap and brought them around to his right side. "Here, Merm," he said, handing Arthur *The Watchtower*. "Bring it to your rabbi. And don't take this stuff too hard. You're still on the buttered side of the bread."

Arthur gave Edward a two-fingered V-for-victory salute but said nothing.

The girls continued to listen to the radio that he could barely hear. They squirmed and bobbed their heads as if dancing in their seats. One of them paused to look over at Arthur. She turned back to her friend and mouthed a few words. The other girl laughed.

Arthur wondered what the laughter was about. It could have been the female nothings his sisters laughed about, it could have been something about him, and it could have been his sitting there talking with Edward. The girls were white girls. He picked up *The Watchtower* and began to rub it slowly against the window where the nasty phrase was written. The front page began to crumple. He could feel the print coming off on his fingers. Jesus or God grew wrinkly but Arthur continued to wipe.

Susan

Joe Costa and Susan stood by the back wall of the cafeteria—lunch duty. Directly in front of them a student named Russell Gingras held up two apples to his chest and sang to his fellow students.

"This may not be how I want to spend the rest of my life," Joe said. He had started teaching six years ago, right out of college.

"You can't touch my apples. They're too good to eat," Russell burbled.

"Boys will be boys." Susan smiled.

"Or boys will be girls," Joe countered. "I wonder if this was what I was like."

"It wasn't that long ago, Joe."

"You're not exactly a grandma yourself, Susan." He straightened his back to get the full authority of his five feet eight inches and turned to Russell. "Russell, you want to keep the vocalizing down? Some people are trying to eat." Amid the clatter of utensils and the clamor of gossip, complaints, laughter, and exuberant chatter, Russell's singing made no difference, but the principal, Mr. Briggs, stressed the importance of adult presence during lunchtime. "Keep 'em honest" was one of the slogans that hung on his office wall.

"Come on, Mr. Costa, we gotta have some humor in our dreary lives." Russell gave a mock-sad head shake. "You ever read *The Return of the Native*, Mr. Costa? Nothin' against Mrs. M but it's about a bunch of miserable people who make each other even miserabler. There's a guy in it that has red skin and he's not even an Indian. And it all happens in England, where they don't play baseball and which is somewhere I never want to set foot on. The book takes place on a heath." Russell paused, as if awestruck. "I never been on a heath and I never want to." With that he flipped the apples up in the air and caught them – one in each hand. He leaned toward two girls in shirtwaist dresses across the table from him and presented each with a fruit: "For the apples of my eye." He darted his eyes from one girl to the other.

Joe gave Susan an elbow nudge. "Happily, Russell has happier things to do than read about miserable people. Happily, what's on his mind are those strategically placed apples. But have you informed Russell and the rest of the gang that most of the books they read here are about miserable people? Or are you keeping that a secret and putting a happy face on Othello and Lear?"

Susan nudged him back. "Keep Shakespeare out of it. And you know about Hardy and me. We're buddies from way back. My childhood in Wessex, Ohio." Susan said this while continuing to scan the lunchroom. There were black faces that sat together. There were more white faces and those faces also sat together. By and large, everyone was polite. But if someone bumped into someone or said a bad word, things could become impolite fast.

"Do you want to do this the rest of your life, Susan?" Joe swiveled his head from side to side as if he were a lighthouse beam. "This school is going to be mostly Negro in five years, seven at the most. Will you be teaching here then?"

"What kind of question is that?"

"One at the back of many minds in this school. And at the front of some minds. As for me, whether it's black, white, or chartreuse, no one told me about lunch duty when I was in college. I thought I was going to deal with Keats, not mashed potatoes."

"I like teaching. You know that. And I like all my students."

"Spare me the educational pieties. I'm sure you do, though you don't have to include Russell. There's a clause in your contract that enables you to opt out in the case of adolescent boys who only have one thing on their minds, and it isn't Thomas Hardy and 'the grimness of the general human situation.'"

"Good quote!" Susan exclaimed and clapped her hands twice. "You've got so much in that young head of yours."

Russell Gingras eyed them warily. "Keep it down you two," he admonished. "We're tryin' to have a serious discussion over here about lit-ra-chur." He nodded to the girls to whom he had given the apples. They raised their eyebrows in an I-don't-know-this-guy look.

"You haven't answered my question, Susan."

"I'm not going to because I don't know. That fair? I don't want to lock myself in."

"You're married with three kids and your mom lives with you. You tell me that when you aren't correcting papers you're driving someone somewhere. You tell me that when you lie down at night and start to read a book you fall asleep. That sounds locked-in to my bachelor ears."

"Actually, Arthur has his license now so he can drive." Absentmindedly Susan fingered the single strand of her pearl necklace, a gift from Stan on their fifth anniversary. "But I'm sure that to your bachelor ears everyone is locked in. You're probably one of those guys with a little black book."

"It's not so little, though." Joe smirked amiably. "Short, dark, and handsome" was how Susan once described him to Lu. She liked standing beside him. He gave off that male scent of sweat and soap.

Mr. Briggs loomed in the cafeteria's far doorway. A tall man who wore three-piece suits, his look was both bland and vigilant—lips buttoned and ready for either a courtesy or command. He could have been a face on a playing card.

"Briggsie should have been a banker. I'm always expecting him to pull a pocket watch from that vest pocket."

Susan tilted her head sympathetically. "He's a dying breed."

"Speaking of watches," said Joe, pointing at the clock on the cafeteria wall. "Another lunch duty has almost passed. Before I forget, I want to invite you to come by on Sunday afternoon. I'm having a few people over to listen to records, talk, and pretend we're cosmopolites stranded in the boorish wilds of Baltimore. It's my effort to do something in life besides correcting sentence fragments. Bring whoever you want to bring

with you, though I have to warn you we'll be listening to jazz —
Miles Davis, maybe Coltrane, that bag." He paused and made
one more rapid head swivel. "Or come on your own."

Amid the din of voices and feet and chairs being
slammed back into place beneath the long tables, Susan had to
raise her voice. "Do I get to meet your current girlfriend?"

"Of course you'll meet her. She'll be offering *hors
d'oeuvres* and keeping a close eye on me." Joe smiled a bashful
smile. "I have to tell you she may be the one who makes me
throw away my black book."

Susan had been to Joe's apartment once before for a
party. He lived on the top floor of a three-story house on the
edge of Roland Park, a garret-like space devoted to the
intelligent clutter of books, magazines, and records. "I'll be
there. I have to admit, though, that I prefer Benny Goodman."

"That's a bit square, Susan." He gave her a good-natured
poke on the shoulder. "I don't want to burst your bubble but
jazz has evolved beyond his magical clarinet." He put both
hands out as if to start fingering an imaginary instrument.

"Hey, you two, have you heard what Gromyko said?"
Sid Colvin stood in front of them. The students called him
"Dusty" for the chalk residue that flecked his dark sport coat by
the middle of each day. He taught social studies, read the
morning and evening editions of the *Sun* each day from front to
back, and actively worried about what he termed "the fate of the
Free World."

"Speaking for myself, since I have been talking with
Susan about topics like Russell Gingras's fondness for apples,
no." Joe bequeathed him the smile that the frivolous reserve for
the serious.

Sid looked downcast. "Well, Joe, some of us pay
attention to the news. And as one of those people I can tell you
that Andrei Gromyko, the Soviet representative to the United
Nations, told the U.S. to not go near Cuba. And if we do go near
Cuba, we could start a war. And you know what that means —
nuclear weapons. *Kaboom!*" A gleam lit up Sid's mild brown
eyes. He liked delivering weighty tidings.

"But, Sid, isn't that what he's supposed to do? Warn us?
And then we warn him about warning us." Joe was still smiling

broadly. "It's like a merry-go-round."

"Gentlemen, if I recall correctly, we have classes to teach." Susan nodded at the staircase in front of them, which was almost empty of students. Sid did get on her nerves. He belonged to the world of Important Things Happening, a world largely inhabited by men obsessed with politics. While the fate of the Free World hung in the balance, she wondered if she had any more Tampax in the house. Despite the coolness of the day she felt a flush on her face. When she got home she would take a Miltown. That usually helped.

"Too bad," said Joe, "I wanted to hear more world news from Sid. But thanks, Sid, for that update. And thank you, Susan, for making a less than pleasant task into a pleasant one." Joe bowed. With a bound he began to take the stairs two at a time.

Susan and Sid watched.

"Youth," Sid opined. He was in his early fifties and liked to lament that he wasn't what he used to be.

Susan began to walk up the stairs but one at a time. She felt weak and paused after a few steps. Then, as if she had not seen them innumerable times already, she regarded the posters for student government elections and tryouts for the fall drama production. She hoped her student Andrew would get a big part. He deserved it.

It was strange how everyone in America lived with these Russian names. It all seemed so far away because it *was* so far away. People went on trips or dreamed about going on trips the way Lu and she did, but there was a big part of the world that no one went to. Yet students walked down hallways there and teachers stood at the front of classrooms and got chalk dust on their clothes, too.

Susan tried to conjure up a vision of her three-floor, brick high school reduced to radioactive rubble. She couldn't. Sid, the town crier, loved to purvey the news, but imagining the consequences wasn't the same thing. Some things were unimaginable. Some calamities were too calamitous. A bell was going to go off in thirty seconds. She had a lesson to teach on intransitive verbs. What did Joe have against Benny Goodman?

Arthur

Since Arthur's high school had more students than it had space for, the school day was divided into two shifts. Arthur attended the morning shift. School ended for him at noon, and on days when he wasn't doing bookkeeping in his father's office or going to the library or shooting pool at Jack's Pool Parlor or at John Silverman's house a few blocks away on North Rogers, he got off the Baltimore Public Transit bus and walked the two and a half blocks to his house.

However slowly, things in school changed from day to day; at the least, one chapter of the U.S. history textbook replaced another. When Arthur headed up the concrete steps of the side porch and entered the kitchen, he entered a world where, at one o'clock on any weekday, things did not change. His sisters were still at school, as was his mother. His father was doing what all fathers were doing—working. At home were Ruby and Seeley, who at that hour were seated on tall, upholstered armchairs that were part of Ruby's Depression-era heritage. They were watching a soap opera.

But one day wasn't another, Arthur reminded himself as he walked through the hallway from the kitchen to the living room where the television resided. America was blowing up in slow motion. Negroes weren't going away and hiding. Martin Luther King Jr. was not going to shut up, though just yesterday a white man punched him in the face while he was giving a speech. King stepped back from the man and then, according to the account in the paper, "spoke calmly to him." The look on King's face was more than Arthur could put into comfortable words. The feelings on his face that Arthur first looked for—fear and anger—weren't there. The face showed hurt—King had been struck—but also seemed serene. Arthur had sat at the kitchen table and given the picture an extra long look. Anyone who had ever been on a playground knew that when someone hit you, you got angry and wanted to punch back. When, on the bus ride home from school, Arthur tried to talk with Edward about it, Edward blew him off with a shrug and the word "unspeakable." The newspaper identified the assailant as a member of the American Nazi Party. Arthur wondered if Mr. Schwartz had seen the photo.

The television was turned up enough for the neighbors to hear it. "And what," Arthur boomed, "are you ladies watching?"

Ruby and Seeley both ignored him.

"It must be *General World*, or is it *As the Hospital Turns*?" He walked further into the room and stood in front of the set.

"Arthur! Move away!" Ruby shouted. "You see we are watching. Is important." She turned to Seeley. "Children in America—no manners. Susie tries with them but no manners."

Seeley nodded perfunctorily.

Arthur stepped aside a few ceremonious feet. "I was just checking to see if you two were awake. You look a little glazed over." He turned to examine the screen, where two immaculately groomed women were bickering: "He doesn't love me anymore." "Whose fault is that?" "Are you telling me it's my fault?" "I'm telling you he told me that you didn't love him." "I didn't love him?!" "Yes, you didn't love him. He told me so." The second of the women smiled scornfully. The first woman began to weep.

"Woe is me," Arthur protested.

Ruby and Seeley both ignored him.

Seeley wagged a finger. "That woman is a crybaby. She done brought her trouble on herself," she said and sighed, pleased with her commentary. Her smooth, light-brown face seemed a bit smoother. She sat back in the uncomfortable armchair and wriggled to make herself comfortable.

"Ach," Ruby muttered. Her voice was low, almost male. When Arthur was younger, the hairs that sprouted on Ruby's chin appalled him. Now that he had started shaving every few days, it didn't seem a big deal. Hair was hair. It wasn't clear whether Ruby was agreeing or disagreeing with Seeley.

Querulous centuries of Jewish history could inform a mere grunt.

Ruby shook her head in disgust. "What do they know about *tsuris*, such women? Some monster has tried to kill them? Kill their children?"

Arthur knew the questions were both automatic and sincere. He also knew that the soaps were women's territory. No one said a word about Seeley taking a half hour to sit and eat her lunch with Ruby while watching a show. It was part of her female work, though the whole matter of what Seeley did still confused Arthur. His father stressed to him that he had to learn to take care of himself, but Seeley made his bed, cleaned his room, and would make a grilled cheese sandwich for him when he asked her, a sandwich he was perfectly capable of making himself. Where was the sense in that?

"These white folks are sad folks," Seeley reflected. "They never pray. They never sing. They never get down on their knees, never give praise to the Lord." She smiled wisely, revealing a number of gold crowns. Arthur's sisters had told their mother that they intended to eat all the sugar they could so they could get cavities and have beautiful gold teeth like Seeley's. Last month Ellen had lain down on the floor and refused to go to the dentist.

"That's what I think," Seeley went on. "They arguin' because they ain't been sanctified. You never see a preacher on this show do you, Miss Ruby? No time for the Lord." Seeley exhaled a low sough of amazement to herself, as if to say, "How could people live like that?" Or maybe it was a sound of dismissal — "white folks be gone." Arthur did not know.

In the meantime, a third person had entered the world of the twenty-four-inch screen, a man in a sport jacket with an ascot — it definitely wasn't a tie around his neck — who started to deliver a lecture to both women about the value of thinking before you acted. The women looked at him with weary veneration, trying to hide their contempt: men spoiled everything.

"I'll leave you ladies to your viewing." Arthur started to head back to the kitchen.

"What you be wantin'?" Seeley inquired.

"How about a grilled cheese sandwich?"

"I'll be soon," Seeley answered. "These people almost over."

Ruby muttered "ach" again, then, "What do they know about *tsuris*?" Though his back was turned to her, Arthur sensed her raising her hands in dismissal. It was too bad Ruby had never been attracted to baseball. She would have been great at razzing the umpire.

The Pepsi in the refrigerator beckoned but Arthur paused to consider the finger paintings by Iris and Ellen that his mother had placed there many years ago. The paintings sagged in various places as if the paint were trying to leave the paper. The tape had turned brown. Every now and then his sisters protested that they didn't want to look at their "kiddy stuff" but Susan said she liked them. The paintings reminded her of when they were little. Arthur felt they still were little but mostly he kept that to himself. They were two and he was one.

Seeley's steps toward the kitchen were deliberate but light. She walked hundreds of steps a day, probably thousands, but never shuffled. She started whistling and humming.

"What's that you're singing, Seeley? Is that a gospel song?" Arthur asked when she appeared in the kitchen. Seeley had a light-blue cotton kerchief tied around her hair. She put one on every morning when she came to work and took it off when she left. She wore a round straw hat to work in the summer and a boiled wool one in the winter.

"A gospel song? What you know 'bout gospel, Mr. Arthur?" Seeley teased. "I don't recall you goin' to church with me but once."

"Sometimes on Sunday morning I listen to the radio. Have you heard of Mahalia Jackson?" In search of potato chips Arthur opened a pantry door. His mother protested that it was hard to keep up. Most days Seeley and Ruby went through half a bag of Utz chips all by themselves.

Pots clanged. Seeley yanked the cast-iron fry pan from a pile in a cabinet beside the gas stove. As if examining it for flaws, Seeley held the pan out. "Do I know who Mahalia Jackson is? Boy, you ask the most foolish questions. You might as well ask me if I know who Jesus is. You must think Seeley was born yesterday." She started humming again but louder.

"I don't think you were born yesterday, Seeley. I didn't mean any disrespect." Arthur stuck his hand in the bag and pulled out a gob of chips. He thought he recognized what Seeley was humming — "Down by the Riverside."

"Get yourself a plate before you start droppin' crumbs on this floor, boy."

Arthur knew that Seeley got down on her knees and washed the floor every other day no matter what got dropped on it, but he went to get a plate. "Seeley, someone punched Martin Luther King Jr. in the face. Did you know that?" He dropped the chips onto the plate. "Someone punched him right in front of lots of people. He was giving a speech."

Seeley scowled at the fry pan in her hand and moved toward the refrigerator. "Someone punched the Reverend? Some white man it must have been."

Her voice wavered and her eyes looked puffy to Arthur. Had he ever seen Seeley cry? "You're right," he said. "It was a white man. In fact he was a Nazi but he was an American Nazi."

"A Nazi?" Seeley pronounced the *z* hard as in *zoo*. After she spoke, her mouth stayed open, as if from bafflement.

"What I think, Seeley, is that Martin Luther King should have punched the white man back. How is a Nazi going to learn anything if he can do that and nothing happens back to him? You know what the Nazis were like. They only respected power. That's how they killed so many Jews. They had power."

Seeley undid the paper wrapper on a stick of butter, then cut a good-sized pat into the fry pan. "Now, Arthur, if the Reverend had punched that white man back, you know what happen? I tell you. Everything fall down in a heap. All the goodness of black folks fall down in a heap. You understand that?"

Arthur nodded and looked down at the floor. He had tracked some dirt when he first walked in.

"There ain't no fightin' back. One fist just makes another." Seeley moved to the stove and placed the fry pan on a burner. "You know what I do every day here? I clean. And what happens to that? People drop potato chips on the floor and get their clothes dirty and dust come from the air and spiders make their nasty webs. You understand me? But I keep workin'. That's what the Reverend doin'. He workin' and he showin' what the white folks done, all the terrible mess they made. He makin' them look. He makin' everybody look. And he ain't goin' to stop workin'." She turned on the burner. "My Lord, I got a sandwich to make."

When Arthur looked up at her, Seeley's eyes didn't seem puffy anymore. The tone of her voice reminded him of his junior high geography teacher, Mrs. Shaw, who made kids stand up at their desk and repeat their wrong answers. She was his first Negro teacher and she was strict. Some days he couldn't stand her; other days he respected her.

"Do I mind what that white man did?" Seeley said. "Course I mind — some no-count white man full of himself. But you can't argue the Lord's handiwork. Hate goes with love — the Bible full of it. The Lord left us here to sort it out. The Reverend understands that. When that white man hit him was he surprised? No, indeed. What else the white man been doin'?" She shook the pan to move the butter around in it. Then she raised a hand to see if the bobby pins that held her kerchief were still in place. "This goin' to burn if I don't pay attention. What I been sayin' to you, Arthur?"

"You were explaining about Martin Luther King Jr."

Seeley took a long observant look at Arthur. "You always listenin'. I give you that credit. Ever since you little, you listenin'." She laughed. "From all that listenin' I guess you must know somethin'."Ruby had begun to stir in the other room. Often she fell asleep after the soap opera and lay there dozing until a gigantic snore woke her up. Startled, she would peer around, then start to raise herself up.

"It's a mercy about the Reverend. I feel I know him. I guess on account of this I do know him." Seeley held an arm out so that she could admire it. Her forearm was bare. Year-round she wore short-sleeved dresses.

Arthur admired it, too. It wasn't that she had an arm; it was the arm's color.

The warm smell of browning bread and melting cheese filled the air. Seeley pointed to a cabinet that held the napkins. "Get yourself a napkin and put it in your lap. I done told you 'bout crumbs."

Ruby looked in through the doorway. "And in here what have you been talking about? Is a debate?" She seemed a little unsteady on her stout legs. Lately she had started using a cane.

"We were talking," Arthur said, "about how Seeley makes the best grilled cheese sandwiches in the world. No one else has a chance."

Seeley lifted the sandwich from the pan with a metal spatula. She started humming again, as if no one else were in the room.

Susan

Susan stood on the landing that led to the upstairs of the house. Arranged around her in the two corners were photographs of her children taken by one of Baltimore's best photography studios when each was five years old and then again when each was ten. She put her hands to her mouth as if creating a megaphone and hollered, "Five minutes! Dinner will be served in five minutes!" No replies came from behind her children's closed bedroom doors.

Her husband, sitting in an armchair, looked up from the *Evening Sun*. "You coddle them," he observed. "The world's going to get blown to smithereens any day now because of these missiles and you're busy coddling three kids who don't know enough to yell 'coming.' *Sheesh*." He often terminated remarks with that sound, a simultaneous acknowledgment and dismissal of whatever disgrace was at hand. Stan had gotten it from Ed Norton, a television character who wore a battered fedora but had a resilient psyche.

"I don't see you going up there to talk to them." Susan stayed on the landing but lowered her hands from her mouth.

"Why should I?" said Stan. "I work all day. They want to eat, let them eat. They don't want to eat, they don't have to."

"You don't make sense, Stan. You say I coddle them but you don't lift a finger. You're their father." Susan could hear the irritation in her voice. It didn't please her.

"The point is that you are calling them. They know that supper is served at six if I'm home. And I'm home." He rustled the front page to show he was there. Nikita Khrushchev's beefy, vehement face peered out from it. "COLD WAR TEMPERATURE RISES" read the headline.

"Maybe they don't know that you're home," said Susan.

"They've been up there all afternoon."

"All afternoon? I could have used Arthur at work. I thought I told him that this morning. Sometimes I think I need to tie a string around his finger." Stan ran a hand over his scalp. "No wonder I'm losing hair."

One upstairs door opened and then another. Quick footsteps followed.

Halfway down the stairs Iris and Ellen paused. "Daddy!" they shouted. They ran past Susan to their father. Each stood on one side of him and kissed him on the side of his head.

Behind them came their brother who remained on the stairs. "Hi, Mom." He turned to look into the living room. "And hi, Dad."

"You were up there reading, I suppose." Stan put his paper down and put an arm around each daughter. They snuggled in against him and made cooing sounds.

"Actually," said Arthur, "I was oiling my rifles. I want to be ready when the Russians show up. This'll be the Alamo."

Stan looked at Susan. "We're raising the next Mort Sahl. Call the people at *Time* magazine."

"I already have, Dad. I'm on the cover next week." Arthur started down the rest of the stairs.

"He's probably looking at the *Playboys* that Grandpa Max gives him," Iris said and made a face at her brother. "All he thinks about is naked women."

"What would a shrimp like you know about anything?" Arthur asked.

"Hold on here," said Susan. "We're about to eat. Ruby's been frying chicken." She gestured to her son, who stood beside her on the landing. "This way to the repast." She paused to observe him. "You're taller than I am. My little boy and you're taller than I am."

"He'll never be very tall," Iris declared. "He's the shrimp. And he has pimples and he looks stupid when he shaves because he barely has anything to shave."

"Your mother's right: can the chatter. You kids sound like the United Nations." Stan rolled the front section of the paper into a tube and pointed it at Arthur. "Didn't I tell you to come to the office this afternoon?"

"Not that I remember, Dad." Arthur looked thoughtful.

"There're more days to work," Susan said. She raised her eyes at her son and then her husband. They nodded reluctantly, as if to say—*and many more rounds to go.* Susan smiled her peacekeeper smile, more relief than gladness, then headed toward the kitchen. "Ruby, we're ready," she trilled.

"I hate Grandma's fried chicken," Ellen grumbled. "It's always soggy. Seeley makes it crispy."

"Don't complain before you've had a bite," her father answered. "Here, ladies, let me accompany you to the table." He extended an arm for each daughter.

Ruby had piled up pieces of chicken on a serving plate. Some pieces looked reasonably fried, others didn't. Susan had offered to help but Ruby refused, saying, "The kitchen is mine tonight." Susan wasn't sure Ruby could even see what she was doing. And even if she could see, Ruby wasn't much of a cook. She tended to hurry; she tended to forget ingredients or go back and add something like salt that she already had put in; she tended to have other things like the saga of her lost-in-America life on her mind.

Ellen reached for the crispiest piece but Stan intercepted her. "We ask around here, young lady. And we thank the cook first of all." Stan nodded to Ruby.

"Thank you, Grandma," Ellen said. "Now can I have that piece?"

"You *may* have that piece," Susan corrected.

"She knows, Mom, that it's *may*, not *can*," Iris said. "She's worried someone else will take that piece."

"I hear Lex Luthor likes chicken." Arthur gave his sisters a villainous scowl.

"Here, here. Let's just eat." Susan eyed the platter and took what seemed like the least-cooked piece.

"Amen. You can't beat that Eastern Shore chicken." Stan took a breast and a drumstick.

Declarations about school accompanied the supper: Arthur's chemistry teacher mumbled; Iris got a ninety-eight on a social studies test; Ellen won a hopscotch match against Katy Fielder, who was "the best hopscotch player in the sixth grade." Stan looked at each speaking child; Susan offered praise; Ruby ate quietly. When Iris made a face to show that her piece wasn't crisp enough, Susan forced a smile back to her — *tough it out*.

After some current affairs beyond the Russians — a hurricane had struck Haiti — and some office talk from Stan — a new account, a business trip next week — the chicken had been consumed. Ellen reached for dessert — brownies that Seeley had baked were stacked on a tray in the center of the table — and knocked over her water glass. Looking at the water running along the table and over the side, she seemed astounded. Then she started to bawl. "This table is too small! I always knock something over! I have to sit and feel Arthur's stupid elbow on me! I hate this table!"

Susan leapt up to grab a sponge. The rest of her family continued to sit and watch the water run off the table edge. "Iris, get another sponge! Ellen, stop crying! Arthur, pick up the serving tray and put it on the counter," she commanded. "This isn't a television show. Help me." She began mopping up the water. "Watch where you step, Iris. Get up, Ellen, don't just sit there."

Ruby shook her head. "Is a small table. Good you had only three children."

"Mom, that's not the most helpful remark," Susan said. She was patting Ellen on the back. "It's only some water, Ellen."

"It got on my dress, Mom." Ellen pointed to a blotch on her lap. She began to wail.

"She's a slob, Mom. Face it." Arthur grinned at his sister.

"And that's not helpful either, Arthur." Susan was wiping the tabletop, which was made from some "miracle product" that appeared to be wood but wasn't. She held the sponge up as if appealing to some higher court. "Stan, do something."

"You're doing fine, dear."

"But I'm not doing fine. I'm wiping this tabletop for the millionth time." She looked at the fraying sponge. A few bits of cellulose had worked loose and were dangling.

"Is a small table," Ruby repeated. "And a small kitchen."

"Mom, shut up!" Susan yelled.

Stan pushed his chair back. "Now, Susan, easy does it. Ruby doesn't mean any harm. She knows she's a guest in this house."

Standing at the sink, Susan wrung out the sponge. "Ruby is my mother. She isn't a guest. She's my mother. I can yell at my mother." Susan knew how this was going. The more upset she got, the calmer her husband got.

Stan looked at her as if observing the weather outside. "You're right," he said. "She's your mother. And she's a guest here."

Ellen stopped crying but Ruby, who had taken refuge in staring down at her dinner plate, raised her head. "A guest? Is this what I am—a guest? I cook and clean and look after the children and what I am is a guest?" She began to sniffle.

"Whew! You can't open your mouth in this house without the waterworks going off. Let's drop it." Stan wadded up a paper napkin and placed it on his plate.

"Sure, let's drop it. Let's drop the fact that this kitchen is too small and this house is too small and that Mom tries to help as much as she can and that we have the money to move but we don't because my husband doesn't want to. Because however much money we have it's somehow not enough. Let's drop all that. Let's drop it that we can't use the dining room because my husband has turned that room into an office away from his other office and if I say anything about it he says, 'I need the space.' Let's drop that too." Susan hadn't stopped wringing the sponge, though there was no water left in it. "But I'll tell you, Stan, tomorrow the house is still going to be here and it's still going to be too small and I'm still going to be wishing we could get the hell out of here. But what I feel doesn't matter."

"Whoa! No need to get worked up, honey." Stan raised his hands as if to ward off further trouble. "And no need to go over this baggage in front of everyone." He beckoned at the children, who had the rapt expressions of onlookers at an exciting sports event. Ruby was blowing her nose. "Ellen knocked over a glass. It's not the end of the world. Those brownies still look swell to me."

Carefully Susan put the sponge down on the edge of the sink. "What I'm going to do is get in the car and go for a drive. Ruby, if you want, you can come along. You kids clean up. Dinner is over." Susan knew she wasn't going to start crying. It was worse than that. She felt like a struck drum — *rat-a-tat, rat-a-tat, rat-a-tat*. She turned to her husband. "I always feel I am being told that I'm the unreasonable one. But I don't think that's true. I think I'm the one who pays attention to what goes on here. I'm the one who deals with the facts of this family." She turned around and headed into the hall to get a jacket and her pocketbook, then called back into the kitchen: "Get moving, kids. You can eat a brownie later. You've seen your parents argue before and you'll see us argue again. Like your father says, the world isn't ending."

"I'll wash," Iris announced to her brother. "Ellen can dry. And you can put things away."

"Since when are you the mother?" Arthur asked.

"Since I've started to become a woman, in case you haven't noticed," Iris answered.

Susan stepped back into the kitchen. While rummaging in her pocketbook for her car keys, she pulled out two soft packs of Salems, each with one bent cigarette left, and a used-up Revlon lipstick. The shade was Perfect Peony.

Ruby had put on a cardigan and stood by the door. Her eyes were red. Stan hadn't moved.

"Let's go, guest," Susan said to her mother as she opened the kitchen door.

Arthur

The two public places Arthur liked to go after school — the local branch of the Enoch Pratt Free Library and Jack's Pool Parlor — were within a mile of one another but, appropriately enough, in opposite directions. Today was a library day. He had stayed after school to go to a meeting of the folk club at City, where he learned some Irish songs from another Jewish kid who joked that his name should be "O'Cohen." Arthur couldn't carry a tune in a paper bag, but joining voices was uplifting and the ballads about doomed heroes and green woods were strangely real. The Ireland of gallows and famines wasn't that remote from the dreadful stories about the old country that Ruby told him. "Is peasants," as Ruby would say.

As he walked from the bus stop down tree-lined Garrison Boulevard, he whistled the mirth of "Jug of Punch" and wondered if Herbie Freilich would show up there today. Herbie was another planet from guys like Rick Scanlon and John Silverman, Arthur's pool hall buddies who only went to the library if they had to. Yet Herbie wasn't what anyone would call quiet. He had opinions about everything, which he could back up because he read so much. Herbie's father was a school principal; his mother taught Latin. The term they used to describe themselves, when he first met them at Herbie's house, was "educators." That seemed more serious than being a mere principal or teacher. He couldn't imagine his own mother using that word. Susan always described herself as "just a schoolteacher."

Each week Herbie toted a brown shopping bag with handles, which he reinforced with another shopping bag. The bag was filled with the books he had read that week and would exchange for more books. It seemed impossible that Herbie could do his schoolwork, help out his Uncle Simon at his poultry stand in one of the markets downtown, sleep at night, and read all those books. But he did.

Arthur read plenty, too, but his tastes tended more to fiction, which Herbie, who was systematically reading through the entire history section of the branch library, despised. A *bocher* with heavy black glasses who spewed saliva when he spoke so that a person didn't want to stand too close to him, he informed Arthur that fiction was "baby stuff—it's just made-up people talking to each other and doing stupid things to each other. It's nowhere."

"And when someone in a history book tells someone else in a history book something, do we know that the person really said it?" Arthur countered. "And don't real people do stupid things to each other? And how about what nations do to nations?"

Herbie grew exasperated. His milky-white cheeks never reddened in anger, but his voice rose to a high pitch, almost a squeal. "They never existed. Why do you want to read about people who never existed? They aren't real. They're *fictions!*" The final word sounded like a curse. Herbie made an ugly face, as if he just swallowed castor oil.

Arthur let it be. It was much safer to talk with Herbie about something remote but real, like the Civil War. Though their sympathies were with the North, they both liked reading about the southern generals. Many a late afternoon on the front steps of the library, they—who had never rode a horse or chewed on hardtack or fired a rifle or seen a bloodied corpse— would discuss battlefield tactics. Why hadn't Lee been bolder at Gettysburg? Why had Longstreet been so dilatory? Herbie jabbed a finger into the air to indicate where Pickett had faltered. Arthur shook his head and pointed to the right of Herbie's descriptive finger. They peered into the empty air. Herbie wheezed. He had asthma.

Herbie went to Poly, another all-boys school but one that emphasized math and science and was City's rival. Poly observed a regular school schedule, so if Herbie showed up it wouldn't be until later. That was fine with Arthur, who wanted nothing so much as to stand in front of one of the long, gray metal shelves and do a sort of impromptu dance. He would move his pointer finger to a book, then skip some books to the right or left of that book, then pause, then draw his finger back. Then, because his eyes were lurching all over the place, he would grab a book that was a shelf or two away from where he had started. Then he would flip the book open—a tiny fluttery sensation on his fingertips before the landfall of a particular page. Then he would begin to read. No matter what the author's reputation was, he never took a book home without sampling it. And somewhere in the middle of the book was better than the beginning of a book. Anyone could make a beginning.

Although the library smelled as if no windows had been opened in thirty years, Arthur enjoyed the stuffiness. The smell he associated with Mr. Schwartz's Europe was of a world ruined by time; this smell was cozy—paper comfortably aging. Today, as he walked toward the fiction section past the white-haired woman at the circulation desk with a small, purple birthmark on her right temple, was like every library day—a dream of books in a largely silent world.

He stood before the H-J section wondering who Knut Hamsun was when a girl walked up beside him, extended an arm in front of his abdomen, and plucked *The Return of the Native* from the shelf. She aimed the book at Arthur, pressed her scarlet-colored lips almost together so that they formed a small opening and blew vigorously. Arthur could see specks of dust scatter in the brittle, artificial light.

"They don't clean the books. I hate the feel of dust on your fingers. It's creepy." The girl, who appeared to Arthur to be his age, looked at the novel in her right hand and then at the fingers of her left hand. "And it makes you sneeze, which is disagreeable." She clutched the book to her chest as if to secure it. She had thin fingers and wore no rings. "I love Thomas Hardy." Like a teakettle, she made a sharp whistling sound. "What's your name?"

Arthur wanted to say, "You're talking too loud and you shouldn't be making noises," but didn't. "Arthur Mermelstein," he replied.

As if she had heard his thought, she moved her head toward him and spoke in an exaggerated whisper. "It's not easy being Jewish is it? Our names are like lead weights. Or targets. We can't hide. I'm Rebecca Farbelman." She made a sort of curtsey though she still clutched the book to herself. "Does your mother teach English at FP?"

"She does." Arthur imagined that her fingers were making an indentation in the cover of the Hardy novel. "She teaches *The Return of the Native*. Thomas Hardy is one of her favorite writers."

"I had her for English last year, but I don't think she teaches this novel" — she brandished it in her right hand — "until senior year. I've read it twice. I love Eustacia Vye. Do you know what Hardy wrote about her?" She didn't wait for Arthur to reply. "He wrote that 'Eustacia Vye was the real material of a divinity.'" She paused for effect. "What do you think of that, Arthur Mermelstein?"

"I guess I should read the book." Arthur stared down at his shoes. He was wearing sneakers, which was good because they were cooler-looking than the loafers his father insisted on when he worked afternoons in the office.

"I guess you should." Rebecca tossed her silky, nearly shoulder-length, light-brown hair back with her non-Hardy hand. "Are you going to ask me any questions about myself or are you going to stand there like a *cheder* boy who's never talked to a girl?" She drew herself up and pushed her chest out, which, even under the sweater she wore, was noticeable.

"*Cheder* boy?"

"Don't you know anything Jewish? That's a boy who's studying the Torah. My father's a rabbi. He talks as though he still lives in the old world of ghettos and *rebbes*. So do I sometimes."

Arthur noticed Rebecca's shoes, which were the scuffed black-and-white saddles most schoolgirls wore. She kept talking. "Would you like to walk me home from here? We live on Oakfield. That's not many blocks away. In Hardy, men walk women home. That's how it should be, I think. Men should be something more than athletes."

Arthur felt a force homing in on him that was not like any he had encountered before. "I like the red ribbon in your hair. Is that from Hardy, maybe?"

"Women used to wear ribbons in their hair so I guess it's in Hardy." She paused as if considering whether to go on about ribbons and Thomas Hardy. "That's sweet of you to notice. I have a bunch of different colors but I like red best. I buy the ribbons at the notion store over near Wabash. I like to sew."

Rebecca and Arthur kept talking as they checked out their books—Hawthorne and Hemingway plus a biography of Jeb Stuart for Arthur, the one Hardy novel for Rebecca—and then began walking toward her house. Rebecca asked three questions for every one of Arthur's, but he asked the question that made her stop in the middle of the sidewalk and take a deep breath.

"My mom's dead," she announced. Her pale face took on a distracted flush. Her lips fumbled for other words but nothing came out.

For Arthur, in that moment, everything seemed to stop. The automobiles traveling along Garrison Boulevard, the sparrows rummaging at the base of a long hedge, the mild afternoon breeze—everything stopped. "I'm sorry," he said.

"You don't have to be sorry. I mean, you didn't do anything. You didn't even know her." Her high, almost flute-like voice seemed even higher, searching for air and not finding it.

The world started moving again—birds, clouds, cars—but Rebecca's face stayed frozen—a contorted stillness.

"Do you believe me, Arthur? About my mother?"

He wanted to look at her directly but couldn't. When he spoke, he tried to make his reedy voice deeper. "People don't make up stuff like that."

Rebecca's eyes flashed. "You are so wrong, Arthur. Don't you read these books in your hands? I mean *really* read them. People will make up anything and then say it's as true as this sidewalk under our feet." She waved Thomas Hardy back and forth like a baton. "People—especially girls—need to make things up. Eustacia made things up. She made up who her husband was and he turned out to be someone else." She halted; the book hung in mid-air. "But I didn't make this up. My mother walked out from between two parked cars on Liberty Heights and directly into the path of a Pontiac Star Chief. That's what it said in the paper—'the path of a Pontiac Star Chief,' as if the name of the car was as important as my mother's name. She was coming home from the grocery." Rebecca's eyes were sad and wild. "What was she thinking? That's the question I ask myself when I'm lying in bed at night. What was she thinking?" Her shoulders slumped. She lowered her head so her face was hidden.

Someone was slow getting away from a stop sign. The car behind blew its horn. Arthur and Rebecca stood in silence. The car blew its horn again.

"Well, who knows what you think of me?" Her voice had hardened. She spoke more to the ground than to Arthur. "If I were you, I'd be scared some. Here you meet a girl who takes out a Thomas Hardy novel and you walk down the street with her and she starts telling you about how her mother died." She picked her head up. "That's not how it's supposed to go. Not in any book."

"How is it supposed to go?"

"Some chatter about your school and my school. I can't imagine, for instance, what it's like to go to an all-boys school."

"It's a lot of guys and no girls."

"I get that already."

"You miss it that there are no girls." Arthur shifted his books from one hand to another. "Here you are, a red-blooded male, and you are dying to see some girls and to be with some girls because—"

"I get that too, Arthur," Rebecca said.

"Right—but there you are all day doing stuff like geometry and U.S. history and shooting the breeze with guys, talking about nothing. So you do that. But. . . ." He moved a hand toward Rebecca's hair ribbon but stopped about halfway there. "I like you," he blurted.

"Ah," Rebecca exhaled. "I think I could like you. I'm sure we'll meet again in the library. I go there a lot. I told you how my father is a rabbi, but he doesn't have a congregation so he makes money by preparing boys for their bar mitzvah. There's usually one droning away in our apartment most afternoons, which leads me to the library. And my father studies the Torah, of course. That's what rabbis do—you know that much." She made the tea kettle sound again.

Arthur realized that his notion of the sound wasn't far-fetched. It came from some vivid tension in her. He tried to think of his own mother being dead. He couldn't.

Rebecca went on. "I have to take care of our apartment for him and for my little brother Isaac. I'm the mother. Right now, I have cooking to do." Her voice was tight but calm. "But I could like you." She smiled, almost merry. Then she turned away from Arthur and toward the street. "Bye!" she shouted, as much to the street before her as to Arthur. Quickly she looked both ways, then sprinted. Her hair flew out behind her.

Arthur forgot to wave back, though he did yell "Bye" when she reached the other side of the street. She took long purposeful strides, turned a corner, and disappeared. He remained in his spot, glued to the earth. It took many seconds before he came back to who he was — a guy standing in the middle of the sidewalk with a lot of blocks between him and his home. He felt thirsty — a cherry Coke would take care of that. A man who walked quickly by him slowed down and looked back over his shoulder at him. Shreds of sunlight spilled through tree branches. Arthur started moving.

Everything about her — how her hair fell, her quick high voice, her breasts in her pointy bra, the red hair ribbon — thrilled him. And questions assailed him. What was it like to lose your mother? What was it like to be a rabbi's daughter? What was it like to care for your little brother and act like a mother?

Arthur lumbered along. The books he was carrying felt heavy one moment, barely there another. He wondered about Eustacia Vye. She was passionate, Arthur knew that much, and she was a heroine. His mother had spoken more than once about Eustacia, about how she was a woman who would not dismiss her feelings. That alone, according to his mother, made her a heroine. He hadn't lied. He should read the book.

There was more: Rebecca seemed romantic in the way that heroines in the Irish folk songs were romantic. He could imagine her standing at a crossroads or on a castle battlement. He could imagine her, rich or poor, in a long dress, exulting or mourning. The past of those songs he had been singing that afternoon felt more real to him: *every word was a river that swept me away.*

He paused at the beginning of the block where his house stood. *Our names are like lead weights.* He looked around as if what was going on inside him had caused an audience to appear. No one was there. He spoke her full name aloud. No one heard. No one applauded. No one mocked him. He began to sing one of the old songs softly.

Susan

Driving over to Joe Costa's, Susan put on the car radio but then turned it off. The quiet felt good. For a time she could slough off the second skin that was her family.

The girls had been invited to a roller-skating party. Arthur had gone over to his friend John Silverman's to shoot pool. Ruby had settled in with her magnifying glass and the Sunday *Sun*, which would provide grist for Ruby's opinions during the coming week. She was keeping a close watch on Fidel Castro, another conniving *royt mamzer* – a red bastard. "To help people, they murder people," was how Ruby summed it up. Aside from Franklin Delano Roosevelt, the politicians of the twentieth century had disappointed Ruby. Susan was inclined to agree. She recalled defining the word "totalitarian" for one of her classes a few days ago. How could there be such a word, one of her students asked. How could things go so wrong?

She had talked with her husband. He was sitting at the dining-room table sorting through the usual flotsam of forms, receipts, cancelled checks, and ledgers. Later, everyone would come together to go to synagogue for the eve of Yom Kippur, but that duty didn't have to interfere with a secular afternoon. She went to services because she was a Jew and a mother of three, not because she believed in God.

Stan was wearing his around-the-house clothes – a white T-shirt and khakis. She had gone up to him, put a hand on his shoulder, and asked if he wanted to come with her to Joe's. She told him about the music and where Joe lived and who he was.

Stan barely looked up. "Is this Joe a beatnik? What are we going to listen to? Probably this Miles guy doesn't sound like the Harry James Band."

Susan drove past a turn she needed to make. She heard

herself sigh. Something your spouse said might strike you as funny one day and then not funny on another day. And sometimes you felt in between funny and not-funny. Sometimes you felt you were being dismissed but there was no place in your marriage to go. You were still there in the room with the person. She told Stan that Joe Costa wasn't a beatnik. He told her to have a good time. He would catch the Colts on the radio.

What stayed with her was the feeling of picking her hand up from his shoulder. His shoulders were still broad and beautiful. She had met him in 1944 and admired him in his uniform. On their first date she had wanted to touch the person in that uniform and be touched by him. Picking her hand up from his shoulder, she felt the emptiness of the air. It shocked her.

When, after a climb of three floors, she knocked on Joe's door, she again felt her hand moving through space. It was strange—a simple action that did not feel simple. Random moments kept announcing themselves to her, refusing to be part of anything. She must have looked surprised when a young woman opened the door.

"You must be Susan." The woman gave a warm, toothy smile. "Joe has told me you are the salvation of his teaching career." She moved aside. "Please come in. I've cleaned up the place some this morning. You would never know Joe was raised neat-as-a-pin Catholic."

Joe rose from a tattered couch on the other side of the big attic room that was a combination living room, kitchen, and bedroom. The couch looked as though a few generations of cats had been clawing at it. "She means that Catholics just keep a crucifix on the wall and a pair of trousers in the closet for church and that's all they have. Deprivation makes them neat." He grinned. "But of course the spiritual riches, the beauties of asceticism . . ." The grin grew until it threatened to split his face, like the Alfred E. Newman character on the cover of the *Mad* magazine that Arthur read every month.

"Susan, my name is Julia Shea. Pleased to meet you." When Julia extended her right hand to Susan, the tight black braid that hung down to the middle of her back seemed to move with her. "You'll have to pardon him. Joe is still ridding himself of his altar-boy youth. It's one reason why he's so messy." She shook her head. "There are many reasons, alas."

"Down with reason, say I." Joe had come up behind Julia, put his arms around her waist, and rested his chin on her left shoulder. He hugged her to him. Joe hadn't been lying about giving up his little black book.

"What, may I ask, is all this Catholic talk? What religious desperadoes have I fallen in with?" The tenor voice—it was musical—came from a corner of the kitchen area where Susan hadn't looked. A Negro man about her age emerged from the corner with a glass of wine. "Here I am—brought up a good American Protestant—and look with whom I am consorting. I need to call the Klan." He halted a few steps away from the others and nodded to Susan. "I'm glad to meet you, Susan. Jarvis Baker's the name. I teach music at City and had your son Arthur in my introduction-to-music class last year. He's a fine student." He stopped to take a sip of wine. "Good *vino*, Joe. And, Susan, you know as a teacher we say 'fine student,' but it's more than a phrase with Arthur. He wants to learn." He took another sip. "Not the steadiest voice on him but he's still growing."

Susan felt her head agreeably spinning as she regarded this man in a tattersall shirt and pleated pants. His smile was unrestrained and cordial, vital yet polite. His skin glowed with an almost yellow tone. He was literally light-skinned—he seemed radiant. That must have been the sun coming in through the windows of the apartment and striking all of them as they stood there. Still, it was a lovely sensation. "Glad to meet you, Jarvis. My learned son is out shooting pool at a friend's house this afternoon."

"Many things to learn in this big world, eh, Jarvis?" Joe had stepped over beside the music teacher and put an arm around his shoulder. They were the same height and build— slender, not big men.

Julia smiled at the scene. "Joe likes to pretend he's grown up and that Jarvis is his younger brother."

"That would be quite the family, wouldn't it?" Jarvis shook his close-cropped head in mock amazement. "That's the American story though, isn't it? Someone creeping into the colored sheets."

Julia continued her narration. "Jarvis and Joe are union buddies, AFT. Jarvis has been Joe's mentor, which is good because Joe needs all the mentoring he can get." She moved toward the men but then turned back to Susan. "Would you like a glass of wine or soda or some of the lemonade I made?"

"Lemonade?" Joe groaned. "We're jazz devotees. Who ever heard of jazz devotees drinking lemonade?"

"Lemonade sounds good. I bet Benny Goodman drinks lemonade." Susan looked over at Joe and raised her hand as if making a toast.

"I'm not much of a drinker myself." Julia said. "Booze makes me sleepy."

Jarvis raised his glass. "I thought painters were bibulous. You know—they paint some, step back from the canvas, take a slug of wine, then go back to the canvas and paint some more."

"Bibulous!" Joe crowed. "You should have been the English teacher, Jarvis."

Julia handed Susan a glass of lemonade and took a long drink from her own glass. She wrinkled her nose. "It's a little bitter but I like it that way. As to painters drinking wine, that's from those stories *Life* used to run about people like Jackson Pollack. You'd think that painters bought more jugs of wine than brushes. I'm not Jackson Pollack."

Joe drew himself up—an authoritative pose that Susan recognized from school. "Well, that's a relief—that you aren't Jackson Pollack. And here I was under the impression . . ."

"You're a painter, Julia?" Susan asked.

"I go to the Institute of Art, so, yes, you could say I'm a painter."

"And a good one, I might add," Jarvis said. "If Joe didn't live in a garret where there was no wall space, he might hang a painting."

Susan felt the earlier part of the day dropping away from her. "What do you paint?"

"Ah, the inevitable question." Joe smiled a commentator's wry smile.

Julia turned toward him and bowed slightly from the waist. "I can speak for myself, sir, thank you." When she turned back to Susan, her face seemed a shade brighter. "I like the abstract abstractionists. I like Helen Frankenthaler especially. Perhaps you know her work? Lyrical—she's very lyrical." Julia nodded toward the room they were in. "The world"—she squinted a bit as she stopped to think—"breathes color. My aim is to get that onto canvas."

"Breathes color? And here I thought the world was a tunnel of black and white." Jarvis pretended to frown.

"Easy on the metaphors, people," Joe commanded. "There're two English teachers in this room."

"I don't know that painter but I'd like to," Susan said. "I love paintings. I love the Impressionists. Not long ago, I read a book about Toulouse-Lautrec. His paintings—their paintings—are so full of life. . . ." She sighed. "I wish I could have lived back then. It sounds silly, but I feel they knew something about life that we don't. And their paintings are like what you said, Julia. They breathe color." Susan looked away from the three people who had been listening to her. "I didn't mean to lecture."

"Why not?" Joe said. "That's why I'm a teacher."

"It's not silly." Julia walked over to her. "There are lots of paintings that make me want to live in the painter's world. That's part of what paintings should do—create a feeling of a world." She took Susan's empty glass from her. "You were thirsty. More lemonade?"

"Yes, it's as good as our maid Seeley makes."

No one was standing very far away from anyone so when Jarvis took a step back, everyone noticed. "Your colored maid, no doubt?" he said.

"Yes, she's a Negro. She's worked for us for many years." Susan felt her voice stiffen with her body.

"Helps to raise the children and keeps the house clean and uncomplainingly puts up with whatever she has to put up with for not much money and takes the bus home every day to some colored part of town? Would that be a fair summation?" Jarvis's voice was distant but brisk.

"She works for her living," said Susan. "I work for my living. You work for yours. I don't see what the problem is. I respect Seeley."

"I'm sure you do." Jarvis halted. He too had stiffened but in a different way. His shoulders were pulled up and his knees slightly flexed. He seemed like a coil ready to spring.

"Hold on, people! This is not sounding like 'How to Relax Your Colored Friends at Parties.'" Joe raised his hands as if to pronounce a blessing. "I call upon the sacred spirit of Lenny Bruce, All-Consuming-Joker and Destroyer of Insidious Stereotypes, to consecrate this social occasion." Joe waved his hands around, a hocus-pocus gesture.

Susan felt somehow frozen in place. She was on an ice-covered pond and a crack was heading toward her.

Jarvis laughed a hearty, from-the-gut laugh. "You're always on the case, little brother. To quote Lenny, 'Ray Charles is Jewish.' I'm not arguing that." He turned to Susan. "No offense, Susan. I heard it in church and it's true: the river is wide."

"Metaphor again!" Joe's hands were still meandering in the air.

Susan sought words but found none. Some of the sudden tension was gone; some was still there. She wanted to bury her face in Jarvis Baker's chest.

Julia came up beside Joe and gently brought his hands down, then held on to them. "Why don't we sit and listen to some of that jazz till Tim and Karen come by?" She looked at Susan. "They're painter friends of mine from the Institute. You'll like them." In a show of female bustle, she headed toward the kitchen. "Now, did I ever get you that lemonade? More wine, Jarvis? It's free of charge."

Susan felt that she had been spun around and was once again facing in the right direction. Julia's braid reminded her of how Iris talked about growing her hair. She remembered Lu's crack about her Catholic schoolgirl flip.

Joe and Jarvis had moved over to the stereo, where Joe was holding up a record jacket—*Kind of Blue* by Miles Davis. Susan saw the photo on the LP's front cover—a close-up of a Negro man playing the trumpet.

"What track is it going to be, Jarvis?"

"I'm feeling like 'Blue in Green.' You know I like to hear that white boy play the piano." He laughed softly. "Some black folks felt it was wrong, giving a white cat that seat. But he can play. He can more than play."

Joe waved a beckoning arm to Susan. "Come to the casbah, also known as the listening area."

"It's really the genuflection area, Susan," Julia called from the kitchen. "Watch out."

"Where Miles is concerned, I can live with some hyperbole," said Jarvis. "He did some dates here in Baltimore, you know, back in the fifties, places like the Club Las Vegas."

"Joe was in kindergarten then." Julia brandished lemonade in one hand and a wine glass in the other.

"If I'm that young, what does that make you?" Joe asked.

"Young enough so that you should be arrested," she answered, then winked at Susan. "I'm actually older than I look."

Susan took her lemonade. She felt she could have stood there all afternoon and listened to their repartee. Joe was funny in school but seeing him here with Julia and Jarvis made him seem both exotic and regular. This ramshackle room with these people and others like them was his life.

Joe put an arm around Julia's waist. "We'll discuss the matter of your age later, miss. Now I'm going to put this long-playing disc on this turntable and put the needle down on track number three. Probably I have to let go of you to do that. Darn." He bent over toward the stereo, which was perched on a low, suitably battered table. "Susan, take a seat please."

Susan sat down on an armchair covered in something like chintz. It felt a little greasy. Like every item of furniture in Joe's apartment, it looked as though it had been rescued rather than purchased. She sat back as best she could.

A piano and bass began a tentative dialogue, then the other instruments joined in, offering their voices but, though time elapsed, it didn't feel to Susan that the music proceeded from beginning to end. It was more like a mood imperceptibly descending. The instruments were just as much talking to themselves as to each other, reflecting and pursuing some vision of feeling but saying only what needed to be said. It was more like a cloth woven from thoughtful sound. It was more like a fragile yet sinuous pulse. When it ended she was surprised. The music felt like a state of grace, something tender and expressive that should go on forever. But it was a trapdoor, too, something she had unexpectedly fallen through. She almost gasped.

"Miles, he's never in a hurry to leave a note is he? That's part of his genius." Jarvis was standing, looking out one of the dormer windows at the rose-pink of a late-afternoon sky. He turned to address the others. "He must be one hell of a lover." Jarvis smiled broadly. "Sorry, ladies, if I offended you."

"No apologies necessary," Julia said. "He does take his sweet time." She smiled a demure smile. "I didn't mean to speak for you, Susan."

"And what do you think, Susan?" Joe was seated on the couch beside Julia. There was nothing antic in his voice; it was almost dreamy.

"It's not what people call a 'tune' is it?" Susan asked back.

Jarvis stepped over to her. "No, it's not a tune. Miles has never been out to entertain folks' ears. He wants . . ." Jarvis paused. ". . . He wants to ravish and enlighten us." He paused again and looked at Julia. "What you said about the paintings, wanting to live in the painting, well, I wouldn't mind living in 'Blue in Green.' Sounds like a painting title, doesn't it?"

He glided back to the window, then raised and lowered his shoulders. Susan was watching. It was as if the music's slow fire had infused his body. She turned to Joe and Julia. "Would you play another one?" she asked. "Don't be stingy, Joe. I can genuflect. See." Susan bowed her head a bit, then raised it. Once more she turned her eyes to Jarvis. "Who is that pianist? He plays like a ghost."

Arthur

"What I don't understand is why the Gentiles don't have a Day of Atonement. Aren't they the ones with something to atone for? Why are *we* atoning? We lost millions in the Holocaust and we're atoning. I don't get it." Arthur kicked at an imaginary pebble. He had on his penny loafers, which he had polished that morning.

Arthur and his father were heading back to the Oldsmobile. Susan had already taken the girls and Ruby home in her car. Every four years his father bought a new Oldsmobile — a "solid" car, "solid" being the opposite of something like "fly-by-night" and one of Stan's highest compliments, as in "he runs a solid company" or "he's a solid starting pitcher."

Stan said nothing in reply but kept walking. He was over six feet tall and took long steps. His pant legs flapped slightly when he walked.

"Sure are a lot of cars here, Dad. Quite a few Cadillacs. Maybe God is on our side after all." Arthur knew his father wanted to get home, but Arthur wanted to hear his father say something — anything.

Stan stopped beside a Ford Falcon. "You know, Arthur, our family is observant but not pious. We don't keep Kosher. We don't light candles on the Sabbath. Every year I mean to light a *yahrzeit* for my mother Minnie but I forget. And your mother is worse than I am. What does she call herself? — an 'agnostic,' which I take to mean someone who is on vacation about God. But we go to the synagogue on the High Holy Days and we remember then that we are Jews." Stan looked up at the cloudless sky and then at Arthur. "So I don't see the point of your question, son. Jews have been atoning on this day forever because they fall short during the year. I fall short, you fall short, your mother falls short." He moved a hand up to check his necktie knot. It had not slipped. Stan never fell short in the necktie-knotting department.

Arthur waited for his father to say more.

"I can't speak for the Gentiles. " He brightened suddenly. "But how could I? I'm a Jew and the Gentiles are another country. I don't understand how Jesus can make everything okay. But that's their business isn't it? " He took a long step, then another. The meaningful talking was over. "Let's go home," he said.

Arthur kept up with him. Perhaps that was how meaningful talking was supposed to be — short if not sweet.

Go home they did, though with its fasting and everybody being in the house and in the way of everyone else, Yom Kippur wasn't much of a holiday. The good news was that the World Series was going to be on television, with Mel Allen calling the game. Arthur was rooting for the Giants to beat the Yankees, who almost always won. The Orioles had a hard time playing .500 ball. A kid who sat beside Arthur in chemistry and who had moved to Baltimore from the Bronx made a point of not letting Arthur forget that the Orioles were "pathetic."

Stan's answer hadn't answered anything but some answer was better than no answer. Whenever his father took the time to notice him as someone who did more than work in the office and go to school, it made him glad. Arthur never talked with his friends about it, but he sensed that they felt the same way: a father was like a ship out on the ocean.

It seemed fair, then, to ask another question in the car on the way over to Grandpa Max's. Everyone was in the car except for Ruby. She and Grandpa Max couldn't stand each other. Their arguments had occurred long ago but that hadn't lessened the bad feeling. "Max," Ruby would say when Stan wasn't around, "he is with gangsters." Arthur couldn't remember Max even mentioning Ruby to dismiss her.

"Why every year," said Arthur, "do we go to Grandpa Max's to break the Yom Kippur fast? Max doesn't observe anything. He sits home on Yom Kippur and eats all day. He probably makes a point of eating bacon and ham. I don't understand, Dad."

His sisters, between whom Arthur was sandwiched, had

been bickering about whether Tuesday Weld's first name really was Tuesday, but out of curiosity they quieted down. Susan rustled the back of her Dacron dress against the back of the front seat. She was listening, too.

Stan turned his head very slightly so he could talk to the backseat but keep driving. "Max is the patriarch, Arthur. You know that word. You're a smart kid. We honor the patriarch. You may not agree with everything a patriarch does but that doesn't make him any less the patriarch. And Max is our patriarch. And for Jews patriarchs are important people."

Once more it was an answer that wasn't an answer— Max with his ever-present shot glass of Jim Beam or Wild Turkey was no Moses—but Arthur said, "Thanks, Dad." His mother rustled some more against the seat back. Iris hissed something to Ellen. Ellen hissed in return. Stan clicked on the car radio to WBAL. A broadcaster was talking about Cuba. Cuba's president had said that Cuba could "become the starting point of a new world war."

"Good god," Stan muttered. "Cuba?"

"Play some music, Daddy," Ellen begged. "We'll even listen to old people's stuff. Anything but the news. I can't stand how they talk. It's like they hold their fingers on their nose when they talk. Please, Daddy."

"I'm getting a headache, Stan. Just turn it off," Susan said. "I should have taken a pill this afternoon." She rubbed her forehead. "I could eat a horse."

When Grandpa Max opened the door for them, Arthur could smell the food. Bertha, the Gentile woman that Max lived with, had been cooking all day. Among other dishes, she made the best crab soup Arthur ever had tasted. As for Grandpa, as Seeley liked to say, he couldn't boil water.

Grandpa Max shook the males' hands and pinched the females' cheeks. He called Iris and Ellen "my beauties," as in "How are my young beauties?" "And how is their lovely mother?" he added while giving Susan a big hug. Grandpa never hid his fondness for women. The pile of *Playboys*, the playing cards with women in scanty clothes, and the calendars with more women in even scantier clothes all testified to that. Arthur felt aroused whenever he walked in, though the underlying odor — cigar smoke and whiskey — kept a lid on it.

"So, Yom Kippur, which synagogue do you go to these days?" Max asked his son. "One of the new ones out on Park Heights, or maybe in the County? It's hard to keep up. The Jews are on the move."

Arthur would have answered for his father: "What's it to you, Max? Arthur's bar mitzvah was the only time you set foot in a *shul* in the last thirty years. You wouldn't know the Torah if it hit you over the head."

"Park Heights," Stan answered. "We move from one to another. It's like shopping. You're trying to get value at a good price."

Max smiled sympathetically. His teeth were invariably decorated with flecks of cigar tobacco. Tobacco had turned Max brown. He wasn't a Negro's brown. He was a human cigar-wrapper kind of brown. He had liver spots on his face and his skull, too, which were gray-brown. Max was nothing to look at, but if Bertha was any indication women were crazy about him. Bertha was fifteen or so years younger than Max and a plentiful, still-shapely woman. She fussed over him as if he were a Hollywood star. Given the acne that came and went on his cheeks, maybe it was a good sign for Arthur. As he stood there in Grandpa Max's living room among Bertha's antimacassars and African violets, Rebecca Farbelman's face and body flashed through his mind — a tingling, secret moment.

Grandpa Max lived in a brick rowhouse near Memorial Stadium that featured a front porch on which Bertha grew geraniums and a tiny backyard with some scraggly azaleas that, as Susan always pointed out, didn't get enough sun. His tavern, to which he went every day even though he was in his mid-seventies, was many miles away on the Old Frederick Road. He had been there that morning checking things out. "*Goyim* drink every day" was one of his refrains.

Not that Max didn't, too. He "tippled," as he put it, which to Arthur meant that he was a meditative sort of drinker, never in a hurry but never without a drink, either. Liquor loomed closer on the availability horizon for Arthur than did sex but was nowhere near as attractive. Classmates would come in Monday morning and brag about having gotten wasted or trashed or wrecked, but throwing up and getting a bad headache seemed nothing to get excited about. Arthur had sipped rye whiskey from Max's glass: it tasted like medicine and gave him heartburn.

"Sit down, sit down," Bertha exclaimed to the Mermelsteins. "It's good to see you. Thank you for coming." While Arthur eyed a *Playboy* on the coffee table, featuring "The Girls of London," Bertha, who varied between hearty and heartier, launched into a series of compliments about how Iris and Ellen were turning into young women and how young their mother looked. The fact of Grandpa living with this rosy, cheerful Gentile woman to whom he wasn't even married was so far from the accepted way of doing things that Arthur had stopped thinking about it long ago. In his mother's words, Grandpa was "a rogue." As for Bertha, Arthur liked her because she never bothered him with those moronic adult questions about what he wanted to be when he grew up, questions that made him want to answer "trained assassin" or "gigolo."

Bertha invited the females into the kitchen to help her serve. She had made blintzes—not the lightest dish to break a fast with but delicious. After beckoning to his son and grandson to have a seat in the living room, Max, as usual, launched into a story about some crony who was in trouble or had barely missed getting in trouble. He sat there vigorously tapping ash on the edge of one of the dozen or so glass ashtrays in the house that bore the Elks Club insignia on them. His eyebrows, which were still black, jumped up and down as he spoke.

"I told Kimmelman—you know who I mean, he ran a hardware store over by Pimlico and had some action on the side—'How many favors have I done you?' And what does he say back to me? 'You done what you needed to do. Those weren't favors.' Talk about *chutzpah*."

Max turned to Arthur, who was pretending to be interested. "That, Arthur, is what's called an 'ingrate'—or *mamzer*, as the Jewish people say." Max paused and flourished his lit cigar in the air. "Just because I don't go to temple doesn't mean I'm not Jewish." He turned back to Stan. "Hell, I'm as Jewish as it gets—a lifetime spent with every *pisher* in Baltimore who could rub two nickels together." Max took a drink of whiskey and made a face, as if he had never tasted the stuff before.

"No one is going to put one over on you, Dad," Stan offered. He had a set number of phrases he used in response to Max's stories. Arthur knew them all — "That's life in the big city" was probably the most common, though "That's the way the cookie crumbles" was another favorite. Arthur wondered about his father's fondness for clichés. His mother wrote down *cliché* in the margins of her students' compositions every chance she got, but maybe that was what it took to make having someone like Max for your father bearable. When Arthur tried to think about Grandpa Max as a father, someone who went out in the yard and threw a baseball with you or helped you learn to ride a bike, he couldn't.

Bertha shouted "We're coming!" from the kitchen and immediately appeared in the hallway bearing a big platter of blintzes. Susan and her daughters followed her with bowls of sour cream and fruit preserves.

"My father took me to Nate's and Leon's Delicatessen when I was a little girl. He said, 'Bertha, you don't have to be one of the Jewish people to eat here.' That's how he said it, 'The Jewish people.' He was a big palooka, drove a truck for the public works, and he could eat like a house on fire, let me tell you." She beamed at the platter. "'You get up from a meal here' — that's at Nate's — 'and you know you've eaten something.' That's what he used to say."

"These people are hungry, Bertha. Let's get to it." Max was on his feet and making his way to the table. His glass and cigar accompanied him.

"Arthur, why don't you offer a prayer before we eat?" Stan said. He was standing by his son and put a hand on his shoulder.

"He doesn't know any prayers, Daddy," Iris said. "Once he was bar mitzvah, he forgot everything."

"Says who?" answered Arthur. "*Baruch ata, Adonai . . .*" When he finished, he gave Iris a curt, I'm-still-the-big-brother nod.

Susan held up a bottle of Mott's. "Drink some apple juice first, children, to get your stomach ready for food."

"Apple juice? What is apple juice?" Max raised his whiskey.

After the initial tastes, exclamations of delight, and praise for Bertha from everyone, Max waved his cigar at Arthur. "So, you worked this summer for Harry Schwartz, I hear. A *shtarker*, Harry, I'll give him that. I knew him when he started out in the rag and junk business. But going around to the jigs day-in, day-out, is that good for anyone? What do you think, Arthur?" He reached for an Elks Club tray and tapped some ash.

"What's a jig, Grandpa?" Ellen asked.

"It means a Negro and it's not a word I want you to use, Ellen," Susan answered. She set her fork down.

Ellen set her fork down too. "But Grandpa used it and he's our grandpa."

"Grandpa is older. He speaks from another time. That's his business—right, Max?" Susan turned from her daughter to her father-in-law. Her look said give-me-some-help-here.

Bertha spoke, however, before Max could. "Grandpa means well. He's got a golden heart, Ellen, but you know he's got a bad word for everyone. That's how he is. He got knocked on the side of his head when he was growing up and he's still got some dents in it. Isn't that right, Max?"

Max felt his skull with his left hand. "No dents that I can feel. But you're asking me a lot of questions. Forget I said that Ellen, honey. Your mom is right. I'm an old guy. Hell, I remember World War I. If you want, I can sing you songs from it." He opened his mouth wide like an opera singer.

"I didn't know you knew Mr. Schwartz, Grandpa," Arthur said.

"Your grandfather knows most everyone in Baltimore," Bertha announced. She sounded proud, as if Max were a mayor or councilman.

"It's true—Paddies, wops, Yids, holy rollers, Polacks, steel workers, society dames." He paused and looked at his almost-empty glass, then smiled. "And a few Negroes, too, thrown in for good measure."

"What's a Paddy?" Ellen asked.

"What's a holy roller?" Iris asked.

Stan stood up. "Grandpa's vocabulary lesson for the day

is over." He turned to Bertha. "Those were delicious, Bertha. Many thanks from my stomach and the other stomachs at this table. A few of those go a long way. Now we should get going."

"But what about playing cards, Daddy?" Iris set her hands firmly down on the table. "We always play cards with Grandpa."

Max started to speak but Stan spoke first. "Not today. We have to get home. Tomorrow is work and school for all of us."

"But I wanted to play cards." Iris still had her hands down as if she were fastening herself to the table. "And I had a question for Grandpa, too."

"You and your sister already have asked a bunch of questions." Stan started to move his chair away from the table. Susan put down her cloth napkin—a Bertha touch— beside her plate.

Iris gave her father a ferocious look. "Okay, but I can ask my question." She turned toward Max. "Did you play cards when you were in jail, Grandpa?"

Arthur, who had been thinking that he wasn't going to get so much as a glimpse of the fabled playmates of London, snapped to attention. The room became still.

"This calls for a drink," Max said. He motioned to Bertha who rose and fetched a bottle. Max poured himself two fingers of bourbon and pondered the glass.

No one said anything. Iris kept her eyes on Max as if he might evaporate. Arthur knew that his sister didn't want to look at her parents. He wouldn't have, either, if he were her.

"To tell the truth, honey, I did play cards in there. There's not a whole lot to do there but think about how you'd like not to be there." He moved his eyes from Iris to Stan. "The cards have been good to me more than not. The cards got me there—I'm sure Stan has told everyone here the story—but the cards helped me live there." He turned back to Iris, who looked more scared than anything. "That means the cards helped me get out because if you can't live there, then you can't get out. For a gambler, which is what your grandfather is, Iris, the cards are your friends. You understand that, maybe? Win some, lose some, but always ready to play." He tapped his cigar but it had gone out.

Stan started to say something but in the same second Iris's face crumpled up and she started crying. She lurched downward so her forehead almost touched the edge of the table. Then she was talking, saying, "I'm sorry, Grandpa. I love you, Grandpa." Then she started crying again. Ellen, who had been looking at her sister with wide open eyes, started crying, too.

"Wow, girls," Arthur said, but no one heard him.

Quickly, Susan and Stan each moved to comfort a child. Bertha stood behind them and made sympathetic clucking sounds. When she spoke, she put an enormous smile on her wide face. "Now, girls, it's all right. Grandpa is here. You'll play cards with him another day. We promise. Right, Max?"

Max appeared startled, as if he had never seen two girls crying at once.

It seemed to Arthur that everyone then ran to the front door. He was the last one, but before he stepped outside Max grabbed his forearm.

"Arthur," he barked. His voice was husky.

"Maybe sometime we'll talk more about Mr. Schwartz," Arthur said. "He's got a thing about Hitler."

"To hell with that cheapskate Harry Schwartz and to hell with Hitler. Listen, Arthur, you're a good boy but there's more to life than being a good boy. You understand?" Max had not let go of Arthur. For an old man, his grip was strong. "One of these days you're going to get yourself a girlfriend."

"I met someone I like, Grandpa," Arthur announced. His voice broke slightly at the word *like*.

"That's good. I'm glad to hear that but what I want you to know, Arthur, is that you want to be a man." He let go of Arthur and reached into a trouser pocket. "So this is for you." He pressed something into Arthur's hand.

Arthur did not look down but thanked his grandfather.

"Don't thank me, Arthur. Just tell me someday you've used it."

Bertha was peeking over his shoulder. "Ramses," she said. "That's a good brand."

Susan

The scent of cinnamon and the commotion of drawers and cabinet doors greeted Susan when she entered the kitchen. Ruby and Seeley were making apple pies. It would be plural because, as Seeley observed, "One pie gets eaten in a minute. If we makin' pies, let's be makin' two." She was right: six people went through a pie in no time. When Stan wanted a snack later in the evening, nothing would be left.

"How was your day, Mom?" Ellen and Iris chorused. They were at the kitchen table slicing peeled apples into the thin rounds Seeley preferred.

"Good, but long," Susan answered. Andrew had stopped by to tell her that he was trying out for a part in *Death of a Salesman*. "Not Willy but one of his sons. I can do either one." She told him she was sure he would get one of the roles. Then she had a student who stayed after school for grammar help and a student who didn't understand why she got a B– on a composition. And she had another student who wanted to talk about why she was having trouble getting her schoolwork done, which had to do with her "getting serious with a guy." After a silence, she said, "Do you understand what I mean, Mrs. M?" Susan nodded. She understood. They talked about not giving all her time to this boyfriend. The student agreed. What would happen when he pulled up in front of her house in his Thunderbird that night when she was supposed to be reading *The Return of the Native* was another story. And then on the way out of school she ran into Sid Colvin, who told her without any preamble that six missile launch sites were under construction in Cuba, according to Senator Keating. "He's a senator from New York," Sid added. Susan felt like yelling at him. How could he teach kids all day and still be interested in this stuff? How could he not be wrung out? How could he care what any senator said about anything? "Thanks for the news, Sid," she mumbled. "Anytime," he answered. If she weren't so tired and distracted, she would have sworn that he was smiling.

Ruby and Seeley were in the midst of one of their symposia about who had it worse—Negroes or Jews. Susan had heard this conversation forever. A year or so ago Stan had wanted to fire Seeley because she told Ruby that the Jews complained too much, and Iris, who had overheard, later asked him if he thought Jews complained too much because Seeley did and Seeley was "smarter than everybody." It took all her wiles to calm Stan down.

"*Bupkis*, that's what the Jews have gotten, *bupkis*," Ruby said. She was vigorously rolling out dough.

"That crust gonna be too thin, Ruby, you keep rollin' that way," Seeley noted. She was grating a lemon rind.

"What's *bupkis* mean, Mom?" Ellen asked.

"Ask Ruby," Susan replied. She looked down at the pile of mail—bills and circulars. Why didn't she correspond with someone? The telephone connected everyone too easily. She couldn't imagine Eustacia Vye blabbing into a machine.

"That word means 'beans,'" Seeley answered. "I been around Ruby long enough to know her language." She chuckled.

"Beans is beans," Ruby pronounced. "Now with the Negroes, Dr. King tells people not to mistreat them." She brandished the rolling pin in her right hand. "Good luck is what I say. The Jews have been telling the *goyim* that forever. 'Show us some respect. Just a *bisl*.' And what has it done for them?" She set the rolling pin down on the counter.

At any moment Ruby was liable to fall into a teary misery that seemed partly her own making and partly history's. For her part, Susan knew she would never parse it out. The trail went too far back in time. Perhaps what her father had walked out on was the habit of grief.

"Look, we've got all the apples cut," Iris said.

Seeley walked over and peered into the brown ceramic bowl. "How 'bout that?" She whistled. "That's a nice job of cuttin'. Now you want the lemon, some of that cinnamon, and the sugar."

Ruby sniffled a little and blew into an ancient handkerchief she kept in the waist band of her skirt. She wore blouses and skirts, or dresses ("ladies' pants are not for ladies"). "A good day for you, Susie?" she asked. Her voice quavered but only a little. Her daughter stood there before her — that was what mattered.

Susan thought she herself might start crying. That was ridiculous — everything good was there in front of her, right down to the apples Stan had bought at a roadside stand out in Carroll County. Still, she felt a strong pang. All day long she had been ministering to people. All day long she had been talking. Here she was again. But the people in this kitchen were fine doing what they were doing. They didn't need her.

"Like I said, Ma, a good day," she answered. "You know me. I was born to be a school teacher."

"I can't wait to get older so I can have you for a teacher, Mom," Ellen said. Along with her sister, she was seated at the kitchen table measuring out tablespoons of sugar from a five-pound sack.

"I'm glad I don't have to wait as long as you have to wait," Iris added.

Ellen stopped measuring and stuck her tongue out.

"When it's time, I'll be glad to have both of you. There's no hurry, is there?" Susan went up to them and put a hand on each girl's head. She loved the feeling of their hair — thick, strong, black hair. She rubbed her hands a bit on their scalps.

"Are you giving me a shampoo, Mom?" Ellen asked.

"Or a massage?" Iris moved her head back and forth, responding to Susan's touch.

Susan raised her hands above her head and suddenly yawned. "Oh, it's been a long day. I need to go somewhere."

"May we go?" Ellen said.

"We're making pies," her sister reminded her.

"I don't know where I'm going myself, Ellen. And Iris is right. You girls are helping out in the kitchen. Seeley and Ruby need you." Susan rubbed her eyes. Probably she should lie down but she didn't want to. Sid Colvin was big on naps. Probably in his sleep he debated Khrushchev.

"I'm going to go for a ride by myself." Susan went over

to the counter where she had put her pocketbook down. "I'll see you all later."

"Mom, will you be back for dinner?" Ellen pleaded. "You have to."

Susan was amused. As a mother, she managed to be both crucial and taken for granted. "I'm sure for one night you can eat without me. Keep a plate warm and don't eat up all the pie." She blew an inclusive kiss. The girls shouted, "Bye, Mom," as she closed the kitchen door.

Without a thought she started the Ford, as if the car would tell her where to go. She knew what she didn't want to do. She didn't want to shop. She didn't want to talk with anyone. Then as she put the car in gear she realized what she did want. Every Sunday she browsed the ads for new housing developments. They were springing up all over Baltimore County, not that far from where she lived but in another world—the suburbs. She wanted to look at houses.

It wasn't hard to find them. You drove out Liberty Road, a two-lane thoroughfare that led to the countryside, where signs heralded Acres and Courts and Valleys and Estates. The land—scrubby woods and cornfields—was becoming streets and houses. When she had first come to Baltimore after the war, the County had seemed far away from the city. It was where the farms were that helped to feed the city. Now those farms were starting to disappear. And off all the roads that penetrated into the County—Liberty, Reisterstown, Park Heights, Greenspring—houses were going up.

The day was perfect. October light suffused the air—dry, soft fire. She rolled the driver's-side window down and let the wind flow over her. If she wanted, she could drive and drive and let that freedom settle into her. It made her recall how Joe Costa had touted *On the Road* to her. "America's novel," he claimed. "We're nomads. We want to keep moving." Susan had picked the book up but the long paragraphs deterred her. And she had to admit: she didn't want to be a nomad. That impulse was romantic. That impulse was for men who didn't want to grow up, much less raise children. She didn't envy Jack Kerouac. There was something sad in not knowing where you were going, something confused, something hopeless.

She turned off Liberty and found herself among streets with British names—Buckingham, Raleigh, Bedford. Her children would be going to the high school out here, not the one that she taught in, unless she switched, too. What Joe had said about the school changing nagged at her. When she brought it up with Stan, he wasn't much help. "Whatever makes you happy" sounded good but didn't offer any insight. Would she feel strange as the school became more and more of a Negro school? Would she continue to learn from her Negro students about how they saw the world? Or would she get tired of it? Would the distance that the Reverend King was trying to span only frustrate her until she finally left? She had heard more than one Negro student say to another, "Well, she's a white lady." Every day she put all of herself into teaching, but it was true— she was a white lady. As a white lady, she could eye these houses and imagine what she pleased. A Negro family would not be imagining what they pleased.

They probably wouldn't try, no more than she would move to a Gentile area. People kept to themselves or the world kept them to themselves or some of both, unless history started to wake up. That was how Joe Costa had put it the other day during a teachers' lounge discussion about Albany, Georgia, and Reverend King. He said he was quoting Jarvis Baker, the music teacher she had met. She could imagine Jarvis saying those words. She had thought more than once of him standing by the window and listening to the jazz. The music, and the vision of him engaged with the music, hadn't left her.

Her head was wandering. She pushed in the cigarette lighter, waited the requisite seconds, and lit a Salem. The afternoon was waning. She cut over on Old Court Road and headed out Reisterstown and then turned off that. The countryside was still present—winding roads, fieldstone and wooden farmhouses that must have been built in the nineteenth century. When she saw a sign for a new development, she took a right and then another right that left her facing a huge field that was sprouting houses.

The building crews had gone home for the day. She pulled the car to the curb, though in fact there was no curb, just bare ground. Everything around her looked raw with promise—

houses you could see through, scraped earth, partial streets, a few huge bulldozers. She hadn't changed from the high heels she wore to work, but she wasn't going to let that keep her from exploring.

The ground was rock hard. Probably they were going to put sod down. She walked up to a split-level that stood on a corner of two nameless streets. The house reminded her of a whale skeleton she had seen in a natural history museum — massive but fragile, too. She stood admiring the structure, then walked up to where the front door would be. A few rickety, temporary steps connected the ground to the door opening. She stepped up carefully and then she was there — in the house. It was large but that was good because with six people they were going to need a large house. She walked slowly, enjoying the echo of her footsteps on the subfloor. Nothing was finished here yet — no windows or doors or cabinets or toilets or showers or drywall. It was more the idea of a house than a real house.

She took another Salem from the pack in her pocketbook, lit it, and blew out a dramatic gust. She had seen the house prices on the signs. No matter what her husband said, they could afford this. She walked up the six steps to the upper level and into the largest bedroom. A closet was being framed up on one side. Two big window openings were on the opposite side of the room. The bedroom was connected to a small room that had a few pipes sticking out of the floor — the bathroom that went with the bedroom.

The pipes looked like stems in search of blooms. The memory came to her of the bathroom sink in the apartment to which she and Ruby moved after her father left. It was porcelain that had turned rusted brown. How many mornings had she lowered her face to that basin? The water was cold as a river bottom. When Ruby complained to the landlord, he would tell her that he would get to it soon. "When is 'soon'?" Ruby would ask. "We need hot water." The man's response was always the same: "If you don't like it, lady, you can move."

Susan ground her cigarette into the plywood floor but then picked it up. The studded walls seemed to call to her: *This could be the place.* The words sounded like a line from some snappy musical from her childhood — spangled hoofers cavorting across a huge stage, everyone singing their lungs out, banishing the hard times. Or maybe Shirley Temple would have sung it. She had loved Shirley Temple.

Along with some apple pie, a family awaited her. The waning light gentled the clay earth and sticklike structures. The sense of promise deepened: autumn might as well have been spring. When she reached her car, she didn't get in. The moment shivered, at once calm and eager; she didn't want to lose it.

There was no romance here. The names the builders gave these developments were laughable. Often as not, the streets were named for their daughters: Judy Lane and Sue-Ellen Court. There was practical possibility here, though. She didn't work every day for romance.

A few crows flew overhead. When she was a little girl, Ruby had told her that in Russia crows were omens, but Susan couldn't recall what they were omens of — probably trouble. She leaned against the car and waved to them.

Arthur

Straws of late afternoon light wandered through the two dusty windows in the central room of the three-room office of Stanley Mermelstein, Certified Public Accountant. Everyone was tidying up papers, closing ledgers, putting plastic covers over the adding machines—calling it a day.

"The Soviets are tough cookies," John Van Borkum stated to the room-at-large. He waved his empty briar pipe to emphasize the point.

"The Russians . . . ," murmured Larry Schneiderman, three years out of the University of Baltimore and known in the office as "Las."

Van Borkum started writing with his pipe on an imaginary blackboard. "They are Soviets. They are an empire. Ask the Ukrainians and the Latvians and the Estonians and the Georgians, if they are Russians. I hail from that continent. I lived through the war." He stopped writing. "The Soviets don't know what fear is."

"Okay, Van, the Soviets are trying to push our button, but what if they do push our button? I mean what if we—or they—push the big button—the you-know-what button?" Las halted as if he were about to pronounce a sentence in a courtroom. "No way we can let those babies stay in Cuba."

Arthur was looking at a wall calendar printed by some insurance company his dad did business with. Every month had a cute photo. October's was of two little kids and a puppy romping in a pile of leaves. Where was the atomic bomb calendar?

"Radioactive corned beef," Lee Berticot said mournfully. He had a huge gut, and of the accountants who worked for Arthur's father, Lee was the most particular about his lunch order. One Saturday when Arthur came back from the North Avenue Market short one half-sour, he thought Lee was going to make him go back.

Stan's windowless door was closed. He was dictating letters to his secretary, Marilee Dorsky. In her late thirties, she did calisthenics at the Y three nights a week, wore spike heels, short skirts, and perfume that reached to the other side of Saint Paul Street. Every man in the office—Van Borkum the worldly Dutchman, Las the young buck, Lee the beefy kind-heart, and even Wally Bright, who wore vest sweaters year-round and lived with his mother—competed for Marilee's attention. Whenever Arthur showed up, she showered him—a child in her mascara-laden eyes—with motherly attention. A couple times the child had to lock the office's bathroom door and jack off into a Kleenex to relieve himself of the excitement Marilee had incited. The act didn't take long, though after the pleasure spurt, he felt hollow—neither boy nor man.

Marilee opened the door from Stan's office and clacked into the room. A whiz at shorthand, she had a steno pad in her left hand and a ballpoint pen in her right. She scanned the men and cocked her brunette head to the side. "What's up, fellas?"

"Nothing major, Marilee," Las answered. "We're just talking about the possible end of the known world—no more Colts, no more Cadillacs, no more crab cakes." He stared down at the floor for a second, as if regretful, then raised his head and smiled pleasantly. Armageddon was no reason to stop charming the secretary.

From the door opening between the center room and the outer room where he and Arthur worked Wally looked on. "Hold on there, Las. The president hasn't spoken to the American people yet. This is all hearsay. You have to be cool and calm in these situations." His large Adam's apple bobbed up and down with determination. Arthur, who was standing beside him, had heard Wally praise President Kennedy for his "strength of character." At the moment, though, trusting the president's prospective words against the fire that could melt cities felt like a very big stretch.

"Wally, you ever had a gun pointed at you?" Las winced. "I hope not, but what's pointed at the U.S. of A are some very big guns."

"From the lower Keys you can almost see Cuba. It's that close." While he spoke, Van Borkum filled his pipe with the Bond Street brand tobacco he favored. "I worked in Miami and I've been to Havana, before all these revolution shenanigans." He started tamping the tobacco with the thumb of his left hand. "I must say the women are beautiful there." He too smiled agreeably at Marilee, who was still standing with her pad and pen.

"I don't know, Van. You've worked all over the world and here you are in Baltimore." Las made a doleful, clucking sound.

Lee Berticot, who had been stuffing papers into a battered briefcase, took the opening. "Plenty of beautiful women right here in Baltimore." He started to smile.

"Okay, guys, knock it off." Marilee put her implements down and threw her shoulders back.

There were moments in the presence of women's bodies when Arthur thought he was just going to lose his mind. He'd fall to the floor and start gibbering. As it was, he groaned involuntarily and took a step backward.

"Marilee's right. This is serious stuff, gentlemen." Wally had taken the floor again. "I haven't had a gun pointed at me, but I don't think our president will let anyone do that to us." Wally emphasized *us*. "He may be on the young side but he's got Irish guts." To clinch his point, Wally tugged at the waist of his sweater.

I had a gun pointed at me. Arthur looked around the room as Van Borkum lit his pipe and blew out a peaceful trail of smoke. "Talking doesn't change anything, does it?" Arthur said. The words were right but his tone was wrong. He sounded angry when he meant to sound world- weary.

Las cocked a knowing eyebrow. "Arthur, you're right. It doesn't change a thing." He paused to put his sport jacket on. "As for me, I've got a heavy date tonight. Let's hope we do more than talk. Good night to you all."

"Ah, Las, to be full of youthful expectation." Van Borkum raised his pipe as a benediction.

Marilee had opened her middle desk drawer and was

rooting through packs of chewing gum, hair combs, and emery boards. "There's that pack of Chiclets!" She lifted her head. "Don't do anything I wouldn't do, Las."

Everyone laughed. In what seemed like a minute Arthur was the only person left in the room.

Stanley Mermelstein's door remained closed. Arthur knew that his father operated on his own schedule. Often he interspersed family trips to restaurants, stores, or Grandpa Max's with a stop at some client's where he was leaving off papers or picking papers up. These stops could last for fifteen or twenty minutes. When he got back to the car, his mother would ask him if he had to make that stop and whether he thought about the people waiting for him. He would reply that he did have to make that stop and that he was making the money that supported the people who were waiting for him. Susan would sigh and subside into silence. Stan would start talking about the Orioles or what Mayor Goodman was up to, and another irritating wait would recede into the uncomfortable distance. Lately, though, Susan had been yelling or "making a scene," as his father put it, rather than sighing.

Arthur sided with his mother. Stan's stops made him feel that everything in life was tinged with business, which was an attitude his father liked to quote: "The chief business of America is business." Sometimes, as a preamble to the business quote, Stan added "There's no getting around it." How, Arthur wondered, did he know there was no getting around it? Had he tried?

When he rapped on his father's door, Stan grunted and then announced that he would be "just a sec." Arthur imagined kicking the door down or, more realistically, taking a bus home. Instead, he picked up the daily business paper of Baltimore and sat down to read about people getting promotions at banks and insurance companies and developers starting up new shopping centers. Various captains of local industry were receiving awards for good works. Why would anyone want to shoot missiles at kindly, industrious America? Mr. Schwartz had told Arthur that the problem with the Russians was that they were more interested in making threats than making money.

A half hour later, Stan emerged from his office. He held

his old brown leather briefcase in one hand and a thick volume of the U.S. tax code in the other. Arthur spent hours in the office putting updates into one or another of the loose-leaf tax code binders. Any human endeavor was more interesting, but "someone has to do it" — another of his father's pet phrases. As if to announce there was more to life than drudgery, Marilee seemed to make a point of wiggling by while he took out one mind-numbing page and put in another.

Stan set everything down on Marilee's desk and looked at Arthur. He started to clear his throat. He had a chronic sinus condition and was always bringing up phlegm. The handkerchiefs that he threw into the laundry basket on the second floor and that Seeley washed made Arthur's stomach turn. "Dad is so goopy," Iris complained. Arthur had to agree with her.

"Arthur, I have to tell you the truth. I'm worried about your mother." Stan squared his shoulders as if preparing to do some physical task. He took a deep breath. Thinking was an act of vigilance. "She reads a lot of books and she has a lot of ideas." His eyes swam away from his son and onto a ledger on Lee Berticot's desk marked *C & N Construction Co.* "Don't get me wrong. There's nothing wrong with literature. There's a lot to be said for books."

"Like what, Dad?" Arthur asked.

"What do you mean 'like what'? You read all the time. Don't get fresh with me, Arthur. I'm trying to talk to you man to man." Stan squared his shoulders even more. He seemed ready to salute a major. He often told Arthur that he had liked the Army because "you knew where you stood." Now he stood before his son. He made the throat-clearing sound again. "As I said, I'm worried. I want you to keep an eye out for her and help her in any way you can. I know she likes to talk to you about books and ideas." He paused, then exhaled a long "Whew!" He seemed amazed, though Arthur wasn't sure what he was amazed about. "The craziest thing is that she thinks I'm involved with Marilee. Can you believe it?"

Arthur felt the floor shift slightly under his feet. "Marilee's married, Dad." He felt embarrassed for the second time that afternoon. He knew enough that there was something called "adultery."

"She is married, Arthur, and she is my secretary, not my mistress."

That last word sounded impossibly strange to Arthur. Where did his father, with his tax codes and legal pads, even get that word? Van Borkum, who claimed to have had a mistress when he lived in Indonesia, was the only person Arthur ever heard use that word.

"Anyhow, keep an eye out." Stan tried to smile and put his arms out to pick up his burdens. "Let's go home. It's been a long day. You're probably starving."

The floor shifted back to where it had been. The usual ton of feelings jostled inside of him: *I met a girl I like — I'm sick of doing this stupid work — I think Mom is unhappier than either of us know — These missiles spook me and I don't know why the human race needs these things — I love you.*

"You're right, Dad. I am starving." Arthur grabbed his school books and moved toward the door. Down the long flight of wooden stairs went father and son, their footsteps tracing a weary song.

Susan

Stan had told Susan that there wasn't much point in going to Parent-Teacher Night because Arthur always did well at school: "He's AWOL upstairs sometimes, but he does his work." Susan felt odd at that moment because her husband so rarely said anything about their children. They might as well have been cows or sheep as human beings. It wasn't that he didn't love them. It was that he was a male with other matters on his mind beside the inner lives of his offspring. Or it was that he didn't know that they *had* inner lives because his own was so harnessed to his work. Years ago she had gotten used to their separate domains: she wasn't reading updates about taxes and he wasn't reading about the Impressionists.

She agreed with him but told him she was going anyway because "teachers owe that to other teachers." "Solidarity, huh?" he half-asked, half-stated. He sounded amused more than anything else. Stan didn't criticize her being in the teachers' union, but he didn't favor it, either. He voted Republican because that was the party of businessmen. She voted Democrat. He thought Adlai Stevenson was "an egghead." She thought Adlai was articulate and charming. It wasn't his fault he hadn't been a general.

Arthur's high school, the stony Gothic dream of some 1920s architects, looked like a cross between a church and a castle. Walking through the metal-locker-lined corridors and sitting through a succession of ten-minute classes should have been comforting. Susan knew what a high school was like and what teachers were like, but as the evening went along and she listened to the spiels about what was being taught in chemistry and U.S. history, she felt more and more unnerved or, worse, enthralled by a dim god who decreed a uniform hygiene of grades, tests, blackboards, lined pieces of paper, and uncomfortable desks. Though every teacher perked up at the mention of Arthur's name, she felt dreary. And if anything, she worried that Arthur trusted books too much. What had Thomas Hardy done for her besides exciting her sensibility and offering the mordant outlook that Joe Costa had quoted? Did it help anyone to know about the unhappy likes of Eustacia Vye?

And what was it that Hardy couldn't even mention though it lay there glimmering like a forbidden jewel — sex? Throughout her tempestuous trysts, Eustacia writhed in the vise of what was natural yet forbidden. Susan's own son was doing his share of writhing these days. Yet whenever she asked Stan if Arthur ever asked him about sex, Stan would blurt "No" and turn to another topic, as if to say, "Why would a father and son talk about that?" But men didn't ask for directions when they were lost, either. Seeley had noted to her that "those stains" on Arthur's sheets were hard to get out. "Use bleach," she answered. Seeley reminded her that bleaching "take the life out of the cloth." "Use bleach," she repeated.

At random moments, she found herself wishing *she* had something to bleach. She fantasized about being one of those Toulouse-Lautrec prostitutes. Her round-cheeked, brown-eyed Jewish face peered out from rumpled sheets. She spent her days and nights in and out of a negligee. Her life went no further than her cunt. She never spoke that word but she thought it. It was a far-fetched vision . . . but it wasn't.

At eight o'clock a bell went off and a voice on the loudspeaker announced that classes were over. Parents were free to go to the cafeteria for cookies and milk. Susan stood at the top of a stairwell on the second floor and thought how little she wanted chocolate chips mingled with chat about college admissions and levels of algebra. What she wanted was to scream and sing at the same time like some of the music her son listened to. As dutiful parents walked by her, she recalled there was a music teacher she knew in this school. She set off toward his classroom.

He was there hunched over a piano, his square-cut woolen necktie dangling in front of him. She stood at the open door of the large band room filled with instruments, music stands, and classroom chairs. As he sampled a series of notes over and over, he seemed to be probing as much as playing them. Then he launched into a sustained sequence. Rich, rising sound struck the lifeless air as if some hope at last had been realized.

"That's from *Rhapsody in Blue!*" Susan exclaimed.

Jarvis Baker raised his head but kept playing until the melody exhausted itself. When he stopped, he rested his hands on his knees and slowly turned toward the doorway. "I didn't know anyone was there. I was pretending I was Leonard Bernstein. He can play the hell out of that piece."

Susan stepped over the threshold. "So can you."

"In musicianship a wink is not as good as a nod. It's about thoroughness and sustaining your attack. Bernstein—he can sustain it, which is tricky because Gershwin goes through a lot of changes in that section." He rose from the piano bench and stretched his arms out above his head. "Excuse me, but it's been a long day. What brings you here tonight, Mrs. Mermelstein?"

"I thought I would see what your classroom looked like." Susan paused and ran a hand down the front of her dress to reassure herself. It was a navy blue dress, solidly colored on top but with tiny white dots on the skirt. It cinched at the waist with a small black belt. Lu, who admitted to spending too much on clothes, had complimented her on it.

"My classroom? If they would just keep the piano in tune, I'd be happy," Jarvis said. "Any of your children play an instrument?" He walked over to his desk and began to sort through a sizable mound of clutter.

"The girls have started flute lessons but they seem more interested in dancing. They both take tap." She looked around at the posters Jarvis had put up: one was for a Mozart festival in Europe; one was for the Miles Davis Quartet. "Where did you learn to play?"

Jarvis looked up from the sheet music, union memoranda, and record sleeves. "I've played since I was a boy. My mama played. But I really learned to play when I went to Howard over in D.C.—excellent music department. Todd Duncan, who was the original Porgy, was a Howard professor." He looked more keenly at Susan, who had not advanced any further into the room. "Of course, you may only know Howard as a name, if that. It's on the other side of the great divide." He was standing very erect now and had shoved his hands into his pants pockets. He leaned his head back. "You can come in all the way, Susan. I won't bite."

"The great divide?" Susan asked. She walked forward until she stood on the other side of his wooden desk.

"You won't find it on any map but you won't find the color line, either. Metaphors never make it onto maps." Jarvis smiled crookedly.

Susan clutched at her small leather pocketbook, then realized her cigarettes were in her car. "I understand. You know that I teach with Joe. You know what my school is like."

"I do indeed. The line is starting to get smudged. Some folks want to outright erase it—uppity ministers with doctorates in theology for instance. Some folks—a whole lot of folks and not just down South—don't." He frowned. Susan could feel his hands dig more deeply into his pockets. The energy of his piano playing stood right there in front of her. His every motion was compelling. She took a small step back.

As it had done that day at Joe's, his face suddenly cleared, the storm passing through him in seconds. She found herself marveling. Her storms didn't do that.

"Well, I need a cigarette." Susan paused. "I guess I'll be going. Thanks for letting me see your room."

"No need to rush off. As a teacher, I'm here to talk with parents and you're a parent. Do you like Gershwin, by the way?"

"I love him. I have a recording with Harry Belafonte and Lena Horne where they sing songs from *Porgy and Bess*. They sing 'Bess, You Is My Woman' together. I love that." Susan moved a self-conscious step forward. "And I remember when he died. I was six years old but I remember everyone saying that George Gershwin had died. I remember someone coming into our apartment and playing a record. I remember how sad people were."

"Funny, isn't it, what we remember?" Jarvis said. He took his hands out of his pockets. The hands were almost out of proportion to the rest of him. He picked up the small globe on

Baron Wormser

his desk and spun it, as if each moment those hands had to have something to toy with.

"It *is* funny." Susan's eyes lingered on the globe. Then she turned toward the door. "Thanks again for your hospitality."

"Would you like to hear that song?" Jarvis asked.

Susan had only taken a step or so. "I'd be honored."

After a final spin, Jarvis set the globe down, went over to the piano, and placed himself on the bench that stood before it. "You can sit right here and watch. Like I said—I won't bite. Growl some, maybe, but not bite." He smiled at his words, a warmer smile.

Susan realized—the thought was like blood thrumming in her veins—how being close to him was what she wanted to do when she walked into the room. Very deliberately, she sat herself down. The billow of her skirt touched his pant leg. She held her breath.

He began to play. Susan could feel him entering the music—the compact body beside hers relaxing even as energy was coursing through him. His hands moved precisely, without hurry, seemingly obeying their own genius. The melody's emotion—yearning and decisive—began to touch her the way it always touched her. The power of a man and a woman coming together lived in that song. In her head she sang the words—"de real happiness is jes' begun."

When the music had spent itself, its aching intensity burnishing the silence, Jarvis held his hands up in the air before him. Slowly he brought them back down onto the keyboard.

Susan didn't move. "That was beautiful."

"Thank you. It's strange music—two Jews speaking through Negroes." He paused and looked down, as if to query his now-still hands. "Maybe that's the best of all worlds. Maybe it's ludicrous. What did the Gershwins from New York City know about Catfish Alley? They imagined it, but I guess that's what we all do all the time—imagine. What else can we do? There's good imagining and there's bad imagining. Our prejudice, our blindness . . ." A bell sounded out in the corridor. "I heard Professor Duncan sing it one day at school. I'll never forget that—sort of like you remembering George Gershwin's death, but not sad. No. It inspired me." He gazed up at the clock on the wall. "Like I said, it's been a long day."

The music had passed; he was asking her to move on. Susan wondered whether she could do it. She could smell him and almost touch the fabric of his cotton shirt. She could feel the warmth of him. The burden of the song lingered there between them — *you is my woman*.

She rotated her legs away from Jarvis so as turn her back to him. It seemed to take whole minutes but in a moment she rose up.

"Thanks again, Jarvis, for the performance. You're talented." Susan started toward the door.

Jarvis waved a hand — dismissing the instruments and music stands as so many sorcerer's apprentices. "This is my world. I'm glad you stopped by to see it." He slumped over. Whatever he had to give, he had given. Under the bleak overhead lights the back of his neck shone a soft beige.

Susan didn't have to open the door because she had never shut it. When she said a small "bye," it was more to the empty hallway than to Jarvis Baker. She checked herself: pocketbook in hand, head on her shoulders, shoes on her feet. Daily life, to say nothing of the relentless headlines, crushed so many feelings. You didn't realize it until you had one.

Arthur

There was no listing for Farbelman on Oakdale in the phone book. Since Rebecca went to the high school where Susan taught, Arthur could have asked his mother to help him but that seemed all wrong. Guys didn't ask their mothers to help them locate girls. He could have walked up and down her street all afternoon. He could have spent every afternoon in the library waiting for her to return *The Return of the Native*. He could have had the sense to get her phone number to begin with.

Unless you were bragging, you didn't tell anything. Guys lived to make fun of other guys. The one course everybody excelled at was Basic Derision. It must have been the first week of school when he asked a classmate for a match to light a cigarette. The guy—Vitalis-oiled and with worse acne than Arthur—looked him over and replied nonchalantly, "A match? Yeah, your face and my ass." As Herbie Freilich liked to say, "Touché"—except in that situation you didn't say, "Touché." You grinned to hide your chagrin, took the match, lit your cigarette, and, after a suitably deep drag, blew out the smoke that saluted the mundane warfare of apprentice men.

Jack's Pool Parlor, run by a longtime pal of Arthur's grandfather named Jack Stein, invited both sarcasm and respect. The parlor was located in the cellar of an old brick building on Liberty Heights. Halfway down the long, narrow staircase that led to the dozen tables, Jack had affixed a sign to the wall that read, "Don't Give Up, Hell Is Near." Maybe that was why Arthur's grandfather commended the place. "You could learn some things from Jack Stein. He's a scholar of life," Max would say.

Despite Max's blessing, Arthur kept his after-school pool hall trips to himself. Going to hell wasn't an activity your parents wanted you to make a habit of. If asked, he said he had been at the library, which earned him a smile and a shrug. And it wasn't as if he were a regular. Unlike his buddies Rick Scanlon and John Silverman, who were, according to Jack, "contenders," he was just an occasional player. If they could have, Rick, whose parents ran a diner in Highlandtown, and Silverman, whose father and uncle owned an appliance store, would have lived at Jack's. And they both had pool tables in their basements.

As Arthur descended the stairs with his two friends, he remarked on the faint smell of piss. "Someone didn't make it all the way down," Rick said. "Or all the way up," Silverman added.

Whatever happened in the evenings, afternoons at Jack's were sedate. In many ways, it felt like school. Jack was the teacher who kept a close eye on the technique of the two contenders and a benign one on Arthur. A few loafers sat on stools and chairs around the room's perimeter or near Jack's huge desk and offered comments about the state of everything. Jack's factotum, Ernie, a man in his forties with a perennial bad haircut and a tic in his right eye, busied himself with sweeping and tidying. Light trickled through the basement windows that faced the avenue but palled before the dangling, always-lit bulbs that hung in metal cages above the pool tables. The brick walls were dotted with posters for boxing matches, touting fighters like Kid Galivan and Carmen Basilio. The air was stale with cigarette smoke, sweat, and time. Jack's was a tomb.

"Jack, how's about a game?" Rick asked the fat, bald man who sat behind what looked like a schoolteacher's desk reading the *Sun*. "You pick it."

"Don't hide behind that paper, Jack," Silverman chimed in. "You know both of us can take you." The tall, thin Jewish boy winked at the tall, thin Greek boy, who winked back. Rick was darker than either Arthur or Silverman. "Maybe I'm the Jew," he liked to say.

An elderly man, slouched in a wooden chair that was missing a spindle in its back, seemed to wake up. He wiped at his eyes with the back of his hand, then guffawed. "Jack was beating hustlers before your father ever laid hands on your mother." He raised his right hand, pinched his nose between his

Baron Wormser

thumb and forefinger, and blew some snot onto the floor.

Jack kept reading. Ernie kept sorting through a bunch of beer bottles in a far corner. Arthur wasn't sure whether it was a game Ernie was playing or a task.

"Okay, Jack, we'll play without you. Where's my good stick?" Rick turned toward the wall where the cues were mounted.

With a rustle of pages, Jack looked up. "You boys ever read what's in the paper?"

"Sure we do," Arthur answered.

"Not you, Arthur, the other two." Jack nodded to the backs of Rick and Silverman, who were selecting their cues.

Silverman turned around. "Course we read the newspaper. We're students. We study current events. We know who Nikita Khrushchev is." He sounded as though he was going to start laughing. "Don't ask me to spell it, though. And *Nikita* — that sounds like a girl's name. How seriously can you take a guy who has a girl's name?"

"Well, Mr. Funny Bones, you may not be laughin' soon." Jack put the paper down on his desk and smoothed it out. "Something's gotta give with these missiles." He stopped his smoothing and folded his large hands together. "I fought in one war and I lived through a couple more. Compared to these missiles, those were pop guns we were shootin'." He paused. "Shit." Another pause. "I guess that's what I gotta say to you boys — shit. And I gotta say, whatever you been meanin' to do, you better do it soon."

"Thanks for the insight, Jack," Rick said. He was hefting a stick in each hand.

"Hey, you *shmegeggy*, you can only use one at a time." Jack looked down at the headlines about Cuba. "You think life's a joke because you're a kid. Well shit, you better wise up."

Arthur had been running a hand over the baize of a table. Each table had a different feel — faster, slower, hard pockets, soft pockets. "Somehow I can see you're not in the best mood today, Jack. My mom and dad were talking this morning. My dad thinks it's no big thing, like two boxers feeling each other out. My mom thinks that maybe we're in a boat drifting toward a big waterfall. You drift along and then suddenly you're

122

over." Arthur walked toward his desk. "How about showing us the art of nine-ball before the boat goes over?"

"Speak for yourself, Merm, about the showing part," Silverman said. He was corralling balls in order to rack them. "Leave Jack to worry about the Russians. That's why he's down here. It's his air-raid shelter."

"Yeah, Jack, that's what President Kennedy is paid to do—worry." Rick had chosen his cue and was taking some strokes in the air in front of him. "You're always telling us to get all the tail we can get and enjoy life. What's with worry?" Rick smiled wide. With a mouthful of big white teeth, he claimed that Greeks could bite through iron.

Tail. Rick claimed not only to have done it but to have done it more than once. As a friend, he had offered both clinical and personal testimony. Arthur remembered every word: *You can't imagine what it looks like. No matter how many pictures you seen, you can't imagine. And it gets wet. It's like a sponge or something. And it smells. That's somethin' the pictures can't tell you — it smells.*

"I'm tellin' you boys to make hay while the sun shines." Jack rose from his desk. His once-white shirt had a big gravy stain down the center and it barely covered his stomach, which he patted with both hands. "Ernie, check these kids out. They're gonna show us how to shoot nine-ball. I'm dyin' to learn."

"Which reminds me, Ernie." Rick stopped swiping the air with his stick. "You said you know a guy who knows a guy on the Block who can get us into the Burlesque, that right?"

Ernie had ambled over to the table. He seemed to be studying Rick's face, as if trying to recall who was speaking to him.

"Ernie knows everybody worth knowin', right Ernie? Ernie was in the fight game." Jack said. "But speakin' of the fight game, you boys want to watch yourself down there. I'm talkin' drunks and punks and soldiers lookin' for a fight—a lotta liquored-up soldiers lookin' for a fight. It's not for schoolboys."

With both hands Silverman held out his cue horizontally across his neck, thrust his chin an inch or so above the stick, and smirked. "Maybe you haven't noticed, Jack, but this establishment that you run isn't a church or synagogue. And boys have to become men. So keep your worries to what's in the newspaper because we're smart." He paused as if to consider. "When we go there we'll wear disguises — wigs and stuff." He made a loud finger snap. "I got it. We'll go as the Marx Brothers. Merm will be the smart one. Rick's almost a wop. He can be Chico. I'll be the one who keeps his mouth shut and checks out the chicks."

"Silverman, shuttin' up fits good on you but I doubt you could do it." Jack turned to Ernie. "I don't know about the younger generation. You try to tell 'em what's what and they make fun of you."

Ernie's forehead was concentrated into frown lines. He spoke slowly. "I'm gonna put you in touch with somebody but you gotta have some money."

"How much?" Arthur asked.

"You're in on this too, Arthur?" Jack laughed an easy laugh. "You must be Max's boy."

"He's got something hanging between his legs," Rick said. "That's all that's required."

Ernie went on gravely. "Twenty bucks from each of you."

"This guy, he take checks?"

"Silverman, I'm tellin' you." Jack waddled toward their table, picking each foot up in the air as if there were puddles on the floor. Once there, he put both hands on the rail nearest him. "After you boys amuse yourselves, we'll play some one-pocket and see how you handle that."

As an answer, Rick leaned over and shot into the diamond. Balls scattered and skittered. Arthur liked this moment of the game as well as anything. You aimed and you tried but the balls seemed to have lives of their own.

Jack raised his hands from the rail. "Nice break. Now start thinkin'."

Susan

"His hands? What about the rest of him? That's what I want to know." Lu rapped knuckles on her kitchen table for emphasis. The next second, however, she drew her hand up and proceeded to inspect it. "My veins are starting to protrude. I'm going to be one of those women who get all stringy-looking like they swallowed a clothesline." She sighed. "More coffee? It's not that instant stuff you serve me, Susan. That stuff's to drink on a rocket ship."

"No thanks. Unless I take some pills, I'll be up all night. I don't need trips to the bathroom." Susan took a tiny sip.

"Up thinking about a Negro man with nice-looking hands who plays Gershwin?" Lu laughed. "I've lain awake and thought about worse things. Did I ever tell you about the guy who wanted to tie me up in bed?"

Susan rolled her eyes. "Lu! You're supposed to be advising me, not telling me another sex story."

"Advising you? You're a big girl, Susan. And I don't know what kind of advisor I am. I could have used some advice myself." She stuck her left hand out. "No ring on that hand anymore."

"I don't know what I'm feeling. It's not love, the way it was with Stan, but something's pulling on me. Something won't let go. And I don't know what to do. What's happening to me?" Susan pushed her cup and saucer away, put her head down on the table, and started crying.

Lu sprang up from her chair. "There, Susan, honey—it's nothing to cry about." She put a hand on Susan's head.

"It *is* something to cry about," Susan stammered through her sobs. "It *is*. He's a Negro man and I'm a mother of three children. Imagine how I feel."

Baron Wormser

Lu took her hand away. She stretched her neck down and around so as to look Susan in the face. "Cheer up. He's a man. There's nothing wrong with being attracted to a man. And so what if he's a Negro? He's not a Martian." She reached a hand out to chuck Susan under the chin. "I've been attracted to some Negro men, believe me."

"Oh, Lu, you've been attracted to every man on earth." Susan sniffled.

"Not your husband for one," Lu answered and drew her head back. "Guys who work with numbers give me the creeps."

"I'm happy I'm safe on that count."

"Being safe doesn't make a girl happy."

Susan reached into her pocketbook, which lay on the table, found a Kleenex, and blew her nose. "Jarvis Baker may be married himself."

"It's tough to know with men. Women walk around with diamonds and guys walk around with hair on their fingers."

"That's not what I need to hear, Lu." Susan dabbed at her eyes.

"I'm sorry." Lu sat back down in her chair but then drew it up beside Susan's. "Feel better for crying?"

Susan peered around the kitchen. Postcards from Ocean City, Virginia Beach, and Atlantic City were taped to the refrigerator door. On the counter beside the refrigerator stood a plastic replica of the Mr. Planter Peanut Man. He was yellow, wore a top hat, and carried a cane. For a large peanut, he was very dapper.

"Maybe you and I should take a trip next summer, Lu. What do you think?" Susan tried to smile but didn't succeed. She put her head down again.

"I think we need to talk this thing through, that's what I think." She nudged Susan on the shoulder. "How about a cigarette, if you aren't going to drink more coffee?"

"Oh, Lu, I feel so stupid. I've barely been around this man. And he's a Negro." Susan raised her head.

"I know he's a Negro, honey. This is 1962, not 1862. You don't have to keep telling me that."

"I have to keep telling myself that because it makes it even stranger. I never thought..." Susan paused. "When I

126

walked out of that classroom the other night, I barely knew where I was."

"If he were a white man would it make a difference?" Lu lit a cigarette for herself. "I forgot you don't like my brand. Maybe a puff?" She proffered the cigarette.

Susan made a face. "Would it make a difference? But a difference about what? What am I going to do beside tell my best friend and go back home and ask my girls whether they did their homework and check on my mom's milk of magnesia supply?"

"You could call him up."

"Call him up? That would be crazy. How could I call him up?"

"Well, you pick up the receiver and you dial the number and you wait for someone at the other end to pick up the receiver and speak into it. People do it all the time."

"Don't make fun, Lu. I told you I don't even know how I feel. What am I going to do? Call someone up and say, 'Hi. I want to talk to you but I don't know why. I'm attracted to you but confused. Oh, yes, and I'm a married woman with a family.'"

"People have done dumber things."

"Is that supposed to be a help to me?"

"Oh, Susan, you look like an abandoned puppy or something. Get a grip." Lu put her cigarette on an edge of an ashtray and with both hands fluffed her hair. "Let nature take her course." She put out a hand toward Susan. "I could use a manicure. When you do what I do for a living, people are always looking at your hands."

"Hands?" Susan groaned.

"Oops, I said the wrong word. That's where we began, isn't it?" She smiled, though more to herself than to Susan. "You never know what will grab a woman's attention."

"I want those hands to touch me."

The wheeze of the refrigerator compressor sounded loud in the silence that followed her words.

"Ah," Lu said. "Now you're saying something."

Susan sat up straight. "Have I? I haven't said half of what I feel. It's the hands but it's the person — who he is and how he talks and my sense there's something there I need to know. I see the problems. And it's true: when the topic of race comes up it can get tense. Why wouldn't it? But there's something at ease about him, something that agrees with this world. And I like that because it doesn't feel stupid or cheap. But . . ." Susan caught her breath. "God, these chairs are hard, Lu."

"Don't wriggle away, Susan. You're saying things you need to say."

"I'm not wriggling anywhere. I said it. Now it's behind me."

"Whoo-ee, girl!" Lu exclaimed. "Do you think saying something puts it behind you? You're the literature teacher. Even Lu knows that life's not that simple."

"It's going to have to be, isn't it? I've got three children a half-block up the street, a mother who lives with me, and a job. And a husband. And the color of my skin."

"Honey, a woman is only as good as she is true to her heart," Lu said.

For a time Susan said nothing. When she spoke, her voice was deliberate. "I agree. That's why I came to you. That's why I've said what I've said. And that's why I'm getting up and going home."

"Hold on, girl. Now I'm going to start crying," Lu said. "Men are the soldiers, not women. You do your duty every day. Give that heart some room. Do you hear me?"

"I do," Susan replied. She did hear. Whether she understood, she couldn't say.

"Good. Meanwhile you need to go in the bathroom and check yourself out. Those tears carved some gouges through your rouge. And your lipstick could use a freshening. The minute you walk in the door, your girls are going to read your face."

"Thanks, Lu." Susan extended a hand across the table.

"I don't know about thanks. I can't say that I expected this, though I thought your dike was going to break sometime. And I don't know how deep whatever you're feeling runs. Getting worked up over someone playing the piano, someone you've only laid eyes on twice in your life — that sounds like a crush to me. I had a crush on Eddy Duchin and then on Tyrone

Power when he played him in the movie. Handsome guys." Lu smiled fondly. "But if you want someone to touch you—that's something else." She looked down at her cigarette, which had gone out. "What I do know is that someone who should be touching you probably isn't."

Susan stood up. "Thanks for the talk. Really, Lu, I do hear you. I feel better. Maybe not clearer, but better." She looked again around the kitchen. "You're keen on Mr. Peanut, aren't you?"

"He's the best sort of man—looks sharp and doesn't talk back."

Arthur

Edward Trumbull got on the bus at Garrison. He saw Arthur right away and walked up the aisle to sit beside him.

"What brings you to the indignity of public transit on a Saturday morning?" he asked. "Don't you have wheels, Merm? Especially in this rain?" Edward took off his hat, a soft crumpled affair, and shook drops onto the floor.

"I'm headed to the library, but my mom took my sisters and my grandma shopping. That's what they do some Saturdays after my sisters' dance class, and that's where the Ford is. My dad's at some meeting." Like lightning—here and gone—a vision of Marilee Dorsky sitting on his father's lap flashed across Arthur's mind. She had no skirt on. He pointed to the book in Edward's lap. "What are you reading?"

Edward read the title aloud: *Booker T. Washington and the Negro's Place in American Life*.

"You doing a history report for Tobey?" Arthur asked.

"I'm reading about my history, Merm. No one has to assign me to read about my history."

"I read *Up from Slavery* a couple years ago. I liked it. He was a brave man."

Edward situated his hat beside the library book so as to not to get it wet. "W. E. B. Du Bois, whom I've told you about, thought Washington sold out black people."

"Did Du Bois walk from West Virginia to Hampton Institute to get an education the way Booker T. Washington did?" Arthur asked. He turned from Edward to look out at the blocks of modest storefronts and rowhouses. Sometimes he felt that Baltimore had existed forever, like the Pyramids or the Colosseum. There was too much weight, too many bricks, too many windows facing too many streets. It depressed him. It felt like drowning in something solid. He turned back to Edward. "I don't know. Walking like that—it's impressive."

Edward smacked his lips in approbation. "I give you credit, Merm. You don't just read a book. You think about it. For his day and place, I'd grant that Booker Washington was a brave man. Anyone who dealt with white people in that world—Jim Crow—and tried to get something for black folks had to be brave. Or smart like a fox. You know he told people they should 'Live down prejudice.'" Edward picked up his hat, stuck both hands inside it and began to slowly twirl it. "I guess we're still living down."

"I don't know if I could walk in your shoes," Arthur said.

"Unless you plan to write something like *Black Like Me*, I guess you're safe." Edward made a dismissive sound that was somewhere between a snort and a guffaw.

"Crazy isn't it?" said Arthur. "How a white man has to pretend to be a black man to tell white people what it's like for black people."

"Wouldn't a lot of white folks feel better today if Martin Luther King Jr. ripped off his face and showed the world a white one? Wouldn't they like to see that? Wouldn't they like to hear him say, 'I was just foolin' around, just actin' the minstrel? I never meant any harm.'" Edward stopped twirling his hat. "Damn." He took off his glasses and wiped them with an inside cuff of his raincoat. When he set them back on his face, he scowled at the rain. "I got to walk some blocks to the *Afro* office. Wish it would stop precipitating."

"What are you, a cub reporter?" asked Arthur. "Like Jimmy Olsen?"

"You see many Negroes running around in *Superman*?"

"You got me there, Edward." The bus lurched to a stop at a red light. "Guess our driver was dreaming more than looking at the traffic lights." Arthur said. "You ever get weary of how white people assume everyone else is white?"

"Weary? Man, you just asked the sixty-four-thousand-dollar question. Weary?" Edward's face lit up. "Weary?" He chuckled to himself.

"I take it you get weary," said Arthur.

Edward was in downright stitches. "Weary?" He took his glasses off again to wipe away a laughter tear. "Go back this afternoon to some of those streets you visited this summer and ask folks if they are weary of white people."

Arthur thought of how Mr. Schwartz prodded him to get out and question people. "Probably that's not necessary," he answered.

"Probably, it isn't. The nutty thing is that white people think they know something. Some senator is always standing up and talking about how he knows the Negro. Has he sat down in a barbershop? Has he shared a meal? Has he gone to church?" Edward looked out the window. "We're near Eutaw. We'll resume our discussion some other time. You have yourself a good day, Merm." He rose, put on his hat and made his way toward the front of the bus.

As the bus pulled away from the stop, Arthur watched Edward hunch his shoulders and start walking. He was no Jimmy Olsen.

A few blocks farther, Arthur got off at his stop; the rain had become a clinging drizzle. He walked past an assemblage of small businesses on side streets—a jeweler, a used-book dealer, a vacuum cleaner repair shop, a beauty salon. At a corner he looked at a newsstand that featured the local papers. "MISSILE SHOWDOWN NEAR," the *News-Post* warned. Thousands of miles separated them, but Kennedy and Khrushchev seemed in their newspaper photos to be gesticulating at one another. Arthur thought of Westerns like *High Noon*. These guys weren't packing six-shooters, though. What had Jack said? *Shit.*

By the time he opened one of the big doors to the main branch of the Enoch Pratt Free Library on Cathedral Street, he felt cold and dank. He headed through another set of doors and then stood still. The huge chandelier-like lights that blazed overhead, the legions of wooden card catalogs, the warm, dry scent of tens of thousands of dozing pages, the vast open lobby, all this performed a kind of resuscitation on him. In Northwest Baltimore he had a home and a bedroom in that home, but this was his mind's home. He loved this building. He breathed in a lungful of air as if he were at the ocean.

"Arthur! Over here!" Amid the library's whispery hush

Rebecca's voice was unmistakable. She had on cherry-red lipstick and a red V-neck sweater to match. The sweater looked old and was too big for her. She had rolled the cuffs up to compensate.

Arthur headed toward the reference desk. A delighted smile was overcoming him. The words tumbled out: "Rebecca, it's so good to see you—really good. I wanted to call you but I couldn't find your number in the book and then. . . ."

"Oh, we have an unlisted number. It's my father's idea. I don't know who's going to bother us, but that's the way he is. Europe made him nervous forever." She moved forward a step or two, right up to Arthur. "Do you like this ribbon in my hair, Arthur? I hope so."

The ribbon was red too. "I do like it—very much." Arthur felt as though he had just come out of a cavern into stunning sunlight.

"Oh, I'm glad of that." Rebecca turned toward the reference desk and the librarian behind it, an older woman with glasses and a gray braid coiled on the top of her head. "Miss Eldred, this is my friend, Arthur Mermelstein. He goes to City and reads a lot. I'm not surprised to see him here today."

Rebecca turned around again. "Do you know about the Boer War, Arthur? I'm writing a report for Mr. Levine, the history teacher who's two doors down from your mother's room. Do you know that the Germans weren't the ones who invented concentration camps? Do you know that the British interned thousands of Boers—those were Dutch people, Arthur, in South Africa—in camps—but not camps like summer camps—and many of them were women and children, and that many of them died? Thousands of them died from things like typhoid and measles. Imagine dying from measles." Rebecca shivered. "Did you know that?" She halted as if coming up for air. The librarian looked as though she wanted to say something but seemed to bite her tongue, which made her head twitch.

Arthur exhaled—part Rebecca-feeling, part misery-of-the-human-race feeling. "Did they call them 'concentration camps'?" he asked.

The librarian gave Arthur a brief but imperious stare. "They did but concentration camps back then didn't mean what they have come to mean in our world," she sniffed, as though it were an etiquette issue.

"It doesn't matter what they were called," Rebecca said. "It matters what they did to people. And the British weren't as good as they made themselves out to be."

Her perfume—lavender and something more muted that he couldn't name—made Arthur agreeably dizzy. "No, they weren't," he said. "They were far from gentlemen." The imperial British engagements of the nineteenth century such as the Zulu War were a military history topic he had mulled over with Herbie Freilich. Herbie and he both found themselves rooting for the natives.

"Do you come here on many Saturdays?" Arthur asked. "I come here when I can. I like it here."

"It's the Sabbath but I'm a girl in high school so I come here sometimes because I have schoolwork to do." Rebecca looked around the lobby. "It's so serious here. I like that." She gave a small sigh of satisfaction. Then she seemed to startle. "You don't go to synagogue, do you?"

"Not on Saturdays, just the High Holidays and once in a while on Friday night."

"You must be Reformed. My father thinks Reformed Jews are barely Jews. He says bad things in Yiddish about them."

"And what do you think?" Though Arthur wasn't more than a foot or two away from Rebecca, he leaned in more closely.

"I don't care. I could marry a Gentile. That's how much I don't care." She looked around as if checking to see whether anyone else heard her. "I don't tell my father, of course. Why bother him?"

Since the topic had moved beyond the Boer War, the librarian made a small shooing gesture. While thanking her for her help, Rebecca grabbed Arthur by the elbow and began to steer him toward the card catalogs. She was about the same height as he was. At first that had bothered him. Now it didn't.

After a few steps she stopped. "Do you have any money, Arthur? I'd like to have lunch. I'm not asking you to pay for me. I'm just checking to see that I don't have to pay for you, because I don't have much money." She looked down at her saddles. Her left shoe had a deep nick in it near the toe. "We're poor. Until I've written all over it, I never even throw out a piece of paper."

"I'm a worker and I get paid," Arthur announced. "What if we go to the Market?"

"Is there a kosher place there? We keep kosher." Rebecca looked gravely at Arthur as if he might not know what *kosher* meant.

"One of the delis there must be kosher. If there isn't, we'll find another place. Let's go." Arthur thought about her willingness to marry a Gentile but said nothing.

"I'll fetch my raincoat," said Rebecca, letting go of Arthur's elbow. "Meet me out on the street. I have to go to the ladies' room, too." She winked at Arthur and sashayed off. He watched her bottom move within her long wool skirt until she disappeared behind a row of card catalogs. A line from one of the hundreds of rock 'n' roll songs he knew lit up his brain: "I likes the way you walk."

While he waited for her, he gazed for the thousandth time at a more monumental sight—the cathedral across the street, a huge neoclassical pile of stone. Arthur thought that the pillars in the front of the building made it look more like a hall for legislators than a church for worshippers. It was a Catholic building, though, which meant in this case that it really wasn't called a "church." It was a *basilica*—a word he always meant to look up but never did.

"There are *shuls* with columns like that in Europe, but they got destroyed." Rebecca had come up beside him. She had on a raincoat that looked like something a detective would wear in an old movie— belts and buckles all over. "They weren't that big, though. The Gentiles like things big." She paused. "Have you ever been in a church, Arthur?"

"No." Arthur stopped. "Well, yes, once I went to the church that our maid Seeley belongs to, near Druid Hill. But it looks different from this thing." He pointed at the cathedral. "It looks more like a wooden house—not so big. It was pretty crowded. But it felt good in there."

"You went to a church with your maid? Your family has a maid? And you went to church?" It seemed too much for Rebecca to take in. Her eyes got large.

Arthur hoped she would collapse on him.

"You're a remarkable boy, Arthur. How many Jews have ever been in a church? We spend our lives walking around and seeing these buildings" — she motioned at the imposing mass on the other side of the street — "and we never go in." She looked down at the sidewalk. "That's what it is to be Jewish — to never go in certain places, to always be looking and watching but never to go in." Her voice trembled.

"I don't know if it's any consolation, but my parents have gone to weddings in Christian churches, all kinds of them. Last summer they went to a Greek Orthodox Church."

"I guess it must be me. I'm cloistered with my rabbi father." Rebecca pulled the collar of her raincoat closer to her neck. "I know I should think the church is beautiful, and I do, though it's cold-looking, isn't it? But what I really feel is that it makes me afraid. No matter how many times I see it, it makes me afraid. It makes me think of what they've done in the name of their god. It isn't fair, but to me they're nothing more than murderers. Look at the British. *They* went to church." She bowed her head. The ribbon that ran across the top of her head had slipped some.

Arthur raised a hand and moved the ribbon slightly. "It was coming off."

"Do you think I'm too sensitive, Arthur? And don't move your hand. I like it."

"I don't think you're too sensitive." He looked at her brown eyes and pallid face lit up by the red lipstick. She seemed like a beautiful clown to him. "And I can keep my hand here all day if you want."

"That's not required." She gently moved it to his side. "Do you like this coat? It was my mother's — from Europe." She started walking. "It's good it's stopped raining. Would you hold my library books for me? That way I can put my hand in your hand."

Susan

Falling asleep hadn't gotten any easier, which meant taking an extra Miltown, which meant feeling groggy, which meant drinking more coffee, which meant going to the bathroom more, feeling irritable, and wishing she could take a month off and sit on a beach in the south of France. Instead she had to fend off her mother, who noted that Susan didn't look good, which was partly solicitous and partly critical, by telling her that she was busy with school (which she was) rather than confessing that she was sick of living in the house she was living in, that she felt her marriage had become more of a mechanical contrivance than a marriage, and that—oh, yes—she kept thinking of a Negro music teacher and feeling palpitations throughout her body that indicated a species of longing she thought had fallen off an internal cliff long ago. When she looked in the mirror that morning, she felt an inclination to start yelling at her bleary face. Then she wanted to weep like one of those petulant fools in the soap operas that Ruby and Seeley watched.

Joe Costa, however, didn't get on her nerves. When he sat down beside her in the teachers' lounge, she looked up from the stack of grammar quizzes she was correcting during her free period and smiled genuinely.

"How's Julia?" Susan asked. "I want to go to the Museum of Art with her. How are you?"

"Julia's moving in with me. We're going to live in sin." He beamed like a boy who had been given an extra portion of ice cream. "Sounds good, doesn't it? It even rhymes. So I'm feeling great. And you?" He leaned back in a battered armchair that signified this was a room for teachers, not for corporate executives. Not that Joe cared about furniture.

"I'm a little tired. I haven't been getting much sleep."

Susan considered Joe's unwrinkled, amiable face. He would never understand. "Nothing that Thanksgiving vacation won't solve."

"That's a ways off, Susan. In case you've forgotten, today is October 22."

"I guess it is." She looked at the Baltimore School Department calendar on the wall. It was hard to imagine getting through this day, much less to Thanksgiving.

Sid Colvin came through the door. It was mid-morning but he already had chalk dust on his jacket. He looked both haggard and elated.

"The president is going to address the nation tonight," he announced.

"Too bad I've got my bowling league," Joe replied.

Susan started laughing. The thought of Joe bowling was ridiculous. He'd be home listening to jazz and making love to Julia.

"You two are strange characters," Sid said. "Here we are at the brink of nuclear war and you two are making fun."

"Sid, if the president and Mr. Khrushchev want to call me up and ask me if they should calm down, I'm glad to talk with them." Joe smiled a jovial smile. "But I don't think that's happening. I'm a little man, not a big man. So I might as well enjoy it. Sound fair?"

"It's not about fair. It's about being interested in the world we live in and teaching our students to be active citizens." Sid brushed some dust off a sleeve to make his point.

"Active citizens?" Joe's voice was climbing. "Who the hell is consulting them about these weapons? Do you think they've liked cowering under desks, as if that's going to save them from oblivion? Active citizens? Ants are more active citizens—and they don't deceive themselves about having more control over their lives than they have."

"Now gentleman, why don't we wait and hear what the president has to say and leave it at that," Susan said. She was pondering a student's paper that claimed *children* was a singular noun.

"Drop the diplomacy, Susan," Joe said. "You just like Jack Kennedy's good looks. And you think that Bahston accent is cute. Pahk the cah."

Before Sid or Susan could speak, the door opened and Cathy Ramsdell walked in. She taught English and coached drama.

Cathy smiled benignly at everyone. "Good news! I've got all my actors for the December play. It's going to be a great cast." She kept her smile in place as if it were a billboard of some sort. She had small perfect teeth.

"Who is Andrew going to play?" Susan asked.

"He's going to work backstage. This isn't a good play for him," Cathy answered. Always onstage, her voice was breathy and earnest. The long scarf she habitually wore had worked its way forward a bit. She flung it back over her shoulder.

Susan set her grammar quizzes down on the coffee-stained table beside her. "Andrew is one of the best actors in this school. He spent a lot of time preparing to be either of the sons. He came in a couple of times after school and talked to me about Arthur Miller and what *Death of a Salesman* meant to him."

"All well and good, Susan," Cathy said, "but it's a naturalist play. Do you expect me to have one of Willy's sons be a Negro and the other not? Calling attention to race would be a distraction. The play is beyond race." She nodded at Susan to indicate she had spoken definitively and walked over to the coffee pot. The silk scarf trailing down her back seemed to nod in agreement.

"Are you telling me that people are going to sit there and get distracted about race because one son is a Negro and the other isn't? Because if that is what you are saying, then you are full of shit." Susan paused. "And you have hurt a sensitive young man who doesn't deserve to be hurt, least ways about the color of his skin."

Both men in the room looked on with mild wonder. This was between women.

"You have no business meddling in my affairs. Do you understand that, Susan? You have no business, much less swearing." Cathy drew out the last words so that they seemed to take long seconds. "I'm the one who makes the judgments about what will work and what won't work. This has nothing to do with color. For the record, as a white woman I have been a

Baron Wormser

proud member of the NAACP."

"Nothing to do with color!" Susan shouted. "You just told us he didn't get the part because he was a Negro. Am I hearing doublespeak?"

"Don't yell at me, Susan. I came in here in a good mood and I intend to leave here in a good mood." Cathy turned her back and busied herself with making a cup of coffee.

"Hold on," said Joe. "Compared to this, the end of the world is child's play. Maybe we could ask the president if he could help out with the high school drama program, too."

"Don't be a jerk, Joe," Cathy said. "I can take care of myself."

"How did Andrew feel about this, Cathy?" Susan asked.

"He said that he wanted to be a professional and he knew that as a professional you don't get every role you want. I think that's admirable."

"Yes," Sid agreed. "That's admirable. We're trying to teach our students good values. That's admirable."

Susan gathered her papers and stood up. "Look, Cathy, I don't think Andrew would tell you the truth, because you have power over him. And I don't think any of this is 'admirable.' I think it's pathetic. I think we cause more harm here than good." She walked over to the door that led in and out of the room. "Tell Julia I'll be in touch, Joe. Good day to all of you."

"Really, Susan, who do you think you are?" Cathy asked but Susan had already headed into the quiet hallway. Fifteen minutes remained in the period.

Arthur

The gravest crisis on the night of the president's speech was the prospect of Ruby missing *To Tell the Truth* on CBS. And though the political situation was unprecedented, Arthur's family ran its usual gamut of responses. His sisters said it was "boring," which they said about everything that didn't concern boys or what they could wear, eat, listen to, or put on their bedroom wall. His father said at the outset, "This is big stuff" and, though it was seven o'clock, fell asleep. His mother murmured while she graded papers that it was too bad all that money that went to missiles didn't go to schoolrooms. She seemed more sad than alarmed. As for Ruby, she wagged a finger at the screen and warned Kennedy about the "Bolsheviks," who were *farbrechers, ganovim,* and other Yiddish words that indicated major trouble. Stan woke up during one of Ruby's tirades but fell back asleep. He'd been working hard but he was always working hard. Arthur made some jokes about Cuban cigars but they fell flat. Probably they should have.

Some of the president's phrases stayed with Arthur: "even the fruits of victory would be ashes in our mouth" and "move the world back from the abyss of destruction." There was going to be a "quarantine" of ships, which confused Arthur because that seemed like a medical word. And if the ships didn't want to be quarantined, if the ships went full steam ahead — the world would have to wait and see. It felt like a lot to deal with for everyone, whether you were the leader of the Free World or some high school kid with an extra ten bucks driving to the record store. An abyss was a frightening place. He looked out the window and saw a little Negro boy going down the sidewalk on a scooter. His shirttails were flapping; his mouth was wide open. He didn't seem to have a care in the world, but as Mr.

Schwartz liked to tell him when Arthur offered an opinion about some street scene, "Pictures deceive.. Don't trust what you see." What were you supposed to trust? What about the photos that led the United States to see those missiles in Cuba and led the president to speak of "unmistakable evidence?"

As he entered The Record Collector, he felt that maybe smell was the sense to be trusted most—Rebecca's perfume or Seeley's fried chicken or what hit him every time he walked into that store—the thin, peaceful scent of cardboard, all those thousands of record jackets sitting there holding their discs, waiting. Larry Fein, who owned the store with his brother Phil, dressed as always in a white shirt and thin black tie, gave Arthur the once-over, and went back to reading the newspaper. Arthur looked around the cavernous, brick-walled space. The store wasn't for casual buyers, people like his mother who every now and then bought an LP in one of the department stores like Hutzler's or Hecht's by someone like Ferrante and Teicher playing *Postcards from Paris* or, even worse, that drippy string stuff of Mantovani's. He couldn't believe her taste in music, though one morning when he was almost out the door she asked him if he knew anything about Miles Davis. She said it was something she wanted to listen to. He did a double take because he was interested in Miles Davis himself—who just last month had been interviewed in *Playboy*. He told her that *Kind of Blue* was on the list of records he wanted to buy.

The store was for people with "taste," as Larry liked to tell anyone who would listen. To Arthur that meant music by Negroes and gypsies, and ballads like the ones he heard in the folk music club. There were lots of other kinds of records in the store, but Arthur was trying to learn exactly who made that music—who Coleman Hawkins was and Lester Young and Cisco Houston and Bessie Smith and Woody Guthrie and Django Reinhardt. It was a big job, especially when you had limited funds. The Negro radio stations kept him fortified with the current music but he wanted to learn about the past, especially when the past wasn't all that long ago.

"Too bad these world leaders don't spend more time listening to music—some Ella, some Stravinsky, a little Gerry Mulligan," Larry Fein said. "The world would be a more peaceful place, eh, Jarvis?"

Arthur looked to the far corner of the store. There was Mr. Baker, his music teacher last year at City. He had on one of those tattersall shirts he wore in school and his reading glasses. "Hi, Mr. Baker," Arthur said, and waited.

"It would be a more peaceful world indeed, Larry, and hello to you, Arthur. What brings you here?"

"I like music," Arthur stammered. Even though his own mother was a teacher and even though Mr. Baker was a good-natured, live-and-let-live kind of teacher, it felt unsettling to talk with a teacher outside of school.

"I remember as much from teaching you, Arthur," Mr. Baker replied. "I myself am here today in pursuit of a recording of *Music for the Royal Fireworks* by George Frideric Handel." He waved a hand over the bin in front of him, which was crammed with classical music records.

"He's one of those three-name guys you told us about," said Arthur.

"Three-name guys! You slay me, Arthur!" Larry Fein cackled.

"I suppose you could call him that, Arthur," Mr. Baker said, "but Blind Lemon Jefferson was a three-name guy, too."

Arthur moved closer to where his teacher was standing so he wouldn't have to shout. "I never thought of it that way. I know Blind Lemon Jefferson was a famous bluesman." Arthur halted—where was he headed? "It wasn't something you taught us in school but I've been trying to teach myself about stuff you don't hear on the radio."

"America tends to go for the Top 40. That's a fact," Mr. Baker said.

One thing Arthur liked about Mr. Baker was how mellow his voice was. He always seemed to wake up on the right side of the bed. And it seemed for-real, not phony.

"Well," Larry said, "you guys can talk about music, but we all may be breathing ashes pretty soon. Adlai Stevenson has been talking to the United Nations to let the world know what we're doing."

"Or not breathing at all," Arthur added.

Mr. Baker set his hands against the mass of records in

front of him as if to brace himself. "It seems to me that Negroes have paid enough dues in this world without getting blown up because of white politicians. I don't see John F. Kennedy marching himself down South. And I have to say I wouldn't mind if a missile were aimed at those crackers in Albany, Georgia, who don't want Negroes drinking out of their precious water fountains." He paused. "I guess that's not what you should be hearing a teacher say, Arthur—but you're no child."

"No, I'm not," Arthur answered. Some of last night's pit-of-the-stomach dread came back to him.

Then, from behind Larry's counter at the front of the store, someone began singing. "Well I wish . . . I was a catfish . . . swimmin' in the deep blue sea." There was guitar and a piano. Then the voice was singing something about fishing. Then the guitar was picking notes that sounded as though they were being played on an acoustic guitar—they were so clear—but this was an electric guitar. The music rang with clean, raw power—pure and sexy at the same time.

Mr. Baker broke into a smile. "You got to love black folks. The women go fishing and find a man." He whistled in appreciation. "Thank you, Larry, for dispelling my choler. And thank you, Muddy Waters, for existing."

"Muddy Waters? That's his name?" Arthur asked.

Larry laughed his semi-hysterical laugh. "You slay me, Arthur. You do all this rooting through the blues records and you don't know who Muddy Waters is?"

"Now, Larry, don't be hard on the young man," Mr. Baker said. "There's a lot of Negroes making music out there."

Arthur barely heard the adults. The music made his insides vibrate. It was almost stately, certainly in no hurry, which was one of Rick Scanlon's lessons about being with a girl—"don't be in a hurry." A piano started trilling, then that guitar came in, picking out notes that were sure and deep. The singer's voice almost drawled.

"Jesus," Arthur muttered when the tune's three minutes had gone by.

"You know a Jew is moved, Jarvis, when they invoke the name of the savior who is not their savior," Larry said, as he moved toward the turntable he had connected to two speakers.

"Want to hear it again?"

"What is that song called? I want to hear it forever," Arthur replied. The next song had started. It was about something called a "mojo."

"'Forever' could be a short time, given the current situation," Mr. Baker said. He pulled a Handel album out of the bin in front of him and began studying the liner notes.

"It's called 'Rollin' Stone,' Arthur. You want to buy the album?" Larry held up the record jacket. It featured a photo of a Negro man with heavy eyelids, whom Arthur took to be Mr. Waters.

"Only if you promise not to tell me again that I slay you," Arthur answered.

"Sounds fair to me," Mr. Baker said. "Eh, Larry?"

"The kid drives a hard bargain. We could use him dealing with the Russkies."

"And I want to pick up *Kind of Blue*. It's for my mom but I'm going to listen to it, too."

"Your mom wants to listen to Miles, Arthur?" Mr. Baker asked.

"To tell the truth, it's not her usual taste, Mr. Baker. She's more the 'Theme from Some Movie' type, but she asked me."

"Good for her, Arthur," Mr. Baker said. "Let's hope we all can keep listening."

Susan

Out of breath after her run from the parking lot, Susan gave Julia a hug, then stood panting in the museum lobby's discreet gloom. Her words came out in a rush. "I know I'm late but I had to talk with a student who wants to be an actor and didn't get a part in a play that he wanted and is upset and then I couldn't find a parking space—which is strange because who would be here on a Thursday afternoon?—but what I really should be doing is getting my hair cut. I'm giving up the flip for something shorter and more French-looking. You know—the French gamin look, like Leslie Caron. My friend Lu says she won't talk to me until I get my hair cut." Susan caught her breath and smiled at Julia. "But look at you with that long beautiful hair. Probably you haven't seen the inside of a beauty parlor since Kennedy was elected."

Julia laughed, reached back, and gave her braid a playful toss. "You're right about the beauty parlor. When you let it grow, it simplifies matters. That's what Cézanne said: 'Those in the know stay simple.'"

"Cézanne! I wonder how often he got his hair cut." Susan pulled a shoe off and turned it upside down. A tiny pebble fell out. "I read about painters but I never seem to meet anyone that I could talk to, so when I met you I thought 'I have to go to the museum with her.' And here I am—on an afternoon when I should be getting my hair cut. I feel like I'm playing hooky."

"I must sound pretentious. Joe says I can't fry an egg without talking art." Julia took a small step toward Susan and looked into her eyes. "You look a little tired. Do you want to sit down before we start walking?" She motioned at a bench nearby.

"I thought I put on enough makeup this morning to cover the under-the-eye rings. But it's not morning is it? Probably I look like a prize fighter in round ten." She stared off for a few seconds. "I feel like one." She stuck her arms out as if to steady herself.

"I've got something to report." Julia hesitated. "I've moved in with Joe."

"Ah, he told me — some good news in the world." Susan grabbed one of Julia's hands, squeezed it, and quickly let go. "I'm happy for you. I can feel how much he loves you. It's something women can feel, and I felt it. It's not the way for women that it is for men. Men are like fish under the sea. They move in darkness." Her voice had wobbled from joyful to somber in seconds. "It's hard to know what they feel. The feelings are there — they have to be — but they don't know. I think Joe, though, has a clue. My husband . . ." She plopped down on a perfectly polished bench and beckoned Julia to sit beside her. "But that's not what I want to tell you now. I want to tell you how when I was a girl growing up in Cleveland, I used to go to the museum on Saturdays. I'd walk around and gawk and sit on one of those benches without backs — like this one — that they put in museums so people won't get too comfortable, and I'd try to feel as though I belonged in such a place. I'd even pretend that I lived there. It was my fairy-tale home. And that was a big deal because I didn't feel I belonged anywhere." Susan opened her pocketbook and started rummaging through it. "How foolish I was. Imagine living in one of these places where the ceiling is so high you can barely see it. And all this cold stone these museums are built out of, like something from Egypt or Greece — it gives me the shivers." She pulled out her compact, flipped it open, and regarded herself. "God, I look like hell." She clicked it shut. "But I'm glad I'm here now with you — a real painter."

"I don't know how real I am. It's hard work. I have my doubts."

"But you're doing it." Susan opened the compact again, applied powder to her face, then pulled out a plum shade of lipstick from her pocketbook.

Julia watched her. "I like that color. Maybe I should start wearing lipstick again."

"I'd feel naked without lipstick," Susan said. "One of the things a woman can't do without—for me, at least."

Julia leaned her head closer to Susan's. "I was wondering. Have you ever painted, Susan? Or maybe, since you're an English teacher, written anything?"

"Finger paints when I was a very little girl. And in high school I wrote a poem or two. One was printed in the yearbook. I've written some lines on the backs of envelopes." She spoke to the air in front of her but suddenly turned sideways. "What sparkling eyes you have."

"But you must be creative, Susan. I can tell that about you."

"I'm not sure what good my creating would do. The world has plenty of paintings and books. And there are people like you who are willing to make a commitment. Let's face it. I barely have time to catch my breath. Sometimes I think my best moments are when I'm fast asleep." She had started to have dreams about a Toulouse-Lautrec-like brothel. The woman in her dreams wasn't herself—she had red hair and was tall—but her name was Susan.

"Ah, catching your breath—my mom had six children," Julia said. "You know the Irish. What's life without a pack of bawling brats? It must be why I like painting so much—the silence." She paused. "My mom was always telling everyone to simmer down and make peace. Too bad you don't see her in any of the pictures of Kennedy and Khrushchev. She tried hard to get us to coexist." Julia laughed softly. "I have to tell you a secret. I'm selfish. I don't want to have children."

Susan made a sort of hiccup sound—a stifled gasp. "Does Joe know?"

"We haven't talked about it. He hasn't gotten beyond wanting to lay his hands on me and do it. He's a little sex crazy." She smiled. "I don't think he wants me pregnant. That would interfere."

"Things happen, though."

"I'm taking the pill. I got a prescription through a doctor that one of my girlfriends at the Institute knows." She looked shyly at Susan. "What do you do?"

"Condoms. Not that we have much sex anymore." Susan

grazed a hand over the smooth bench. "He's tired or I'm tired or we're both tired or we aren't tired but say we're tired. Or we don't say anything. It isn't even there. But I didn't need to tell you that, did I? I'm sorry."

"Telling the truth is nothing to be sorry about. Friends tell each other the truth."

A guard walked over to them and pointed to his wristwatch. "We'll be closing, ladies, in a half hour." He nodded to affirm his official capacity, then padded off on soundless soles.

"He's tired of hearing us blab. An Irish and a Jew, we could talk all day," Julia said.

They rose up together, hoisted their pocketbooks, and headed toward the museum's inner entrance. Susan stopped, however, before they got to the door.

"Julia, I have to ask you a little more about not having children. Do you mind? If you do, you can tell me."

Two tweed-suited matrons paraded by. Julia raised her eyebrows to their backs, then winked at Susan. "High-society bitches," she whispered.

Susan suppressed a giggle. "It's hard for me to imagine. My children matter so much to me."

"And if you never had them?" Julia asked.

Susan shuddered, a quick rise and fall of her shoulders. "My life would be empty. Maybe that sounds stupid but that's what I feel." She looked down at the marble-like floor. Maybe it really was marble.

"No, not stupid. But I want to do something on my own. It's not that I don't want to be with someone. I love Joe. But I want to do something only I can do, as an artist." Julia took Susan by an elbow. "Let's keep walking."

"Being an artist seems so murky." Susan put a hand to her lips. "I'm sorry. That's not a very good word."

"But that's it. It *is* murky. That's why I have to trust myself." Julia let go of Susan's arm and faced her directly. "Look at me. I'm twenty-four. It took me time to find my way to art school."

"Because?"

"Because I didn't trust myself. Because I'm a woman and

everyone in my family — bless them all — looked cross-eyed at me when I said I wanted to be a painter. 'How are you going to make a living?' 'I'll wait tables.' 'Then you don't need to go to school to wait tables, do you?' Then my aunt or uncle or cousin or, yes, my Mam or Dad would give me a smug smile." She paused. "I can't stand that smile. It can destroy every hope and wish."

They were ambling through a series of galleries, looking as they walked, sometimes stopping and looking longer.

"But what about you?" Julia asked. There was an edge of exasperation in her voice. "What about these paintings? What about the books about painters that you read? What about going to the museum when you were a girl?"

"That's not trust," Susan said. "That's on-looking. That's curiosity. That's my fairy tale."

With those words they entered the museum's prize collection — many Matisses, Picassos, and the Cézanne titled *Mont Sainte-Victoire Seen from Bibémus*, which they especially wanted to see. For a while — time suspended in the museum's cushioned quiet — they stood entranced by the Cézanne.

"I had a professor," Julia said, "who said Cézanne was brutal — the hardness, the determination. But there's peace, too. A painter can create a separate stillness." Julia turned from the painting. "All the talk about modern art, the isms, just distracts. Peace is something else. Art — real art like this — can teach us that peace. And I'm not ashamed to say that."

Some part of Susan that wasn't considering what task she had to do next and what she had to do after that believed Julia. Some part of her took in not only the earnest young woman Julia was and the glory of the canvas in front of her — of mountain, quarry, and pine trees mutely existing in the miracle of light — but took in, too, the gathering late afternoon and her children and her mother and her husband seated at his desk in his office, and there at the furthest edge of the moment, the vast cold ocean and the ships with their cargoes of missiles bound for Cuba — took in the whole of it, the taut, implacable being of it. Then it all dissolved into a silent moan.

"We've still got some minutes," Julia said. "Let's look at a few others."

On the room's far wall hung a large watercolor of a group of circus performers by Picasso. An old woman washed dishes in the foreground. Another woman held up an infant. A harlequin observed a boy in tights who was balancing on a ball. The whole of the painting was suffused with an impossibly tender, rose-sepia color.

"Look," said Susan, pointing. "It's my family."

Arthur

Arthur had read John Hersey's *Hiroshima* and knew that what the bombs did to people was barely comprehensible, that many survivors envied the dead. But this wasn't the Second World War. There was no war going on except for the cold one. What he read about in the newspaper — charges and countercharges — weren't in the nightmares he'd had since he was a little kid of the sky turning orange and exploding so that there was no more sky and him disappearing into that blackness, his body a feather in an infinite wind. What he read about now was too daily to find frightening. It was only words. But it was more than words. It was like a playground game of chicken, except it was being played with missiles. And although he had never seen a missile face to face or walked around where one was installed or been in a factory where they were assembled, the missiles were real. Though their function was to turn people into ghosts, the missiles weren't ghosts at all. They were sitting in underground silos in the Upper Midwest. Day and night, soldiers were on duty there waiting for a phone call. And missiles had been sitting in Cuba, where other soldiers were on duty waiting for a phone call. Maybe the notion of the phone call was what was most frightening — some human being who had given up on human beings.

He was standing outside the burlesque house. It could work out — Rick Scanlon said it would be "easy street" — or it could not. He felt self-conscious but needed to say something. "Well," he began, "Khrushchev is dismantling the missiles. I guess JFK knew what he was doing." Arthur blew out a stream of air and stamped a foot on the ground as if it were January. He even rubbed his hands together. "That blockade did it."

"Merm, we're waiting to get into a striptease joint and

you're talking about missiles. Give it up. Tobey's not going to quiz us." John Silverman spat authoritatively and peered into the dim light of the alleyway off East Baltimore Street. The reflection of a neon sign pulsed above his head — "GIRLS!"

Rick Scanlon rubbed his hands together, too. "Tobey, he's hell on wheels, isn't he? Dates and facts, dates and facts — you start seeing double in there. To me, though" — his voice became deeper and less eager — "it's hard to take this missile crap serious. Who they kidding? All the good-looking women in this world — why blow it up? These politicians can get their hands on any piece of ass they want — our guys and I bet their guys, too. Their women may be Reds, but they're women." He sighed. "Man, I'm worked up and I haven't seen anything yet."

Silverman smirked. "Hope you shot off your rocket before you came here."

"You mean my missile, Silverman, and when I shoot it off, it's got a target."

Silverman turned to Arthur and motioned toward Rick with his right hand, as if he were pointing at something in an exhibit hall. "Listen to him. He fools around a few times with an Eastern High girl and he's Casanova."

Arthur thought of Rebecca. He couldn't imagine telling her about what he was doing, but there was no reason to tell her. You didn't have to tell everybody everything. Unless you had a father like Silverman's who let John use his projector to show stag movies.

As if he had read Arthur's mind, Rick started in on the movies. "You think this'll be like the stuff your dad has?"

"What are you talking about?" Silverman sounded aggrieved. "That's on a movie. There are real women on the other side of that wall." He flicked a hand at the grimy brick façade from which a few tatters of burlesque posters dangled.

"You're pretty philosophical, Silverman," Arthur said, "distinguishing between what's real and — "

"Hey, fuck you, Merm."

Before Arthur could swear back, the side door of the burlesque hall creaked halfway open on decrepit hinges. A voice rasped, "You Ernie-from-the-pool-hall's kids?"

"Yes," replied Arthur, who had been picked as the group

spokesman. The word felt formal but he was jazzed. He could have started barking. Silverman was right — this wasn't school.

The door opened more, revealing a short man with wide shoulders and a big head. He had on a pale pink shirt and a bow tie. His eye brows were bushy like the old movie actor Peter Lorre, and his voice was deep like Peter Lorre's, as if someone were speaking from a cellar in the man's chest. It was eerie. He seemed made out of wood. "You kids got the money?"

"You talking through a ventriloquist, mister?" Silverman asked.

Arthur stepped hard on Silverman's right foot. Rick stepped on the left.

"What you say, kid?" the short man asked.

"He said that we have the money," Arthur answered. "Right, Silverman?"

Arthur and Rick kept pressing down on Silverman's feet.

"Yeah, we have the money," Silverman gurgled, then whispered, "get off my feet, you assholes."

"That's good," the short man said. "Step right up that little staircase against the wall and be quiet. A show's going on. This is a theater."

"That's what I told my mother," said Rick. "I'm going to the theater. Mothers — all you have to do is tell them what they want to hear."

Arthur led the way. He didn't know what to expect, but he had expected something beyond a narrow hallway lit by a bare bulb and a man with a bow tie holding his hand out to take their money. After taking their bills, the man beckoned them to go through an unmarked door and take seats in the back. "Don't cause no trouble, boys. Trouble ain't a good thing."

"Thanks for the wisdom," Arthur muttered, but the short man had already headed down the hall toward the back of the building. There was a hitch in his gait as if one leg were shorter than the other.

"That must be where the dressing rooms are," Rick said. "But we have something else to do right now."

Although many sensations hit Arthur when he walked in, the strongest was the mingled raunch of sweat, hair cream, and tobacco. It smelled like the laundry basket in gym class where you threw in your towels, tee shirts, and jock straps, but even stronger. He made a gagging sound. Any woman who walked into this place—and he didn't see one in his first look at the crowd in front of him—would need a pint of perfume to ward off the odor.

"Smells like spunk," Silverman observed.

"What's that guy up there doing?" Rick asked. "We're here to see women, not some idiot in a baggy suit."

The three of them found places in the back row. The seats were wooden and bolted to the floor. "I guess no one's going to pick one of these up and hit someone over the head with it," Arthur said. When he sat down, the seat bottom felt sticky but he tried to ignore it. This wasn't a Sunday school social, as Grandpa Max would have said, though it was unlikely that Max had ever been to a Sunday school social. No doubt Max *had* been to this establishment—more than once. He had an autographed picture of the stripper Tempest Storm on the desk in the little room on the second floor of his house, the room he called his study. "I know what you're studying in there, Max," Bertha liked to say to him.

The man up on the stage, which was smaller than Arthur thought it was going to be—in fact, smaller than the stage in his high school—was telling jokes. He wore a beat-up fedora and held an extinguished cigar in his left hand. His voice sounded groggy: "I been seeing a school teacher. I like her. She's got no principals and no class."

"What's with this guy?" Rick asked again. "I can sit in the back of geometry and hear Tony Cappazuco tell bad jokes."

"That's part of the scene," Arthur answered. "Comics come on between the acts." He was sitting in the middle of the three of them. He also was trying not to place the whole weight of his bottom on the seat, but knew that was impossible.

"You been here before, Merm? How do you know?" Silverman asked.

"Merm knows everything," Rick answered. Then he poked Arthur in the ribs. "Well, almost everything."

After a few more jokes, the comic told the crowd to give a big hand to "a lovely little lady with some major assets—Cupcakes Carson." The curtain went down and a piano started to play a slow strut.

"Now we get some grinding and bumping," Silverman said. He grunted at the prospect.

The curtain, which looked heavy and ancient, slowly rose and a blond woman minced onto the stage. She wore very high heels, a tight sequined dress, a cape around the dress, and long white gloves. The dress covered up practically every inch of her but once she started dancing to the piano music — and Arthur immediately saw it was dancing she was doing, not just shimmying and swaying — the suggestion of what lay beneath the dress made itself powerfully felt. She glided and dipped and slowly twirled. Arthur wondered how someone could walk in such shoes, much less dance in them.

"Va-va-va-voom!" hollered a soldier a few rows in front of them. He swung his private's cap around his head as though it were a lariat. "Take it off, honey! Take it off!"

For an unbearably long time nothing happened in that department. The woman smiled at moments and at others seemed dreamy, as if lost in what she was doing. Then she paused, turned her back to the audience, twitched her bottom to a slow drum roll and began to peel off the gloves.

Arthur felt himself starting to get hard. If the sight of her taking off a pair of gloves did that to him, what would happen later?

"Boner time," Silverman croaked.

Cupcakes flung the gloves to the side of the stage.

"Throw 'em here!" hollered the soldier. Some whistling and hooting followed his shout but to Arthur it seemed that most of the guys in the place didn't want to say anything for fear of missing a moment. You could feel their attention. They were studying.

By the time Cupcakes got down to the pasties that covered her nipples and the little spangled patch in front of her crotch, Arthur was aroused — but also disappointed. He wanted her to go on forever. It was delicious, how she was in no hurry and how she danced around the stage as if in her own world yet aware of what she was doing in every motion and of who was watching her. She bowed at the end, and when she did, Arthur and everyone else could see the perfection of her breasts. She held the pose for some seconds, then straightened up and blew a calm kiss before strolling off. The piano jangled a final run. More hoots mixed with cheers exploded from the audience.

"Wow!" Arthur yelled.

"Easy does it, Merm," Rick said. "The night is still young."

Arthur began to say something, but he saw the bow tie guy tugging at Silverman, who was sitting nearest to the end of the row. "You boys got to leave now."

"What are you talking about? We just got here," Silverman said. He turned to Arthur and Rick. "Am I right? We just got here. We paid good money."

"I don't care when you got here, you got to leave. There's a plainclothesman in here and he's spotted you and if he wants to make some trouble, he can do it." The bow tie guy arched his shaggy eyebrows to show he was serious. "I don't mean to give that cop a dime of my money tonight. You hear me, boys?"

The piano was starting up again. The comic shuffled across the stage while holding up a placard that read "Empress Lola."

"We're not going anywhere," Silverman said.

Although it was dark at the back of the theater, Arthur could see clearly what appeared in the right hand of the bow tie guy—a switchblade. A kid in his mechanical drawing class had shown him a similar weapon one afternoon while their teacher was in the hall yakking with another teacher. It was slim and the blade was long.

"Am I making myself plain, boys? If you come home to mommy with a big cut on your face, you're going to have to do a lot of explaining." He gave the blade a little swish in the air.

"You win, mister," Silverman said. He rose from his seat. Arthur and Rick followed him.

"Lola, honey, take it off!" the soldier shouted.

The bow tie guy followed them to the outside door and opened it. "Good evening, gents. Say 'hi' to Ernie for me." Then he closed the door. They heard a lock clicking on the inside.

They stood there in the alleyway. Someone out on Baltimore Street was yelling. The words weren't distinct but the voice carried—loud and drunken.

Arthur looked down at the pavement. An empty pint of whiskey — Four Roses — lay unbroken as if someone had placed it there reverently.

"Asshole," Silverman sneered.

"Him or us?" Rick said.

"Silverman used the singular noun, but I'd say it was both," Arthur answered. "As for me, this is the second time in six months I've had a weapon in my vicinity."

"In your 'vicinity'? What the hell are you talking about?" Rick waved his arms around.

"When I was driving around this summer for Mr. Schwartz — the landlord I worked for — a guy pulled a gun on us." Arthur paused. "I've never told anyone."

Silverman, who had been lighting a cigarette, turned to Arthur and stared as if to make him out better in the alley's scant light. "Holy crap! That's no joke. What happened?"

"Nothing. We drove off. He never fired the gun."

"Empty threats. That's why we were assholes." Rick grimaced. "We should have stood up to him. We should have said 'Make us.' We should have acted like men. No wonder he called us 'boys.'"

Silverman put his hands in his pockets and kicked at a beer cap on the pavement. "To tell you the truth, I didn't know what to do. Did you know what to do, Merm?"

"I didn't want to be there. That's about it."

"God damn!" another voice on Baltimore Street bellowed. "God damn it to hell!"

"Look, how about a cigarette for Merm and me, Silverman?" Rick asked. He adjusted the knot of his tie. They had dressed up as if they were going to the real theater. "One thing I know is that we'll be back here. We'll walk in the front door and we'll sit as long as we want. And no jerk with a knife's going to touch us."

"Hey, how's about those cupcakes?" Rick whistled a wolf's whistle.

"Man, I'd like to work in that bakery," Silverman said.

They began walking toward Rick's car a few blocks over, on Redwood. Arthur felt his footsteps on the sidewalk in a way he never had before. He was here in Baltimore and though everything was far from all right—like the bottom of his pants and the switchblade—everything was not all wrong either. He had seen something he had hungered to see—not enough of it, but some. It was more than an anatomy lesson. It was a seduction. Even from the back row the premise he carried with him every day about a woman's body was true: nothing equaled that flesh. And now he was walking with his friends and making jokes about the guy with the bow tie and the soldier who kept hollering. And nothing was coming down from the sky—no rain or apocalypse, no angels like in *The Watchtower*, and no bombs. You couldn't make out the stars above the glow of the city, but that was okay. They were still up there.

Susan

Sometimes when she and her girls were playing a game like Monopoly or Clue, it seemed to Susan that her own life rose up from the board—a rectangular vision. That was silly. It was, as she pointed out when the girls became petulant or pouty, only a game. But the feeling wasn't silly. She moved around and around. She made decisions. She landed on the same square as other people. Yet the feeling that came to her as she rolled the dice and moved her token was that she wasn't moving. She stayed in one place. She could neither win nor lose. People emerged from bankruptcy or accumulated properties, but she was more like the board itself, something that was a condition and a fact.

It occurred to her, as one of her daughters considered whether to mortgage a property or put down a house, that she should invent a game called "Mother-Daughter-Wife-Teacher-Homemaker" that women could play. They could be all those things at the same time and go around a board that said things like "Argument with husband over moving to the suburbs" or "Daughters bicker over favorite cereal bowl" or "You dream about someone who isn't on the game board but won't leave your mind." Instead of going to jail, however, you would sit in your bedroom and wonder what you had done with your life. Or you would take a Miltown or go for a ride in the car and hum something from the Hit Parade of 1943 to yourself. Then you would draw a "brave face" card and go forth.

She thought about the game board on this early November Saturday morning when, after she had graded half a stack of themes about *Oliver Twist* (1. Describe the different sorts of thieves who populate this novel. 2. Compare and contrast the worlds of the city and the countryside.) and lit another Salem, she wondered where, aside from Marvin Gardens, her life was going. She went into the living room where Ruby was studying the front page of the *Sun*. While she was crying at Lu's kitchen table a few weeks ago, the world had passed through a crisis. It seemed remarkable—but was it? Men who represented nations threatening other men who represented nations: that was routine. The unhappy progress of the human race could be measured by how sticks and stones had become more than sticks and stones. She remembered Einstein's remark that the release of atomic power had changed everything except for human thinking. Lately her son had started announcing his own headlines. Yesterday's was "Apocalypse Avoided but Human Race Will Keep Trying." She asked Ruby if she wanted to go to the movies. Among other things, Susan was bored.

Ruby wasn't the easiest person to take to a movie. She didn't move well; she couldn't see the screen clearly. What made it particularly difficult, though, was Ruby's penchant for talking back to the picture. She had done this her whole life, or at least as long as Susan had known her. As a child, Susan sat in terror that her mother would be removed by an usher. Then she would have to decide if she was going to follow her mother or stay and watch the movie. It never happened but always seemed possible. She spent a certain amount of time elbowing Ruby, placing a finger to her lips and softly going "*sssshhh.*" Ruby would quiet down, but fifteen minutes later she would again speak to the screen. Susan could never decide whether it was utterly the child in Ruby or utterly the frustrated adult.

If she didn't ask Ruby to go with her, Ruby's feelings would be hurt, which would lead to another kind of trouble. Ruby would sulk and then ask Susan if she still loved her and whether she—Ruby—had been a good mother because she had tried to be a good mother . . . and similar talk that led into the grim night of the past. If Susan said something about wanting to be by herself, Ruby would shake her head in puzzlement. "By yourself? Why to be by yourself?" At this point Susan might start crying, though this was another vague zone where Susan wasn't sure whether the tears were about Ruby's distress or her own. Probably they were about both. That would fit the game board Susan was inventing—"You cry over milk spilt this morning and milk spilt thirty years ago."

Even a movie about a man who spent his adult life in prison was better than the confines of her house. It would offer the spectacle of another world. It would present some people who weren't named Mermelstein and who didn't live in Baltimore. It would make her feel that life was charged with meaning, however confused, rather than the low-grade randomness of a stranded mother whose family was variously occupied. And she did pay attention to movie stars. She liked the lead actor, Burt Lancaster. He couldn't be Jewish with a jaw like that. He must be Irish or Scotch. For a few hours she could feast on his handsome face.

The theater showing *The Birdman of Alcatraz* was one of those downtown picture palaces built in the twenties that took tawdry inspiration from every architectural period—Egyptian-Gothic-Versailles. She remembered going there with Stan on one of their first dates in Baltimore. She had been impressed with the theater's size and impressed with him. He was level-headed but sweet. He wanted to make good but he wasn't pushy. And he emitted that basic chemical that men emitted—a strength that would not wait. Where had that gone? Into the fog of columns and ledgers, the dither of money? When she looked around the faded lobby, she felt low. Whatever glamour had once been there had thinned out and worn down. Whatever gilt had been on the columns had flaked off. The very air smelled tired.

Ruby remained quiet during the movie. She moved her neck forward to peer more intently at the screen. She didn't complain. At one point—around when Robert Stroud, the convict played by Burt Lancaster, got a microscope from the kindly prison guard—she fell asleep, though not for long. When, toward the end of the movie, Stroud, who had been denied parole again and again, told his wife that she should leave him and then he and his wife put a hand up against the glass panel that separated them as if to touch one another, she whimpered, but so did Susan.

There was more there at that moment than heartache. Susan felt anger about Stroud's telling his wife to leave him. How could a man tell a woman who loved him to leave him? He thought he was being honorable, but what did honor have to do with love? It wasn't a marriage in any conventional sense — he in prison and she on the outside — but there had to be more to love than convention. Didn't love always invite a degree of impossibility? Wasn't that what she was teaching her students about Clym and Eustacia? If things worked out badly, then things worked out badly. Better sorry than safe. Yet who was she to talk?

Susan dabbed at her eyes and offered Ruby a tissue. She remembered what, on many days, she forgot — that she loved her mother.

After the movie ended and the credits had played, Ruby needed time to collect her stout self and make her way up the aisle. She paused at the door that led out onto the lobby as if surveying an endless plain. She sighed — Ruby was a champion sigher — and lowered her head slightly as if determined to bull her way forward, although there were only a handful of people leaving the show. Her hat — a little pink felt square from 1938 — tilted precariously. Her cane began to search its way across the burgundy colored carpet.

Susan looked down and noticed how worn the fabric was. When she looked up, she saw Jarvis Baker.

"Imagine seeing you here on a Saturday afternoon. This must be your mother." Jarvis smiled at both of them. He had on a tie as if he were going to work. In one hand he held an Ivy-style poplin cap. "I just saw Arthur not long ago at the record store." He kept smiling, as if the sight of a sad, angry woman groggy from taking an extra Miltown the night before and her tottering mother gave him pleasure. "I must be on your family's radar."

Susan tried to smile back. Ruby emitted a small squeak. Being greeted by a Negro male in a public place was as bizarre as visiting Alcatraz.

"Yes, Jarvis, this is my mother — Ruby Sofritz."

"Pleased to meet you, ma'am," Jarvis raised his cap in salutation.

"Pleased to meet you," Ruby mumbled. She leaned heavily on her cane.

"Jarvis teaches music, Ma, at the school Arthur goes to. Last year he took his class." Susan turned back to Jarvis. "Did you say you saw Arthur at a record store? He didn't say anything about it to me. He did buy a Miles Davis album — for both him and me — but he didn't say a word about you."

"He talked some about Miles. And he talked some about you. But you know how that is, Susan. If males told females about everything going through their heads . . ." He winked. "I teach a hundred or so of them every day. I know."

Susan nodded a jittery nod — this was all happening too fast and was too unexpected. She turned to her mother and asked Ruby if she was okay.

What was she saying? Was meeting a Negro man in a movie theater going to affect her mother medically?

Jarvis cocked his head and gave Susan a long look. He said nothing.

Susan was certain his next words would be: "Well, it was good to see you but I have to get going."

"Would you like to have a cup of coffee and talk?" Jarvis asked. He fumbled a bit with his cap. "That was a serious movie. I could use some conversation. I was hoping someone I knew would be here." He paused and gave Susan another long look. "You've got nothing against hoping, do you?"

"Yes. I mean no, I've got nothing against hoping, but yes, that would be wonderful." Susan turned again to her mother. Ruby's eyes looked frozen with fright, the way they did when they were at the beach and Ruby, who couldn't swim, walked out a yard too far into the surf. "You'll enjoy this, Ma. It's good for you to get out and see new people."

"Good for me?" Ruby answered. "Milk of magnesia is good for me."

Standing between her mother and Jarvis, Susan felt she needed to be able to speak out of both sides of her mouth. She put a hand on Ruby's shoulder while swiveling her head toward Jarvis. "My mom is feisty."

"I like feisty women," Jarvis replied. "Let's find a coffee shop." He paused and frowned, two thin but deep lines. "The mixed nature of our party won't be a problem downtown. Read's integrated quite a while ago and set the tone." He spoke slowly to Ruby and Susan as if he were an interpreter of some sort. "Negroes think twice before they enter a public establishment. And Baltimore, well, Baltimore is the Deep South of the North. There are places in this town where my face is not wanted." Easy with the truth, he grinned with a boy's mischief. The lines disappeared.

Ruby nodded; her hat slipped slightly. "That is why the minister is important—civil rights for each person."

"The Reverend King, Ruby means," Susan explained. She pushed Ruby's hat back on the top of her head, then touched her own head. She had left the house without putting a hat on. Since she had gotten a haircut, she felt more exposed. What surprised her was that she liked the feeling.

"I understand. And, as you can imagine, I agree." Jarvis took a step. "Please let me lead the way."

Susan's head was a jumble of *maybes*: maybe Jarvis had been bored, too . . . maybe fate was bringing them together . . . maybe Ruby was the worst person in the world to have with her . . . maybe she should stop thinking and let life happen.

When, after a very slow progress punctuated by pleasantries about how many people were out shopping, they sat down in a coffee shop off Howard Street, Ruby looked about furtively. The Gentile world retained a mysterious and forbidding savor for her. Mirrors, doors, floors, windows— somehow everything was different.

"They have coffee here?" she asked.

Jarvis laughed. "It's a coffee shop, ma'am."

Susan laughed, too. "I'll order it for you the way you like it, Ma." She looked directly at Jarvis, who was seated across from her in the booth. "Ruby likes a lot of milk in her coffee. My girls tease her that it's more like milk with coffee than coffee with milk." She put her hands palms down on the Formica table top that separated them. Her wedding ring stared up at her. "So what did you think of the movie, Jarvis?"

"I'm glad I didn't take my wife. I don't think she could have handled it. Too grim."

Something dipped and then crested inside Susan. "Too grim?" She braced herself against the back of the booth. Her insides kept moving.

Jarvis ordered three coffees. Susan appended an explanation about milk in Ruby's coffee. The waitress snapped the gum she was chewing but said nothing.

"The way that prisons work is grim," said Jarvis, "how one senseless act leads to what the voice on the soundtrack called 'a vast boiler of despair.' But the birdman wasn't despairing. To me the ending wasn't grim. You saw Stroud talking about where he was being transferred and how he could go for walks there. He didn't seem grim. Maybe we make too big a deal about freedom." Jarvis smoothed out the top of his cap that he had placed on the table. "And when I say 'we,' I mean the human race — everyone." He stopped the smoothing.

Ruby took off her hat and set it carefully on the table top. She patted her sparse white curls. "But what about the minister? He is for freedom."

Susan realized that when Ruby spoke, she was cringing. Any second now, she expected to hear "the *shwartzer* minister."

"He is for freedom," Jarvis agreed, "but I don't have to repeat what's in any civics text." He stopped and poured a teaspoon of sugar into the coffee that arrived while he was speaking. "What matters most is the inner freedom that the birdman had. I'm not sure who can give us that. We have to earn it — each of us."

"But what about the injustice of his still being in prison? Hasn't he paid his debt to society?" Susan's mouth remained open: *I sound like a teacher.* A few more years of belaboring the obvious and she would be another Sid Colvin.

"Plenty milk," Ruby observed. A smidgeon of creaturely satisfaction crossed her face.

Jarvis idly stirred his coffee. "There's no shortage of injustice. I can speak to that, but I think Robert Stroud stopped caring about that. Justice or injustice — it didn't matter to the birds. He wasn't Saint Francis but he — a murderer — became a gentle companion to the creatures. Who among us can say that?" Jarvis seemed to have entered a reverie. "But what do you think, ladies?"

The eyes of a white woman making her way to the front door lingered on Susan for a few cold seconds. When Susan opened her mouth nothing but air came out, the cloud of feelings within her. Then she spoke slowly. "'The first duty of life is to live.' I think I'm quoting correctly. And I agree. But not many of us are made of the stuff Robert Stroud was made of. Some of us are women, like the woman who married Stroud and whom he told should pretend that he was a dead man. What could she say to that? What were her female feelings supposed to do with that?" Susan paused. She hadn't touched her coffee. She was leaning toward Jarvis but she was looking not so much at him as past him. "But not many of us have put ourselves in that extreme a position."

Jarvis almost whispered. "Due to the color of our skin some of us are born in that extreme position. Jail or no jail—all our sayings issue from that place."

His words grazed Susan—a tree that fell not on her but close by. She knew such words might be coming—her Negro students had told her much the same thing many times before—but the mystery lay in the timing. She didn't know at what moment the words would arrive, or from what shadow they might emerge. And she didn't understand, though she kept trying, how the shadow wasn't a shadow but a brute presence. She shook her head dumbly. She felt heard and unheard.

Ruby reached suddenly toward her hat as if to make sure it wasn't going to fly away. Susan gave her mother a quick sideways glance. Whatever limit Ruby had for this situation had probably been exceeded.

"Well, "Jarvis said, "the movie gave us plenty to think about. I wish Hollywood did more of that. And who knows? They got to lifetime convicts, someday they may even get to Negroes." He picked up his cap. It was a light blue color. "Why don't you let me pay for this? I'm the one who wanted to come here."

Susan could feel Ruby's alarm—*a Negro paying for me?* "Why don't we make it a Dutch treat?" Susan answered. "I'm so glad we got a chance to sit and talk. And we don't have to go yet. How is school going for you, Jarvis? Have you seen Joe lately?"

As if from inside one of those glass booths that quiz show contestants sat in, she watched while Jarvis took her cue and began to make appropriate small talk. Ruby drained the bottom of her coffee but said nothing. An unhappy calm descended on Susan. She was near this man who brought up something that she didn't know was in her, something she had no idea what to do about beyond extending her hand across the table top and touching him. It seemed simple, but wanting could make any hard thing seem simple. Her hand stayed at her side.

A waitress slammed in the register's cash drawer. A counterman called out an order. This crowded moment might be as close as she would get to Jarvis Baker. Prisons were more than bars and cells: was that what Jarvis was saying? She thought of the newspapers that week announcing that the missile tensions were over. The Free World had been ready to blow itself up for the sake of freedom. Did the Free World know what freedom was? When the wardens lectured Stroud in the movie, the last thing they seemed was free. There was no freedom in retribution. There was no freedom in certainty.

"I must go to the bathroom," Ruby declared. She turned toward the aisle, swung her cane out, and raised herself carefully. "Watch my pocketbook, Susie." She trudged off.

Jarvis smiled crookedly. "Your mother wouldn't be thinking that Negroes are thieves, would she?"

"Paranoids don't discriminate. The whole world is after her pocketbook."

"Well"—and Jarvis exhaled—"I try to not take much personally. I don't always succeed, of course. When I was playing that tune the other day, I felt you were listening. You were listening with your whole body. You were tense, though. Even when I finished, you were tense." He leaned forward, his face not far from Susan's. "Music is supposed to ease us up. Surely you felt that."

Susan felt a blush coming on. "Your playing took me somewhere I haven't been in a long time. Maybe never."

"Now, now, there are long-playing records and I know you own some." Jarvis leaned back, put a hand into a pants pocket and drew out some change. "You know I'm a married man, but I'm a man all the same. I don't know if you are flattering me or teasing me or you don't know yourself, but I know the Gershwin brothers spoke a heap of truth. And I know the truth runs in every direction—even through the color line." He examined the coins in his palm. "It's been good talking with you today. You're a woman of feeling and intellect. Perhaps we'll meet again at Joe and Julia's." He threw down several quarters. "Make sure to let your mom know I didn't go near her pocketbook. And I know that my money is more than the price of my coffee." He snugged his cap on and was out of the shop in a few brisk steps. As he was leaving, an elderly white man in seersucker came up to the door. He hesitated before stepping in; perhaps he was in the wrong place.

Susan looked toward the door and felt—how could she not feel?—like the birdman: time might seem to stand still—dusty, confining and stale—but it could never flow backwards. Jarvis had ended the conversation where he wanted to end it. She was left with her heart fluttering in the cage of her fears. He would mock a white lady thinking of a cage. It wasn't fair, though, to compare cages. That seemed one more thing the birdman had learned.

When Ruby returned, she looked at the empty side of the booth. "The *shvartzer* is gone? He speaks well. Is a teacher? He went to college, to university?"

"Teachers go to college, Ma, to become teachers. You know that. He went to Howard."

"Harvard? Is a good place."

"Howard!" Susan shouted. "Not Harvard! Howard!"

Ruby recoiled. A man at the counter slowly spun around on his stool and stared at the two women.

Susan bowed her head. Dizzy with feeling, she breathed in hard, as if she had climbed an impossible set of stairs. When she looked up, she could see, even through Ruby's thick glasses, the trepidation in her mother's eyes. When she spoke, her words were deliberate, like someone reading a confession. "I'm sorry, Ma. I didn't mean to raise my voice. Howard is a university in Washington. It's well respected. Most of its students are Negroes. Jarvis Baker went there." She picked up a spoon and dipped it into the cup of coffee she hadn't touched. She raised the spoon and dipped it, raised it and dipped it.

The man spun back around on his stool.

"I never heard of it. But what do I know, an old *sotsyalist* in America?" As if to avow who she was, Ruby grazed her own cheek. A bit of powder adhered to her pointer finger. "And what is for dinner tonight?" she asked. "Chicken? Lamb chops?"

Baron Wormser

The game board Susan had thought about that morning came back to her. Instead of "Chance?" there would be a space on it that read "What to make for dinner?" An image of a huge steak would be circling around a woman's head.

"Let's make meatloaf. The girls will be bringing a friend back for dinner. Stan and Arthur will be hungry from working all day." Susan put the spoon down. "It won't take long but we need to get moving." She looked out the plate glass window at the street and the people hurrying by. The image of Robert Stroud in his cell came back to her — his calm, resigned face. He never asked any doctor for any pills.

Susan pushed the coffee cup and saucer away from her. Jarvis's coins lay there on the table top. She replaced one of his quarters with one of hers, then turned quickly to her mother. "Don't forget your pocketbook, Ma."

Arthur

Iris and Ellen told him that no one went out on a date on Sunday night. Susan asked him if he had brushed his teeth. Stan told him to take it easy on the gas pedal. Ruby wondered if he could find the movie theater—"Is a big city, Arthur." He told his sisters to bug off. He waved a toothbrush at his mother. He assured his father he was no lead foot. He explained to Ruby which streets and roads he would take. His sisters made faces at him. His mother smiled. His father said, "Okay, kiddo." Ruby croaked something in Yiddish.

He was going with Rebecca to see *The Miracle Worker*. He didn't care what anyone said, though it wasn't as if he hadn't been on dates before. Silverman and he had taken girls out on double dates, but the girls who were his date had always been friends of Silverman's girlfriend, which meant that the evening was more about seeing if two people who had never met before could find a spark beyond "What classes do you take?" and "What do you like for music?" They hadn't, which meant a goodnight peck on the girl's cheek and Silverman's needling Arthur the next day about how he had to step up more with women.

When he knocked on the door of the apartment where Rebecca lived with her father and brother, he was perspiring with excitement. No one in his house had asked him whether he put on deodorant, but he had. The door opened suddenly. Rebecca's father, a large man with a thick black beard, stood before him. He extended a hand, but only slightly. "You are Arthur?"

"I am, sir. Pleased to meet you. It's an honor." Arthur grasped the rabbi's hand and shook it firmly. In the hallway behind the rabbi, he could see Rebecca. She had on the same sweater she had worn on that Saturday in the library. Arthur had come to understand that she didn't have many clothes and that the hair ribbons were a way of being stylish. Tonight she had on a violet-colored one. She was waving to him with both arms like someone beckoning to a search party. She was smiling her big, red lipstick smile.

"And you are Jewish, Arthur? You have had a bar mitzvah?" As if searching for Semitic qualities, the rabbi studied Arthur's face.

"I am Jewish and I have had my bar mitzvah." Arthur paused. "It was a wonderful ceremony."

"Yes, of course." The rabbi turned to Rebecca but spoke to Arthur. "She is my precious daughter. You take care of her. You understand?"

"Yes, sir. I understand." Arthur took a tentative step toward Rebecca, although there wasn't much room between the rabbi and himself.

"Arthur is a responsible young man, Daddy," Rebecca said. "He is an honor-roll student at City College. He is the son of one of the English teachers at my school."

The rabbi turned back to Arthur. "Enjoy yourself tonight. Young people should enjoy themselves." He tried to smile, a fumbling of the lips that reminded Arthur of Ruby's trying to smile. Smiles had been left on the other side of the ocean. The rabbi stepped aside for Rebecca to come forward.

"I will, sir. I . . ." He halted. Rebecca stood beside her father. Her hair was just washed and shone with pale light. A lilac fragrance filled the air. A feeling began to rise up in him, but it was not one the rabbi needed to hear about. "Thank you, sir."

"Bye, Daddy." Rebecca took Arthur by the arm and they were out the door.

In the car on the way to the movies, Rebecca sat not over by the window, the way his mother sat in the car with his father, but not right up against him, either. Rebecca was worried about her father. "He wants to move to Israel. He doesn't like it here. He keeps saying that he has tried but he doesn't like it here. He says things like 'I want to die among Jews. I don't want to die with these *goyim* and their missiles and their Christmas.'"

Rebecca moved closer to Arthur. "What am I going to do? I don't want to go to Israel. I don't care about the missiles or about Christmas. I want to stay here."

Arthur took his right hand off the steering wheel and gestured to the air. "That's tough. He's your father."

"Yes, he's my father, but soon enough I'm going to be a grown woman. And I have guys who are interested in me already. One would marry me tomorrow if I let him."

Marry me—the words seemed unbelievable to Arthur. They both were only in high school, taking tests and reading books, looking out a picture window at adulthood. *Marry me*—the words seemed impossible.

"I don't like him enough to eat a hamburger with him, much less marry him." Rebecca moved even closer. Now she was right up against him. Her wide skirt made of some ugly wool spilled onto his pant leg. Arthur quivered. "The fact is, Arthur, I like you. You're gentle. I like that. Maybe you aren't a man yet, but you will be." Rebecca placed a hand on his right thigh. "You will be."

Arthur tried to lick his dry lips but didn't have any saliva. He needed to be responsible—to keep the car on the road, to pay attention to the other cars and the street signs and traffic lights. He also needed to put a hand on Rebecca's hand. "I like you too."

Rebecca laughed. "I should hope so." She leaned a shoulder into his shoulder.

In the movie theater they didn't hold hands. Rebecca kept hers demurely in her lap and stared mesmerized at the screen. When Arthur looked over at her, she seemed to be barely breathing. Then, near the end of the movie, when young Helen Keller said the word "water," Rebecca grabbed his upper arm with both her hands and squeezed it hard. She made a low, indistinct sound as if she were trying to form some word herself. For the remaining few minutes, right until Helen came out on the porch and kissed Annie, her teacher, Rebecca held on tight. Her grip hurt but the attention felt good.

On the way back to Rebecca's house, Arthur expected her to talk about the movie but she was quiet. It wasn't every day that you witnessed a child grappling with such handicaps or a teacher who was so fiercely dedicated. Rebecca fingered the long necklace of glass beads she was wearing. Again and again she touched her hair ribbon. She didn't look at Arthur. When he asked questions about what she thought of the movie, she only said "yes" or "maybe," as if he weren't there at all, as if she had gone into the world of Helen and Annie and the deaf and blind fury, and not come back. He was a little scared. Her silence was unsettling, something brought not to light but to darkness. Rebecca looked intently out the window at the streetlights and houses and shadows as if she were seeing Baltimore for the first time.

When he pulled the car up in front of her house, she told him to go around the block and park the car in an alley. "Right here is good." She pointed. "Over by this garage with the trashcan beside it. No one comes by here."

Arthur turned the ignition key to off.

Rebecca turned toward him but her eyes were shut tight. She stretched her arms straight out before her, level with her shoulders. They hung in the air between the two of them, her hands almost reaching Arthur but not quite. "I want you to help me, Arthur," she said. "I want you to touch me and I want you to make me go crazy." She paused. "Do you hear me? I can't stand it anymore. I want you to make me go crazy. I'm not going to open my eyes." Her hands moved a little closer toward him. "Do you hear me?"

"I do."

"Good. You don't have to kiss me." She put her hands down at her side. Her eyes remained closed. "You don't have to talk either."

Arthur put his hands where her breasts were beneath the sweater. Slowly he began to move his hands over them. He had dreamt of this but doing it made his whole body feel electric.

"That's nice but it can be nicer." Rebecca pulled back from Arthur's hands, tugged her sweater off and began to unbutton the blouse underneath it. She moved from button to button surely. "I don't need eyes for this, Arthur," she said. Her shirt lay open. "Now touch me more, not roughly but passionately. Like a lover."

At the sight of her bra — it had a little bow in the place

between the two cups—Arthur's breath, heart, and pulse all stopped. Not everything stopped, however. He was hard, which got in the way some but was not going to stop his hands' work. He began to touch and feel.

Rebecca started to groan, an involuntary pleasure sound from the back of her throat. For a stupid second Arthur thought she was snoring. He drew back.

"What are you doing, Arthur?"

"Take off your necklace. It keeps getting in my way."

"Oh, silly." She moved her hands back and undid the clasp. It dropped onto the seat.

Then his hands were back on her. He found the clasps of her bra and without fumbling undid them.

"That was good, Arthur. Now I take back what I said about kissing. I want you to kiss them, especially my nipples."

He pulled the bra straps off her shoulders and let the bra fall into her lap. Then he bowed his head slightly and began to kiss the soft firmness of her breasts and then her nipples. The texture of her nipples—almost pebbly—surprised him.

Rebecca began to gently whinny. She arced her head back slightly. Her arms remained at her side. Her eyes remained closed.

Part of Arthur's head knew there was more to what could happen than this—he hadn't forgotten the prophylactic Grandpa Max had given him—but part of his head felt that nothing better than this could possibly happen. Her nipples grew hard. She whinnied more and moaned more, too. Time seemed like a pat of butter that Seeley had dropped into a hot pan. It sizzled, melted, and then evaporated.

He was in his mother's car. He was nowhere. He was a tongue on her breasts.

Then he heard Rebecca's voice. It seemed far off, as if coming from outside the car. "Look at your watch, Arthur. Is it ten-thirty yet?"

His watch—for a second he wondered what a watch was. Then he pulled his head away from her chest and looked at his wrist. "It's ten-fifteen."

Rebecca opened her eyes. "I have to be home by ten thirty." She pulled the front of her blouse together. "Oh, Arthur, you did it! I felt crazy. Your mouth is wonderful. But what about you? You must be . . ." She reached toward his pants.

"I am," he muttered.

Rebecca undid his belt buckle, then moved her fingers inside his boxers. It didn't take long. When she raised her hand, she held it out between the two of them. "Do you want to taste?" she asked.

"No thanks."

"Well, I can't walk into my father's house with this on my fingers." She began to lick, then paused. "It doesn't taste like a food."

Arthur looked down at his watch. "Seven minutes."

Rebecca finished licking and put her bra back on. Then she turned her back to Arthur. "Place your hands over my breasts and squeeze them—not too hard but so I can feel you touching me one more time."

He pressed her toward him. He kissed the base of her neck.

"That was sweet. Now I'll neaten up. I've got a little perfume to dab on." Rebecca grabbed her small pocketbook, which had fallen to the car floor. "I know there's more to this than what we did, Arthur. And I know that you know. But this is what I wanted to do first." She pulled out a tiny vial. "I keep a little bottle of perfume that was my mother's on my dresser." She opened her wide brown eyes even wider. "Sometimes I feel that grief is going to split me right open. Now I know better." She opened the passenger side door and began walking away.

Arthur leaned toward the empty seat. "I want to see you again."

"Good," he heard Rebecca say, but she didn't turn around.

The word loitered in the night air. He sat there with the passenger door open, in no hurry, the scent of Rebecca lingering, the thrill of her hand on him lingering, too. Around him the city slept, its indifference a species of calm. When he did start the car and put the radio on, Ray Charles was singing "I Can't Stop Loving You." Arthur had seen him on television. Listening now, he could picture the blind man wearing those dark glasses, sitting at the piano, and bobbing his head as he played the music. You could feel him feeling the song. There were no lines or limits: he *was* the music. Then Arthur came back to Rebecca and how her face had looked with her eyes shut—trust become ecstatic. And then he recalled a scene from the movie when Helen clutched her doll to herself as if her life depended on it. That was how people put it: "as if life depended on it." But it did. There was as much to feel as there was to see. There might even be more.

Susan

"Does anyone know how hard English teachers work?" Arthur came in from the kitchen bearing a slice of the pineapple upside-down cake Seeley had made the day before. A smear of brown glaze decorated his upper lip.

Susan looked up from the theme she was correcting. "Do you know what a fork is, Arthur?"

"I do, but I like to lick the sweetness off my fingers." Arthur waggled the index finger of his right hand and stuck it in his mouth.

"Charming. You pick the crumbs up."

"Sure, Mom. I'm a big boy. Now what about my question?"

"About English teachers?" Susan extinguished the cigarette she was smoking in a large glass ashtray that had BPOE inscribed on it, a gift from Grandpa Max. "Other English teachers know and their families know and that's about it. We're like the title of that Joseph Conrad story — secret sharers."

Arthur sat down on one of the wing chairs in the living room. He drew his legs up underneath him and continued to eat the cake with his hands.

"Don't touch that chair with those hands, Arthur. Seeley just waxed that wood."

"I wouldn't think of it, Mom. And I'm licking my fingers carefully. I'm like a cat." Arthur threw his legs out over the side of the chair. It was uncomfortable no matter how he positioned himself. "Do you like being a secret sharer?"

"You're full of questions tonight, aren't you?"

"Don't get Jewish with me, Mom, answering a question with a question. And don't start in with don't-you-have-more-homework-to-do. Like Joe Friday said, 'All we want are the facts.'"

Susan set down the pile of papers on the coffee table in front of her. A red pen fell to the floor but she let it lie there. "Helping young people is important. They need to be able to speak and write and learn what a good book is. All of that matters if we are ever going to live in a better world." She paused. "There are days, though, when I wish I were more visible in the life beyond my school. There are days when I feel I'm on a raft and the world is too far away. But maybe I've just written 'run-on sentence' one too many times."

"So do you think *The Return of the Native* is a good book? That's a tough call, isn't it—saying one book is good and another isn't?" He placed the last piece of cake onto his tongue, then closed his lips and made an *ummm* sound.

"I'm glad you like the cake, Arthur. Seeley got the recipe from someone in her church." Susan stopped to pull a pill off her sweater. "You know I think *The Return of the Native* is a good book. I don't teach books unless I think they're good books. And I don't mind if my students disagree with me—up to a point." Susan smiled slightly. "I just want them to see that someone like Thomas Hardy was a serious writer, someone who wasn't afraid to show how much feeling went into people's lives." She paused. "And, though it could be confused, how much that feeling mattered."

"Every time I go to the library I avoid that book. I'm afraid to read it because Rebecca—you know, the girl I went out with the other night—is like you. She's crazy about it. What if I don't like it?"

"I'm sure she'd appreciate it that you read the book. I'd appreciate it. I still remember the talk we had about *Lord Jim*. It must have been last spring."

Arthur held up his hands to show how clean they were, then placed them in his lap. "Do you ever talk about books with Dad?"

"With your father? No, I don't. But you live here. You know that. Why do you ask?" Susan reached toward the pack of cigarettes on the coffee table, took one out, and lit it. "Don't ask me for a cigarette, Arthur. The answer is No."

"I can afford my own, Mom, and I don't like your brand

anyway. Menthol tastes like a bad chemistry experiment. Yuck. But I asked about Dad and you and books because kids wonder about their parents. Because I notice that Dad isn't here some nights. Even after he's worked all day, there's more work to do."

What came into Susan's head at that moment was a woman's face that was reproduced in a book she had been reading about the painter Manet, a woman standing behind a table at the *Folies Bergère* — a melancholy face graced with sensual full lips.

"Mom? Are you there?"

Susan blew out some smoke. "I'm here. Your father has been busy lately."

"It's not tax season, Mom."

"He's been busy." Her voice was brisk. "While we're at it, let me ask a few questions. Should I assume the necklace I found in my car is Rebecca's? I have it in my pocketbook."

"You should assume that." Arthur stood up and began to massage the base of his spine with both hands. "Why don't we get rid of these stupid chairs?"

"Hold on, I'm still asking the questions. And besides, you know these chairs are Ruby's and you know that Ruby doesn't have much in this world."

"And I know I should feel sorry for Ruby even when she makes bad chicken and complains every other sentence."

"Arthur!"

"Sorry, Mom."

Susan extinguished her cigarette. For a second she looked at her lipstick on the filter as if surprised to see her lips on it. "How come you didn't tell me that you ran into Mr. Baker at the record store?"

"Is this a quiz?" Arthur let his arms dangle and moved his weight forward so he was on his toes. "I'm getting tall but I need to be taller."

"I wondered why you didn't tell me."

"Guys aren't supposed to, Mom. You know that. They're like nations with missiles."

The woman in the Manet painting, a barmaid, returned unbidden to Susan. The woman's eyes directly engaged the viewer. She was aware of being looked at. She was, after all, a woman in a very public place, a sort of cabaret or theater that was filled with men. Yet the feeling that came from her was enigmatic, her gaze at once blank and penetrating. The mystery of her female presence was palpable. And the painter understood that. He didn't push it away, nor did he make too much of it. He accepted it.

"Do you like Mr. Baker?"

"Mom, you know I like Mr. Baker. He and someone like Mr. Tobey are in two very different leagues. With Mr. Baker you feel like he's opening things up for you. With Mr. Tobey everything's already decided. 'Turn to page 108.' That's Mr. Tobey."

"I get it." Susan looked away. "And do you like Rebecca?"

"Mom, ease up with the questions. Let's not ask any more questions. Let's just talk with each other."

They eyed one other, then relaxed into silence.

"Your father and I are thinking about separating." Susan was staring at the pack of Salems but didn't pick one out. She reached over and swiped at some speck on the table before her. Then she looked at her son, who had plopped back into the wing chair.

"What the hell? Separate? What do you mean?"

"We weren't going to ask a lot of questions, Arthur, if you recall. We were going to just talk."

"Whew!" Arthur blew out an exaggerated air stream. "You have to tell me why, Mom." He grimaced as if he were going to start crying, but no tears showed.

"I guess I do. Because your father and I don't talk about what I care about. Because your father spends so much time working. Because I'm tired of pushing your father to do things he doesn't want to do. Because of me." Susan halted. "But that's a big topic. Don't tell your sisters. Don't tell anyone, not even Rebecca, especially not Rebecca because she goes to my school." Susan drew her legs up to her chest but kept her eyes on Arthur. "I don't know where we are headed. I thought I should tell you because you're the oldest and because you understand a lot. I don't want to treat you like a child."

Arthur brought his hands together and interleaved his

fingers, as if getting himself ready for a task. "Thanks, Mom. I mean it. Thanks." His voice was shaky. "I don't know what to say. Dad told me to sort of keep an eye on you."

"Keep an eye on me?" Susan asked.

"He's been worried about you."

"Worried? And he told you about it?"

"He did."

Susan got up, went over to her son and mussed his hair. "You need a haircut."

Arthur bowed his head but said nothing.

Again, Susan saw the woman in the painting. There was something proud in the woman's eyes, something that no one could touch or invade or seize. Or was the woman simply weary, very weary? The world had told her more than she wanted to know.

A clatter on the stairs interrupted her thoughts. Iris and Ellen stood in their pajamas on the landing. "Mom, you have to listen to this Joan Baez song we learned," Iris announced. Before Susan could say a word they began singing: "Come, my love, let's take a walk. . . ."

"'Banks of the Ohio'!" Arthur shouted. "He kills her because she won't marry him."

The girls continued singing. Their faces were determined — they were performing — but their voices were soft and light. Susan closed her eyes and listened. "Lord, I saw her as she floated down."

Arthur

Mr. Tobey's classroom proclaimed his patriotism. Color reproductions of portraits of American presidents, along with photos in black and white of the more recent ones, lined the wall above the blackboards on the side of the room opposite the windows. The wall above the blackboard in the front of the room was covered with reproductions of colonial American flags. Mr. Tobey especially liked to point to the Don't-Tread-On-Me flag and tell the boys how that was the real American spirit. His favorite president was Teddy Roosevelt. There were sayings by various eminences on the back wall, people like Horace Greeley, Abraham Lincoln, and General Patton. Edward Trumbull asked Mr. Tobey at the beginning of the year if he was going to put some words of Martin Luther King Jr. up there. Mr. Tobey smiled a bland smile—a modest incision on his small, sallow face—and said he would think about it. The first quarter of the school year was nearing its end. There were no words by Dr. King on the back wall.

"History is now," Mr. Tobey liked to remind his classes, which, outside of the classroom, his students turned into "History is a cow." When, after taking attendance, he told his second-period history class that he suspected it was "just a matter of time before those bombers are removed from Cuba and this whole thing is done with," he waited a few meaningful moments before intoning his favorite phrase. He went on to say how important it was that the United States had stood up to the forces of Communism, how the United States had taught the Soviet Union a lesson that it would not soon forget.

"It's been a little tense over these couple of months, but we're still standing. I'm proud of us." Arthur pondered his teacher for what seemed like the one millionth time. Like a lot of teachers, Mr. Tobey wore more or less the same clothes every day. He had two v-neck sweaters—one had an argyle pattern on it and the other was a solid pale green. Today he had on the argyle. He had on his blue tie, not his brown tie or his gray tie. Arthur looked out the window. A few leaves danced in the breeze, refusing to fall to earth. He watched them flit and flutter. The best thing about history class was that Mr. Tobey barely noticed what was going on. He just as soon would have talked to a room full of shoes or orange peels as human beings. Or it seemed like that, which was fine because Arthur could sit and gaze out the high windows and daydream.

Today, though, he wondered if his mother was for real about his parents separating. Her face had been serious in that way adults could get serious, where you sensed they knew something bad and were only telling you part of it. The part they weren't telling you was worse than the part they were telling you. It was like when Ruby talked about the Holocaust. Her words were ghosts but her silences were monsters. He sighed. It wouldn't be bad to be a leaf in the wind—no worries and no thoughts, floating through space. You wouldn't know you were in Baltimore or Berlin or Tokyo. Then he wondered when he would touch Rebecca's breasts again. Even in the dusty deadness of the classroom, his prick stirred. He didn't want to be a leaf after all.

John Silverman sat on one side of Arthur's desk and Herbie Freilich on the other. Today, Silverman was drawing a side view of a 1959 Chevrolet Impala. Arthur thought that it wasn't a bad likeness. The fins looked sharp and the overall proportions seemed right. Silverman would have taken mechanical drawing every period if the school let him. On the other side, Herbie Freilich was reading a life of John D. Rockefeller that he had in his lap. Herbie would look up occasionally and notice Mr. Tobey, push his thick glasses back up on the bridge of his nose, and then dive back into his book. No one in the class took notes because Mr. Tobey based his tests and quizzes on the textbook. As long as your textbook was open on your desk, Mr. Tobey was okay with you. When he asked a question it was usually, "Wouldn't you agree with that, Mr. So and So?" He called the boys "Mister." All you had to do was reply "Yes, sir" and Mr. Tobey was happy. He was like a toy train that went around and around on a fact-filled track.

Arthur looked down at his desk. He had a notebook full of blank pages beside his textbook. Maybe he should write a poem to Rebecca. Or maybe he should write a letter to his mother about how confused he felt, how grown-ups were supposed to work things out, not just give up. Or maybe he should make a paper airplane. He ripped a page out and started to fold the paper when he heard Edward Trumbull's voice. Edward sat in the first row. Back in September he had explained to Mr. Tobey that Negroes didn't like to sit in the back of anything. One of the other Negro guys promptly told Mr. Tobey that he was fine with sitting out back. More than once, when he had overheard some of those same guys talking, he had heard Edward's name and the phrase "full-of-himself nigger."

"Why should I care about those bombers, Mr. Tobey? I can't vote in many parts of this country. I can't go out to eat in many parts of this country — or this city for that matter. And the fact is that if I tried to buy a house in most parts of this very city, I'd be brushed off or told to go back to Africa. Do you expect me as a Negro to feel good about some missiles that aren't in Cuba?" Edward's voice was calm, as if he were reading from the textbook about the Louisiana Purchase. Sometimes Mr. Tobey actually read from the textbook. "Just to put to sleep those of us who are still awake," was how Herbie Freilich put it.

Mr. Tobey made a choking sound but then cleared his throat. The sound reminded Arthur of his father's habit of throat clearing, though Arthur didn't think that Mr. Tobey had a sinus condition. Mr. Tobey had a teacher-as-pontificator condition. "Edward, I appreciate your thoughts but I don't think you understand."

"I do understand, Mr. Tobey. I understand very well. That's why I said what I said."

John Silverman motioned to Arthur to view his Impala. He was doing the hubcaps, which featured a lot of ray-like lines around the perimeter. It was slow going. In some ways Silverman was impetuous, but in others he was methodical.

"Well, Edward, to put it bluntly, we all could have been incinerated. That's something to care about."

"That's what I *am* talking about. I can't eat a crab cake in places in this city and I'm going to be blown up because I'm an American. It doesn't seem fair." Arthur could only see the back of Edward's head but he knew Edward was smiling his take-that-you-ignoramus smile.

Herbie looked up from his tome. "Rockefeller's bought up all the refineries in Cleveland," he whispered to Arthur. "I give Tobey a minute, maybe two, before he blows his stack."

"We're all in this together as Americans." Mr. Tobey gestured at the presidents above the side blackboard.

"I don't see any Negro faces there," Edward replied.

"Wish I had a finer lead for my pencil," Silverman said to Arthur.

"You're doing a fine job, Silverman. You're an artist," Arthur said.

"That doesn't mean, Edward, that we aren't all Americans who have shared in the American experience." Mr. Tobey's voice had gotten louder.

Someone in the back of the room softly swore.

"If you call being left out 'sharing,' then I respectfully disagree with you, Mr. Tobey." Edward tapped a pencil on his desk for emphasis.

"Tobey goes over the edge — now," Herbie muttered.

Arthur nodded. Rebecca's body had come up in his mind again. Or it had never left.

"Edward, this is getting us nowhere. I was pointing out to the class" — and Mr. Tobey waved an arm at the other boys — "that history is now. We have lived through a historic moment."

"Yeah, Edward," said Bob Caramullo, a starting linebacker on the varsity team who sat over by the window. "It was a historic moment. And we didn't get fried." He started chuckling.

Arthur nodded again to Herbie but this nod meant *Caramullo is psycho.*

Herbie nodded back in agreement.

"I've spoken my piece," Edward said.

Arthur thought of Seeley's voice and then the voice of Martin Luther King Jr. Were Negroes the only people in America who had any dignity?

"I agree with Edward," Arthur announced.

"Who asked you?" said Caramullo.

"Now boys, boys, easy does it." Mr. Tobey walked over to the row of seats by the windows. "A classroom is a place for give and take. All opinions are welcome here."

"Look at that hubcap." Silverman was almost crowing. He held up the paper to examine it better. "Damn!"

"What was that, Mr. Silverman?" Mr. Tobey asked.

"Nothing, sir. Just following the discussion."

"Well, that's good. Now, today we are going to learn about the women's suffrage movement and Susan B. Anthony."

"Did someone say 'women'?" Caramullo asked. He leered appropriately.

Arthur looked out the window. The leaves were gone. A few clouds were scudding across the unincinerated city. Several nights ago he had a nuclear bomb nightmare. What he recalled were people running down a street and screaming; their mouths open like the gate to hell. But soundless, the way screaming was sometimes in dreams. He kept waiting to hear something but it never happened.

Mr. Tobey was pointing at some dot in New York State on a map in the front of the room. Arthur didn't wish anything. This class would end. It always did, even if Arthur didn't believe in *always* anymore.

Susan

She should have said "no" to Lu. She should have said that her husband was away on a business trip and it was a Friday night and she was tired from teaching all week and all she wanted to do was stay home and read about the painter Manet. She knew if she said that, though, Lu would tell her that was all the more reason to come by and have a drink or two with Lu's current boyfriend and "put on a happy face."

Lu's boyfriend, a genial guy in his forties who sold cars for a living, tried to put a happy face on everything. He told jokes, one after another: three-guys-go-into-a-bar jokes and two-lawyers-meet-St.-Peter jokes and little-Jimmy jokes. Between drinking strong highballs and listening to punch lines, Susan felt her sense of where she was and what she was doing begin to waver and dissolve. It hadn't happened in a long time, but she was drunk. She even started laughing at the jokes, as when little Jimmy kept pointing at insects and truncating their names so that when a cockroach ran across the kitchen floor and he said to his mother, "Will you look at that big cock," Susan whooped.

As the night wore on, however, and as Lu and the salesman kept trading longer and more suggestive looks with one another, and as the jokes became one relentless skein in which little Jimmy met St. Peter in a bar, Susan felt ill. She looked at the bottom of her third tall glass and the salted peanuts in a ceramic dish that had "Ocean City, Maryland" inscribed on its side and the salesman's glistening forehead and Lu's bullet bra asserting itself beneath Lu's thin sweater and she felt that she was going to start crying. Or screaming. Or heaving. She managed to get up from the couch and wish the lovebirds good-night and stumble back up the street to her house and bedroom.

Lu wasn't ignorant. She knew that "business trip" could

be a euphemism, that it likely *was* a euphemism. She could sniff "man trouble" a downtown block away. When, just two days before, Susan came through the front door, it was not surprising that Lu stepped back and said, "That bad, huh?" Lu even wrinkled her nose. Maybe people were more like dogs and cats than they liked to think. Susan had reprimanded a student the other day for using the word "bitch" in the hallway. "But it's in the dictionary, Mrs. M," he said in his defense. "That's no excuse," she replied. He shook his head — that you-can't-win-with-teachers shake. Bitches in heat and prowling tom cats — who was she, lying in an empty bed, to deny it?

Susan turned over on her side. No natural sleep was forthcoming. Her stomach felt as if she had swallowed several pieces of glass. Had she lost her husband? She had seen his secretary, who had long nails that could rake down a man's body and make him cry out in sweet pain.

Susan held out her own hands in the dark. She hadn't had a manicure in years. Lu chided her for neglecting herself: a woman's nails were part of a woman's power over men. Susan had laughed.

The man who hummed the upbeat, 1942 innocence of "I've Heard That Song Before" was gone. He wasn't humming any tunes anymore, at least not to Susan. Maybe the impasse about moving into a new house was his way of telling her he didn't want to move anywhere with her. Men were like that. They didn't know why they said what they said, but that didn't mean there weren't reasons.

The house's silence lulled her, then put her on edge. Arthur had gone to see that long movie about D-Day with a couple of his friends. Tomorrow he would tell her what he felt he should tell her — that and nothing more. Her girls were starting to be like that, too — more in their own worlds. Only Ruby let everything out. And even Ruby sealed off parts of her woe. She had not pronounced the name of Susan's father in decades.

She wanted to talk to someone. It was three fifteen in the morning and she was awake and she wanted to talk to someone. That didn't seem like a lot to ask.

She could smell her husband's scent on the sheets, both

salty and earthy — but no husband.

No sleep either.

There must be a dream for her to walk into like a museum of art, like a palace, like an office or school on a Sunday morning when no one is there, everything in place and waiting to be noticed. There must be a dream for a woman in the middle of the night still tipsy and feeling her stomach crawling toward her mouth — not a nightmare but a dream.

Stan would show up late tomorrow afternoon and say nothing beyond pleasantries. Stan would show up late tomorrow afternoon and talk about his trip to Philadelphia and tell Susan a funny story about an incident in an elevator or having lunch with a client, and then smile at her appreciatively and say how glad he was to be home. Stan would not show up. He would call and say that he was detained. Or that he was not coming home for a while. Or he would not show up or call. The phone would sit there on the table in the downstairs hallway — a relic and silent admonition.

Susan rolled over, away from the scent.

There must be a dream she could walk into. She didn't need a new dress for it or new shoes. She didn't need a code word. She didn't need to know anyone she didn't already know. She didn't even need a manicure. Someone would greet her and tell her that everything was fine because everything was fine — a roof over her head, three beautiful children, a profession she cherished.

But someone else, someone like Lu, would say, "Who are you kidding? What are you doing in this dream? Scram!"

Susan started, although she had not dozed. Her skin felt prickly and cold. It was November. She needed to tell Seeley to get another blanket out.

Blanket.

Susan saw it — the blanket she had on her bed when she was a girl. It had four stripes on it. Someone told her it was a Hudson's Bay blanket. She remembered looking it up — where Hudson's Bay was. They didn't own an atlas. They didn't own many books at all — *David Copperfield* and a book of stories by Sholem Aleichem were the two she remembered best, but down the hall from them lived an old Scotsman who had a beautiful atlas from the 1920s. She remembered that Canada was colored pink. Why were certain countries given certain colors in the atlas? How had Ruby gotten that blanket? What colors were the stripes?

She had never been to Canada. She had never been to France. She had been to Florida with Stan before Arthur was born. She had never been to California. She had been to New York City several times. She liked Chinatown and the Staten Island ferry.

She wanted someone to touch her and love her, right now. If she wasn't going to sleep and dream, she wanted that.

There was someone who could do that, but she hadn't the courage to pick up a phone and tell him there was a world beyond what her ever-wary mother said in passing in a coffee shop, there was a world where the two of them could sit down and get to know one another. And, yes, she knew that he was married and she was married, but that didn't mean that there weren't surprises in this world. Literature, as she liked to tell her students, quoting a professor of hers, was "the art of surprise." She was the one who prized imagination. That was why she taught the books she taught.

She lay on her back and tried to imagine what it would be like to have Jarvis's body on top of hers, the force of him bearing into her. She scrunched her eyes shut to see better in her mind's eye, but when she opened them again after some seconds there were only the dark room and the feeling that she had lost her way and not noticed, that she was grasping at ridiculous straws.

Morning was far off.

Slowly Susan pulled the blanket off. She sat on the edge of the bed but didn't move. Her stomach felt pukish. Her head hurt. She felt for her bedroom slippers. She didn't want to turn her bedside light on. Even though no one was up, she didn't want anyone to see her like this.

She kicked the slippers away and rose from the bed. Quietly she opened the bedroom door and tiptoed to the bathroom. The feel of the carpet under her bare feet was delicious. She felt weightless.

Lu had told her there was a newer pill, a better pill. What

, its name? It was something scientific sounding. It began .th an *L*. Lu said experts recommended it. There were ads for it everywhere, Lu said, like the ads that Milton Berle made for Miltown. Uncle Miltie. He was a funny man, funnier than Little Jimmy jokes.

I live to laugh and I laugh to live.

Susan flicked on the fluorescent light above the medicine cabinet. In the mirror she looked as pale as a sheet of writing paper. Her eyes were craters. Maybe she should put on some lipstick. She thought of the pensive woman in the Manet painting, at once looking out at the world and into herself. You felt her presence, how her abundant flesh possessed an endangered soul, how despair and competence both could be calm, how her face was attentive yet dreamy. She would have to show a reproduction to Lu sometime. Or she should talk with Julia about it. Julia would know the painting. She would understand how the woman called to her.

But what did it matter? What did her reading about the lives of the artists and looking at their paintings do for her? She was still who she was — a half-orphan rattling around in her half-life.

She was falling. She was standing there in the bathroom but she was falling. And she wanted to fall further and not stop falling. It wasn't a bad thing to be falling.

Susan opened the medicine cabinet. A brownish, congealed scrim coated the cap of Arthur's tube of acne cream. A hard white stick of something — it almost looked like a pencil — lay on its side. Stan applied it to his face if he cut himself shaving. There were three brands of aspirin plus one of children's aspirin. Listerine in two sizes. And a bottle of milk of magnesia.

Jarvis Baker's hands came to her again. She envisioned them striking the keys, their delicacy and force. She wanted to hold that sight, hear the music once more, but another scene invaded her ragged mind: Sid Colvin in the hallway one day after school telling her that there might be a nuclear war, and her standing there and having no response but boredom, so sick of the din of men and the ministrations of terror that all she could do was yawn.

It's funny how a theme / Recalls a favorite dream.

She was falling. She was sick of everyone's words. She was sick of her own. Sick and tired.

She placed both hands on the edge of the sink and kept them there. The cold tiles didn't feel as kind on her feet as the carpeted hall had felt. She raised a hand and took the bottle of her pills from its place on the right side of the middle shelf. She paused, then gave the bottle a little rattling shake. She unscrewed the top and looked in. There were plenty.

Arthur

"Arthur, what's all this hush-hush about you asking to see me and talk? I feel like Eustacia having an assignation." Rebecca resumed trying to drink her milk shake through a straw. The straw emitted a blobby, stifled sound.

"Read's makes a thick shake, huh?" Arthur said. He sat across from her in a booth in the soda fountain area of the drugstore.

"I don't like to just glug down a milk shake. I'm a lady." Rebecca put her glass down and wriggled a bit to apprise Arthur of her ladyness. "Anyhow, you must have something on your mind. Or maybe your getting me here was just a pretext because you're so crazy about me and want to see me every minute you can. Even in public places." She thrust a demonstrative hand at the rest of the store. "Maybe we could shop together for Q-tips."

"Something bad happened to my mom." Arthur averted his face so that he was talking more to the wall of the booth than to Rebecca.

"She hasn't been in school."

"You're right. She hasn't."

"Do you want to tell me why?"

"I do but I can't." Arthur kept his face averted.

One of the milk shake machines behind the soda counter began to make its whirring noise.

"Look at me, Arthur. It's okay to cry if you need to. I can hear it in your voice. I've cried an ocean, maybe two." Rebecca hunched forward.

Slowly Arthur turned to her. He felt like a marionette, a heap of limbs and strings. "That's kind of you." His words were wobbly. He paused and breathed in. "How do you do it? Live without your mom."

"Oh, Arthur, is it that kind of bad for you? Your mom's not dead is she? God forbid." She slid her hands toward him. "Hold my hands."

"If I touch you, I'm going to bawl. I don't want to do that." Arthur shook his head as if to ward off his tears. "But no, she's alive. She's going to be okay." He looked down at Rebecca's thin hands. She had on some shade of red fingernail polish. He couldn't fathom how women sorted out all those colors.

"That's a relief, Arthur. But for me, you know that . . ." Rebecca stopped and stared into space.

Arthur waited for her to continue. He hadn't meant to put Rebecca on the spot but the spot was there, staring back at them.

Other conversations and noises—the clatter of plates, a cash register's buttons being pushed—were going on around them, but a voice was speaking directly to them. Arthur felt himself trying, through the welter of his feelings, to get the voice into focus. It was like trying to adjust a blurry TV. There was a girl standing next to their booth, though, and she was speaking.

"Well, isn't this something, here in Read's Drugstore, two sweethearts sharing shakes? Rebecca, you didn't tell me about this guy." The blond teenage girl smiled violently, then gave her carefully combed hair a careless toss. She began to toy with the tiny links of a gold necklace.

Rebecca turned her face away.

The girl continued to pose.

Arthur said nothing. It wasn't as though she had introduced herself to him. Or cared to know who he was.

The girl gave her necklace one more casually ostentatious touch. "I don't want to be interrupting anything important." Her smile had turned to a simper. "I'm here to get something for my mom. You know how that is—parents." She gave an emphatic sigh and then nodded, as if pronouncing a blessing. "So good to see you, Rebecca." She turned to walk away but not before giving her hair another practiced toss.

"Ever want to kill someone?" Rebecca asked.

"I can't stand the New York Yankees, but I never wanted to kill any of them."

"Guys have it easy, Arthur. They just knock each other down and then get up. Girls knock each other down with words. They don't shut up. And you can't fall down because if you do, they won't let you back up." Rebecca drew her lips together and frowned. "You don't have to know her name, but last week she came up to me in the lunchroom and told me how much she liked my 'hand-me-downs,' how 'quaint' they were." Rebecca paused. "She smiled then too, like she was doing me a favor. Acknowledging that I existed — what a favor."

Arthur put his hands on top of Rebecca's.

"I told her I made my own clothes, thank you very much." Rebecca smiled a bleak smile. "I'm going to have to do everything on my own. To make my way in this world I'm going to have to do everything on my own. No one is going to help me."

Arthur framed the sides of Rebecca's face with his hands. "I think no one is going to help me, either." He tipped his head forward and brushed his forehead against hers.

For a time, the arch their heads formed stayed in place. Then Rebecca drew back.

"You haven't told me what happened," she said, "but I can guess. I can guess a lot of bad things. I'm good at it. Life's giving me lots of practice. Plus there are the books I read." Rebecca looked around vacantly. Her eyes were misty.

"It's bad. I knew you . . ." Arthur couldn't go on. The suffering inside him had gotten keener, but that wasn't Rebecca's fault. He had wanted to talk with her about what his mother had done. He had to talk with someone. And even though he could barely say anything, she understood. He could feel, though, how suffering didn't stop with him. It had no borders. Like a flooded river it spilled out, not just over his heart but other people's hearts, too. And his mother was alive. It wasn't like what had happened to Rebecca.

"I guess we should drink our milk shakes," Arthur said.

"I guess we should. It was sweet of you to treat me, Arthur. Unlike some people, you have some manners." Rebecca was crying but her face seemed more distracted than miserable. The tears seemed an afterthought.

Arthur stared at his glass. "Wow, this is tough."

"This is tough," Rebecca repeated. She brushed delicately at her tears, then a smile began to glimmer.

In some of the songs Arthur had been listening to, the men said they would do anything for their women. It was starting to make sense to him.

"Maybe that's what God said after he made the world. 'Wow, this is tough.'" Rebecca shook her head in perplexed wonder.

"It's probably not in the Torah." Arthur put a hand on Rebecca's cheek. "If you're here in the world, it can't be too tough."

"That's probably more the milk shake in front of you than me. But I'll take the compliment." Rebecca dipped her head toward the straw and began to suck.

Out of the corner of his eye Arthur saw the blond girl. She had been watching them. He didn't want to kill her but he wouldn't have minded if the floor of Read's Drugstore gave way and she fell forever.

Susan

"You hear what she did to herself?"

"Tricia down in Emergency told me. Sad story."

"Not the first, not the last."

"Doesn't make it less sad, though."

Susan wanted to sit up but a weight on her head kept her down. The room was dark. It was night. Or it was day and the blinds were shut tight.

"What they have her on?"

"The usual. They knock themselves out with one thing. We knock 'em out with something else."

Susan had been left behind. She was a little girl and there was a class trip. The school bus had taken off and she was left in the classroom by herself. She tried the door but it was locked from the outside.

"Any special mess to clean up?"

"Maybe her soul."

"I've done harder. Where'd you get those shoes? They look comfortable."

"Same place you buy yours. One of those Jew stores downtown."

Susan could see herself in a yellow dress she had liked when she was in the fourth grade. Ruby had sewn it. It had a little vest that went with it. She wore it on special days. But what were her special days?

"Probably has children."

"Unh-unh. What kind of mother does something like that?"

"You seen her life from the inside?"

"That's you, always looking at the other side. Some things don't have other sides."

"It may not be good but there's another side."

A phone rang down the hall.

"I can't imagine getting that miserable. I'd go out and have some fun."

"Fun can wear a person out much as work."

"I'd like to try."

The two voices laughed.

Susan had left the childhood classroom. She was in what everyone called "the real world," in a hospital, in a bed. She would leave soon. She would have to talk to her daughters, her mother, her son. Her husband. She would have to tell some friends. She would have to lie to many people. Or she wouldn't lie but would endure their glances. *Do you know what she did?* She wanted to start speaking now. When she tried to clear her throat, she made a dry rattling sound.

"That her snoring?"

"Could be. People snore different. My husband's like wind through a tunnel."

"Men are like locomotives."

"I don't mind it if they put the energy into other nighttime activities."

"Nighttime activities—that's a fancy way of talking."

"I'm a fancy girl."

The voices laughed again but more raucously.

Susan couldn't move. It didn't matter. Her voice was lost. She had lost everything except for these two women talking.

"You never know with these cases. Some of them are bound to do it. There's no stopping them. And some of them turn the corner."

"And what do you think about this one?"

"I think we should take our break now."

Two sets of feet shuffled from the room. A heavy door closed.

Susan saw the faces of her daughters and her son sitting at the kitchen table, looking at her. She wanted to cry but couldn't. She saw her face at the table, too. There were tears on it. In the sightless dark that reassured her.

1963

When Edward informed Arthur that "a group" was going to picket Mr. Schwartz's office and asked whether he wanted to be part of it, since Arthur had told Edward that he understood there was more to do about civil rights than offer an opinion in Mr. Tobey's history class, Arthur had the presence of mind to reply with nothing more than a semi-interrogative "really" and let Edward speak more about why his boss from last summer had been targeted. And, after a tilt of the head that Edward favored as a means of making someone know that he was fixing his total attention on the person, Edward explained that the intent of the picketing was to call attention not just to discrimination but to people who were taking advantage of Negroes, people who were going about "their daily business of keeping Negroes down." And he told Arthur that the demonstration offered him a chance at "something like atonement." Harry Schwartz was no longer just a name to Edward.

They went back and forth about it, with Edward mentioning the chance of their being arrested and Arthur saying that his father knew a bail bondsman. When Arthur agreed to it, Edward made a crack about needing "some white legs." "Could be a new baseball team," Arthur replied.

Walking back and forth on the North Avenue sidewalk in front of the H & B Real Estate Corporation with a sign in his hands—"Fair Housing for All"—Arthur didn't feel he was atoning (that was Edward ringing his bell the way Edward liked sometimes to ring his bell)—but he did feel he was part of a history beyond Mr. Tobey's blather. A dozen or so other people—including a few other white people—were also there. Some cars slowed down to look at the protesters and their placards; more cars—most, in fact—went by without a look. No newspaper reporters from the dailies or TV cameras were present, nor were there any police. This was between the group of message bearers and Mr. Harry Schwartz, who presumably was sitting inside, overseeing his empire of rowhouses.

Arthur had told his father that he had something important to do after school with a girl. He was seeing Rebecca more and more and was coming to understand that his father would cut him some slack in that department. "A woman is no small thing in a man's life," he had said to Arthur and given him a playful tap to his shoulder. His father wasn't one to bestow playful taps. Arthur wondered what was happening in his father's life, but there was no asking about that. Whatever your parents served, you took. His mother had her stomach pumped; his father stayed away from the house some nights; but no answers were forthcoming from either of them. Neither one was talking about separation. It was strange, how you lived right up close to people, the very people who literally made you, and you knew so little about them. Maybe that was healthy. Sometimes, if you were honest about it, you didn't want to know.

The five o'clock sun reflected wanly off the plate-glass window of Mr. Schwartz's enterprise. The name of his company was written in an elaborate serif that took up the top third of the window. Arthur had learned one day while driving with his boss that the B in H & B stood for Blanche, Mr. Schwartz's wife who had died years ago. Arthur had difficulty imagining Harry Schwartz being married. His wife may have been his accomplice, though. "Like attracts like," Grandpa Max used to say while ogling Bertha. "H & B": people could share darkness, too.

A young woman who was carrying a sign identical to Arthur's came up to him. "Are you Susan Mermelstein's son?" she asked. The woman had a long braid and very pale skin. She wore jeans that had various streaks and blobs of paint on them. Not long ago Arthur and his father had argued about wearing jeans. Stan thought they were "unacceptable." Arthur asked him, "Unacceptable for what?" Stan answered, "For being my son." Then he said, "Next question?" A guy in Arthur's sophomore-year physical education class claimed to have slugged his own father. It seemed that at some point you had to do that, that you could only put up with "next question" for so long.

"Yeah, I am," said Arthur to the woman in jeans. He lowered his sign slightly.

"I know your mom. I go to the Institute of Art and she teaches with the guy I live with. I know she's had some troubles but she's a cool lady. You're lucky to have her for your mom."

"Yeah, I am." Arthur hunched over. He wished the woman would go away. Talking about your mother to a stranger was embarrassing. He kept his head down. "Let's hope we accomplish something today."

The young woman did a sidestep so she could speak to Arthur's face. "Every time white and colored people get together in public to protest, it accomplishes something. Every single time."

When he looked up, he saw the young woman's face, but beyond the startling color of her eyes, which were like jewels of some kind, maybe emeralds, he saw the squat eminence of Harry Schwartz advancing toward him.

The picketers parted to let the landlord through. The young woman stepped back. She was light on her feet. Maybe she was a dancer, Arthur thought, while in the same mental moment he was falling into that uncanny stillness of the-world-has-stopped. That was how it was when the robber pulled out the gun or when Rebecca told him her mother was dead or when he stood outside his parents' bedroom door that morning back in November and heard his mother fall to the floor.

The stillness wouldn't last. He had come to learn that. Whatever terror informed it, the moment was still a moment. If he looked around, he would see cars carrying people on their way home from work. If he looked up into the pale spring sky, he was likely to see birds flocking and preparing to roost. That reassured him. Not many feet away, a Negro woman pulling a wheeled wire cart laden with groceries navigated around the protesters. She walked heavily but steadily.

"So, *boychik*, what brings you here? I didn't pay you enough last summer? Or you have decided that the root of race problems is someone who actually has something to do with Negroes. Is *that* what you believe?" Mr. Schwartz was right in Arthur's face but his voice was calm, almost bemused. He could have been reciting the names of horses to another railbird at Pimlico.

Before Arthur could reply, Edward was speaking. "I'm one of the organizers of this protest, Mr. Schwartz, and a reporter for the *Afro-American*. It's come to the attention of the community that you are not giving the community what it deserves for what it is paying you. We are here this afternoon to let the world know that and to create some dialogue with you."

"'Dialogue'?" The word came out thick with saliva and disdain. "I can call the police on you people, and you want 'dialogue'?" He turned from Edward to Arthur. "What is it with the world? I haven't been through enough *tsuris*?"

"Things have to change, Mr. Schwartz." Arthur stood up as straight as he could. His sport jacket had gotten tight on him.

"Change? What else does life do? Am I standing on a muddy road in Galicia? Am I waiting for the czar or the kaiser to start a war?" A tremor had come into his voice. "Answer me. Any of you." He pivoted to face the small group around him who were listening. "Answer me."

"I can answer you, sir," Edward began. "We've had enough and we won't be denied. How it looks from where you are standing and where we are standing is very different. Arthur is right. Change has to come. You can't go on charging people for houses that don't meet the standards of the day."

"Standards? What are you saying? You probably don't know what a furnace looks like or how much a plumber costs," Mr. Schwartz said. "You probably keep your nose in a book like my friend Arthur. You probably think you know something." Mr. Schwartz turned slowly to examine each face gathered around him. "I have no doubt that you are good people. But you are wrong to be here today and hold these signs up in front of my place of business. You are wrong. Do you hear me? What you are doing is what Hitler did. Maybe you have heard of *Kristallnacht*. Maybe Hitler is more than a name to you."

Edward cleared his throat but said nothing. The woman with the long braid who knew Arthur's mother was buttoning the front of her cardigan. It was going to be a cool night.

"This has nothing to do with Hitler, Mr. Schwartz. Do you understand? Not everything has to do with Hitler. To make everything come back to Hitler is nuts." Arthur moved toward his former boss as the others moved away. "Nothing can get better if we stay stuck in the past. That's why we're here today." Arthur paused. "And don't throw our words back at us."

Mr. Schwartz reached out to Arthur and put his hands on Arthur's shoulders. "You're a well-meaning boy, Arthur, but—"

Arthur yanked the old man's hands away. "Don't tell me I'm a boy! And don't say 'but'! I hate it, how there's always a *but*. I don't want there to be any more *buts*. We're choking to death on *buts*." Arthur's throat burned. He was yelling.

The ever-melancholy look in Mr. Schwartz's eyes became even more so. The landlord walked away a few steps but then turned to address the little band of protesters. "I wonder some days why I came to America. I know why, of course. I was brought here to live, that was the first thing, to live, and to have an opportunity. Even as a boy I understood that." He halted; his words had come out slowly. "And I have had an opportunity. I appreciate that. But every day it pains me how little the good people in this country understand anything. It pains me how much they are fools. It pains me that they have nothing better to do than stand outside my office holding up signs and pretending they are doing something important." He looked up, searching the twilight sky as if it might have something to tell him. Then he looked across the street. "You'll excuse me. I have a bank deposit to make." He nodded to no one in particular. Like a second thought, the tails of his suit jacket flapped behind him.

"What you said, Arthur, is the truth. Don't take it too hard." The woman with the braid was speaking.

"Julia's right, Merm," Edward said. "All this Hitler stuff, your boss is lost in the past. That's how it is. So many people are lost in the past."

An older Negro man, his hair gray at the temples, came up beside Edward. "I'm Ralph Jenkins from the NAACP. This man, Harry Schwartz, has been on our list of out-and-out slumlords for a long time. We have got to make this public. Nothing changes if it isn't public."

Arthur nodded, though he hadn't heard much of what was being said. He was still back with Mr. Schwartz. The look in those eyes had been more than sadness. There was the wound of betrayal, too. Probably word would get back to Stan from Mr. Schwartz: "So, did you know your *boychik* was parading outside my office with a sign the other afternoon? Is that how you raised him?" Those were questions but they would not be questions. They would be accusations.

"Merm, are you listening to us?" Edward took off his glasses and stepped up to Arthur. "We're saying that you did the right thing. We're saying that if you don't confront people, they aren't going to change."

"I heard you," Arthur answered. Gently he pushed Edward back. "I heard you."

Susan held on tightly to her pocketbook, a black leather bag Lu had given her for her birthday a few years ago. No one was going to take the bag from her but it was comforting to grip. Some of her life was inside the bag, including a container of tranquillizers. She was ashamed of what she had done — she had told her mother and her daughters she had gotten sick, and the confused and hurt look in their eyes said "Tell the truth" — but she couldn't. She left it at that, which meant there was another shame on her. Yet there was no leaving it at that. Her husband and son both knew; she had told Lu and Julia outright. What came over her that night seemed impromptu, some bottom note calling her that never had called before. But as the weeks and months went by and she returned to her life, assuring everyone that she was fine — regular and normal — she understood that it hadn't been impromptu at all.

In the first session with the psychiatrist with whom she was working she explained that her father had abandoned her mother and her. That absence was her foundation. Nothing — not even the love she felt for her children — could change that. When something shifted in the fabric she had created — whether caused by suspicion about her husband, which she told the psychiatrist about, or longing for another man, which she didn't — she was in peril. The thought depressed her. She seemed permanently vulnerable, one of those doomed souls Thomas Hardy wrote about. When she went to the museum a week or so ago, she couldn't even look at the paintings. It was absurd but she felt she had betrayed them. She walked out, stood on the museum's front steps, and smoked a cigarette to calm down. It didn't work.

The Calvert Street office of James Millman, Certified Marriage Counselor, was somewhere between sterile and indifferent. There was no artwork, not even a reproduction, on the plaster walls, nor were there any photographs of anyone on the large steel desk Susan was seated in front of. Maybe that was intentional. Maybe Mr. Millman didn't want to put too much of himself, beyond a few framed degrees, in front of his clients. Or maybe he had no imagination. Susan didn't want to think that because she wanted to hear someone with some imagination talk about what she and her husband could do about their marriage. She and Stan weren't doing a very good job of it—she knew that.

Since her overdose Stan had wavered between solicitous and wary. Neither attitude helped much. When he was solicitous, asking how she was and what she was doing, it felt insincere, more that he was concerned about her being crazy than about loving her, more that he feared she was going to make more trouble. When he was wary, it felt the same. She felt like a specimen or a social-work case rather than a wife. They made love a few times in the fragile weeks after she came home from the hospital, and those times had been tender and hopeful, but after those weeks, after she re-entered the workaday world, they returned to a peck on the cheek and being tired at night. Her marriage was the way it was before—that was her doing too, she knew that—but Susan wasn't sure if she should leave it, to say nothing of how to leave it. Slamming the front door with a suitcase in her hand wasn't going to do it. Then what?

She had been talking to Julia on the phone. Though Julia was much younger than Susan, she seemed to understand in a way that Lu, despite her experience, didn't. It was Julia who suggested the marriage counselor. Though the idea of talking about their troubles to a stranger, however much of an expert, didn't appeal to Stan, Susan was forthright: if he couldn't bother to talk with a third party, then why were they living together? She knew he hated questions like that. He somehow wanted nothing to happen. He somehow wanted to live in a state of suspended animation, dangling in the current of life. She didn't say that to Stan, though. He would have dismissed such thoughts as "poetic." Perhaps they were.

Mr. Millman was a pudgy, balding man who spoke very deliberately but had a lisp that turned s into sh. As she clutched her pocketbook and looked at him rather than her husband beside her, Susan thought there was something comic about him, as if he were mocking his professional gravity. She tried to straighten up in her cushioned armchair but felt herself sinking more than rising.

After informational pleasantries, the marriage counselor asked them each for a brief summary of why they were there. Stan explained that his wife had tried to kill herself and that he was worried for her. "And for our children," he added. When asked about how he felt, he replied, "How am I supposed to feel?" He felt "disturbed." He called himself "a straight-ahead guy." "This is new territory for me," he said. He leaned forward to emphasize his point. His voice had been steady but now it had a blur in it: "new" meant "scary."

Mr. Millman took notes on a legal pad but was silent except for an occasional "I shee" or "Could you shay more about that?" Susan appreciated that. The rumors about what happened to her had elicited more than enough bracing consolation. Cathy Ramsdell had come up to her in the teachers' room, thrown a palsy-walsy arm around her, and announced with stagey bravado that Susan would "get through this." After a few lost seconds, Susan mumbled some chipper adage. What she should have said was, "What the hell do you know?" She had come to despise the cheapness of optimism. The more people tried to cheer her up, the angrier she felt.

She intended to let Mr. Millman hear some of that anger and some of the guilt burning inside her. The sessions with the psychiatrist hadn't changed her status as a mother who had attempted suicide. She had been grateful for the psychiatrist's ever-reasonable words but they didn't exculpate her. It was hard to imagine what could — or whether anything should.

Still, she had come to this office today to talk about how things were for her. She told the marriage counselor about how she wanted to move because it was too crowded in their house and the neighborhood was changing and how she was sick of bickering about money because they had enough money to buy a house but her husband refused. She told him how she was the one who had to deal with everyone in the house plus teaching and how she was weary. She told him that although she tried to be focused each day, she felt lost. She even told him how she admired John F. Kennedy and her husband didn't.

"And this led you—" Mr. Millman started to say.

"This led me to try to kill myself, along with a pile of collateral grief such as my father abandoning my mother and me, and my never getting over it."

Stan looked at her for the first time since they had sat down. "Never getting over it? Something that happened that long ago?"

"Just because I don't talk about it, doesn't mean it's done with."

Mr. Millman raised his pencil as if it were a baton. "It's important here that we hear each other rather than bicker with each other."

"I don't think we're bickering, Mr. Millman. Just trying to make ourselves understood," Susan said.

Stan repeated, as if speaking to himself, "Something that long ago?"

"Often, Mr. Mermelshtein—"

"Call me Stan."

"Fine, Shtan. Often people carry within themselves childhood memories and hurts—we call them 'traumas'—that shtay with people all their lives. Those traumas attach themselves to ush and don't let go." He halted. "Unlesh we tell them to go."

"Tell them?" Susan echoed. "Is it that easy?"

"No, it isn't, but we have to take a poshitive attitude, even about negative things." He lowered his pencil.

Susan attended to the voices of the counselor and her husband but she was drifting. She replied to questions about how she felt now and what she was trying to do in her life, but she noticed how the counselor's tie tack was in the shape of a golf club and how there were spider webs in the corners of the ceiling.

"Susan? Did you hear me?" Stan was peering at her. His face was part concerned, part petulant.

"I need to say something," Susan answered. "To both of you. It's that I don't think there's any 'because' about me, as in 'I tried to kill myself because . . .' The fact is I was wrong about what I said about my father. I don't think there's a reason for what I did that I can put into a sentence or two. I'm unhappy. I have plenty of good things in my life. I know that. I do. But I'm unhappy. And what I don't know is what to do about it."

"Well, that's why we're here today," Stan said.

Susan turned toward her husband. "Are you having an affair? Tell me the truth."

"No." After he said the word, Stan looked away from her.

"Maybe that's why I'm unhappy." Susan leaned over, put her pocketbook on the carpet next to her seat, and straightened herself up. "I don't believe you." Both men looked harder at her as if expecting her to say something more.

She didn't. However insufferable or just plain wrong her words were, she wasn't taking them back. She had said the words in front of someone else; it didn't matter whether or not he was one more keeper of the mental gates in a miserable, light-starved room that smelled like an old closet. When she had looked at the pills that night, the moments had caught up with her. Now she felt a moment releasing her. It seemed like magic — but hard-won magic. She almost smiled.

"I can't make you believe me," Stan answered. "I shouldn't have to, either. I'm your husband. I care about you."

Susan didn't reply. The wanton impulse to smile kept leaping around inside her.

"We aren't going to shee closure on thish today," the counselor said.

"That's good," Susan said. "We need to get all this out into the open."

"What's 'all this?' I told you I'm not having affair. I have business meetings in D.C. and Philly and they keep me overnight. I'm working hard for my family."

"No one accused you of not working hard. Just give me a phone number where I can reach you," Susan said.

Stan didn't reply. He tugged at one of the lapels of his sport jacket.

"You know, Mr. Millman," Susan said, "Your office is a little dingy. You might want to get on a ladder and clean those cobwebs. People might get the wrong idea about your line of work."

The counselor's mild eyes drifted upward. Susan rose in her seat. "Let's go, oh possible adulterer of mine. Our time here is up."

Stan nodded toward the man behind the steel desk — *see what I'm up against.* When he turned toward his wife, she was gone.

Arthur

"I know we haven't talked much lately, Arthur," Susan said.

Arthur continued to adjust the rearview to his satisfaction.

For a change Susan was seated on the passenger side. Under her feet were some chewing gum wrappers and old grocery lists. Seeley's neat cursive could be discerned, along with Susan's scrawl. His mother typically kept her car immaculate. It would take ten minutes to clean up but she hadn't found those minutes yet in the months since "the incident," as his father called it, as if a spaceship had crashed in their backyard. That was how it went. Susan was still his mother but in some ways, "incident" ways, she wasn't. Or she wasn't the mother she used to be. She couldn't be.

"That's Dad's line, Mom. You don't want to be taking his line. Then he'll have nothing to say." Arthur started the car, then let it idle for some seconds. "Your engine sounds a little rough. When's the last time you had the plugs changed?"

"I haven't been to the garage in a while." Susan looked blankly at her son. Arthur noticed how dark the rings under her eyes were. She hadn't put on that powder she used to cover the rings. They almost looked like bruises.

"Maybe you should think about it." Arthur paused. "You know, you don't have to do this today, Mom — go and buy clothes with me. I'm old enough to buy a shirt on my own."

"Look in your mirrors when you pull out, Arthur," Susan warned. The car was parked in front of the Mermelsteins' house. Few cars went down their quiet street.

"I do, Mom. I'm the one who's driven around East and West Baltimore for days on end. Relax."

"I'll try. It's easier said than done. I . . ." She looked

around vaguely as if unsure where she was.

Arthur stopped at the light at Gwynn Oak and Liberty Heights. He was headed to the Oxford Shop on Greenmount. Rebecca had told him she liked the button-down shirts he wore. If they made Rebecca put her hands on him, he wanted more of them.

"I'm glad to talk, Mom. Why don't you tell me what you did to yourself? Why don't you tell me why you're still living with Dad? Why don't you tell me why we're all walking around in our house acting as though we know what we're doing, when we don't?" Arthur looked over at the marquee on the front of the Ambassador Theater — *Dr. No*, which he'd already seen twice, once with Herbie and some other guys and once with Rebecca. He'd told Rebecca she was sexier than Ursula Andress.

"What happened is what I told you. I accidentally took too many pills to help me sleep. I was disoriented from being up and from drinking at Lu's." She rolled down her window. "It's already getting warm."

"It's been warm before in Baltimore, Mom. Hell learned from Baltimore. Was it an accident? Can I ask you that?" Arthur paused. "Whoops. *May* I ask you that?"

Susan smiled. "You may. It was. Let's let that be the end of it. Fair?"

"Fair — but it doesn't feel like the end of it. It feels like a roll of something that's only been unrolled so much. There's more to unroll." Arthur stopped for another red light. They were about to pass by Jack's Pool Parlor. Silverman and Rick were probably there right now. Rick claimed he wasn't going to go to college, just hustle pool for a living. Silverman said Rick had a five-pound weight between his ears.

"Probably you shouldn't forget," said Susan. "Things that happen that surprise us, we shouldn't forget — good or bad. I just wish . . ."

"Wish what, Mom?"

"Wish that something good would surprise me." Susan looked away from her son, then started crying — not heaving tears and shaking, but crying softly.

"Hey, should I pull over?" Arthur started to move the car toward the curb.

Susan kept crying and nodded her head.

Arthur pulled up behind a Mercury Comet—you didn't see many of that kind of car. Or maybe he just overlooked them. They weren't much to remember. He figured he would be ready in a year or so to buy his own car.

It made him sad when his mother cried. And he didn't want to be sad.

Gradually Susan settled down and blew her nose into a tissue she fished out of her pocketbook. After she used the tissue, she held it away from her as if she wasn't sure what to do with it.

Arthur looked over at his mother. It was frustrating trying to understand her when she didn't seem to know herself what was going on. It wasn't fair. She was the parent. There were rules. She was supposed to know.

"Arthur," Susan said. "How come you haven't told me about the demonstrations you've been involved in? Did you think I'd be angry with you?" Her voice was off-key but determined, like a little girl trying to be a grown-up. She looked at the tissue in her hand and let it fall to the floor.

The questions didn't surprise Arthur. His mom talked on the phone for what seemed like hours with the young woman who went to the Institute of Art. The subject of Arthur and demonstrations had surely come up.

"I didn't want to bother you. I figured you had enough on your mind already." Arthur stretched his arms out in front of him. It felt good to be taller. Seeley assured him that he wasn't done growing: "Plenty of inches still in you." He was going to be over six feet.

"That was thoughtful of you." Susan began to rummage in her pocketbook.

"You need a cigarette, Mom?" Arthur asked. "I've got some Marlboros."

"What shape am I in that my son offers me cigarettes?"

"Question answering a question, Mom, means 'I don't have to answer it.'" For something to do, Arthur waggled his fingers and held the steering wheel by pressing his palms against it.

"What if something happens, when you are picketing?

217

What if someone gets angry and becomes violent?" Susan put her pocketbook down—no cigarettes there.

"Are you telling me I should be afraid?" Arthur raised one hand and snapped his fingers. It was a gesture he'd been working on. "I know I just did what I told you not to do about answering a question. But really—is being afraid a good thing? Doesn't the racial trouble come from fear? We don't know each other—white people and Negroes—and that makes everyone afraid."

"I'm not telling you to be afraid. I'm telling you to be careful."

"I appreciate that, Mom—I do. But the point of the protests anyway is to be careful about how we act. Martin Luther King Jr. is not a careless man. He knows how much hate is out there. James Meredith walking through all those screaming white people in Mississippi is not careless. Careless is the last thing they are. It's everyone else who's careless."

Susan leaned over and began picking up the litter on the car floor. "Do you believe me when I say it was an accident?"

Arthur exhaled—a puff of invisible darkness. "That's not a reply to what I was just talking about, but yes, I do believe it was an accident. I can't imagine you leaving us."

"I can't imagine that, either. I wouldn't. But I keep wondering what the world has to do with me." The words came out like a singsong. Susan sat back up and patted the seat between Arthur and herself with her left hand, as if there were some reassurance in its solidity. She placed a little trash pile on the other side of her.

"Mom, it has everything to do with us—not just stuff like Cuba but like the Negroes who really are a part of this country and who are starting to buy houses in our neighborhood, which I think is great because everyone should be able to live everywhere." Arthur started the car again but didn't pull out. "I want to be part of what the world has to do with us, like Edward, the guy I go to City with, who's a serious character. I like that. It's nothing against my other friends. Herbie's serious. He reads so much history you'd think he was pals with Winston Churchill. But he's not serious the way Edward is."

"I can see why you're doing what you're doing. It's not

that I don't think about the news. All I'm saying is to be careful."

"Look. I'm using the side-view mirror. How careful can a guy be?" Arthur reached toward his shirt pocket. "Want a cigarette, Mom? It seems like you could use one." Arthur pulled out a crumpled soft pack. "You could picket too, Mom."

"You're right," Susan said. "I could."

His mother's words sounded dreamy. Again Arthur thought that she was the parent and had to know more than he knew. That was home base in the game. But he knew, too, that he was not going to forget opening her bedroom door and seeing her lying naked on the floor, not awake and not asleep. She looked like a wounded animal, not his mother.

Susan

"I know you, Susan." Lu gestured not to Susan, who was driving, but to the passenger side window. "You want to keep all the cute men to yourself. I don't believe any of this killing-yourself stuff. You took a couple extra, that's all." She gingerly fingered her bouffant. "I've taken a couple extra, you better believe it." She turned to Susan, her right hand still up against the skyscraper of her hair. "How do I look?"

Susan said nothing. When she had told Lu about the Sunday afternoon get-together at Joe and Julia's, Lu invited herself, telling Susan that she shouldn't be going places alone. Susan hadn't argued the point. Although she was surrounded by people—children, mother, husband, maid, students, fellow teachers—she felt solitary. It wasn't all a bad feeling. Some part of her had emerged from the session with the marriage counselor feeling that she was okay in and of herself. It was strange. She felt she could drift away, though she had no idea where she might drift to. She felt tentative but that was better than numb.

"What do you tell people about what happened to you?" Lu asked.

"Is that your idea of being good company to me?" Susan lifted her hands off the steering wheel for a second and exclaimed, "Oh, boy! What a friend you are!" She put her hands back on and kept talking. "I've already consulted Emily Post about it. 'Tell people you went on a vacation. Immediately change the subject so they don't ask where.'" Susan looked out at the large Tudor-style houses of Roland Park and wondered whether any Jews lived in them. What if she wanted to move there? "No, I didn't consult Emily, even though she knows everything, because people don't ask me straight out. If they did,

I'd tell them I had an accident, because that's the truth. I had an accident."

"Nothing is an accident," Lu declared.

"God, Lu, you sound like some of my students," Susan said. "Maybe you should teach English. Have I talked to you about fate and Thomas Hardy?"

By the time Susan was walking up the winding staircase to Joe's apartment, she had finished relating the plot of *The Return of the Native*. Though she told Lu that the title of the last chapter had the word "cheerfulness" in it and that a wedding occurred, Lu made a face. "What an unhappy book," she said. "I never want to read it. Life's unhappy enough."

As she paused before the apartment door, Susan thought of defending Thomas Hardy. Instead, she raised a hand to knock but the door opened on its own.

"I heard your footsteps. Welcome." Julia opened her arms.

After a hug, Susan took Lu's hand and brought it forward. "This is my neighbor Lu."

"Delighted," Julia said. She and Lu exchanged a look that was friendly but wary. Braid and bouffant were miles apart. Susan had warned Lu that her friends might be considered "arty."

"Susan, so glad you could make—and that you brought a friend," Joe smiled. "I assume she's a friend." He winked.

Right behind Joe was Jarvis Baker. He too was smiling. "You never know with Susan. She keeps her cards close to her chest."

Susan suppressed a sigh. "Do I?" She tried to make her voice bright but it came out gloomy.

"Well, everyone, as Susan's longtime friend I've got to say she can let it all hang out. She can drink with the best of them. She even knows some dirty jokes." Lu, who had taken in Joe's wink, winked back at him. It didn't take Lu long to do her scouting. She had told Susan that "Jarvis Baker is yours but otherwise I'm going to keep my eyes open."

A man joined the knot clustered around Susan and Lu. He wore a blue oxford-cloth shirt, chinos, and sneakers. "Hello, ladies, I'm a teacher at the Institute and a painter. Ned Kimball is the name." He extended a hand to the air in front of him and Lu immediately grasped it.

"Let's move into what I call the living area and what Joe calls the listening area," Julia said. She motioned toward the dilapidated couch and the up-to-date stereo.

"Susan, in your honor, no less, we're listening to Miles," Joe said. He was squiring her, her elbow in his hand. In a lower voice he said, "Your friend's hair-do is a turn-on."

"She attracts men like a magnet. That's her purpose in life. And she enjoys it." Susan turned her head to see Lu smiling her come-hither smile at Ned Kimball. Julia had told her that Ned "went both ways." Susan had to pause a minute to realize what that meant.

"And how are you?" Joe asked. "That's an out-of-school question. You don't have to say that you can't wait for the next pep rally or a chat with Sid about the next crisis of the Free World."

"Did I hear someone say 'Free World'? Where can I join up?" That was Jarvis, who had sat down beside Susan on the couch.

Susan couldn't help but feel his proximity. She could smell him—a light, sweaty musk. A flutter began inside her, precipitate wings trying once more to escape the cage.

"Don't start in on that one, Jarvis," Joe said. "We know that story." He was on his knees sorting through a pile of records. Everyone else had sat down.

"Do you?" Jarvis answered. "Driving here today I drew a very long look from a policeman when I stopped at the light at Roland and 40th. He was just checking me out, a Negro driving in the white zone." Jarvis paused and leaned back. "You never know what mayhem is on a Negro's mind. I carry a few hatchets around in my trunk."

Lu put a startled hand up to her bouffant. "I never thought about it. You mean you have to be careful where you drive?"

"That's one thing I mean, yes."

"That's not right," Julia blurted. "That's why I'm out there with people picketing." She turned to Susan. "Including your son, Susan."

"My son?" Susan asked. She still hadn't gotten control of her voice. It had an ominous edge, as if she were warding off a spirit.

"You didn't know Arthur has been picketing? I thought I told you." Julia frowned.

"You did and I know. He and I have talked about it but . . ." Susan looked around vaguely, as if searching for words.

"Boys," Lu chirped. "They do all kinds of things." She gave Ned Kimball a coy look, then turned back to Susan. "Someone told me Arthur spends his share of time at that pool hall near Garrison Boulevard. Not that there's anything wrong with pool halls." She turned again and eyed Ned. "I like a man who can shoot a game of pool. Those cues are sexy."

At any moment Lu might go into concupiscent orbit. As for Susan, she wanted to fall sideways into Jarvis Baker's lap and let him cradle her bursting head.

"I'd be proud of the boy, Susan," Jarvis said. "He's doing his part. He's standing up for what he believes."

Joe began to wave a record jacket, but Julia cut him off. "You're right, Jarvis. It's easy to feel that Doctor King can do all the work. It's easy to say that things will get better. But look at the Northwood Theater. If the Morgan students and other people hadn't stood outside with signs, if they hadn't gone inside and gotten arrested, it would still be segregated."

"The Northwood wasn't open to Negroes?" Lu asked. "I just saw *Irma la Douce* there. I love Shirley MacLaine. She's so spunky."

For a second, Susan thought Lu was going to get up and do the can-can. "Oh, Lu, to hell with Shirley MacLaine."

Lu took on a pouty look but Susan continued. "I'm proud of Arthur, pool hall notwithstanding. What's been hard to understand is that when one group loses their rights, everyone does. Everyone is lost."

Jarvis raised a hand to testify, then placed it — a friendly, confirming presence — on Susan's knee. "Martin keeps saying it — how everyone loses — but when they tell a Negro where to eat or live or work, white people believe they've won something. What has that policeman today won?" He paused. "You should have seen his eyes. Empty and mean. And mocking."

To Susan the adjectives seemed like bottles on a wall—targets Jarvis was blasting one by one.

"Every Negro knows those eyes. But what every Negro wonders is what they did to deserve those eyes." Jarvis's voice tightened. "I'm sitting in my car with Handel running through my head, conducting, and . . ." He looked away from everyone. "Damn."

Joe began to speak, but again Julia was there before him. "If you try to tell a joke, Joe, I'll brain you. I'm smaller but I'm formidable."

"She wields a mean paintbrush," Ned Kimball added. He had been through more than one conversation like this, but never with an actual Negro present—not that he was going to tell the present company.

"Okay, no jokes." Joe shrugged. "I just don't want Jarvis to feel on the spot. I get nervous when we start to speechify." He stroked the record jacket. "And I have some great music to play for us."

"Speechify—that's something white and black folks can both do." Jarvis said. "Even those southern bastards in the Senate, you have to hand it to them. They can speechify."

"Yes, my fellow senators," Joe began to declaim, "I'd like to comment extemporaneously on several incidents that have come to my attention in recent days this month of May in the year of our Lord 1963 that have been reported in the press in my home state of Alabama, fairly and judiciously I might add, and that have drawn attention in the, shall I say, liberal northern press that seeks to portray police dogs and nightsticks and tear gas not as friends of the Negroes, whom we cherish as our unofficial chattel, but . . ."

"Joe!" Julia shouted through a giggle.

Jarvis took the moment to remove his hand that had lingered on Susan's knee. He looked sideways at her. It was only a second but Susan felt what was there: a man noticing a woman.

"I thought, Julia, you would rather listen to Miles Davis playing trumpet than to me filibustering." Joe blew a kiss. "I'm not as stupid as I appear."

Susan leaned back on the couch, but the cushion was too

forgiving. Her shoulder blades could feel the wooden frame. That was how Joe lived—close to the bone, no frills. She had tried to fill in every crevice—and where was she? Or what was she? According to her psychiatrist she was a recovering suicide, a term that made no sense. She breathed in the man next to her. Even Listerine would smell good on him.

"Last time Susan was here, which was a while ago," Joe halted as Julia shot him a watch-what-you-say-look. "Well, we played some tracks from *Kind of Blue*. And though we have moved on lately from Miles to some of his sidemen—"

"Joe, stop being a disc jockey," Julia interrupted. "Who needs more wine?"

"My, you two sound like a married couple already," Jarvis observed.

"I don't think it's that bad," Lu added.

"As I was saying, though we have been playing more Cannonball and Trane lately, the fact is that there's no denying Miles."

"Amen!" whooped Jarvis. "I'll drink to that." He raised his wine glass. "Even fays dig him."

"Now, Jarvis," Joe said. "I thought I could go a whole afternoon and not experience reverse denigration."

"Sorry, chief. Something got into me." He sipped some wine. "This is a lot better than what's drunk on the street corners of our fair city."

"So as I was saying, we're going to play *Kind of Blue*. And we're not going to talk while we play it. If you have to talk, raise your hand after the cut is over and I will recognize you. As certified union hep cats, we . . ."

"Joe, you're a tyrant," Julia said, though she was smiling.

"No, I'm just a high school teacher who likes jazz. Right, Susan? Right, Jarvis?"

In agreement, Susan and Jarvis chinked their wine glasses.

The first track began. She had put on the LP once with Arthur and it was good, she and her son being together and making small but appreciative talk after listening, her son telling her some of the history he had gleaned from liner notes and the owners of the record store he liked to go to. She had put it on herself a few times, too. Hearing it at Joe and Julia's was better, though. Being with others brought her closer to the music, how it was private but was made by a group of people to exist in the world of other people, how it wasn't trying to knock you over, how it created a moody current that carried a person along, that said *Listen — you are alive. Every note matters.* It was as if the music represented another stage in the evolution of human beings, one that was happening right now. That was a large claim, but this quietly startling spontaneity felt so unlike what she had grown up with. That music — the big bands like Glenn Miller — was vibrant, but simple. This music wasn't simple but its intimacy wasn't daunting. It trusted its intuitions. She exhaled for what felt like the first time that afternoon. She could trust, too.

Arthur

"Something's happening." John Van Borkum reached for his pipe.

"Darn right," Las Schneiderman almost whooped. "It's only May but the Birds are contenders."

"Don't get your hopes up," Lee Berticot said. "There's a team called the 'Yankees.'"

It was mid-afternoon break time, a ritual long observed at the offices of Stanley Mermelstein. Sometimes Stan came out of his office and talked with his employees; more often he kept his door closed.

Many days Marilee Dorsky was behind that closed door with her boss at that mid-afternoon hour but today she was in the main office. She wore jerseys that tended toward two sizes: tight and tighter. Today was tighter. Arthur already had made two trips to the water cooler by her desk.

"I doubt Van is talking about baseball," Marilee said. She detested sports. Even the Colts, who were more a religion than a football team, meant nothing to her.

"Thank you, Marilee." Van Borkum was going through his ritual pipe filling. "I meant the Negroes here in the United States. Something big is happening with the Negroes."

Arthur liked how Van liked to talk about what was in the news. When he had described to Rebecca the people in his father's office, he had called Van "worldly." Things *were* happening and Arthur was becoming part of them. Yet in the office it seemed as if there was only the treadmill of work.

"I hate to act wise with a smart Dutchman, but you're not saying anything we didn't know." Las snorted. He wanted to talk baseball.

"I don't think Americans understand what is

227

happening." As he spoke, Van Borkum struck a match.

"Don't start in about Americans, Van." Wally Bright was standing in his customary perch in the door frame between the two employee offices. "We're doing just fine. And President Kennedy knows his stuff. If he can deal with the Russians, he can deal with some unruly Negroes."

Burdened with a lingering boner, Arthur got up awkwardly from his desk, then took his place beside Wally. "Who is 'we'?" he began. "Does that include Negroes? Or does it only include good ones not 'unruly' ones."

"Oh, boy," Lee Berticot sighed. "Here we go—current events." That afternoon, like every afternoon, he was busy consuming two packages of Tastykake Jelly Krimpets.

Wally turned to face Arthur. "Of course it means Negroes. Who said it doesn't?"

Arthur could smell Wally's hair cream. The stuff must have been made from dead cats and bald tires. Arthur, who wanted to look like some of the folksingers—not the Kingston Trio but the real ones—was trying to space his visits to the barber so his hair could grow longer. His father believed in a haircut every two weeks.

"I think I know what Arthur is getting at," Van Borkum said to the room at large.

"Let Arthur say what he's getting at." Marilee was tending to her nails with an emery board. Until he met Marilee, Arthur had never even heard the word *cuticle*. His mom didn't paint her nails or shape them. They were just nails. Rebecca always had her nails painted. It was part of what she called her "allure."

"Why do Negroes have to go through all this grief to get what they should have in the first place?" Arthur asked. "What I mean, I guess, is why aren't there any Negroes in this room?"

"In this room?" Lee Berticot sounded dumbfounded. He was licking jelly filling off the fingers of his right hand.

"That's what I'm getting at about something happening. It's something big, something that's going to change everything," Van Borkum announced. He took a contented drag on his pipe.

"Everything?" Lee asked.

"Stop talking like a chorus, Lee," Las said.

Wally took a measured step into the room. "I'm not sure about everything changing, Van. There's some Communists connected with this Martin Luther King. You know what that spells?" He paused for B-movie effect. "That spells trouble."

"Communists?" Lee had finished with his licking. "You can't beat Tastykakes. Communists?"

"Lee, stop it! You're driving me nuts." Las rose halfway from his chair.

"Easy, Las, Lee is just registering the common man's confusion." Van Borkum smiled indulgently. "As to your charge about Communism, that seems, to a European like me, to be a red herring—no pun intended."

Lee opened his mouth but said nothing.

Arthur swiveled his head to take in everyone in the room. "The white world is spinning on the wrong axis. That's got to change."

"'White world'?" Lee asked. "Whoa!" He turned to Las. "Sorry about that, Las. It just slipped out."

"And aren't you part of that axis, Arthur?" Wally asked. "And what if that kind of remark is just what the Communists want? What if all these protests are acts of subversion? What if the Kremlin . . ."

"Hold your horses, Wally," Van Borkum interjected. "Don't drag the Kremlin into this." Van inhaled and held the smoke. He was pondering.

"I don't think you guys get it," Arthur said. "Some Negro could throw a brick through our office window and you'd be wondering why he threw that brick. None of this is real to you."

At that moment, Stanley Mermelstein thrust his office door open and strode into the room. He wore a suit jacket, a white shirt, a striped tie, dark trousers, and Florsheim shoes—the uniform. "Lovis Construction," he said to Marilee. "That letter has to get in the mail today."

"Here 'tis, Mister M." Marilee waved a piece of paper. "All it needs is your John Hancock."

Arthur wanted to keep talking, but it was time to return to depreciation schedules and tax forms. Lee brushed some

Tastykake debris off his desk. Las made his usual show of moving papers from one pile to another. Van Borkum tapped the contents of his pipe into a glass ashtray. After a long look at Marilee, Wally retreated to his desk. Arthur remained by the doorway.

"Arthur, I'd like to speak with you," Stan announced and turned back toward his office.

"A summons to the inner sanctum, I don't know what this bodes for you, Arthur," Las loud-whispered.

"Inner sanctum?" asked Lee.

Before Las could rebuke him, Van Borkum spoke: "It means a place that a person can retreat to and be left alone. 'Sanctum' comes from the Latin *sanctus* and means 'holy.' Originally it was a religious term."

"Couldn't have said it better myself." Las gave Van a pointer-finger salute.

Arthur said nothing but wasn't excited to open his father's door.

"Take a seat, young man."

"Young man" signaled something seriously parental. Arthur's stomach began to knot.

"We haven't talked much lately. You know how it is, even after the tax season, all the extensions we have to deal with. But how are you doing?" Stan picked up a paper clip from a silver bowl on his desk and moved it from one hand to another.

Arthur gazed attentively at his father's hands. Usually the clip stayed for ten seconds or so in one palm before the transfer. Grandpa Max did the same thing, but with a coin.

"Uh, I don't know, Dad, the usual." His mom used that opening sentence; his dad used that opening sentence: Arthur wished they could all write a new script. He started to say something more but saw that his father's face was starting to change color.

"The usual!" Stan yelped. "Demonstrating with a bunch of Negroes outside the offices of Harry Schwartz is 'the usual'? Lying to me about seeing your girlfriend is 'the usual'? Don't fool with me, Arthur." Stan dropped the clip back in the bowl and scowled. "I've been holding my fire about this but I'm not holding it anymore. Don't tell me it's 'the usual.'"

"Well, you're right, Dad, that's not usual. That's something different in my life." Arthur sucked in some of the hot air from the radiator beside his chair. The weather had turned cool. Arthur coughed but more than he needed to. "You've got me there, Dad."

"What am I to make of this diversion, Arthur? You don't have better things to do than bother someone who paid you faithfully last summer and took you under his wing?"

"We weren't bothering him. We were respectfully demonstrating in front of his office."

"'Respectfully demonstrating'? What, may I ask, does that mean? Did you ask him? Did he invite you?" Stan picked up a clip again but clenched his fist around it.

"It means what I said. It means I have the right to make my views known. It means I'm not a slave to Mr. Schwartz. It means I don't think the way Mr. Schwartz treats his tenants is just."

"Making money isn't about justice," Stan replied.

"Maybe that's the problem, Dad. Maybe the world would be a better place if there were some justice in making money. Maybe money shouldn't control everything. Maybe—"

"Look, Arthur, I'm talking here. I'm your father who knows a lot more than you know."

Arthur shook his head no but said nothing.

"This won't do, Arthur. You're embarrassing me. I probably don't have to tell you that Harry called me. He was polite but he was upset. I knew he was wondering what kind of father lets his son run around with rabble rousers—Negro rabble rousers at that."

"There were other white people there. In fact there was a woman there who knew Mom."

"That's wonderful, Arthur, just wonderful. Let's drag your poor mother into this, too."

Arthur got up from his seat and leaned his hands on his father's desk. "Why is she 'poor,' Dad? Why did she try to kill herself? Why don't we talk about that instead of me holding up a sign?"

"Arthur . . . ," Stan began.

"Look, Dad," said Arthur, "I found her lying on the

floor. I tried to talk to her. I called the ambulance. Where the hell were you?"

"Don't yell at me, Arthur. I'm your father. You don't yell at your father and you don't cuss." Stan opened his palm and looked down at the clip he was holding. He seemed surprised.

"I don't think you have anything to tell me, Dad, about anything. That's what I think."

Stan dropped the clip on his desk. The tiny sound seemed enormous. He too stood up. "I have plenty to tell you, Arthur, but I'm too upset right now and I might say things I might regret." He started to walk around the desk toward Arthur but halted abruptly. "It's best at the moment if we declare a truce and talk more another day. I don't like the tone of this—not one bit."

"I can buy that, Dad."

"But I want you to promise me there will be no more demonstrations with Negroes on your part. I want you to promise me that."

"I can't do that, Dad," Arthur said. "You raised me not to make promises I can't keep." He tried to smile but his face was too tense with feeling.

"I did. But . . ." The word drooped in the stuffy air.

"I'll go back to work." Arthur almost sprinted to the office door. "I've got a lot of payables to do."

"Yes," his father muttered. "You do that." Stan was staring down at his empty palm.

Out in the main room Arthur ignored Marilee's what-happened-dear-boy look. He stopped at Las's desk. "It wasn't so bad," he said.

Las smirked. "That tough, huh? You weren't in there long. Sounded a little loud out here."

"It means," Arthur answered, "what you want it to mean." He continued on to the far room and the accounts payable for Pulaski Hardware, Incorporated.

Wally Bright was putting some lead in his mechanical pencil. He couldn't stand regular pencils. "Don't interrupt me, Arthur," he said. "This is painstaking work."

"I wouldn't think of it." Arthur sat down at his swivel office chair. His left leg was jigging nervously. Numbers in columns—at first they seemed like hieroglyphs but then they came into focus. He began to write down more numbers.

Susan

On top of the emotional fog of each day—her wondering who she was and where she was headed—were images from the TV and newspaper that had barged into Susan's soul and would not leave. Perhaps the main one, even starker than the water hoses knocking people down or the barely leashed dogs that brought to mind the world of slave catchers and overseers or Bull Conner himself, the so-called public safety commissioner of Birmingham, Alabama, snarling at the world beyond Birmingham and defying it to change what he considered unchangeable, was the sight of the children marching in Birmingham, some no more than seven years old but clearly aware of what they were doing. She saw the pictures of them being put into paddy wagons. Some were grave-faced; some were smiling: little boys in white shirts and dark pants, little girls with pigtails in dresses.

To say that it wasn't right was to say nothing. Susan knew that. She found herself crying at moments that didn't seem like times she should be crying—while entering grades in her grade book late at night or driving on her way to some errand. Something inside welled up and had to get out, and though Lu and Julia both told her it was understandable because, after all, she was dealing with a lot each day, still she felt that it wasn't all her doing. She felt that the events had filled her with faith and despair in large but equal proportions. She felt, too, that those children knew something she didn't know but should know. And that made her feel ridiculous—she, a grown woman. Next to those children, the missiles everyone talked about last October seemed inconsequential. She knew that wasn't strictly true. As Arthur liked to remind her, the planet was still studded with them. The red phone still sat by the president's side. But the picture of those children walking toward the city hall of Birmingham, Alabama, was both beautiful and unbearable.

When she brought it up with Julia, who was more than sympathetic and who was busy picketing and marching herself, Julia said she understood but then started talking about the speeches being made and the numbers of people being arrested and the headlines those arrests provoked. It was a "movement," as she put it, and that movement was headed inexorably toward its goal. Susan appreciated that, but both the joy—the children clapping and chanting and singing—and the agony—mere children being arrested—were too much for her. She had been naïve but she also had been unaware of how much spirit a small vessel could hold.

Susan tried to explain how she felt to Arthur, but he was impatient with her: "It's okay, Mom. I get it, that you have feelings." He knew she had fissures in her. For that matter, so did her husband, who kept telling her she would feel better and that they "would get back on track." Stan had a cliché for every occasion. That the occasion might overwhelm the cliché wasn't part of his thinking. But why would it? He didn't linger on those photos. He didn't study those children with their earnest, elated faces. He didn't take them personally; yet there seemed no other way to take them. It seemed a crime not to take them personally.

Though she had observed him only a handful of times, Jarvis Baker seemed to Susan to slide through it all, an acrobat of equanimity. Susan continued to discuss with Lu about how she could make an overture to him, how all she had to do was pick up the phone but she hadn't done it. She couldn't bring the feeling down to earth. "Would you rather pine away?" Lu chastised her. Susan had no good answer. All she had to do was to think about it, and history—hers and the nation's—seemed to stand in her path.

Perhaps because she walked around feeling that, however vicariously, she was living through an extraordinary time, when, after a union meeting she had attended, Jarvis invited her to follow him over to his house in her car to have an iced tea and "hear some Gershwin," his words were not unexpected. The surprise she talked to her son about had proclaimed itself naturally. The thoughts and scenarios she had involving Jarvis Baker — what Lu called her "schoolgirl fantasies" — fell away. He motioned to where he was parked on North Avenue, then scooted across the street. She stood a second admiring him. He was lithe as flowing water.

Jarvis's house was near Lake Ashburton, a stucco rowhouse with a begonia-festooned front porch.

"My wife, who's away visiting her sister in Wilmington, likes plants. I figure my forebears grubbed in the earth enough for me." Jarvis was speaking from the top of the five steps up to the porch. Susan stood on the sidewalk below him. "It's not like Little Willie Adams' place — you know who he is because everyone in Baltimore knows Little Willie — but it's home sweet home. White folks used to live here but then we showed up. We're like lice. Or worse, much worse."

Susan felt she should protest Jarvis's words but knew he was speaking the truth. She wanted to sell her house more than ever. Just that morning she had said to Stan that a person could kill herself on account of not being able to get into the upstairs bathroom. He didn't think she was funny. She thought it was healthy that she could joke about it.

An older woman stepped out on the porch two houses away. She was tying on a large straw bonnet as she moved. "Hello, Jarvis!" she trumpeted. She could be heard a half block away. "When's Kitty coming back?"

"Monday. She and her sister get together, there's no pulling them apart."

"I met that woman. She's an AME lady, I recall." By this time the bonnet was on and the woman was walking in the other direction from Susan and Jarvis. A long violet-colored ribbon hanging from the rear of the bonnet jounced with each step.

"Your stopping by will be in the *Afro* tomorrow." Jarvis laughed. "It's a wonder Lucille didn't take a photo."

"I'm not trying to stir up any hornets, Jarvis. I just . . ." Susan put her hands beside her hips as if she were a soldier awaiting an order. Standing up straight, she couldn't help but feel her midriff stretching the front of her A-line dress. More than one night she had drowned her sorrows in chocolate ice cream.

"No hornets. My wife understands I can invite

whomever I want to invite into our house. If she doesn't like it . . ." Jarvis paused. "I guess you know we don't have children."

"I didn't. I don't know much about you beyond that you like jazz, do union work, and teach at City."

"Well, come in and learn something." He held open the aluminum screen door.

Susan had that feeling she had whenever she entered Max's — the dimness of a space where light entered only from the front and rear. Rowhouses always felt cave-like. She looked around, and gradually the furniture and decorations revealed themselves — overstuffed chairs from the twenties and thirties, not unlike what her mother favored, and a big dining room table made of oak.

"It feels very solid in here," Susan said.

"Negroes need heavy furniture. It keeps them in their place."

"Oh, Jarvis," Susan said.

"My comedy is in proportion to my anxiety. But with you, dear lady, I feel not anxious at all. I feel myself." Jarvis moved toward the kitchen in the back of the house. "Not sure what that is, of course — 'myself.' But I like the notion. Sugar and lemon in your iced tea?"

"Both."

"I keep a pitcher in the ice box. I wish iced tea came out of the faucet."

Susan remained standing as Jarvis opened doors and jangled spoons. On the wall opposite from her hung a framed photograph of a big family, ten people in all. It looked as though it was from around the turn of the century — everyone very serious and in their best clothes. They were Negroes — but why wouldn't they be? Where did she think she was?

She and Jarvis seated themselves on two of the chairs and drank their iced tea. They talked about the union and the up-and-down weather — it having turned hot now — and the march that was being talked about, a big one in Washington.

"Hard to believe there's never been a time when that many Negroes congregated in a public space. It's like we've lived in a closet." Jarvis set his tea down on a coaster on a side table. He looked down at the glass. "My wife is particular about making rings on the furniture." He sighed. "Part of me feels proud that we're going to march, that white people are going to see us. But part of me" — and he looked at Susan — "is blue. 'How long' — that's how the song goes." He hummed a bit of melody.

"I don't know that song," Susan said. "I don't know many of those songs — the blues — but I can imagine that it's hard to acknowledge — the 'how long.'" Susan didn't avert her eyes from Jarvis. "Or maybe I can't imagine."

"You can, dear lady, and you can't. What's hard to face is the pity of it. The last thing I want is pity." He raised his arms at an angle to his torso and began to slowly rotate his hands. "Got to wake up my wrists. I said I was going to play you a tune." He rose and headed to the upright piano that stood in the middle room.

Susan wriggled a bit in her seat to see Jarvis better. The sun wasn't coming in directly but still it was hot. Although she was wearing a slip, the seat of her dress felt clingy.

"How about 'Summertime'? It's a good song any time of the year." Jarvis played a few warm-up scales — a breeze stirring a lake's surface — then stopped. "Why don't you come over and sit beside me on the bench, the way you did that night back in the fall." He struck a black key, its sound more plangent than musical. "I haven't forgotten. It was back when the world almost blew up."

"No forgetting that," Susan said. The words came out too brisk, more in pursuit of authority than feeling. A terrible awkwardness possessed her. She took short steps toward the bench as if on a balancing beam. For a second she closed her eyes — Jarvis's back was to her — then opened them and reached out to touch Jarvis's shoulder and steady herself. They weren't big rooms; it hadn't been many steps. Slowly she removed her hand. She sat down beside him, arm touching arm and leg touching leg.

Jarvis dove into the song, strong from the first but savoring each note as if not wanting to part with it, just as he had commended Miles Davis's playing. To Susan the insistent languor of the music, the near insolence of its yearning, felt like a thick, exquisite cloud enveloping her. She had heard the song countless times—it was almost an anthem—but no one had ever played it for her. A recording was someone playing on some other day; this was right now.

They sat in stillness after Jarvis finished. Then Jarvis put a hand on Susan's hand. "Susan," he said. "This is ridiculous. I want . . ."

Susan moved her head toward his.

He grabbed her shoulders and kissed her, softly but fully.

She kissed back. As she dissolved into the kiss, she felt herself moving forward, not just meeting him but pressing herself into him.

When they pulled their heads back, Jarvis rose, went around the bench and pulled Susan up—his hands under her shoulders—as if she were a sack. He pushed the bench toward the piano, turned her around, and drew her to him. Susan mumbled something. It could have been "God" or not a word at all, only a sound. Their hands leapt around on one another's backs—clutching and grabbing as if the other person might disappear. For some moments they couldn't find one another's lips but when they did the kiss lasted—as obliterating as a depth of water.

Susan gasped, then trembled when they let go. Close up, Jarvis looked even more handsome, his face delicate yet fierce with feeling. There was something essential about him that called her back to the first time she met him, something pure yet sensual, like music itself. "Are you prepared?" she asked.

"Am I prepared? There's no fallout shelter here," Jarvis replied.

"Oh, Jarvis!" she laughed. "I'm not on the pill."

"I have a whole box of you-know-whats upstairs."

"Let's go up there, then."

Jarvis offered his hand to her. "Just like that?"

"Just like that."

"You are some kind of gal."

In the bedroom, while taking her clothes off, Susan was surprised by her own calm. However strange it was, the scene she found herself in didn't feel dreamlike. She lingered to examine a small run in one of her nylons. She laid her dress out carefully over a chair with a caned seat. A breeze riffled the curtains in the back windows.

"I like to go slow," Jarvis said.

"Four months ago I turned forty," Susan said. "I'm in no hurry." She lay down on the top sheet of a big, antique metal bed. As she lay there — Jarvis had gone into the bathroom — she kept waiting to feel self-conscious, sprawled out as she was, an object of flesh. All she felt, though, was the sharp chaos of desire.

Then Jarvis was standing at the foot of the bed, naked and smiling, his tawny skin mild in the mid-afternoon light. "I like a woman with some meat on her bones. Too many white women doing all this diet nonsense, like they're trying to become air." He touched one of Susan's feet. "Women speak the earth — no two ways about it." He paused and considered her again. "Jewish people all have brown eyes?"

"Just like Negroes," she answered.

They both laughed.

Then he was on her, heavier than she thought he would be, muscled and smooth and deliberate. He was slow but not languid. She tried to feel each kiss but the core of vigilance inside her had dissolved. She felt herself spreading out over the bed. When he thrust himself inside her, she was wetter than she could remember. Then again, no one had ever kissed her where he had kissed her.

"Oh, you butter," he moaned to her.

Intent on her body's sensations, she said nothing back. She was thrusting with him, at once holding onto him and rocketing in her own ether. Then something broke loose: shouts, cries, and whimpers.

"Scream your head off, baby," Jarvis whispered. "Scream your lovin' head off."

When it was over, it wasn't. She knew she would return to who she was. She knew her car was parked down on the street. She knew that street led to other streets and eventually to her house. But she was here snuggled onto the shoulder of a Negro man lying beside her. If the history that littered each day and that spoke through mere children was telling her anything, it was telling her that no one knew what could be.

"Women like me," Jarvis announced to the ceiling above

him. "And my wife knows that."

Susan dug into the hollow of his shoulder a little more. "They should like you."

A ceiling fan was whirring above them, the sound gentle but insistent. It could have been music.

Arthur

Arthur knew what Larry Fein was going to say when Arthur walked in: "Arthur, you haunt this place." And he did. But he added that another such haunter already was there — "your music teacher, Mr. Baker, from City." And not only Mr. Baker but a guy Arthur had brought to the Record Collector a few weeks ago who kept turning up every couple of days "like this is the library or something," Larry said. "I guess the gang's all here," Larry further offered and turned back to his habitual *Sunpaper* spread before him.

Edward raised a hand in greeting. "Paul Robeson, I want to listen to everything he did. And you, Merm — in search of the reality of Negro music?"

Jarvis Baker whistled. He was in what looked to Arthur to be his favorite place — the classical bins — and had three or four LPs out. "Easy does it, Edward. There's reality in all music. Remember how I played Chopin for your class, and Stravinsky? Are you going to tell me, young man, that some music is more real than other music or that one group has a special hold on reality?"

"I was just teasing Merm — I mean Arthur." There was a blush in Edward's normally authoritative voice. Edward had special respect for Mr. Baker. There were a handful of Negro teachers at City; many schools in Baltimore didn't have any. And Baltimore had integrated its schools in 1956, though (as Edward explained to Arthur more than once) that was a lie, since there still were neighborhood schools a Negro couldn't attend because a Negro couldn't live in those neighborhoods. Edward labeled integration "a band-aid on a gunshot wound."

"I don't know, Jarvis," Larry said. "It doesn't get any more real than the country blues." He started to sing about

242

someone who owned a Rolls Royce car but had become a fallen star. The words came out as a drawled, Jewish-southern lament.

Arthur was formulating a sentence about the blues teaching him that feelings went beyond skin color, but Edward spoke first.

"That old stuff's going to give Arthur the wrong idea," Edward said. "Negroes nowadays don't like that stuff, those sharecroppers from Mississippi growling and moaning. It's no help. Mississippi is the land of bondage."

"And murder," Larry added and shook his newspaper. The civil rights leader Medgar Evers had been shot to death a few days ago. Arthur had read about it. He was going to be buried in Arlington National Cemetery, but Arthur knew that whoever shot him, assuming anyone would bother to arrest him, would not be convicted. It was one more reason why, when Mr. Tobey started talking about justice in America, Arthur put his head down on his desk.

"What are you saying?" Arthur looked cockeyed at Edward. He pulled a record from the bin. "See this? See what the title says? *King of the Delta Blues Singers.* Robert Johnson takes me to a different world."

Edward smiled his trying-not-to-condescend smile. "Merm, I don't need to be taken to a 'different world.' I live there already."

"Now, I'm over here looking at Verdi operas, young men," Jarvis Baker said, " —you remember Verdi from my class? —but I can't help but overhear you and I have to say again that music is for everyone, that no one group owns a musical experience."

There was that rich voice of Mr. Baker's. Arthur wondered why he didn't sing more in the classroom. Maybe he had some of the blues in him. Maybe he didn't want people to know.

"With all due respect, Mr. Baker," Edward said, "Negroes have their own take on life that emerges from their unique experience. What other people take from it is going to be partial, if not predatory."

"I may not agree with you, Edward, but I could listen to you all day." Larry shook his head in admiration. "You are one well-spoken young man."

Jarvis Baker put a record back in the bin, then rested his hands lightly on the mass of records in front of him. "You're young, Edward—smart but young. Heartbreak, to name one musical theme of the blues, is universal. Maybe those Mississippi Negroes come from a deeper sorrow. I won't deny history. But a woman leaving a man is a woman leaving a man. You hear me?"

Arthur and Edward exchanged glances over the wooden bin that divided them. Mr. Baker was a teacher but this wasn't the classroom.

"I'm with you, Jarvis," said Larry. "These gentlemen probably haven't experienced that yet."

Wary-eyed, Arthur and Edward exchanged another glance.

"Well, the blues can prepare them," Jarvis said and tossed a glance at the two of them. "Of course, the man can leave the woman, too."

"Does it always have to be sad?" Arthur asked.

"Depends," Jarvis said.

"Depends," Larry said.

Sometimes, when adults equivocated like that, Arthur felt he wanted to maim them.

"It doesn't matter," Edward declared. "Mississippi is what you leave. Mississippi is what's wrong. There's no point groveling in that dirt."

"Wait a minute, Edward," Jarvis Baker said. "No one is groveling. You listen to the stuff Arthur is listening to on those scratchy old records and you won't hear anyone groveling. Pride can be stuck in a corner but it's still pride. Pride can even laugh."

"Sometimes," Larry said, "I wish I had a tape recorder in this store. People wouldn't believe it. They think I'm just here selling music. They don't understand what happens here. This place is an academy." Larry looked around the huge, record-crammed space he presided over. There wasn't much decoration on the brick walls beyond a few posters, including one of the crooner Johnny Mathis that Larry kept saying he was going to take down. "I'm going to miss this old building."

"You're moving, Larry?" Jarvis asked. His voice was lighter but concerned.

"Out toward the edge of Roland Park," he replied.

"Damn," Jarvis said. "The white world."

Larry went on. "Two times in the past two weeks someone's tried to jimmy the door. I don't want to work in a bunker."

"But if you leave, Mr. Fein," Edward said, "who's going to take your place here? And what message does that send to the Negro community?"

"I didn't make the world, Edward. I'm a businessman and I want to keep eating." He grabbed the black tie he wore every day and began to fiddle with it, rubbing the material between his thumb and index finger.

"But it isn't right, Mr. Fein," Edward said. "It isn't right to give up. People can try to break into your store anywhere."

"Don't hector him, Edward." Jarvis Baker had picked up his LPs. Arthur noticed that his pants were pleated. That was sharp—pleated pants. And different—his father would go to the moon before he wore pants like that. Anything the least bit stylish, Stan consigned to the world of "zoot suits." Arthur had never seen such a thing but sympathized instinctively with the men who had worn them.

"Again, with all due respect, Mr. Baker, I wasn't hectoring." Edward pulled out one of the Paul Robeson records from the bin. "You know how this man was treated. He went through an inquisition. He couldn't even get a passport to *leave* this country. Am I supposed to forget that? How am I supposed to live?"

Arthur felt as though he had walked into a family quarrel—or not a quarrel but one of those times when someone tried to explain something important to someone else, the way he tried sometimes to explain himself to his parents. He knew how that usually turned out.

Jarvis Baker walked deliberately toward Edward but stopped a few feet from him. "You've got Paul Robeson in your hands. You can hear him sing. You can feel the strength in that voice. No one can take that away from you. And that's how you are going to live." He paused and sucked in a breath. "Does it make sense? Does being a Negro make sense? Do we always have to choose one thing over another—George Frideric Handel

245

over Ray Charles? Or maybe not, maybe we don't, maybe we can live with more, not less." He extended an arm out as if to place it on Edward's shoulder but realized the young man was not near enough to him.

He looked over at Larry Fein, who was brooding over the picture of Medgar Evers in the *Sunpaper*. "It's a shame you're moving, Larry. There's something precious in these walls." Then he looked at Arthur, who was gripping the edge of the record bin with both hands as if to hold steady. "Wake up, Arthur."

Mr. Baker smiled but Arthur couldn't tell if his music teacher was happy or unhappy. Probably both. Feelings always seemed a step ahead of words.

"I'm trying, Mr. Baker," Arthur said.

"I keep looking at this picture" — Larry was speaking to all of them — "and I feel how sick I am of people paying with their lives."

A woman wearing a trench coat and carrying a huge pocketbook opened the one door into the Record Collector, took a few steps but then stopped. "Am I interrupting something?"

"Nothing that can't be started again," Larry Fein said. "May I help you?"

Susan

It felt strange to Susan to have a secret. There had been mysteries in her life, her father's disappearance being the overwhelming one, but secrets were different. Secrets were something that a person held on to that couldn't be seen but that felt somehow visible, as if someone peering intently enough at a body could detect them. You could think something was secret but it wasn't to other people. They could tell, for instance, that you were in love—or something like love. Susan knew that from working with young people. With Lu it took all of three steps into Lu's kitchen for her to guess what had happened. "Look at your face!" she exclaimed. "Bingo!" The two women hugged giddy hugs.

"How good was it?" Lu asked, to which Susan replied, "Very good." They hugged again. "And your husband?" Lu asked. "Still my husband," Susan replied. They both smiled awkwardly, though Lu's smile became coy. "I bet you're just being the ever-polite English teacher. I bet 'very good' means 'super.'" Susan smiled an obliging smile. Lu clapped her hands. "Hon, you look like a woman should look. I can tell. You got your pot stirred."

There was no arrangement with Jarvis. They had Joe and Julia to bring them together socially, or she could say she was going off to do union work. They had gone to bed two more times and the feeling of him inside her, of over and over pulling him into her as if his own powerful movements were not enough, wasn't going to leave her. Ambushed by pleasure, she felt how a bed was the basic kingdom, the one all the others depended on whether they acknowledged it or not. Yet the talk around the pleasure, before and after, was just as important: she never had encountered a soul like Jarvis's, one that was tested every day yet was open to the likes of her. They laughed about that—the likes of her. When he teased her about enjoying the sex or overcoming "etiquette," as he termed it, to be with a Negro man, it wasn't mean-spirited. It was amused as much as anything. She didn't feel condescended to; she felt encouraged.

The ghost of disappearance was no longer calling to her, nor was Thomas Hardy's customary bleakness. "Why did she have to be sacrificed?" one of her students had once asked her when the class was talking about Eustacia drowning herself. It was a good question. When she looked in the medicine cabinet mirror these June mornings, she saw less and less of the woman grabbing that bottle of pills on that November night.

A secret took up room, though. Susan felt even more cramped in her house. Even the bedroom was no longer hers. Ruby would trudge upstairs, her heavy footfalls like cannon reports, and knock vigorously on the door. "*Bist du* sick, Susie?" she would shout. When Susan wanted to sit and read downstairs, her daughters swarmed her with anxious love. Or they voiced their wants—a bigger house or a television in their bedroom or a dog. They debated what to name the dog, even though Susan told them they were not getting a dog anytime soon.

There was the reality of her neighborhood, too. One of the two Negro teachers in her high school had come up to her back in March and asked about her house. When Susan stammered, the woman chuckled. "I know how these things work. I've been by your house and I like it—that privet hedge out front and that side porch. You let me know. I don't mind busting a block." Susan hadn't said a word to Jarvis about her house, but she didn't have to. His school was never out of session.

Calling a realtor was her idea. She and Stan communicated about the simple things—bills and Listerine—but she had given up on getting him to talk about moving. She would present him with the numbers. He respected numbers.

Clarence Goldstein of Goldstein Realty, Incorporated, extended a fishy hand to her while jerking his head around, taking in every detail of her living room. Susan tried to smile but couldn't, not that the realtor cared. He rapidly explained to her what the situation was.

"In five years this will be an all-Negro neighborhood. You can hang on, or you can be one of the first ones to leave and get the price you deserve for your house. I'll have to do an appraisal, but I walked around the outside. The house is in good repair. Nice grounds, too. Those roses look high class." While he talked, he kept rubbernecking. Susan had the feeling that the house was more real to Clarence Goldstein than she was.

"Mr. Goldstein," Susan began.

"No need to be formal, Susan. I prefer to be on a first-name basis with my clients." He was talking past Susan's right shoulder to the door that led down to the basement and through which Seeley came with a basket of folded laundry.

Seeley gave Mr. Goldstein a sharp glance. Susan often marveled at how quickly Seeley could size up a white person.

"This is Mr. Goldstein, Seeley. He's a realtor." Susan gestured to him, but he was already striding toward the stairs that led to the second floor.

"Uh-huh," Seeley said. "Movin' day comin', I imagine."

Clarence Goldstein didn't deign to look at Seeley. He did say that he liked the built-in closet under the staircase landing. "Good use of space there, Susan."

Seeley trundled by him and up the stairs with her load of Mermelstein clothes. She kept her eyes straight ahead of her.

"Let me lead you around the house, Clarence," Susan said. His name stuck in her throat. It seemed like a name you'd give a pet bird.

"Very good. Let me just make a few notes." He began writing on a sheet of paper attached to a clipboard. Susan realized that she should have asked Lu to be there. Lu would be appraising the appraiser and joking about his checkered sport jacket and his TV-announcer voice.

Ruby emerged from the same door that Seeley had just come through. She took off her glasses and rubbed her eyes. Susan had given up saying anything to Ruby about her sight. She was going blind, that was a fact. "Who is this?" she asked. Ruby would never address a stranger directly. She was still a little girl standing on Rivington Street, clinging to her mother's skirts.

"Mr. Goldstein, Ma. He's a realtor. You know, he helps people buy and sell houses."

Ruby gave him a look as if he were a plate of pork chops set out on the Sabbath.

"Pleased to meet you. You are . . ." Clarence Goldstein looked to Susan for help.

"My mother, Ruby," Susan said. She felt the impulse to bury the moment and Clarence Goldstein in a torrent of words: *Her husband, who was also my dad, left her in the twenties and she never got over it even though that's a long time ago and she lives with us because she has nowhere else to live and she's cranky but she's my mom who's going blind and I don't know how I'm going to deal with that, a blind person, but I guess I will because that's the story of my life although just a few days ago I was in bed with a Negro man and could be arrested for that in many states including the one in which you and I both reside. The term, I believe, is* miscegenation. *Should I have entered into this liaison back in the mid-fifties and become pregnant by him I could have been sentenced to the penitentiary for up to five years. God bless the state of Maryland.*

"Susan." It was Mr. Goldstein. "Let's look at the dining room, if that's all right with you." He did have that newscaster voice, at once self-important and droning: "The Dow Jones was higher today, closing up sixteen points."

Seeley came back down the stairs. She was singing softly to herself. Some of the music coming from Arthur's room these days didn't sound much different from Seeley's songs.

Susan was knocking the palm of her right hand against her ear as if trying to get some water out of it.

"The dining room, Susan?" Mr. Goldstein was already standing there. He had put his clipboard on the dining room table and cupped his hands around his mouth to make a megaphone.

Ruby came up to the dining room threshold. "Mister, you should watch that table. Susie's husband works there. Easy to make scratches but hard to get out. Is a good table."

Clarence Goldstein snatched up his clipboard.

Seeley came up beside Ruby and put the empty wicker basket down on the floor. "Polishin' that table is a Monday mornin's worth of work." She spoke loudly. "No need for startin' any scratches. Is that right, Miss Ruby?"

"Is trouble," Ruby declared.

Clarence Goldstein had stuck the clipboard under an upper arm and pressed it close to his side. "I have a list, Susan, of people who would be eager to see this house," Mr. Goldstein said. He smiled but also seemed forlorn.

"Plenty of colored gonna like this house, Mrs. Merm," Seeley said. "My older sister's daughter Elvira lookin' for a house. She work for Social Security." She looked through the opening into the dining room, where the realtor stood at attention. "That the government, Mister Real Estate. That serious money."

Seeley had asked Susan for a raise last week, to which Susan acquiesced immediately. Stan told her she had to draw a line. She had given Seeley three raises in six months. Susan told her husband to leave her alone.

"And the rest of the house," Clarence Goldstein was saying.

"Is moving?" Ruby asked.

"Don't worry, Ma," Susan said. She put a hand on her mother's shoulder. Ruby smelled sour. Some days she didn't shower. She said she was afraid of falling down. Plus, it was too dark in the shower, according to Ruby. What was "too dark" for someone going blind?

Seeley had picked up the basket and moved to the basement door. "Plenty to see down here, Mister Real Estate. This where Ruby live and I work. Nice down here—cool in the summer. Never need no fan."

"You have a busy household," the realtor observed.

"Maybe I'm not quite ready to sell yet," Susan replied.

"Come again?" he said. He put a hand up to an ear as if he had a hearing problem. He looked like he was playing charades.

"You heard me. I'm not sure I'm ready to sell yet." Susan thought of Jarvis Baker's body on top of hers. Involuntarily her pelvis twitched—a good gremlin. "I still have to talk to my husband about this and then there are my children and they need to be consulted, but I'm sure I'll be in touch."

Baron Wormser

Ruby had sat down on one of the cushioned dining-room chairs. She looked around absently. Susan knew that her mother was about to enter some byway of lamentation. In her own head another internal screed was forming.

She pushed an unresisting Clarence Goldstein through the front door. He gave her his business card and said he would be in touch. Susan didn't doubt that. She thought of the list of potential buyers. Her leaving would be a boon to some worthy family. Was that how she should look at it? Arthur said that the Negro newspaper, which Arthur's friend worked on and which Arthur had started to read, was full of ads for houses like theirs but not so close to the county line. Maybe they shouldn't sell yet, though. Maybe more was going to happen. Maybe some of the blocks Jarvis had been around would start to become real to her. Maybe her history would start to catch up with his.

"Don't cry, Ma," Susan called into the dining room. "We've got four solid walls around us. There's nothing to get upset about."

Ruby shot her daughter a skeptical look but said nothing.

Clarence Goldstein's card was still in Susan's hands. She began to tear it up.

Arthur

"We're not doing that tonight, Arthur," Rebecca said.

Arthur's hands were still on the steering wheel. "What?"

"You're not listening to me. In your mind you've already got my blouse and bra off." She smiled, though more preoccupied than amused.

"What's wrong with that?" Arthur raised his hands and held them out, then started shaking them. "Look! If I can't touch you, I'll go crazy."

"Don't be goofy. I hate it when you're goofy. That's the problem." The smile was gone. "I could smoke one of your cigarettes, but it's a bad habit."

"If you do it once in a while, it's not a habit." Arthur put his hands back on the steering wheel. Rebecca was right. The moment Rebecca got in the car, his pecker went into overdrive. He scrunched his legs together.

"We're moving to Israel the first of the year — the calendar year, not the Jewish year. My dad has made up his mind. I'm supposed to go with him unless I get married. Then I have my own life here. Then I don't have to go." Rebecca spoke resolutely, a little speech she had rehearsed before her bedroom mirror. "That's why I don't want you to touch me tonight." She moved sideways on the car seat and put a hand on Arthur's shoulder.

He scrunched his legs harder. The merest touch did it. On other nights, Rebecca had laughed at her power.

"You're not exactly someone who's going to marry me, Arthur. That would be safe to say." Rebecca's fingers danced absentmindedly on Arthur's shoulder.

Arthur peered in front of him, a pilot at the helm, but there was nothing out there to distract him. They were in an alley near Rebecca's house. It was dark, neither a moon in the sky nor a streetlight near. He could make out a few stunted trees growing alongside a chain-link fence. They were what Mr. Schwartz, who knew even less about nature than Arthur, called "weed trees." He hadn't seen Mr. Schwartz since the picketing day.

"Israel's in the desert," he said. "It must be hot there, even hotter than Baltimore."

Rebecca took her hand away. "I don't want to talk about geography, Arthur." She took a deep, unhappy breath. "Oh, I wish you were more grown up."

"But—" Arthur began.

"I know you better than you know yourself, Arthur. Women think about people. I don't know what men think about, but it's not the way that women think. Men are like my father. I'm more of an object to him than someone with feelings. Or I'm an object who's liable to start crying."

Arthur was relieved to be grouped with men rather than boys. Still, some failing was being counted against him that he couldn't envision. He thought of protesting but knew that Rebecca was right. He didn't think about people the way she did.

"Say something, Arthur," Rebecca tugged at the sleeve of his Orioles T-shirt. She barely knew what baseball was. When Arthur had suggested they go to a game, she looked at him as if he were proposing a trip to Antarctica.

"I don't want you to leave," he said.

The languid silence of the night seemed to seep into the car after Arthur spoke. They both sat there listening to nothing. Then they heard footsteps coming down the alley. Then they heard a voice: "Evenin' folks. Just out to get a sip o' this night air." An older Negro man peered into their car. "Don't let me stop you from anything." He laughed gently and shambled away. At the end of the alley there was a ravine down which he disappeared.

Rebecca shivered. "That was scary—someone coming up like that. Last week there was a rape a few blocks from here." She clutched Arthur's arm.

"What's scary? He's just some old guy out for a walk.

There's no law against taking a walk." Arthur put his other hand on Rebecca's to reassure her.

She wrenched herself away. "Maybe I should move. I bet there are no Negroes in Israel." She drew her knees up on the seat and hugged herself. "Why are you so interested in Negroes, Arthur? I don't get it. They just make trouble."

"What are you talking about?" Arthur's voice rose. "It wasn't Negroes who practiced slavery or killed the Jews or, for that matter, tried to keep Israel from becoming a country." Arthur felt the shrillness in his voice but couldn't help it. In fact, it felt good. How many times had he sat with Mr. Schwartz and listened to his craziness, his *that's how it is, Arthur*?

"You're a fool, Arthur. You're more of a fool than I thought you were. Here I need to get married if I want to stay in America and you're telling me Negroes weren't the Nazis. What a genius you are."

Arthur leaned over to Rebecca. Her neck was there right in front of him. He planted a loud, suctioning kiss on it. She wriggled and flung her arms out, but he kept his lips on her. When he let go to breathe, it was only for a second. He kissed her again as hard as the first time. Her rigidity started to melt. He could feel that. Her arms now dangled at her side.

"Oh," she said. "Oh."

Arthur drew back but again only for a second. He turned her face toward his and kissed her lips. He could feel her lipstick — Rebecca always slathered it on. She didn't kiss back but she didn't pull away either. He was holding onto her, convincing her. Or he was letting her go.

He felt her breath on his breath. It was gentle and electric, that mingling. The world was their mouths.

She put her arms around him, but they still were limp. He could feel the weight of her exhaustion. When, slowly, she began to clutch him, it was as though she were coming back to life. And when the kiss was over, she still held onto him, but almost fiercely, her chin planted on his shoulder, her arms encompassing him.

He had no idea how much time passed; as in a fairy tale they were children in a dark woods holding on to one another. Though he felt Rebecca's breasts pressing against him, sex seemed, for the first time between them, to be elsewhere. They hadn't gone all the way because Rebecca wasn't going to let anyone do that with her, "a rabbi's daughter," until she married, but they had come to the verge. In their last car session, Rebecca had nothing on but her panties and had ground herself into Arthur, who was grinding back. "Dry humping" was the phrase Arthur recalled from guys like Rick, but it wasn't dry. When he shot off, Rebecca screamed, laughed, and started crying in the space of thirty seconds. Now they were more like Hansel and Gretel.

And she was crying now, so faintly that Arthur wasn't even sure it was crying. It sounded more distant than near, but then she picked her head up and leaned away from him and continued to cry. He sensed that the sound, hesitant yet wracking, was traveling from some awful depth, from the hole of her mother's death. He had no idea what to do. Despite their clinging and his kissing, there seemed no comfort in him for her.

When she finally stopped, she dabbed at her nose with a handkerchief embroidered with little five-cornered stars. Rebecca had told him that her mother had done that work and had taught Rebecca to embroider. "I'll make someone a good wife," Rebecca had said about her female handiness.

"It isn't just that we have to stop all this, Arthur. It's that I have to make some big decisions. I've been postponing them. I haven't wanted to face them." She twisted the handkerchief idly. "There are things about you I don't understand, like why you've become interested in Negroes so much. But that's your business, isn't it? Probably no one really understands another person all the way through, anyway. But—" and she paused and let the handkerchief rest in her lap—"I've been seeing this guy I knew from FP who's graduated and whose dad has a good business— a furniture store—and he's nuts about me."

"And he'll marry you tomorrow if you want," Arthur said. "And you'll be able to do with him what you can't do with me." It wasn't a hard thought to complete. "I hope it's someone you can stand."

"I can stand a lot of things, Arthur. His family may not be happy but he said he'd elope. We could drive up to Elkton."

"And then you'll be married. You'll be safe."

Rebecca leaned back hard into the car seat, pulled off her summer shoes, a pair of nondescript flats, and thrust her pale legs up and out onto the dashboard. Her cotton skirt—she had told Arthur she had sewn it herself—dangled around her knees. Looking over at her pure, unnerving female presence, Arthur felt the most drastic longing.

"What makes me sad, Arthur, is that I want to find out who you become. And I want to be near you when I find that out. I don't want to hear it secondhand." She pressed her toes against the windshield as if bracing herself. "Do you remember that day when we met in the library?"

"Of course I do." The words came out dazed.

"I'd seen you for months there in the library. I was curious about you. Who is this guy who reads these novels? Finally I figured out how to get your attention. I figured out that Thomas Hardy would help me." She angled her head toward Arthur and smiled weakly. "And he did."

"God bless Thomas Hardy, the dark eye of the blind universe."

"That's not bad, Arthur. Did you just make that up?" Rebecca almost squealed, despite herself.

"Who knows what I can make up?" Arthur paused. "But it's not going to be with you." It was stagey but he had to say it, a period at the end of a hopeless sentence.

"No, it isn't." Rebecca brought her feet down and wiggled them back into her shoes. "I feel more of a mess than when we tangle, Arthur."

"I don't want this to be this way." Arthur's head slumped onto the steering wheel.

"Neither do I, but it is," Rebecca replied. "Drive me up to my house. I don't want to walk."

Susan

"You ever see those before? You're holding 'em like you got a grenade in your hand."

The voice was close to her. Susan turned around, a bunch of collard greens in her right hand. One fat leaf drooped over.

"They're best cooked with bacon fat. Some ham doesn't hurt either." Jarvis Baker smiled his usual born-on-the-morning-of-the-world smile.

"Jarvis. Imagine you being here at Lexington Market." The joy of seeing him jumped right on her. She smiled a dizzy dame smile.

"Frankly, it's more 'imagine you being here.' When did you get interested in collard greens?"

"Seeley, our maid —"

"Yes, your colored maid. I remember her name."

Susan watched his smile thin. She hurried on. "Seeley's always talking about these greens, and I thought I'd let her prepare some for us. Or maybe I'll cook them. I can cook."

There couldn't have been more than a foot or two between them. It was as if he had sprung up through the cement floor, a miracle in brown slacks and a Ban-Lon shirt.

"It's good to see, Susan, how the other half eats. And that's a fine bunch you have there. My wife and I patronize this market."

Though the last sentence was meant to make her squirm, Susan resisted. "I need to put these in a bag, Jarvis."

"Your son told me I might find you here. I called the house and then drove over."

"Arthur?" Susan asked. She couldn't avoid the catch in her voice.

"We had a brief chat. He's planning to participate in the protest at Gwynn Oak on the Fourth. I guess you know that."

"Sort of." Susan took a brown paper bag from a pile nearby and stuck the greens in them. The bag was too small; more of the greens were outside than inside.

"It gets complicated, doesn't it? Your son is demonstrating and you've gone to bed several times with a colored man, but you have a colored maid and you probably, or maybe definitely, want to move out to the Jewish part of the County because there are no Negroes out there to speak of." Jarvis laughed but there was no mirth in his voice. "And that bag is not working for you, Susan. Those greens are going to escape."

"Did you want to see me, Jarvis?" she asked.

"Apparently, though I could use some greens myself. Maybe I can show you the fine points of ham hocks, too."

"I wanted to see you." Susan heaved the words out, then looked down at the inadequate bag. "I'll hold these, Jarvis, and you put another bag over the top part. That should do it."

"And what if someone sees a colored man helping you put your greens in a bag?"

"Now you're making fun of me."

"Why would I want to do that?" Jarvis had taken a large brown paper bag from a nearby stack and slipped it over the other bag. "And I wouldn't say I was making fun of you. It seems a legitimate question. You never know who you're going to run into here. Hopkins professors, some politicians too."

They looked around at the stalls full of pastries, meats, seafood, vegetables, fruits, dairy products, pickled this and preserved that: everything an appetite could want. The air smelled of brine and peaches, crab spice and cinnamon, butter milk and corned beef. Every shape and age of person was there — sniffing, swallowing, grabbing, licking, pinching, hefting, chewing, appraising, savoring. The air smelled of bodies, too. A few half-hearted fans blew the heat around.

"I hope heaven is like this," Jarvis observed. "These big-aisle supermarkets are one more bad white-folks idea."

Susan felt a pang. She and Ruby loved supermarkets. Her being at the downtown market was a fluke. She didn't want to be at home. She wanted to humor Seeley. She didn't know what to do with herself. She wanted to experience a slice of Baltimore that she hadn't experienced in a long time. She wanted to enjoy by herself the state of near love she was in.

"Coming over to my place this afternoon?" Jarvis asked. "I did track you down. Not that I'm in a hurry. We could share a bite. I'm hungry." He eyed her bag. "Your greens won't wilt. Collards have steel in them. That's what's kept Negroes standing upright—gospel and greens."

"Do all roads come back to the same place?" Susan asked.

Jarvis started to frown but stopped. It left him looking quizzical, like an actor who had forgotten his lines. "The my-being-a-Negro place, you mean? Does the world let me forget that place? Can I sit down and eat a meal with you in most of this city and forget that place? Can I go into Hutzler's Department Store and try on a suit? Or will I be asked to leave because I can't go into a dressing room because I might contaminate an expensive piece of clothing? And what if right now I asked you to hold my colored hand, to make a public proclamation?" He extended a hand to Susan.

She looked at the hand over which she had expended so much feeling and let it hang in the air. "You know I can't do that."

"Do I?"

Around them, people hustled by, intent on their next purchase, almost shouting their demands: "I'll take two of the ripest you got." "Make it snappy." "Go easy on the fat."

"I think people are looking at us," Susan said.

"Let them look. It's a free country."

"Don't force me, Jarvis. I didn't—" Susan looked around distractedly.

"You didn't mean to say what you said?"

Jarvis's voice was too calm, a feint before a storm. The smile he showed her was more armor than ease.

"You buyin' those greens, lady?" the stall proprietor asked. An old man, he looked to be from somewhere in Eastern Europe, one of those Iron Curtain nations that rarely got into the Cold War news.

"She is. I'll pay for them. We're going to go right home—" Jarvis paused—"where we live together and cook them up." Jarvis took back his extended hand and reached for his wallet with it.

"Jarvis!" Susan hadn't meant to raise her voice. She looked down at the bag of collards. She wanted to throw them away.

The grocer shuffled out from behind his counter. It was hard to tell how tall he was because he was so bent over. "Lady," he wheezed, "is this guy botherin' you? Cuz if he is, I can do somethin' about that." He turned to glower at Jarvis. One of the grocer's cheeks was blotched red, as if only half of him were angry. But that wasn't true. However doddering he was, he was ready to fight, all seventy-plus years of him.

Jarvis leaned back. A line of sweat that Susan had not noticed before gleamed on his forehead right below his hairline.

"I'll take these vegetables, sir. Everything is fine." Susan shrugged her pocketbook off her shoulder, located her wallet, and paid the man, who had not taken his eyes off Jarvis, who was now rocking on his heels. Somewhere nearby a fan hummed dully.

She grabbed Jarvis's hand. "Let's go." She squeezed it and tugged on it to get him moving. He looked at her with astonishment.

"All of a sudden—" he began.

"All of a sudden, I woke up," she said. "Did you mean it about cooking the greens at your house?"

The ancient grocer continued to eye Jarvis. Although nothing had happened, Susan realized that he might call the police. She also realized that if anyone should be calling the police, it was Jarvis.

Hand in hand they turned a corner. Susan recognized a deli counter she had stopped at earlier in the afternoon. The man behind the counter was eying the two of them. His look wasn't so much unfriendly as baffled.

At the market's doors to the street Jarvis stopped and let his hand fall from Susan's. "I don't have to thank you, because I can take care of myself. I wouldn't be standing here now if I couldn't. I don't have to be indifferent, either. I'm not."

261

Susan nodded. She was focused on his face, the warmth that came from it and the determination, too. Looking at him, she sensed once more how much she could lose all sense.

"I want to be with you again, Susan, but I'm not sure how I want to do that. I'm not who I was ten minutes ago. That's how it works with us Negroes—to go back to that place. Moments open up that can swallow us alive—or not alive."

A white woman with a handcart filled with grocery bags trundled by him. She stopped before the door, which Jarvis opened for her. The woman regarded him briefly and grunted. As she walked off, Jarvis mimed the words "You're welcome" to her back.

When he turned to Susan, he swallowed hard, his mouth caught in a wry twist. "As you can see, that's what's funny about dealing with white folks. They think being a Negro is like being a tree or a stone. Except that a tree or a stone can't open a door for them." Jarvis raised his hands in a show of exasperation, then laughed a scoffing laugh. "That's why the change has to come. They can't go on like this. We can't either."

"And that puts you and me where?" Susan asked. Though she didn't want to, she still felt the deli man's eyes on her. The thought of her home and everyone there came to her, too. When she looked at Jarvis, his eyes were downcast, his usually mobile face blank. She wanted to be instinctive, to reach out to him. There were no pills in her system tranquillizing her, only the sum of her past life. She held the bag of greens more tightly.

He looked up. "You're going to suffocate those greens. Look what they've been through—almost started a race riot."

Susan watched Jarvis's face try to right itself. She moaned—her longing escaping her.

"Hey, Jarvis." The voice walked up to them in the form of a lanky Negro man dressed much like Jarvis but wearing a bright yellow golfer's cap. "Long time, no see." The man took in Susan. "Out shoppin'?" It wasn't clear to whom the question was addressed.

Jarvis and Susan exchanged a brief glance.

"Yeah, I was shopping but they didn't have what I wanted," Jarvis answered. "How you been, Reggie?"

Susan stood there flatfooted. Her mind was flatfooted, too. Despite all the years she had lived in Baltimore, she had never witnessed two Negro men greeting one another.

"Can't complain," the man named Reggie answered. "And how're you today, ma'am?" He doffed his cap and bowed slightly.

"I'm Susan Mermelstein and I'm fine," Susan answered. She sounded like a grade-school child.

"Susan works with me in the teachers' union," Jarvis said. "We bumped into each other down here." He motioned airily to indicate the vagaries of coincidence.

"The union, huh? Well, Jarvis, I know there's no holdin' you back. You one man can play both sides of the street." Reggie gave Jarvis a broad wink. "I'll be toddlin'. Good to see you. And nice to meet you, ma'am." He nodded to Susan. "Truth is — I'm good with the union. Tell you why. Because the justice ones — they's helped the colored." He turned back to Jarvis. "We got a memory for who's been good and who's been bad, eh, Jarvis? We a regular bunch of colored Santas. No toys to hand out, of course." He gave a little wave with his cap to both Jarvis and Susan, then began to amble down Saratoga Street.

"Reggie — I know him from the neighborhood," Jarvis said. "He drives for one of the Jewish furniture companies."

"Jewish furniture companies?" Susan asked. They had drifted out of the market and onto the sidewalk.

"Excuse me," Jarvis snapped, "but people use 'Negro' freely enough as an adjective — why not 'Jewish'? How many times have I picked up the *Sun* and read about a 'Negro suspect'?"

Susan startled but spoke immediately. "It doesn't excuse the newspaper, but I'm not sure if it's good to put religion together with furniture. Maybe it's silly, but it makes me nervous."

"Yeah, doesn't it?" Jarvis answered. "I've been nervous forever. Words start off innocent and end not-so-innocent. Sometimes they don't start off innocent at all." He paused to look at Susan. "As for descriptions, I don't mind putting 'good-looking' in front of 'woman.' You are all there in that dress you got on." He raised his wrist watch. "Too bad I've used up my time with you today."

"But—" Susan began. She held out a vague hand toward Jarvis.

"Harder than being teenagers, isn't it?" he said and smiled. "Maybe I should consult with Arthur about how he manages his affairs. I suspect he has some female companionship by now."

The smile and patter asserted that he was back to being himself, though Susan wasn't sure what that state was. Just today she had seen at least three different Jarvises. And he had seen a few Susans, too.

"It is harder, isn't it?" Susan said.

"We'll get together again. I know that." He looked tenderly at her, a look that was meant to ravish her and did. The world around her on the busy Saturday-afternoon sidewalk fell away. Her body felt syrupy and keen at the same time. She could have fainted.

No holdin' him back, Susan thought. As he started to head off, she waved the bag. "With ham, is that what you said?"

He called over his shoulder: "With Jewish ham."

Arthur

"Seems like we're always on the bus together," Arthur said. He sniffed the warm air. Although the windows were open to the pleasant day, the old school bus held the memory of thousands of bodies. The plain green seats had an oiled sheen. Time and sweat had worn them down but they retained a human essence. Arthur sniffed again.

"You turning into a dog, Merm?" Edward asked and smiled his wide, gummy smile. "How about a stick of gum for my man?" Edward pulled a pack of Juicy Fruit from the pocket of his clean white shirt. "Give your jaw something to do beside talk."

Arthur liked how Edward made a point of being nonchalant in these situations. Most guys at City thought Edward was stuck up, but the more time Arthur spent with him the more he felt it was the opposite. In his carefully spoken way, Edward was cool.

"We should have each other over to dinner," Edward said. "Takes forever to get out to the County." He surveyed the wooden and brick houses and their leafy yards, "I walk down some of these streets and people would run inside and call the cops. 'There's a Negro out there,' they'd say, except they're likely to use another word than 'Negro.'" He yawned. "I surmise we'll hear that word today."

Arthur nodded. He suspected Edward was about to launch into one of his disquisitions about the state of the nation and the history of everything. That was okay with Arthur. He wasn't about to tell Edward how much his stomach was churning. He couldn't really say why. It wasn't the prospect of being arrested. He knew there were going to be cameras and that the police knew that, too. Everyone that morning in the big church on Lanvale Street stressed that the protest was to be a peaceful one. How could it not be, with all these religious people involved? In front of Arthur were seated two rabbis and a number of ministers. There was even a Catholic priest on the bus.

It was hard to fathom—how Negroes weren't allowed to swim in a certain swimming pool or go to an amusement park and ride the rollercoaster and shriek and wobble around afterwards. Would the world end if that happened, the way the *Watchtower* people always were predicting? Edward joked to Arthur that if he went to a swimming pool and got in, the water would turn brown. And, crazy as it seemed, there might be white people who thought that. A classmate at City named Kurt liked to brag about his father, who had been one of the *Sturm Soldaten* in World War II. He wore a belt buckle that had the lightning-bolt-like *SS* on it. Unless he had to in class, Kurt never spoke to a Negro.

One of the rabbis on the bus was talking to the priest. Arthur wondered if they knew each other or were just comparing notes on God. His own family was not very Jewish. Arthur's bar mitzvah was more notable for the cakes Seeley had made and the amount of whiskey Grandpa Max consumed than for any religious feeling. When he went to Hebrew school, it always seemed that the teachers were trying to make things meaningful that shouldn't be made meaningful. God was weird, Arthur thought. Wasn't that the point of God? Wasn't creating people a fundamentally weird act? How all-knowing could God be if he did that? Bringing the heavens down to earth for a bunch of bored kids who would rather be playing touch football on an autumn afternoon seemed a waste of everyone's time.

Edward was talking about the Harlem Renaissance and what Negro writers had done for American literature and how here in Baltimore a Negro couldn't ride on a carousel. What kind of justice was that? Arthur knew that was a rhetorical question. His gum was losing its flavor, but he continued to work his jaw.

When he left the house that morning, he told his parents he wasn't sure when he might be home. His mom gave him the usual "be careful." His dad told him to watch out where he parked, since the church where they were gathering was in a

Negro section of the city. That probably was the best they could do. He knew that his mom sympathized with what he was doing. She even said that she should be doing something, too; Arthur was honoring the Fourth of July "in a real way." Arthur pointed out that staying in their neighborhood would be doing something, but she only shrugged. He had to admit that not wanting to move was partly selfish. He didn't want to spend the remainder of his high school years in some ugly box in a cornfield.

He was partly peeved with his mother, too. She continued to have a hard time making up her mind about anything, as if she were going through some permanent Eustacia Vye crisis. He finally had gotten around to reading *The Return of the Native*. At least now he could understand what was happening when his mom started talking about what he now understood had to be one of the world's unhappiest couples, Clym and Eustacia. And at least she wasn't crying as much as she used to. Sometimes she even seemed happy, as if she wasn't so much a "be careful" mom but someone exuberant, someone who was more than her responsibilities. She had started to actually ask him what he was listening to up in his room. A day or two ago, he had heard her singing to herself out on the patio. The songs were stupid, Arthur thought, stuff about Paris and springtime, but maybe she would move on to Ray Charles soon.

His dad wasn't sympathetic but told Arthur that Arthur needed to learn for himself. That meant: If you want to act like an idiot, be my guest. Lately his dad had been around the house more. Arthur was tempted to ask him if Marilee was mad at him, but he didn't have the guts — not yet, at least.

Losing Rebecca tugged at Arthur every day. Though he listened to his parents and the guys at work and his pool hall friends, he didn't really care what anyone said or did to him. Part of him hoped that a cop would bash his head that afternoon. The blood would be real. It would be better than a girl telling him he wasn't grown up enough. He thought of Rebecca naked and groaned.

"Something bothering you, Merm?" Edward inquired.

"Nothing a civil rights protest can't fix," Arthur answered.

"Good thing you aren't a Negro, then," Edward said. "We always return to our skins."

Arthur had that mildly ticked-off feeling that Edward often provoked when he one-upped him about race. "What's wrong with that?" he asked Edward. "Where the hell are we supposed to return to? Isn't everyone supposed to accept him or herself? Isn't that what this is about today — acceptance?"

"No need to get huffy. I'm not Sigmund Freud, but it feels like you have more on your mind than the plight of Negroes who want to ride the Wild Mouse at Gwynn Oak Park."

Arthur sighed, but then he thought of Ruby's endless sighs and tried somehow to retract it. It was gone, however, to wherever sighs went. "I rode the Wild Mouse once. It's pretty great if you want to feel like you're made of Jell-O."

Singing came from the front of the bus. A stout Negro woman stood up and began to slowly sway. The song was "We Shall Overcome."

Arthur and Edward began to sing, too. Arthur enjoyed this part of things, how, no matter what was going on, there was bound to be some singing. He thought Negroes were geniuses that way, though Edward sang no better than he did. Worse maybe — Edward's nasal bleat reminded him of the old men at an Orthodox synagogue.

A few more songs were sung, spirituals like "I'm on My Way to Freedom Land," which made Arthur think about how real heaven was to some people — like Seeley, for instance — while to him heaven seemed like more craziness of the *Watchtower* type, and then the bus driver hollered "Gwynn Oak Park, folks," and everyone gathered themselves up, which meant for Arthur that he threw his gum out the window, got off the bus, and walked toward the entrance to the amusement park, which featured a large oval sign announcing "Welcome to Gwynn Oak." A Ferris wheel loomed high above.

Arthur and Edward both pointed at the sign but didn't say anything.

A lot of people who hadn't come on buses to protest segregation, hundreds and hundreds and hundreds of white people inside the park and some outside the park, were yelling. Arthur had focused on how the protesters were going to be arrested for trespassing. He hadn't thought about other people being there.

"White nigger! You! White nigger!" shouted a woman in a sundress who had zeroed in on Arthur. He could see the veins standing up on her neck. Her face was red and purple; she looked as if she were going to explode. Arthur's stomach flopped again. When he had picketed places like Mr. Schwartz's office, no one around him seemed to care much one way or another. This was different: these people were boiling angry. They had signs that said things like "White People Have Rights Too" and "Keep Gwynn Oak White."

"Let's be thankful they don't have guns," Edward murmured.

"How do you know?" Arthur asked. They were standing in a large group near the park entrance. Patrol wagons were nearby. Arthur could see some of the first people who had come, including some ministers, being led or carried off. It didn't take long. You trespassed and you were arrested. Arthur had never seen so many police.

The hollering lady was not letting up. Arthur wondered if she knew him from somewhere. He didn't recognize her. Maybe he should go up and talk to her and try to explain what they were doing. The air pulsated with screams from the white people.

Arthur started to make a comment to Edward but a Negro man came up and held out two picket signs. "I want you boys outside the park. We got plenty of people to be arrested. I want you out there with these signs telling the world why we're here."

"But—" Edward said.

"No *buts*," the man said. "Do it."

"Yes, sir," Edward responded. Arthur heard something gruff in Edward's voice, something not like Edward. He had told Arthur that he intended to be arrested. He was tired of carrying signs. "White people know what we're saying. That's not the point. The point is to make things happen."

The two of them joined a line of people by the street. When Arthur looked over at the hecklers, the woman in the sundress was still going strong.

"That woman keeps looking at you, Merm," Edward said. "You know her?"

"Never saw her before in my life," Arthur answered. Edward and he were walking along side by side, brandishing their signs: "Gwynn Oak Park — For Everyone."

"White people all look alike, don't they?" Edward chuckled. Then he put on his trouble-I've-seen face, his history face. "I'm going back to that crowd and I'm going to lay myself down and I'm not moving till I'm arrested."

Arthur understood. That was what nonviolence was about. You made them deal with the fact of your body.

"Don't feel that you have to follow me. In fact, I wish you wouldn't. This is my thing." Edward reached out to Arthur's shoulder and pulled him so they were no longer side by side but facing one another. "You're doing the right thing, Merm, being here. I know you don't have to do this. I appreciate that. But you aren't me."

Some of the white people had taken up a chant — "Two, four, six, eight, we don't want to integrate." Almost like counterpoint — a word Arthur had learned from Mr. Baker — many of the protesters were singing, their words — "We are not afraid" — mingling with the taunts. Arthur looked up at the sky where a flock of starlings was wheeling around. A car drove by and honked. Another car drove by and a guy Arthur's age leaned out the window and shouted something. "Disgrace" — it was something about disgrace. In one of his hands he held a small American flag attached to a stick.

Edward had left the sidewalk and was walking toward the entrance. Some of the protesters were lying on the ground while others were being carried into patrol wagons and buses. They hung limply in the officers' arms, dolls stuffed with spirit. The white people who were chanting had changed their words: "Two, four, six, eight — we still want to segregate." A man spat on a Negro minister who was lying on the ground. Another white man slapped the spitter on the back. They both laughed.

In their white T-shirts and greased-back hair, Arthur saw, they weren't anything out of the ordinary. Maybe that was the point. Arthur's textbooks were always telling stories about famous people doing famous things, but meanwhile the world was full of people like these guys. They were having a ball, elbowing each other, grinning and pointing at the minister, who was still prone. They didn't even seem angry.

Arthur kept walking back and forth with his sign. He felt hopeful. He looked once more at the guys standing by the minister. He felt hopeless. He was doing something that needed to be done. He was doing something futile.

The eye of the harrowing, uplifting storm had come to Baltimore. He paused and listened. Above the jeers and songs, he could make out another sound: people on the rollercoaster. Their shouts echoed with fear and joy.

Susan

Iris regarded the Duncan Hines chocolate layer cake Susan had made that afternoon and the candles on it with what looked like horror. Everything—the dinner of Iris's favorites, including succotash and crab cakes, the small talk at the table about how the summer was going, even the absence of mosquitoes on the side porch—had gone the way Susan wanted it to go. However up in the air her life was, however much she jumped every time the phone rang, it felt this evening that her family still was a family. Even Ruby praised the food that Susan and Seeley had cooked and said how beautiful the birthday girl was—a *"shayna madela."*

Iris didn't look very beautiful at this moment. Snot was starting to run down over her upper lip, and when her sister made a motion toward her with a tissue, she pushed it away.

"What's wrong, Iris?" Susan asked. She tried hard to keep her voice even. Lately, Iris had been telling her that she had a right to her own feelings. Susan wasn't about to argue.

"Would you blow out the candles?" Arthur asked. "And wipe your nose. I don't want to taste your mess."

Iris gave her brother a get-lost look.

"I don't want your daggers, Iris. I just want some cake," Arthur responded.

"Susan," Stan said.

"Don't make Mom take care of everything," Iris said. She wiped the back of a hand under her nose.

Ellen made a face at her sister and muttered "gross."

"Too bad, Ellen," Iris said, then made a loud sniffle.

Susan held her breath and waited. No wonder she never wanted to be a drama coach like Cathy Ramsdell. She had a family.

"If anyone wants to know why I'm crying it's because I'm getting older and I can see we aren't the people we used to be." Iris looked down so that she wasn't talking to anyone in particular.

Ruby said something under her breath in Yiddish, then started to lament: "Not the people, *oy*, not the people."

"Now, Iris—" Stan began.

"Don't 'Now Iris' me," Iris said.

Stan began again. "Young lady—"

"Don't 'young lady' me."

"Just blow the candles out, Iris, will you, before there's wax on everything," Arthur said. "It's your damn birthday, for Christ sakes."

"Arthur!" Stan glared.

Iris smiled wanly, inhaled, and then blew at the candles. She blew again. On the third try the last wavering flames went out.

"Did you make a wish?" Ellen asked.

"It's best if we keep the wish secret," Susan said. She tried to muster a motherly smile but failed. Along with the low-grade anguish of a fraught birthday celebration, she felt, at this inauspicious moment, Jarvis Baker's hands on her. She tried to push the hands away but they wouldn't budge. The hands roved up and down her body. Susan had slept with him six times now. Lu, ever the fount of unhelpful wisdom, told her that "getting laid for real can scramble any woman's brains." Jarvis greeted any sign of Susan's concern as to the whereabouts of his wife with a calm, almost whimsical dismissal. "She's out toddling," he would say.

"She wished for world peace, Ellen," Arthur said. "Now let's eat."

"Peace," Ruby declared. "Not between Communists and Wall Street. Only *sotsyalists* will bring peace."

Stan began to tap his fingers on the table.

"Iris, please cut the cake for us," Susan said. She moved the pile of dessert plates in the center of the table toward her daughter. "The birthday girl is welcome to the biggest piece."

"Where did you get those plates, Mom?" Ellen asked. "All those flowers on them, they look like they're from the olden days."

Iris heaved her shoulders, a spasm of feeling without tears. "I'll cut the cake but I still feel bad. It's like we're all going off in different directions." She hefted the silver cake knife and began cutting slices.

"I agree," Arthur said. "Maybe we can be the anti-*Ozzie and Harriet*—Dad always at the office, Mom looking distracted, sisters learning to spell the word *puberty*."

"Shut up, Arthur," Iris said.

"Iris, there will be none of that language here," Stan commanded. "How's about some of that great looking cake for me?"

Susan had the impulse to yell. She didn't lack for material: "I'm having sex with a Negro man. It's a good thing in my life. He's alive to me. And I'm becoming alive to him." Maybe Arthur was right. Their TV program could be *Meet the Mermelsteins*, which would be a different kind of show, one where happiness wasn't dispensed like mayonnaise and difficulties didn't evaporate like air freshener. Her words wouldn't kill anyone, though she couldn't be sure what they might do to her mother.

Iris handed out pieces of cake and served herself last. Everyone started eating, but she didn't touch her fork.

"Mom and Dad, I want to know when we're going to move," Iris said. "Ellen and I need to have our own bedrooms. And we need to have another real bathroom. And we want to go to school out in the County. And you don't tell us anything." Iris paused for emphasis. "I hate that."

"Now, Iris—" Stan started to say, but Arthur cut him off.

"I like it here just fine. You can go to school with Negroes. Mom teaches them and gets along with them fine. A lot of my classmates are Negroes. My friend Edward—"

"Drop dead," Iris blurted. She shot a quick look at her father but kept talking. "No one cares what you think about Negroes. If you want to protest everything, that's your problem. Ellen and I have other concerns."

"Your problem, Iris—" Arthur began, but Susan cut in.

"I don't think this is a good way to spend a birthday."

"It's my birthday, Mom, and I should be able to talk

about what I want to talk about. I'm not a baby."

Susan nodded but said nothing. The yelling impulse hadn't gone away.

"It's time for Dad to clear his throat and make a pronouncement—right, Dad?" Arthur said. He licked his fork while making an appreciative sound.

"Arthur," Stan said. "I can live without that tone. And I can live without your comments, Iris, about our moving. We'll move when we're ready to move. We don't want to do anything rash."

"You always have the last word, Daddy. It isn't fair," Ellen said.

Everyone, except for Ruby who had nodded off, looked at her as if they had forgotten she was there.

"It *isn't* fair, Stan," Susan added. "You said 'we' but you mean 'I,' not 'we.' Are you the dictator of this family?"

There was silence. Then a car drove by slowly.

"That's not helpful, Susan," Stan said. He put the fingertips of his hands together to make a steeple.

"It *is* helpful, Stan. The truth is always helpful."

The car came to a stop further down the street. They heard a tire rub against the curb, a dense squeal.

"That's Danny Glickman," Arthur said. "He always hits the curb. What a ding-a-ling."

No one responded.

"This is Iris's birthday. Let's keep it festive," Stan said.

Ellen pushed some crumbs around on her plate. Arthur whistled a few notes from "Sweet Home Chicago." Susan realized she was gripping the edge of the table. Ruby quietly snored.

Susan got up from her seat and asked who would help her clear the table. Ellen raised her hand. Arthur said, "Sure, Mom." Iris said nothing and neither did Stan. The half-eaten cake seemed to slump slightly. Everything got started but nothing got finished. Everything became more complicated. That's what the days bred—complications. She touched her mother gently on her shoulder. "Ma, wake up. Wake up, Ma. I'll help you get downstairs."

Ruby looked around startled. "Is still a birthday?" she

asked.

"Oh, Grandma," Iris whispered. The words trembled with sadness.

Susan didn't move her hand from Ruby's shoulder. It was comforting.

Arthur

No one in Arthur's immediate family had died. Max's wife had died long before Arthur was born; Ruby's husband had disappeared. He might be dead or he might be sitting beside a swimming pool in Palm Springs. The only people whose deaths he knew intimately were in books — people like Eustacia Vye and Jay Gatsby. Those were people who had to die. The world they lived in couldn't abide them. Sometimes it spooked Arthur to think how the real world might be like that too, but, like the atomic bombs, that was a fright to be pushed aside. "Put off until tomorrow, what you can avoid today," Alfred E. Newman said in *Mad*. That seemed like reasonable advice about some decisions.

Being in the hospital wasn't one of those decisions. Bertha had called their house, and Susan had called the office, where she learned that Stan was in his car headed to a meeting with a client. Arthur took the phone from Marilee and told his mother that he would go to the hospital. Though he couldn't say what it was, Grandpa Max meant something to him. After Rebecca broke up with him, he stopped carrying around the condom Max had given him. It depressed and rebuked him. He couldn't even look at the *Playboys* at Max's anymore; her real body made those posed bodies look pathetic. He was living in the worst of no worlds.

Under the fluorescent light, his grandfather, propped up in his white johnny seemed like something that had washed up on the beach — shapeless, pummeled, and emitting a bleak, medicinal scent. Susan was seated at the bedside and told him that Bertha had gone to the cafeteria. Otherwise the room was empty of people — no doctors or nurses, interns or orderlies. Arthur had pictured someone official at Max's side, saying something soothing. Someone was, but Arthur's mother was not a medical person. She was telling Max in her gentlest voice that he was going to feel better soon.

Max seemed to be listening to her. He had the habit of paying attention to women. "Once they figure out what's wrong with me, I'll be top drawer," he said to Susan, then turned to Arthur. "How you doing, sport?" Max's voice seemed hollowed out. The rumble was there but thinner. That must be pain, Arthur thought, or what they're sedating him with. Since the morning his mother fell, pills had become more real to Arthur.

"What happened, Grandpa?" Arthur asked. He had walked over to the far side of the bed but had a hard time looking directly at Max. Max's face seemed caved in, as if someone had pressed against it with a weight. His eyes were glazed. His flabby cheeks had a sickly, yellowish cast.

Susan answered. "Max passed out and Bertha called an ambulance. They've started to do some tests. So far as they can tell, it wasn't a heart attack. He has chest pains, though. He's short of breath."

"I've felt better, Arthur," Max said. He tried to sit up more in bed but could only rock a bit from side to side. "And the docs don't like cigars and whiskey. Killjoys. Means I'll have to get the hell out of here soon." He beckoned with his left arm, the one that wasn't hooked up to an IV bag. "So tell me what's happening in the world. What've I missed?"

"Stephen Ward killed himself," Arthur answered.

"Who the hell is that?" Max asked. He tried to say something else but began to cough. It was an awful sound — harsh, deep, and desperate. Arthur became afraid that Max wouldn't stop, or that he would pass out.

Susan grabbed one of Max's hands and held it. After many scary seconds, the cough subsided. Max looked even weaker than before. Arthur felt more uneasy. This was a place he never had been.

"Stephen Ward was a doctor in Britain," Susan said. "He apparently worked as a procurer for rich men. Some of them were politicians." She stopped. "Haven't you been reading about it in the paper, Max?"

Max shrugged.

"It's called 'The Profumo Affair' because a government minister named John Profumo was involved with one of the girls,'" Susan went on. "It's titilating and tawdry, which sells papers."

"Mom means it's about sex," Arthur interjected. He expected his grandfather to smile but Max didn't.

"Stephen Ward took sleeping pills and killed himself." Susan announced. She might have been reading the attendance roll at the beginning of a class. She pursed her lips but didn't say anything more.

The feelings that had haunted Arthur since his mother's suicide attempt were still there. They kept pushing against some shut door inside of him. He could have said, "Like you tried to do, Mom, huh?"—but that didn't seem very constructive. It seemed, though, that it was up to him to get his mother to consider what things had been like for him since then. She talked to him about Martin Luther King Jr. and Thomas Hardy and even about their listening to a few more of the jazz records Arthur had bought—bebop—and how different that music was to her and how much she was starting to like it, but for them to talk about the panic Arthur had felt that morning seemed too close to him and too close to her.

"Killed himself? That's no damn good. I want to see the Orioles win the pennant. Is that right, Arthur?" Max tried to wave the arm attached to the bag but realized he couldn't. "Damn this thing," he said.

"Sure, Grandpa," Arthur mumbled but then roused himself. "One of these years—it's coming."

"I wonder if he needed to kill himself," Susan said. Her words didn't seem addressed to anyone special. It gave Arthur a shiver. What he felt when he walked in the hospital was true: no one near him had died. Someone had wanted to die, though, someone he loved.

"What was that, Susan? I'm not much company," Max said.

"You're not supposed to be company," Susan answered. "You're supposed to get well." Susan smoothed the skirt of her dress, a gesture Arthur had seen her make a few thousand times. Today she wore a green dress without sleeves. A yellowish belt made of some coarse material cinched the waist. Rebecca had told him how his mother had a sense of "American style." Arthur had nodded politely. All he had wanted to do was get Rebecca out of her clothes. Once upon a time his father must have felt that way about his mother. But now? It couldn't feel good to get older.

"That's right, Grandpa. Your job is to get well," Arthur repeated. He looked at his mother, though, not Max, when he spoke.

"There's a lot to live for," Susan said.

From where he was standing, Arthur stared out into the hallway. A nurse was pushing a wheelchair. The girl in it seemed around his age. Her head lolled to the side and was covered by a bandana. The wheelchair made a reassuring, mechanical creak — round and round and round.

"I'm going to the March on Washington, Grandpa," Arthur said. He moved a little closer to Max. He wanted to make sure that Max heard him.

"The march for the Negroes?" Max asked. His eyes remained unfocused but for a moment his voice was stronger.

"That's the one," Arthur answered. "A lot of famous people are going to be there giving speeches and singing. Joan Baez is going to be there."

"Joan who?" Max closed his eyes. "Truth is, there's worse people in this world than Negroes. Japs, for instance."

"I may go too," Susan said. Her voice was husky. She looked placid enough, but Arthur wondered what was going on inside of her.

"That right?" Max asked. "Big day for America, I guess. Not as big as VJ Day but a big day."

The syllables in "America" were spaced out, drifty. Arthur thought of his transistor radio late at night and how the disc jockeys sounded like that. They were far off and disembodied, though. His grandfather was right in front of him.

"You might go, Mom?" Arthur could hear the wobble in his voice. He hadn't thought of asking his mother.

"I might," she said. She stood up from her seat.

Susan and Arthur looked from one another to the patient. Max had fallen asleep. His head drooped forward from the stem of his neck—a large, bald blossom.

"Do you think Grandpa will be okay?" Arthur asked.

"He wants to keep living. That should count for something," Susan answered.

They both stood gazing at the old man's skull. It was ugly but it was beautiful, too.

Susan

"You ever cheat on your husband before?" Jarvis asked. "It's a form of escape. Maybe not *The Great Escape*, but I'm not Steve McQueen, either." Jarvis lifted a glass of iced tea to his mouth. "I read he does his own motorcycle stunts—one crazy white man." After a small swallow, he put the tea back on the table. "Needs more sugar." He reached toward the dispenser on the table.

Susan looked to the left of Jarvis's head, out the window at the people passing by on Howard Street. "No, I haven't. I have to say, I don't like the word 'cheat.' It doesn't seem like the right word."

"There's no forgetting you're an English teacher, Susan," Jarvis said. He smiled at her. Susan thought that if Jarvis were a lamp with three switches for brightness, this smile was the middle wattage—alert to the humor of the situation but not overwhelming. Mostly his smiles delighted her. They were part of how he had decided to live his life. She wanted to reach across the table, put her hands on his shoulders, and kiss him. Instead, she busied herself with the club sandwich she had ordered. Whatever they represented as a white woman and a Negro man, they could show they were hungry. She didn't have much of an appetite, though.

"It's more like following a feeling. It's not as though I set out to wrong my husband," Susan said.

"Word always gets back about these things. We're sitting here in public. Anyone can walk in at any minute. We made a rendezvous in a movie theater and sat next to one another in the darkness. We touched one another in that darkness." Jarvis took a bite out of his sandwich. "Heat got to you, Susan? No appetite today?"

"I fantasize every summer about going to Maine, where

a hot day is seventy-eight degrees. But it's just one of my fantasies." Susan pushed her plate toward Jarvis. "You're welcome to some of mine."

"You like the movie, by the way?" Jarvis asked. He took a long drink of tea.

"It's a man's world, isn't it?" Susan asked. "Men make wars, men create prisoner of war camps, men escape from them, men kill the escapees, and men make movies about the whole thing." Susan paused. "I like looking at Steve McQueen. He may be crazy but he's cute." She raised her own tea to her lips. When she put the glass down, she rattled the ice in it a bit, then looked at Jarvis. "And do you 'cheat'?"

"I spread the love around, if that's what you mean," he answered. He didn't smile, though. He didn't frown, either. He was presenting a fact.

"So I'm a lucky recipient."

"You may not have seen yourself as having any to spread around, Susan. But you do. The way I see it, the world needs all the love it can get."

"And your wife?"

"The same as your husband."

Susan watched him put a half-teaspoon more sugar in his tea. "That's more sugar than it is tea, Jarvis."

"Keeps me sweet." He smiled the low-wattage smile.

Again, she wanted to reach across the table and kiss him. It was awful. Everything in the coffee shop was mundane except for her feelings.

"My husband doesn't know about us," Susan said.

"You sure?" Jarvis asked. He swallowed the remnant of one of the sections of the sandwich. "Not a bad sandwich. Not like my mama could make on some good Jewish rye bread, but not bad."

"And your wife knows about your love-spreading?"

"That's between me and her, Susan. You got part of me but you don't have all of me." It was Jarvis's turn to look steadily at her. "You look awfully nice in that dress, Susan. That's one beautiful set of breasts on you. Make a man smack his lips."

"Jarvis!" Susan almost yelped. She bowed her head.

Baron Wormser

"Easy does it, girl. We're in public. Remember what happened in the Market. That old Polack was about to kill me."

When Susan looked up, she saw that a waitress clearing a table was eying her. There was more contempt in the woman's eyes than alarm. That probably was better.

"I didn't mean to," Susan said. "I—"

"I get it. You're a lady and what I said wasn't proper. I understand that. My wife is a lady, too." Jarvis looked around slowly. He reminded Susan of one of the prisoners in the movie, a man whose job it was to get rid of the displaced dirt from the tunneling for the escape. Like that prisoner, Jarvis's movements were so slow that people would not recognize how much he was taking in. Maybe white people never thought that Negroes noticed them to begin with. "If you never hear what people really think, you may assume they have no thoughts," Jarvis had told her.

Susan's sandwich lay uneaten. "Now, you got to keep some flesh on your bones, but if you're going to waste that, I can help you," Jarvis said. He pulled the plate to his side and picked up one of the stuffed quarters.

"This is driving me crazy, Jarvis," Susan said.

"And what is 'this,' if I may ask?" Jarvis snapped a finger and beckoned to the waitress. "More iced tea, please. Many thanks."

Susan felt it—how every motion and word was calibrated, every politeness and every look. And she adored Jarvis for being so natural. Did that make her a fool or merely wishful?

The waitress nodded ever so slightly; she was a strong-jawed mountain woman who could be found on any block of some Baltimore neighborhoods, a year or ten years out of West Virginia but never in her heart having left the scrap of earth that was home.

"You know what I'm talking about, Jarvis," Susan said. The sadness welling up inside her felt like more than her body could contain.

"You mean the neither-here-nor-there quality of our coming together, the higgledy-piggledy quality of it, the teeter-totter of emotion, the uncertain coloration of color?" Jarvis was

284

almost leering at her.

Susan didn't mean to push him to this place, but she had. She dabbed at her mouth with a paper napkin.

"Nothing to clean from those lovely lips, Susan. You've barely taken a bite," Jarvis said.

The sadness felt calm, too. Her incoherent love was not going to equal his good-natured lust, but there was no reason it should. Having received numerous gifts of feeling from Jarvis, she was, as her father-in-law would have put it, "ahead of the game."

"I want to go on the march," Susan said. "Would you help me?"

"Help you?" Jarvis asked. "Hire a limousine, perhaps?"

"I want to go on a bus with other people—with your people." A conspirator, Susan kept her voice low. The waitress seemed to be lingering at the next table, wiping it more than it needed to be wiped.

"With my 'people'?"

"Quit it, Jarvis. I want to ride on a bus with some Negroes. Can I make it any plainer?"

"My, my, my," Jarvis laughed. "You'll allow my amusement, I hope. Truly the wheel is turning. White folks have spent forever not wanting to be on a bus with Negroes." He looked away from Susan. "I can't really say how much I feel about you, Susan. Probably I don't know. But the fact is—you touch me." He paused. "Even when I don't want to be touched."

The waitress was folding up her cleaning cloth very carefully. Susan thought of men in the synagogue folding up their prayer shawls.

"Sure, I can put you on a bus. I know my share of Baptists, AME's, Methodists. Nobody needs heaven more than Negroes." He smiled, but it wasn't the easy switch Susan was accustomed to. It was uncertain, almost fumbling. It was more like the word Jarvis was teaching her to use—*blue*. "Sue feeling blue?" he would say to her. Sadness came and went, the plaything of moods; the blues hung on. "A debt you never can pay," was how he put it.

For a time neither of them said anything. To Susan it seemed more frightening than their talking. When they were chattering, they were being like the others in the coffee shop on a busy street in downtown Baltimore. Now they were somewhere else, their silence begging to be noticed.

"I get you anything else?" The waitress was speaking to Susan.

"I don't think so, ma'am," Jarvis answered.

The woman didn't turn her head to him but pulled back so fast she bumped into the table behind her.

"Watch out there," Jarvis warned. He let his eyes rest on the woman for a few seconds and then, as she walked away, turned to Susan. "I'll put you on a bus," Jarvis said. "I doubt if I'll be on it, because I'm not a churchgoer. Personally, I think if there were a God He would have thrown a few bricks through the car windows of a few southern politicians by now." Jarvis reached for his wallet. "That's my problem, though. My father wants to go to D.C., says he wants to see it for himself — all those colored people standing up for themselves."

"I'd like to meet your father, Jarvis," Susan said.

"That would be something, wouldn't it? Maybe you'll take Ruby and I'll take my father and we'll all go to the movies and sit here afterwards and talk. Maybe my wife will come, too." He pulled out some dollar bills. "Of course, what we don't know can't hurt us." He paused. "White folks taught me that."

"In that case I'll bring my husband along," Susan said. "We can start another Congress of Racial Equality."

Jarvis rose. When he pushed his chair back, it made a thin scraping noise on the linoleum. "Probably one such organization is enough. As to your husband, I'd be intrigued but I can't say it's necessary. It's like what you said about the movie: men always wind up being men." He pushed the chair in carefully so that it didn't make a sound. "Women are another story." He winked at her so fast it didn't seem to happen. "I doubt, dear Susan, if we are finished with one another."

As he walked through the door, Susan waved goodbye to him. She felt the waitress watching her. She could admit it — the watching thrilled her. She began to eat the rest of her sandwich.

Arthur

For the past month Arthur had been slipping out of the house once everyone was asleep, getting in his mother's car and driving around Baltimore for a couple of hours — not in pursuit of anything special, like the burlesque houses on the Block or Jack's pool hall, but just driving for the sake of driving, being by himself and listening to the radio. He had found a truck stop out on Route 40 that was open all night. He could get gas there, and they had a diner, too, with thick milk shakes and great cherry pie. You could get other things there, too, he learned one night when a woman in a very short skirt approached him in the parking lot and asked him if he was "interested." He said he didn't have any money on him. "Too bad," the woman said, "You're kind of cute," and she swished her ass off into the night.

He didn't hide the driving from his parents, but they didn't say anything to him. It surprised him when they were cool about something, though it may have been more that they were distracted by their own troubles. He could feel the frostiness between them but it was hard to know what it meant. It seemed worse than when they had arguments, because when they argued they usually made up. Now they never made up, but he was starting to understand that their grudges were their business. He was moving away from them, not toward them.

What he *was* moving toward, he didn't have a clue about. That was okay. He felt safe in the car — not invisible, but in his own cocoon. He rolled the driver's-side window down and felt the night air. Some nights it was still plenty hot but better than the infernal daytime. He drove through the endless Gentile neighborhoods of Baltimore, places where not a single Jew lived, not just the fancy areas but the working class areas, too — miles and miles of little houses with little yards, or rowhouses with porches and minute plots of grass in front and TV antennas on their roofs. He couldn't believe people lived in each and every house. And he couldn't believe how everyone cared so much about who lived next door. Sometimes he wanted to holler out the window, "Wake up—Jew driving through." He took his time taking off from the red lights and stop signs. The least he could do was linger in a foreign country.

It wasn't thinking about prejudice that interested him on these nights anyway. He got enough of that with Edward. And he wasn't going to forget all those people screaming their hatred at Gwynn Oak. What he liked about these nights as he drove block after block and mile after mile was listening to the songs. Out of the darkness came endless music, not only the local Negro stations that played rhythm and blues and even some jazz, but after midnight the stations from farther away, places like Cleveland and Buffalo. That seemed amazing but there it was, right in the car dashboard.

Edward liked to tell Arthur that integration was a two-way street. White people had as much to gain, maybe more, from being with Negroes. "Negroes are inherently expressive people. Inside or outside of church, the Lord is in their bones," Edward had proclaimed recently. Their music certainly proved that; it had soul with a capital S. Something crucial was being dispensed, and at least for him, sitting there and fiddling with the dial, it was free of charge.

One night could feel like many nights and that was part of the beauty of the driving, too, how one song became another. The joy of it was that there always was another song, always another voice, always another set of words and feelings. The songs came from worlds Arthur knew only dimly, but that didn't stop them from making sense to him. The music of white people—"pop," as it was called, sentimentality pretending to be real feeling, one small letter removed from "pap"—seemed almost comically thin compared to someone named Solomon Burke singing "Loneliness, loneliness, it's such a waste of time." 'Singing,' however, was an inadequate word for what Solomon Burke was doing . He was testifying (a word Arthur had learned from Seeley), he was sobbing, and he was communing with something Arthur couldn't spell out but trusted—the unwieldy mystery of the human heart and how some things — like Rebecca getting married — happened the way they happened and left a person standing alone, a person who cared for another person. "When you're waiting for a voice to come in the night / and there is no one there / Ah, don't you feel like crying." Solomon Burke might as well have been singing to Arthur alone. And he was — that was the gift of it.

Arthur had been singing that Solomon Burke tune in his head, over a commercial for "more Parks sausages, Mom," when he pulled the car over to the curb. He was not far from where his grandfather lived, near the stadium. He had a dark feeling about Max, how he might not leave the hospital alive. Arthur turned the ignition off and sat there with the nighttime stillness. Moths swarmed the streetlight not far from his car. Seeing Max lying there in that vast white bed without his familiar cigar and whiskey had been a shock. He had thought Max would flick ash and play poker forever.

When Arthur started the car again, the radio rushed right at him: "This is my man, the child-man, the harmoni-cat, the genius. Who am I talkin'? What am I talkin'? I'm talkin' Little Stevie Wonder. I'm talkin' 'Fingertips.' Can you, can you, can you, can you move to this groove?" The voice belonged to a local disk jockey — the Midnight Man. He'd be laying down this patter until six in the morning, rhyming and two-timing, as he liked to put it. Arthur turned up the volume.

It was as if right there in the Ford Fairlane a party had started — a sound party. People were clapping. A band was playing. Little Stevie was playing his harmonica and intoning a few lines of song. Above and beyond that, it felt that the universe had gathered into one loose but powerful braid of music and had no intention of letting go. When the song was over — and the disk jockey played both sides of the single, parts one and two — it continued in Arthur's head.

"I like that!" the Midnight Man brayed. "I like that cat! Cool and nobody's fool, blind but he can shine — Little Stevie Wonder!"

"I like it too!" Arthur yelled back at the radio. "I like it too!" He turned onto 33rd Street, where Memorial Stadium stood. It was strange to see it at night with no one there. Some lights were on in front but the parking lots were dark. Over the years his grandfather had gone to a couple of Oriole games with Arthur and Stan, but he tended to get fidgety. Baseball was too slow for him. He needed a home run or a great catch every couple minutes but that wasn't baseball. Max always brought a flask with him.

Police lights shone suddenly in Arthur's rearview mirror, coming out of nowhere. He winced, pulled over, killed the motor, and waited. He had already gotten a ticket in a speed trap out in the County and had to go to three Saturday classes so he wouldn't lose his license. He hadn't been going fast now, though. Could they give you a ticket for going too slow?

The policeman shone a flashlight in Arthur's face. "Just out driving, son?" he asked.

"Yeah," Arthur answered. "Just out driving."

"Nice night for it," the policeman observed. "You've got a dead left taillight. You know that?"

"No, I didn't, officer."

"Probably your parents' car?" The policeman turned off the flashlight. "You give me your license and registration and I'm going to write up a report. It says that you need to get this fixed. If we pull you over again, you get a ticket. Sound fair?"

"Sounds fair."

The ballpoint pen that the policeman wrote with was barely visible in his meaty hand. Patiently he scrawled the information. "Probably a good idea to head home now, since you have that light out. We want everyone to drive safe."

"Sounds like a good idea," Arthur answered. Inside himself he exhaled.

"You like baseball?" The policeman nodded toward the stadium.

"I do."

"I was just thinking of Bob Boyd tonight. You remember him, a Negro guy, played first base?"

Arthur looked at the policeman's face. He must have had bad acne when he was Arthur's age. His cheeks and nose were pitted.

"They called him 'The Rope' on account of he hit so many line drives. When he got a fastball he liked, he'd rip it."

The policeman shook his head. His cap tipped a little to the side, as if it were a size too large for him.

Arthur wondered how much the cap weighed. With its visor and badge affixed to the front, it seemed heavy.

"Stick with the Orioles, kid. One of these years they're going to do it." He hitched up his belt but didn't move. "Everything comes around sometime," he said, then turned his back and strolled toward his car. He started whistling. It was one of the Irish rebellion tunes Arthur had learned in the folk music club—"Roddy McCorley." Arthur began whistling himself. The policeman turned around, tipped his ungainly cap, and then got into his car. Arthur whistled even louder.

As he drove through the vast, quiet city, his home of black and white, North and South, aching feelings and thoughtless answers, he sang to himself—aloud, not in his head— "Young Roddy McCorley goes to die."

"What's a procurer?" Ellen asked.

Susan and her daughters were standing in front of the bank of elevators on the ground floor of Hutzler's Department Store on Howard Street. Susan was thinking about how she needed to buy some underwear. When she was shopping with her daughters, she usually forgot that she needed clothes, too. She wanted them to be sexy. Jarvis had teased her about her underwear: they were more like bloomers than panties.

"A procurer gets ladies of easy virtue for men," Iris answered.

"'Ladies of easy virtue'? What does that mean?" Ellen asked.

"Guess," said Iris. "You've been reading about that British man in the newspaper."

"Girls," said Susan, "this isn't the time or place to be talking like this."

"Why not?" they chorused. Their synchronicity was frightening. Susan didn't have to search for high fidelity; her daughters were stereophonic.

Susan put an arm around each and drew them back from the elevators.

"Actually, Mom, I have something real important I need to ask you right now," Iris said.

"More important than what I asked?" Ellen giggled.

"Is it about clothes?" Susan asked. Susan dropped her hands to her side and regarded her older daughter, who stood beside her in a madras skirt and white, short-sleeved blouse under which could be seen a bra that gave Iris's breasts a conic shape and that Iris insisted was the right bra for her. It didn't just seem that Iris was a different person every day; she *was* a different person. Even Ellen, who was her sister's faithful shadow and critic, couldn't keep up with her. At random times Susan found herself trying to think back to her own early adolescence. She remembered boys looking at her differently. She almost could summon up the emanation in a classroom or hallway, an atmosphere charged with sweaty, unholy electricity. What a rancid, exciting time of life.

Susan sighed. "As you know, we're here to shop for clothes, Iris. Again I'm asking you whether this is the right time and place." They had moved forward a few steps toward the elevators. People—mostly women—milled around them or stood there waiting. The air reeked of perfume, cologne, and deodorant. Susan knew she should take the girls by to say "Hi" to Lu, who would spray the girls with something new. It was a ritual; Lu was a priestess of sorts.

"There isn't any right time, Mom. Some things don't have right times."

Susan glanced at her other daughter. Ellen eyed her sister but said nothing. A pang of worry shot through Susan: Ellen was too passive, always watching her sister. Susan shook her head. As a mother, how many crossed connections did she discern each day?

"Why are you shaking your head, Mom?" Iris asked.

"Am I?" Susan asked. An elevator opened before them; people exited with packages, bags, and boxes. The elevator operator, a Negro woman, stood patiently waiting for the next human wave to enter.

Susan and Ellen moved toward the elevator, but Iris remained where she was. Because they were already a few steps away from her, Iris raised her voice. "Here's my question," she said. "Do you still love Daddy?"

The people around the Mermelsteins stopped for a second, as if the question might be directed at them. Then they focused on the woman Iris was defiantly staring at. Susan could feel those nearest to her hesitating. Here was some free drama; they wanted to hear the answer.

Susan moved back toward her daughter, as did Ellen.

"I wonder about that too, Mom," Ellen said, though her voice was much quieter than Iris's.

"What makes you think I don't love your father?" Susan asked. Her voice was level. She moved her eyes from one daughter to the other.

Someone near them exulted, "What a bargain!" A woman wearing a pink hat with a flimsy little veil, the sort Mamie Eisenhower wore, turned toward Susan.

"Come on, Mom," Iris said. "You must think we're idiots. You and Dad are always contradicting each other, always picking at each other. You never even sit down with each other. Just because you don't fight doesn't mean you're getting along."

"We worry, Mom," Ellen added. Her voice remained quieter than her sister's.

"I'm not going to lie to you. You're my girls." Susan looked around. The woman in the hat had looked them over and moved on. The elevator opened again. The Negro lady took a quick look at Susan, as if to say, "*You still here? Can't make up your mind where you're going?*" "I don't love your father the way I used to," Susan said. "I don't think he loves me the way he used to."

The girls said nothing. Susan thought one or more likely both of them were going to start crying. Their faces had that look—their eyes unfocused, their lips tensing.

"I wanted a half-slip," a woman nearby said to another woman. "But they have only full slips in my size. I guess I'll have to go to Stewart's."

"Or Hochschild's or Hecht's," the other woman added.

Standing there, Susan felt that she and her daughters formed some sort of living sculpture.

"Thanks, Mom, for being honest. It's hard for us to live with you guys," Iris said. A startled look came into Iris's eyes. She rubbed them with her palms. She wasn't going to cry.

"So does that mean, Mom, you're going to get divorced?" Ellen had moved closer to her sister. The resolve in her daughters' voices pained Susan but made her proud, too. If anyone were to start crying at this moment, it would be Susan. Speaking about the absence of love made her love for her daughters stronger: right there on the hectic, over-scented ground floor of Hutzler's her heart seemed to be coming asunder.

"Well, look who's here," a familiar female voice announced. Lu inserted herself between Iris and Ellen and put an arm around each of them. "How are my favorite raven-tressed beauties?" The many bracelets on Lu's wrists rattled. "I'm on my lunch break. Why don't we go to the Quixie together?"

Iris gave Lu a quizzical look. "We're crummy," she pronounced.

Susan was thinking now about the comic operas that Jarvis had told her about and how much they had to do with *Porgy and Bess*. Lu's coming up to her daughters seemed like a scene from one of them. Perhaps the women all around, clutching bags and boxes, would—chorus- like—start singing. "Shoppin' time and the livin' ain't easy." That was something Arthur would come up with. She had picked up one of his *Mad* magazines recently and couldn't put it down: there was so much to make fun of.

"We were talking, Lu, about the state of my marriage," Susan said.

"Ah." The syllable came out distended.

Lu took her arms off the girls and folded them up crosswise against her chest. "It's a big topic. This—" and she beckoned to the shoppers around her—"is probably not the best place to discuss it."

"That's what Mom thought," Ellen said.

"What do you think, Lu?" Iris asked. She was twisting a strand of hair in her right hand. Susan felt another love pang. Maybe she should break out into song. Arthur, who was turning into an authority on everything about the races, said that was one problem with white people—they didn't sing enough. He had shown her a headline about Birmingham that read "Sirens Wail, Horns Blow, Negroes Sing." Arthur didn't have much of a voice but Susan heard him singing in the shower or in his room. When his sisters mocked him, he sang all the louder.

"I think your mom is a wonderful woman," Lu answered. "I think she deserves to have a life of her own."

"What's that mean?" Ellen asked.

A woman barged into Susan. "Whoopsie!" she exclaimed. "I can barely see over all these purchases."

"If you'd like, I'll take some of them off your hands," Susan said.

The woman gave Susan a sharp look and scurried off.

"That was cool, Mom," Iris said.

"Yeah, that was cool," Ellen repeated.

Lu and Susan exchanged winks.

"I think it would be great if we went to the perfume counter and I let you experience some new fragrances." Lu waved a hospitable arm. She had told Susan more than once that cosmetics were on the ground floor because they were most important.

"What about lunch?" Ellen grumbled.

"We'll eat later," Susan answered. "It won't take long. Lu's making a kind offer to you girls."

"You never answered Ellen's question, Mom, about getting divorced," Iris said. She had her feet planted again.

The elevator opened once more and the operator looked out at them. "Miss Lu, how you doin'?" she said.

"I'm fine," Lu chirped. She waved her arms about and shook her bracelets.

Ellen tugged at her sister's sleeve. "Let's go smell some stuff, Iris."

"Yes, let's do that, Iris," Susan said. As she took one of Iris's hands, she felt a force moving through her. The words leapt out: "Everything's going to be okay, honey." She looked into her daughter's frowning face and lifted Iris's hand with her own.

"We have a new Hermès product I'm very excited about," Lu said and started to head off with Ellen.

The words Susan had spoken were words that her own mother had never said to her—not once. They felt strange in Susan's mouth, but that was pardonable. Someone had to start saying them. It might as well be a confused, love-starved, love-struck mother of three. What was even stranger was that she believed the words.

"A new Hermès product," Susan said. She swung their arms forward and ventured a step with Iris.

"Don't be an echo, Mom. I get enough of that already." Iris grasped her mother's hand more firmly.

Arthur

"It's her," Iris announced, extending the phone receiver toward her brother. She made a face that translated into something long and hyphenated: it's-your-ex-girlfriend-who-dumped-you-which-I-know-about-even-though-you-didn't-tell-me-you-dodo.

"It's *she*," Arthur corrected.

"Don't be a know-it-all, Arthur. Mom's out again so she can't pat you on the back."

"Look who's talking." With one hand Arthur grabbed the receiver and shooed his sister away with the other.

"I don't blame Rebecca," Iris said. "What can she see in you?" She flounced out of the hall, where the phone sat on its own small table.

The moment between Arthur's putting the receiver to his ear and saying "hello" was a time-hole—narrow and deep. He fell into it but at the same time a feeling—both warm and wary—was grabbing him, holding him up.

"Arthur?" Rebecca's voice asked.

"Yes, hi, Rebecca." The constriction he felt in his throat eased a bit. Arthur looked down and was surprised to see his tennis-sneakered feet. They were a reddish-orange from the clay courts at Druid Hill. "How are you?"

"If I were okay, I wouldn't be calling you, Arthur." Rebecca's voice was shaky. Arthur knew that voice from his mother: it came after a woman had been crying.

"What's the matter?" Arthur moved the receiver away from his ear. He didn't want to hear the answer. Then, in the next second, he moved it back.

There was silence on her end of the phone. Arthur put his other hand up and pressed on the wallpaper. At his high school, it was a standard detention exercise—you put both hands out against the wall in front of you and held up the school. If the teacher saw you were just resting your hands, he added on minutes. It seemed like the Marines, but it made you think about getting in trouble.

"Do you love me, Arthur?" Rebecca asked. Her voice was steadier but desperately forlorn. "Why did you give me up? Why didn't you fight for me?"

"Give you up? What are you talking about? You told me you were getting married. You told me I was a kid." The wall in front of Arthur started to pulsate. He drew his hand back.

"Don't raise your voice."

"Don't be my mother."

"Oh, Arthur," Rebecca started to sob. "I've made a mistake."

Arthur thought of the soap operas that Ruby and Seeley watched. Women said ridiculous things like "I've made a mistake" and started crying. Men never seemed to say those things. Arthur sucked in some air. The wall had gone back into place.

"What mistake?" Arthur asked.

"Don't be thick, Arthur. It's my getting married." Rebecca's voice kept changing. Now it sounded hoarse and spent.

"What can I do?"

"You can listen to me. My girlfriends are jealous or they're self-righteous or just plain mean. They think I'm getting what I deserved. They think I'm a conniver. They think all the books I've read went to my head."

"Did they?" Arthur was aware he was asking too many questions, but he was curious. He didn't know what else to do.

Rebecca sighed. "Maybe they did. I think of what Eustacia said to Clym, 'You are no blessing, my husband.' But my husband wants me to do bad things with him, Arthur, unclean things. I saved myself and now I'm with a pig. What you and I did together was innocent. You loved my body. My husband only wants to use my body. It's not the same." Rebecca's voice grew louder. "It's not the same. Do you understand? It's not the same. He wants a slave, not a wife." She started sobbing again.

"I do love you," Arthur gasped. He could feel his insides being twisted.

The sobbing went on. There was something primal to it that stunned Arthur. He didn't know about a lot of things—he knew that—but this was like the grief he had read about and heard about from Ruby and Mr. Schwartz. This was that place where a human being felt caught the way an animal in a trap was caught. No creature should be in that agony.

"It's sweet of you to say those words, Arthur." Rebecca was talking through sobs but they were lesser sobs.

"It's not sweet. It's true. And you're right. I gave you up because I didn't know what to do. I didn't know how to step up."

There was silence but it didn't feel as terrible. He waited.

"I don't know what to do, Arthur. I want to run away but I don't know where to run to. My father would never forgive me if I left this marriage. He wanted me to go to Israel. When I confessed to him what I was going to do—because I had to tell him—he was unhappy. Of course. But he said he wouldn't stop me." Rebecca sniffled. "I don't have much of anything now, Arthur. And the worst thing is that I'm afraid."

The banter of guys about cocks and cunts, the bragging about what happened last night ran through Arthur's head. You liked it and the girl liked it and that was that. It was simple—the instinct of the parked car. But it wasn't simple.

"Are you there, Arthur? I need you to say something."

Arthur ground his teeth. He wanted to touch her and see her. In his head he had tried to push her away because he didn't know what else to do. He wanted to smile at her lipstick and her hair ribbons. "It's going to be okay. You're strong and it's going to be okay."

A bleak laugh came from the phone. "Oh, I'm strong—even when I'm afraid I'm strong—but whether it's going to be okay—that's another story."

"It will be. I know it." Arthur paused. "You can come live with us."

This time Rebecca's laughter was deeper. "Live with your family? Haven't you told me there's not enough room in that house for all of you already? Where would you put me—in a cupboard?"

"We're going to move sometime soon into a big house out in the County. We'll have more rooms than you can count."

"That's kind of you. Who knows? I may take you up on it." After a silence—Arthur could feel Rebecca thinking—she spoke very distinctly. "You don't know how much I wish you were older, Arthur. You don't know how much. I can see you in a way you can't see yourself. It tears at my heart. I know how good you could be to me. You don't know how much I want someone to be truly good to me."

"Ah," was all Arthur could say. It wasn't for lack of feeling. It was because of too much feeling.

"I need to get off the phone, Arthur, but I need for you to say you will take my calls when I can call. I need to hear that."

"Of course I will. Are you kidding?" Arthur nervously swung the phone cord. He wanted to crawl through the receiver to her. "Can I see you?"

"Maybe. I don't know what's going to happen. I have a cousin in New York. I may just leave." Her voice had turned crisp, determined. "It's been good to hear you, Arthur. Don't forget me."

"Forget you?" he said, but she had hung up. His words lingered there in the hall. He put the receiver down and looked around to see where he was.

Iris walked in from the kitchen. "I need the phone now, Arthur."

Arthur couldn't say anything to her. He shook his head no, then yes.

"Are you okay?" his sister asked.

"Yeah, I'm okay," he managed.

"You can tell me the truth, Arthur. You're my brother. I'm not a fool."

"You're right. You're not a fool. I'm the fool."

"Don't be hard on yourself. We've got a lot to deal with right here." Iris paused and looked up and down at her brother. "Do you love her?"

"I do."

"I knew that." Iris moved a step toward him. "Is she in some kind of trouble?"

"Yeah, she's in trouble."

Iris opened her arms.

Arthur moved toward her. Carefully he put his arms around his sister and hugged her. It meant something, but it wouldn't bring Rebecca to him. He had not understood, but now he understood more. He pulled back from his sister as a chill shook his body. Standing there, he felt at once older and younger than his age. There was no question: he needed both ages.

Susan

Susan's wedding anniversary was never merely an anniversary. She and Stan had married in the month and year of the atomic bombs. She could make something of that or she could not. Love hadn't cared, nor had history. The war that took boys from rural Tennessee and ranches in Wyoming and the tenements of New York and said, "Now you will die long before your time in a place you never knew existed" was going to be over. She remembered crying out of both relief and agony. Right there, right at the beginning, a two-headed creature was inside of her. She had started to write a poem: "Take two aspirins / drop two bombs / kiss two soldiers / mourn two children." That was as far as she had gotten. She had never known what to do with that creature. There was no reason to think she ever would. The books she read and the thoughts she thought and the life she led were straws in a fire that mocked all books and thoughts and lives. When the missile crisis, as they called it, came and went, she almost came and went, too. Looking back, that made sense to her.

Her husband was not one to forget their anniversary. He sent flowers in the morning, delivered by a cheerful man from the florist on Liberty Heights who asked her if she was "the missus of the house." They were roses. Stan knew she grew tea roses. He did know some things. She tended to forget that.

Stan had suggested that they "dine" (a special word in Stan's parlance) at the Chesapeake on North Charles Street. The Chesapeake was run by a Jewish family and offered lots of rich food in a cushioned atmosphere. It was more spacious than the Pimlico and not as gourmet-minded as Danny's, to name two other Baltimore restaurants they had been to on previous anniversaries. Stan liked to quote the Chesapeake's motto: "Cut your steak with a fork, else tear up your check and walk out." Stan liked steaks. Susan usually wanted something made with crabs, something that went with the restaurant's name. She liked that about Baltimore, how it had its own cuisine.

Sitting across the table from her husband, Susan felt at a loss. There was much to say but she didn't think she could say it. In her head, she had tried out some opening lines, but they all seemed too abrupt. She didn't want to be abrupt. She kept talking and thinking about truth, but, as she seemed to be learning, truth was gradual.

"What I like about the Chesapeake is that it's reliable. You're never going to get a bad meal here." Stan put the menu down and smiled with satisfaction. "And it's not too loud in here. The Pimlico can get a little loud."

"Do you wonder who gets to eat here?" That had not been one of her opening lines. That had flown into her head unbidden. For a second she hoped that Stan had not heard her.

"People with the money to pay for the meal get to eat here," Stan answered.

Susan looked at her husband and almost smiled. This was as good a way in as any. "I wonder what would happen," Susan said, "if Negroes tried to eat here."

"They'd be served, of course." Stan picked up his linen napkin and put it on his lap. He hadn't ordered yet, but, as he liked to put it, he was "reporting for duty."

"I don't see any Negro customers here tonight," Susan went on. "Not even any African diplomats."

Stan laughed. "Yeah, the diplomats, those guys from the *Afro* who went into restaurants and dressed up like Africans. Said they were big shots. What country did they say they were from? 'Baboon'?"

"Gabon was the country."

"And the governor had to say that restaurants should serve African diplomats. Pretty smart of those guys dressing up like that. You gotta give them credit."

A waiter appeared and took their drink order—an Old Fashioned for Stan, a Singapore Sling for Susan.

"It's cruel, isn't it, that they have to masquerade to make their point." Susan looked into the hazel eyes of the father of her three children. She wanted to still love him. He had been the fixed star that guided her life. He had been like a faith to her.

"We could use some rolls. Let me get the waiter's eye," Stan said.

"I asked you if you thought it was cruel and you start talking about rolls."

"I'm hungry. People go to restaurants because they're hungry—no crime in that." He waved in the direction of their waiter.

"You're right. There isn't any crime. But I was saying something I thought was important." Susan had the sensation she was on top of a wave that was moving toward a distant beach. It was disconcerting—she didn't know where she was headed . . . but also comforting—she was headed somewhere.

Stan continued to wave but turned to his wife. "You look great in that dress. It becomes you." He smiled his charming, I'm-being-attentive smile.

"Thanks, but I still said something to you." Susan held her hands out a few inches away from herself and slowly moved them down the front of her dress. Someone desired her. She felt better about stepping into a dress because she could imagine stepping out of a dress. "You know what happened at Miller Brothers, how Leonard Bernstein walked out because they wouldn't serve a Negro in his party, a violinist in his orchestra. It was shameful. It makes us look like hicks and bigots."

The waiter appeared with rolls and butter. Another waiter appeared with their drinks.

"To us," Stan said and raised his tumbler toward Susan.

"To us," Susan replied and chinked her glass with her husband's. She took a deep drink.

"Whoa, you'll get through that in a second," Stan said.

"I need to get through it in a second."

"This is our anniversary. There's plenty of time for everything."

"That's what the white people have been telling the Negroes: there's plenty of time."

Stan took a meditative sip. "It's a little sweeter than I like."

"Damn it! Stop making small talk. I'm telling you

something." She took another deep drink.

"What are you worked up about?" Stan set his drink down. "We're here to enjoy ourselves, not worry about where Negroes can eat. They're walking around Baltimore and they're all fed. I don't think we have to worry about them. Anyway, you're the one who wants to leave the neighborhood."

"Your oldest daughter was dripping menstrual blood in the hall while you were in the bathroom shaving last week, so don't talk to me about our house. I'm talking about the right to walk in a restaurant and not have to concern yourself about whether you'll be served or not."

"You like this Leonard Bernstein?" Stan regarded his glass but didn't pick it up. "He's a long hair, isn't he?"

Susan pulled her seat back a few inches.

"Hey, I just asked some questions. Don't get testy. Finish your drink."

Susan quivered. Before she spoke, she reminded herself to speak slowly and distinctly. "I don't think you understand. We aren't living in some prehistoric bubble. Things are occurring all around us—important things. There's more to life than getting your rolls."

"How come, Susan, you think I'm a dumbbell? How come after years of marriage you start telling me stuff that isn't even about me? I'm not in the headlines. And I don't want to be." Stan raised his glass up to the light. He sighed. "I didn't come here to argue."

"Neither did I." Susan felt the stirring of contrition but resisted it. "You don't get it."

"Don't be too sure of that, wifey." He leaned his head in toward Susan. "I've got a temper, too. You can only push me so far."

Susan drained her drink, then put her hand up and snapped her fingers.

"What are you doing?" Stan hissed.

"Ordering another drink. It'll help me talk better about nothing. I can order another drink, can't I? Or do I have to ask permission?" She leaned back. She felt better for saying something that spoke to reality, but she felt false, too. The whole, simultaneous truth seemed more than her mouth could hold.

Someone has made me come to life. I can't marry him, but I feel much better than I've felt in many years. I never would think of killing myself. That's good, isn't it? I don't know why I'm still with you. I don't know where to turn. Can you help me?

"You —" Stan began but Susan interrupted.

"I'm going to the ladies. Order me the crab imperial." She rose unsteadily, her head rollicking from the alcohol. All around her, groups of white people were enjoying themselves. The smells tantalized: prime rib, peppery spices, the perfume of the bejeweled women. The Chesapeake wasn't a cheap date. As she began to walk, she could feel the press of her girdle. Jarvis liked her body the way it was. He called her "a full-grown woman." Maybe she would leave the elastic encumbrance in the ladies' room.

She stopped and sneezed. Three different voices said, "*Gesundheit.*"

It would take her a while to remove her girdle, but Stan would wait. That was his nature. And if he didn't, then he didn't.

She thought of August 1945, when the calm horizon of time had been taken away forever. It was an incongruous vision to have in a crowded restaurant, but most of the visions she had been having lately were incongruous. Too much didn't fit into the approved compartments.

Once again the aromas came to her. People were busy shoveling food into their mouths or chattering. She forgot what she should say, could say, would say. She was here on this night in her own skin and possessed of her own appetites. It was no small thing: so much had been ruined — and so many.

Arthur

Edward thought it would be good for Arthur to meet Edward's family on what Edward termed "the eve of a great event." And so — a reasonable-seeming locution that Edward favored — Arthur found himself seated at the dining room table of Professor and Mrs. Trumbull and their three children. Like Arthur, Edward had two younger sisters who also teased him. Edward referred to them as "the pests."

Susan had coached Arthur about his manners: "No elbows on the table, no holding the soup bowl up to your mouth, no reaching across the table." He assured his mother that he would be a perfect gentleman. Normally he would have protested that he wasn't a child, but this time her caring touched him. *Treat these people with respect* was what she was saying. She had told Arthur that she was going on the march, too. That was all they said to each other about it. He liked that. Her reasons could be her own. That left more room for his.

The Trumbulls' dining room reminded Arthur of Grandpa Max's. There was a big, dark wooden table in the room's center and cabinets in the corners filled with plates and cups and even a huge tureen. Edward said the Trumbulls had a lot of "kinfolk." At Christmas, there might be twenty-five people at their house. That seemed wonderful to Arthur. If you were Jewish, it was hard not to envy the Christians their big day.

Max was still in the hospital. He didn't seem any worse, but he didn't seem any better, either. When Arthur walked into Max's room a few days ago, Bertha was sitting there crying.

Arthur sat beside Edward at the dining room table. It was set very carefully — doilies under bowls and serving plates and a big pitcher for water. At Arthur's house, if you wanted more water you got up and went to the sink. Professor Trumbull engaged Arthur in conversation while the food was being brought to the table. He was a big man, well over six feet, and peered at Arthur through thick glasses. He spoke slowly, each word carefully enunciated.

The talk wasn't any big thing—school and what Arthur had been reading lately. Edward seemed to make a point of being silent while Arthur replied. Having your parents talk to a friend of yours could feel awkward no matter what your skin color was, though when Mrs. Trumbull, who told Arthur to call her "Iona" because that was her name, announced that everything was ready and that it was time to say grace, Edward lit up. Maybe, Arthur thought, it was the food, or maybe Edward had gotten bored listening to his father. Edward was so like his father it could feel too close. When kids at school called Edward "Professor," it wasn't a compliment.

Edward's father, who was wearing a white, short-sleeved shirt and a black tie and black pants, stood at the head of the table while everyone bowed their heads and said a few words about the Lord blessing this meal. "We thank you for this bounty and for the presence of Arthur Mermelstein, a friend of our son Edward's." Arthur kept his head down. The customary "dig in" at his house was less than prayerful.

Everyone murmured "Amen," but before Mrs. Trumbull could begin to offer the plates of food—baked chicken, green beans, sweet potatoes, and gravy that smelled so good Arthur wanted to drink it right from the boat it was in—Edward said that he wanted to say a few words. His sisters mouthed words back at him; his parents moved their heads slightly to the side in the way that Arthur recognized his own parents did sometimes, indicating *well we had the kid and we have to live with him.*

"I think it's important before we eat to acknowledge that we are on the cusp of a historic occasion and that the words of one of our forebears should be heard." Edward's sister Labelle, who was three years younger than Edward, was scowling so hard she could have started a thunderstorm two states away, but Edward went on. His other sister, Cherise, sighed loudly.

"I wish to speak some words by Frederick Douglass. They are as follows." Arthur thought Edward was going to pull a piece of paper from a pants pocket but he didn't. Instead he took off his glasses and spoke from memory: "We were hemmed in upon every side. Here were the difficulties, real or imagined — the good to be sought, and the evil to be shunned. On the one hand, there stood slavery, a stern reality, glaring frightfully upon us, — its robes already crimsoned with the blood of millions, and even now feasting itself greedily upon our own flesh. On the other hand, away back in the dim distance, under the flickering light of the North Star, behind some craggy hill or snow-covered mountain, stood a doubtful freedom — half frozen — beckoning us to come and share its hospitality." Edward paused. Labelle glared; Cherise fiddled with her silverware knife.

"Frederick Douglass, as you know," and Edward made a point of nodding to his sisters, "lived for a time in what he termed 'the Christian city of Baltimore,' a city that endorsed slavery and whose inhabitants termed him "a damned nigger," among other things. I think it's only fitting that we remember those before us as we take a further step in our struggle to be free."

"Amen, son," Mrs. Trumbull said.

"Amen," said Professor Trumbull, a half beat behind her. "Those are important words for us to hear."

After the professor spoke, there was one of those table silences that Arthur recognized from his own house: manners and hunger canceling one another out.

"Now may we eat, Daddy?" Cherise asked.

Edward shook his head in mock disgust. "One thought in your head, Cherise, and it isn't the history of your race, I'm afraid."

"Now, Edward," Mrs. Trumbull said. "Cherise is a growing girl."

"She could grow and think at the same time," Edward replied. "What kind of message are we giving to my guest here?"

"Maybe we can talk later about those words, Edward." Arthur regarded the gravy boat with longing. "I'm hungry too, though."

Everyone looked at Arthur and then laughed — even Edward.

As they ate, the conversation focused on the next day. Professor Trumbull quoted A. Phillip Randolph, who had quoted Frederick Douglass when he announced the march: "He who would be free must himself strike the first blow."

"We've struck a lot of blows already, Pop," Edward said. "How many blows do we have to strike? And is a march like this a real blow?"

It couldn't help but feel strange to Arthur. He was being careful to watch his elbows and he was complimenting Iona Trumbull on how good the chicken was—almost as good as Seeley's—while around him the history of subjugation was being discussed. And Arthur knew it wasn't just history. Its tentacles included roller coasters and Harry Schwartz's rowhouses and dressing rooms in department stores and lunch counters and even water fountains. It made him think once more of that woman at Gwynn Oak and how it wasn't that he especially loved Negroes, although their music alone seemed precious, but that he couldn't stand the stupidity of prejudice, of that woman's gaping mouth.

"The blows have glanced off the beast time and again. It's true," Professor Trumbull said. He looked more at Arthur, though, than his son. That made sense: his skin made him a representative of that beast. He had read Frederick Douglass himself and remembered one sentence in particular: "I loathed them as being the meanest as well as the most wicked of men."

"But we have the Lord to sustain us," Mrs. Trumbull said. "And the Lord will carry us forth tomorrow because the Lord has never failed us."

The conviction in her eyes was riveting. Arthur had seen the same thing in Seeley's eyes when she was talking about "the Reverend" or her church. Lenny Bruce wisecracking about Religions, Inc., was one thing. This was a vast other.

"My Iona is a wise woman, Arthur," Professor Trumbull said.

"And a great cook, Daddy," Labelle said. "What's for dessert, Mom?"

Mrs. Trumbull smiled. "Who said there was dessert?"

Labelle stuck a hand under her chin and made a pouty face. "You always make dessert when we have company."

"Arthur's not company. Arthur's my friend," Edward said. He wrapped an arm around Arthur's shoulder.

Everyone at the table looked at them. Mrs. Trumbull smiled again, but to Arthur it was a different smile — a little sad perhaps, some depth he felt but couldn't see into.

"I don't care what Arthur is," Labelle announced. "I want to know if there is dessert."

Edward pulled his arm back and leaned forward. "If you had something on your mind, Labelle, beside your stomach, maybe it would work better."

"Don't start sassing me, Mister Edward," Labelle shot back.

Mrs. Trumbull pressed her palms against the table and rose up. She was a good foot shorter than her husband. "I've made peach pie. Is there anyone here who likes peach pie with vanilla ice cream?"

Arthur raised his hand.

"This isn't a classroom, Merm," Edward said. "A simple 'yes' or 'no' is adequate." He gave Arthur a light shove on the shoulder.

This feels like another home. The thought flowed through Arthur like a song. He wasn't that beast. He never would have to be.

Susan

"Lord's sakes, Mrs. Merm, how in the world you bein' here?" Seeley made a hand clap, then turned to the woman beside her. "Mrs. Merm's my employer."

"Well, isn't that somethin'?" the woman replied. "How do you do?" The woman had a purplish-colored handkerchief in her hand and waved it a bit.

Susan remembered that weeks ago she had agreed to give Seeley this Wednesday off on account of what Seeley called "a personal fact." Seeley had asked for days off before and Susan never inquired further. She knew that Seeley had three grown daughters and numerous grandchildren. There was no shortage of occasions requiring her presence.

"I'm on this march too," Susan said.

Seeley had a red barrette in her gray-black hair and when she shook her head in wonder, she seemed almost girlish. "Now, Mrs. Merm, I got to ask who put you on this bus with all us Baptists? I bet there's some Jewish buses goin' today, too."

"Lot of buses," the woman beside Seeley said with an air of authority. "Folks on the B & O, too."

"Jarvis Baker got me on this bus," Susan said. "He teaches music at City College. I work with him in the teachers' union."

"Jarvis Baker," Seeley said. "I know that so-and-so. His wife AME, though."

The other woman nodded.

"He calls the house sometime, don't he?" Seeley asked.

"Yes, he does," Susan answered. She hadn't known what to expect today, but she hadn't expected to be talking to her maid. Maybe Jarvis had stage-managed this surprise. There were a number of other buses she could have gone on; he arranged for her to be on this one. Maybe, though, this was what was supposed to happen. Maybe that was the idea behind the whole day. Susan could have driven over to Washington but she wanted to be on a bus. Her request had continued to amuse Jarvis: "When a white woman wants to sit on a bus, that folksinger is right—something's damn sure blowing in the wind." They talked about going in a car with Joe and Julia, but Jarvis was against it. "This occasion is personal," he said. "My father is going with some buddies. My wife thinks the whole thing is low class. The person I need to be with most is me."

"You have a good day, Mrs. Merm," Seeley said. "Goin' to be a long one. Walkin' and then speeches. I got to warn you: some of these Negro preachers can talk all day."

"Talk the sun down from the sky," the woman beside Seeley said.

"Take a seat, madam," the bus driver announced to Susan. "We are about to commence."

"A good day to you too, Seeley," Susan said. She began to walk toward the back of the bus. At least she had had the sense to wear comfortable flats. She had some salve in her pocketbook if her feet began to ache.

"Seat here, ma'am," an older Negro man said and nodded to Susan.

"Thanks," Susan replied. She made a show of being ladylike, smoothing the underneath of her skirt as she sat down, then sitting very erect, pocketbook in her lap. She was so many things—excited, abashed, anxious, curious. The bus was bound for Washington, D.C., but it was bound for more than that and she felt it. Something good was trembling inside of her.

"Goin' to be hot but not too hot. Good you got yourself one of them." The man nodded at Susan's big straw hat. "My name's Wiley Jones." He extended a hand.

Susan shook it, giving herself a second to feel his hand before letting go. "My name's Susan Mermelstein." She paused. "I'm a schoolteacher."

"Well, that's nice to hear, Susan," Wiley said. "My mama was a schoolteacher, taught sixth grade in Virginia and then here in Baltimore. Myself, I'm a barber by trade." He smiled pleasantly.

Susan breathed him in. Wiley smelled of powder and pomade and aftershave.

"Have you been doing that a long time?" Susan asked. She wanted to chat but wasn't sure of the decorum.

"Most of my life." He put his hands together on his small paunch. "One thing white folks don't much interfere with. You don't see many barber shops puttin' out signs, 'Negro hair cut here. Please come in.'" He was still smiling but Susan felt that knife's edge she knew from Jarvis — amiable pain.

"That must be a benefit," Susan said. "To be left in peace."

The smile bent a bit more. "Peace? That's for sure — hard to get enough of that in this world."

"Martin Luther King is so important for all of us, isn't he, because of that, because of peace?" Susan asked.

Wiley angled himself to better regard Susan, his back resting in the corner between the seat and the bus window. "Martin's one of the Lord's. He's takin' on that power. He — " Wiley looked down to examine his folded hands. "He's usin' the only power we have. He's sayin' to white people that it's your Bible, too. You best live up to it."

"I see," Susan said. She still sat very erect — an attentive student. "There must be laws — " She didn't know how to finish the sentence.

A silence lay there between them, neither comfortable nor uncomfortable. Wiley began to twiddle his thumbs. Someone behind them was telling a joke. Someone else was humming.

Susan started the sentence again. Again she hit a wall. She had grown up transfixed by her own form of suffering. Others seemed to be mere background, part of life's sanctioned woe — Thomas Hardy country. How wrong that was, yet understandable. To feel that the immutable wrongs were mutable was more than most days could bear.

Wiley's smile broadened. There were lines that ran down from his temples into his cheeks that seemed to have been carved there. His skin was ebony colored. "I guess we opened the door pretty fast between us, but then I guess that's what this day's about. I know Seeley up there, so's I know you, too. I know

Jarvis Baker, too." He waved his hand as if to dismiss some complaint or annoyance. "Martin's makin' them look at their mighty laws. He knows who these white people are—how couldn't he? Bein' a Negro is like bein' a shadow. But he knows you got to put your ticket on the counter and collect your parcel. Freedom is our parcel. It's time for us to collect, time for us to be seen."

"You are eloquent, Mr. Jones," Susan said.

A thickset man in the seat behind them leaned forward. "Don't attend to a word that barber says, ma'am. Wiley cut hair and talk all day. He talk to the rain, he talk to a brick wall, he talk to a dead person. He just like to talk." The man snorted and drew back.

"Some truth in that, some truth in that," Wiley murmured. "I been cuttin' Jarvis' hair since he was a little boy. I seen him grow up, become a man. He still comes round to my shop—loyal." Wiley whistled to himself, a note of wonder. "That's somethin'—when someone's loyal. Not enough of that in this world."

Susan wanted to hold up her end of the conversation but wasn't sure what she was holding. Jarvis wasn't loyal to his wife, but that wasn't the topic under discussion. Who knew what he told other people? And this day wasn't about her attraction to a loyal patron of Wiley Jones's barber shop. Even Ruby had talked about the march: "The Negroes standing up, every person standing up—is good."

"You sit like that all the way to Washington, your back gonna hurt something terrible," Wiley remarked.

Susan made a show of exhaling. She slumped a bit. "These seats aren't very comfortable."

"Baptists get a school bus, they're happy. Don't need no Greyhound. They so full of the Lord, most anything make them happy. Seeley one of the happiest women I know." Wiley cocked his head. "Probably you know that. But listen up. They gonna start singin' soon." He chuckled. "I know them. They gonna start singin'."

The man behind them leaned forward again. "Why don't you start it off, brother? You got enough wind to lift the roof clear off this old bus."

Baron Wormser

Wiley looked at Susan. "You may not know the words, Susan." He paused. "But I reckon you can learn."

He took a deep breath. Susan felt something being sucked out from the warm morning air and into Wiley's chest. Then, without preamble, his voice boomed forth: "Paul and Silas were bound in jail, had no money for to get their bail. Keep your eyes on the prize. Hold on!"

People began clapping. Susan began to clap too.

Arthur

You never knew. A few nights before the march, John Silverman called Arthur up. They hadn't seen each other for over a month. Silverman was working on one of the delivery trucks in his family's business and had a steady named Lauri with whom he was "making progress," as he put it earlier in the summer. Silverman wanted to know if Arthur wanted to go to the march with him: "I figured you were going but I've got a car, gas money, and I want to get out of Dodge. Plus I'm curious. Plus there's gonna be a lot of women there."

"You're planning to fornicate in front of the Lincoln Memorial?" Arthur replied.

"If the chance presents itself."

"Dream on."

Silverman had heard about Rebecca. "I'm doing better than you, Merm."

"Go fuck yourself."

"That's my man talking. See you soon."

Silverman showed up in a 1960 Impala convertible, two-tone, powder blue and white.

"Where did you get your hands on this machine?" Arthur asked as he got in.

"The cool thing to do, Merm, is jump over the side and into the seat. That's why there are convertibles." Silverman massaged the top of the steering wheel with both hands. "It's my older brother's. I told him I had a rendezvous with history."

"Bullshit." Arthur was putting on a pair of sun glasses.

"I know some stuff about my brother he doesn't want our parents to know."

Arthur gave the dashboard a confirming tap. "Quite the car, maybe you're right about the women."

On the way over to Washington they talked about Martin Luther King Jr. and nonviolence. Silverman said he couldn't do it. He couldn't let someone hit him and not hit back. "It's not human," he said. Silverman had a way of putting his lips together as if he was about to play the trumpet. It was how his face got serious. He was as serious as Arthur had seen him.

Arthur's picketing hadn't put him in any real danger. He'd been yelled at, like at the park, but he'd been yelled at on the playground in the third grade. The people who went down South, the people who lived down South—they had been in danger. They still were. Edward had spoken to Arthur about nonviolence, about how once you put your hand up to retaliate you were lost. Even when it felt good to strike back you were lost, because you had given up your "righteousness." That was the word Edward used. "You have to give up your power to gain power," Edward said.

"So if someone kicked you, Merm, you'd just let him kick you? You'd just say, 'kick me all you want'? That what you'd do?" The convertible seemed to sluice through the air. A soft roar pummeled Arthur's ears.

"You know what?" Arthur said.

"What?"

"That's what I'd do. I wouldn't say anything, but I'd take it."

Silverman shuddered. Arthur could tell it wasn't from the breeze going by them.

"No way," Silverman said. "No fucking way. Tell it to the Nazis."

They were silent for a lot of miles. Then Silverman turned the radio on, but they were too far from Baltimore to get the station he wanted and he didn't know the stations in D.C., so he turned it off.

"Maybe I'm not as brave as I think I am," Silverman said all of a sudden.

Arthur didn't reply. It didn't seem about being brave. It seemed about holding onto something that you couldn't let go of, that if you let go of it you were lost. He couldn't define what *it* was, though. He thought back to all the religious people on the bus on July Fourth. He should have talked to them.

After they parked the car on a side street and walked for what seemed like a mile, finally arriving at the Mall in mid-morning, Arthur's stomach jumped with excitement. There were a fair number of people there already, but with every minute many more people were coming, seemingly an endless number of people gathering to walk down Constitution Avenue — mostly Negroes but lots of white people, too, and all sizes and shapes and ages, children and old people, even someone who went by him in a wheelchair.

"Crazy," Silverman said. "It's a sunny day but it's raining people." He turned to Arthur. "This is more people than a Colts game."

"Hard to believe anything could outdo the Colts," Arthur said, then ducked Silverman's mock punch.

"Hey!" someone shouted. "You boys foolin' around over there. Come here and give us a hand."

Silverman and Arthur saw a Negro man beckoning to them. He had a bunch of signs leaning against his body and as they neared him he lifted a sign for them to read: "No U.S. Dough to Help Jim Crow."

"How about carrying a sign? Some of my buddies couldn't make it today." He pointed at some other Negro men. Dressed in work pants and T-shirts, they looked rumpled and tired. "We drove here through the night from Detroit."

"Jim Crow," Silverman mumbled. "That's some kind of whiskey, isn't it?"

"What you say, son?" asked the man who had been talking to them. "What you say?"

"He's a little confused, sir," Arthur said. "He knows that Jim Crow represents the illegal segregation policy that, although sanctioned by Supreme Court decisions, has marred any real notion of democracy this nation might put forward, inviting ridicule from the Soviet Union, for instance." Arthur looked down at the bit of sun-baked grass he was standing on, then up at the cloudless sky. The spirit of Edward seemed to have attached his tongue.

"One knows nothing and the other knows everything." The man held out two signs. "You two are separate but equal." He grinned. "My name's Ray. And you boys are — ?"

"Tonto and the Lone Ranger," Silverman answered. "But John and Arthur to our many fans."

Another one of the men from Detroit came forward, took a toothpick from his mouth, and looked them over. "Sometimes I can't believe what Noah let in the ark."

Arthur grabbed Silverman by the elbow, thanked the men for the signs, and started to steer his friend toward the Washington Monument.

"Do you think this is a joke?" Arthur asked.

Silverman made that tight lip face again. "No. It's the opposite, Merm. I'm afraid inside." Silverman didn't have on sunglasses. His eyes looked startled, almost glassy.

"Afraid?"

"Yeah, afraid. I can feel, standing here, that what I thought I knew means nothing. Just talk. And that feels good in a way, like it makes me feel lighter or something. But it makes me afraid, too." He paused and looked about vacantly. People were milling around them, brushing up against them, people everywhere. "It's stupid. But that's how I feel."

Arthur felt embarrassed. Edward's sorts of words were of no use.

"You got to help me, Merm," Silverman said. "I'm not diddlin' you."

The Jim Crow signs were dangling from their right hands. "Pick your sign up, Silverman," Arthur said.

Silverman stared at him.

"Just pick your sign up and start walking beside me. Do it."

Silverman looked down doubtfully. He made a sputtering sound, then hoisted his sign.

"This is what they mean when they say 'sea of humanity.'" Despite the crush around him, Arthur didn't have to raise his voice. A lot of the people were silent.

Silverman nodded. "You might not believe me, Merm, but I think I see your mother up ahead, maybe a half block or so. She turned around, like she was looking for someone. I could see her face."

"Could be."

"There's no catching up with her, though," Silverman

said. "And now I lost her." He paused. "Do you think we belong here?"

"We live in Baltimore. We go to City. We ride the buses and walk the streets and go into stores and restaurants. We're not just kids along for the ride."

Silverman didn't say anything back. He didn't nod either. What he did do was hold his sign up higher.

It felt as though they were being carried rather than walking. It felt as though the whole of the history book Arthur had lugged around for a year had spilled out into the faces around him. Some enormous dam of uncountable days and years had broken.

A few more yards forward brought them up beside an old woman who motioned at them with a furled umbrella. She seemed not just old but very old, older than Ruby, older than Max, her face an intricate web of wrinkles and creases, her light-brown skin almost translucent. She was small, too, no more than five feet. She was dressed in black.

Arthur realized that what she had motioned with wasn't an umbrella. It was a parasol, something he had read about but never seen.

"You boys help me along today and I'll buy you each a Coca-Cola." She bent toward them. Arthur reached for her instinctively so that she wouldn't topple over, but cat-quick she grabbed at his arm. "I've lived most of my life right here in Washington, District of Columbia, and I've been waiting for this for a long time, 'cept I didn't know I was waiting."

"Neither did I," said Silverman. "Neither did I."

"I got a passel of stories," the old woman said. She held on to Arthur's arm.

"That's great," Arthur said. "Tell us some."

Acknowledgments

Deepest thanks to those who helped along the way: Nina Ryan, William Patrick, Rachel Basch, Lewis Robinson, Michael White, Hollis Seamon, Joan Handler, Joan Levinstein, Michael Steinberg, Peter Agrafiotis, Marc Estrin, Elaine Ford, Michael Fleming, Richard Miles, Susan Hammond, Christopher Holt, my wife Janet, and my sister Sherry, to whom this book is dedicated.

Two books in particular were a special help to me: *Not in My Neighborhood* by Antero Pietila and *The Baltimore Rowhouse* by Mary Ellen Hayward and Charles Belfoure.

About the Author

Baron Wormser is the author/co-author of twelve books. From 2000 to 2006, he served as poet laureate of the state of Maine and has been the recipient of fellowships from Bread Loaf, the National Endowment for the Arts, and the John Simon Guggenheim Memorial Foundation. He grew up in Baltimore, where he attended Baltimore City College and the Johns Hopkins University. He teaches in the Fairfield University MFA Program in addition to being director of educational outreach for the Frost Place in Franconia, New Hampshire.

CPSIA information can be obtained at www.ICGtesting.com
Printed in the USA
BVOW07s1747120114

341557BV00002B/66/P